BADD ENDINGS
BOOK 4

BADD
Endings

BOOK 4

A NOVEL BY
AUTHOR ZEE. W

www.zbookpublishing.com

www.zbookpublishing.com

ZBook Publishing, LLC
P.O. Box 2085
Stone Mountain, GA 30087
www.zbookpublishing.com

Badd Endings
First Edition
ZBook Publishing, LLC

ISBN-13: 978-1-941689-04-2

Dedication

I DEDICATE THIS book to all the readers who motivated me to keep going. Thanks for giving me a chance. Although the Badd Series has come to a conclusion, your enthusiasm and passion for the characters will forever live in my heart.

Thank you for your support.

—Author Zee. W

Contents

1: Brock Badd 1

2: Mona Badd 11

3: Brip Badd 27

4: Taffy Badd 36

5: Dalla Badd 45

6: Billy Badd 54

7: Mona Badd 69

8: Lera Badd 80

9: Bobby Badd 88

10: Mona Badd 99

11: Brock Badd 112

12: Billy Badd 124

13: Mona Badd 131

14: Brip Badd 141

15: Taffy Badd 151

16: Vinchi Badd 160

17: Billy Badd 168

18: Vinchi Badd 177

19: Brip Badd 184

20: Mona Badd 191

21: Bobby Badd 199

22: Dalla Badd 206

23: Vinchi Badd 213

24: Brock Badd 220

25: Bobby Badd 229

26: Mona Badd 236

27: Taffy Badd 242

28: Billy Badd 250

29: Brock Badd 258

30: Dalla Badd 262

31: Bobby Badd 267

32: Lera Badd 273

33: Brip Badd 280

34: Brock Badd 288

35: Mona Badd 296

36: Lera Badd 299

37: Taffy Badd 302

38: Billy Badd 305

I

Brock Badd

I STARE DOWN AT Lady L, who Tony has tied to a chair. At any moment, it looks like her frail body is going to topple over. Her lanky arms lay limp at her side, and her pointy shoulders are slumped over, creating a small hump in her back that defines her spine. Her neck looks as if it can't bear the weight of her head anymore. Without the costume of hair and makeup, she almost looks unrecognizable. Angelo tried to get her to talk by taking away the beauty she cherishes, but it didn't work. Now, Angelo is gently placing a bottle of water against her mother's cracked lips. She urges her to take a sip, but Lady L refuses. She hasn't spoken a word in days, and for the past two days, she has declined food and water. Lady L is rebelling.

Angelo looks at me with guilt and compassion in her eyes. I can tell she feels bad for what she has done to her pathetic mother, but I have no sympathy for this woman. I need her to talk, so I demand answers.

"Where is he?" I calmly ask while standing over Lady L with my arms folded. "I know he's alive. Does he know she died? Does he know my mother kill—" I clear my throat and correct myself. "Does he know she's dead?"

Lady L musters up enough strength to look at me and laugh, and I know why. It's because she knows what I did. Her heckling laughter quickly turns into a coughing fit, and Angelo pushes the bottle of water back in her face. Again, she refuses and drops her head. Pouring the water in her hand, Angelo smears it across her mother's dry mouth.

"You got to drink something, Lady L," Angelo pleads. "You want to die like this?"

Angelo darts her eyes when Lady L doesn't respond, giving me a desperate look, but I'm not moved.

The stories about the dangerous love affair between my mother and Carlo Lucky weren't just rumors; they were facts. I know it was him who she was writing to, although she addressed each letter with *My Love*. Their love affair was real. My mother loved this man like he was her soulmate. She talked about my brothers and me a lot in the letters. In one letter, she said how she could see him in my eyes, how Billy had his heart, and how Bobby had his mind. She was worried Papa Badd's influence had tarnished Brip. In one of the last letters she wrote to him, she detailed a plan to take Brip and leave with him, but Carlo Lucky never showed up because my father killed him. At least that's what I thought. It's what we all thought, but there was one last letter between them—dated only days before I killed her—that proves Carlo Lucky is alive. Or at least he was. I only read the first page, but there was more. They were planning to escape together. Now how were they going to do that if Carlo Lucky had been dead for years? How would that be possible?

I learned the truth about who we all were in her last few letters. She told Carlo that before they left, she had to tell us the truth. She said she was going to come clean to me, saying we deserved to know. And she did. She told me, but I was so full of fear that I didn't let her finish her story. I didn't allow myself to hear everything she had to say, because back then, I only cared about two things: the Ranch and my presumed father.

I wonder if Carlo Lucky waited for her. I wonder if he thought she backed out the deal. He was going to help her leave the Ranch. They had a plan. The last pages of that letter detailed it, but Lady L wouldn't give me the rest. Her and Ace only gave me enough to tease me. Although I have Ace's mother and sister under my control, they are holding me captive. However, the truth can set them free. I need answers more than I need blood.

How was this possible? How did Carlo Lucky father four children with my mother under my father's nose without him knowing? How is he still alive? *Is* he still alive? If he is, what does that mean for my brothers and me? What does it mean for the Ranch? My mother was almost free before I stopped her. Free to love. Free to smile. But, I put an end to it all. I killed her twice.

My mother detailed in the letters all the horrific things my father did to her—the violent physical attacks, the rapes, and the verbal abuse. All under my nose. My mother was dying slowly under all of our noses. If it weren't for the hope she had in being with the love of her life, she would have taken her life a long time ago. I looked at her all those years like she was weak, when really she was strong for enduring the abuse for so long, and all while staying beautiful and graceful. How could I have had so much respect for a man who treated my mother like garbage? Like she was less than a human.

Carlo Lucky gave her strength; he was her hope for a better life. In the letters, she would tell him that they would be together soon. It was never the right time for her to leave. It took years for her to plan her escape, and I fucked it up. She asked for his patience. I guess he had no choice but to give it to her. She wrote that soon, they would have the rest of their lives together, but I ended that dream. My mother deserved to be happy, though.

I never knew how much I didn't know about her until I read her letters. She was thoughtful, supportive, patient, positive, and charming. She loved my brothers and me more than life itself. She mentioned us in every letter, turning our faults into strengths and only seeing the good in us. She wanted us away from my father, but she knew that couldn't happen. It was too dangerous. She worried about me the most. She wanted me to be nothing like him, but I'm exactly like him. We were the reason she stayed so long—the reason she endured the physical and mental abuse inflicted by my father. Carlo Lucky was my mother's last chance at love, and I took that from her. Then I took her life.

"She ain't looking too good, Mr. Badd," Angelo says to me.

"Get her to talk," I coldly reply before turning to walk away.

"She ain't gonna be able to talk if she's dead," Angelo responds, raising her voice.

I spin around and give her a stern look. She backs down, lowering her head.

"You do understand why you and your mother are here, right?" I look her in the eyes and then down at Lady L, who is looking more and more like a corpse by the minute.

"I understand, and I want to help you. I told you that before, sir, but this ain't working."

"Well, what do you suggest?"

Angelo is hesitant for a moment before asking, "You got any coke?"

"You think I just have that shit lying around?" I say, slightly offended.

I'm nothing like her brother or her family.

"It may be the only thing she won't refuse. Get that powder in her nose, and she'll get to talking. I promise," Angelo replies.

I look down at Lady L and back at Angelo, then shake my head. This woman is getting more pathetic by the second. How could the same man who my mother was in love with love this woman? Lady L and my mother couldn't be more different.

"I don't like drugs," I tell her.

"But you want answers," Angelo says humbly and extends the bottle towards her mother's lips again, but Lady L remains stubborn. "Can we untie her? I don't think she's much of a threat."

"I'll see what I can do," I say, referring to the coke. "But if this doesn't work, I'm holding you responsible." I mean what I say, and she knows it. "For now, she stays tied."

TONY BUSTS THROUGH the door with so much force that I draw my pistol, thinking we are under attack. It was risky coming back to the second Ranch, but it's the best option for me right now. I waited a while to give Kong and his crew time to raid the place in their search for me. I only returned once they cleared me from this place. This Ranch has always been my haven to think my way out of fucked-up situations. Here, I can focus and succeed in taking back the Ranch. If they come for me, I'll be waiting to silence them one by one. Tony and I are a two-person army. I got my weapons, my safe houses, and my cameras to back me up. Nobody is catching me off guard. Not here. Besides, I know this Ranch like Billy knows the main Ranch.

It's been almost two weeks since I was last here. Since then, everything has been dead silent. I don't know what's going on. For all I know, they could be dead. I expected Mona to find a way to call me by now, but she hasn't, and it's making me nervous as fuck. That's why I had to call in the bigwigs. I need help.

"Mr. Badd, they here…they here…they coming," Tony says in one breath.

Tony's a good soldier, but he gets easily excited. It takes a lot to keep him calm. My hat goes off to Dalla for being a master at handling him.

"Stand your ground, soldier," I tell Tony, who straightens his posture and draws his weapon. "We don't need that." I place my hand on his arm and lower his gun. "They're here to help us."

"Scrappy, too, right? They gonna help us get Scrappy?"

"Yes, but if any of them act up, you know what to do, right?"

"Boom," Tony gestures with his gun.

Tony is one of the best shooters I've ever encountered. He doesn't waste bullets. Every bullet he loads in his clip fulfills a purpose, and he's good at unloading and reloading his pistol in record time. If I could clone this nigga, I would.

"Go greet our guest," I tell Tony. "Then bring him to my office."

Tony spins around like he's about to take off running, but then stops, takes a deep breath, and walks outside with more composure. I lock the basement door and head down the hall to my office to prepare for this meeting. I'm shocked he got back to me so quickly. It usually takes him months to respond to others—if he responds at all, but it only took Stein days to respond to me. I'm not sure if that's a good thing or a bad thing.

Stein is like an urban legend. Few people have ever seen him in person, yet he knows all the right people. I don't know if Stein is his first name or last name. If he's everything my father described, it's probably neither. You got to be deeply connected to know a man as resourceful as Stein. He can make the impossible possible, and you only call him when all else fails. Stein was instrumental in helping my father develop the Ranch. He took my father's vision and made it a reality. Again, he made the impossible possible.

My father told me about Stein years ago when he was training me to take over. He gave me the card that I'm now holding and made sure to tell me only to call Stein if the Ranch is in true jeopardy. I look down at the white linen card that has nothing but a phone number printed on it. Even after all these years, the card hasn't tarnished. It's still crisp and clear. I wasn't sure if the number was the same, but when I called, someone answered on the first ring. It was a woman. When I told her who I was, she gave me a date and time for an in-person meeting without even asking what I needed. At first, I was leery. Why would a man, who is basically a ghost, agree to meet me so quickly? Could it be a setup? I definitely didn't want to question Stein. I was taught to respect him too much ever to do that. It was a gamble, but at the end of the day, I had a good feeling about it. So, I agreed.

Stein has been on our payroll for as long as I could count money. We pay him ten percent of everything we make, and I wire the payments to a shell account—nothing anyone can trace. I never miss a payment. My father would always say, "You pay Stein before you pay the light bill. You pay him before you pay yourself." That's how important this man is. I thought long and hard before calling him. I had to be sure I needed him. But I can't take back the Ranch on my own. Sure, I could build an army, but this whole takeover needs to be kept silent. I don't want outsiders to know what's going on. If word gets out that the

Ranch has been taken, then we look weak to our clients. Plus, it would take me weeks to do what Stein can do in a day, and time is not on my side. My family's life is in danger. Our business is in danger. So, I need this shit handled as quickly as possible.

When I hear Tony's footsteps rapidly approaching, I place the business card back in the lockbox that I keep in my office drawer and stand to my feet. I then take a deep breath and prepare to greet a legend.

"He in there," I hear Tony say from outside the door. "Go," Tony tells him, sounding annoyed. "There," Tony says.

I can envision him pointing at the door.

"It's okay, Tony," I call out. "Let him in."

A man like Stein isn't used to opening doors. He probably walks right through them.

Tony opens the door slowly and in walks a short, average-build Spanish man wearing a fedora and a nicely tailored suit. Dark shades cover his eyes, and he's carrying a black leather briefcase. His free hand is balled into a fist. I don't know if this means he's anxious or nervous. I don't like that I can't see his eyes. I also don't like that I don't know what's in his briefcase. He appears to be a little younger than me, so I know he's not Stein.

He stands in front of my desk without saying a word. His stance is robotic as if he has been programmed to move a certain way. My eyes lead to the briefcase and then to Tony. Reading my mind, Tony reaches for his gun, but I stop him. I don't want any trouble.

"Stein?" I hesitantly say while extending my hand for him to shake, but he ignores me.

I look up at Tony, who appears to be just as confused as me.

"Did Stein send you?"

I try to get the man to speak, but he doesn't. He's standing in place, not moving and barely breathing. I bet he's not even blinking underneath those shades.

Taking a deep breath, I think about my next move. I could get

Tony to draw his attention and grab the briefcase, or be patient and trust the process. Before I have a chance to decide, I hear a phone ringing. I instantly look down at the burner phone I have lying on my desk. It's not my cell phone ringing, though. It's coming from the briefcase.

As if that were a cue, he sits in the chair in front of my desk and, with the precision of a soldier, places the briefcase in his lap. He then pushes a button, and the briefcase pops open. Tony and I both jump a little. I give Tony my *"it's okay"* eyes, and he removes his hand from the butt of his pistol. The man takes out the cell phone. It's an iPhone. He answers it without saying hello, then presses the speaker button and holds the phone in the air with a stiff and steady arm.

I carefully take a seat, not taking my eyes off the man. I hear nothing on the other end of the phone.

"Stein?" I say out loud.

Seconds later, he responds.

"This is Stein."

Nothing more. His voice is mature. It's that of an older and wise man. I can tell he only speaks when necessary. Every sentence he expresses must mean something. It has to be productive. His voice is raspy. Almost as if someone took a cheese grater to his throat. From his tone, it seems he's had his fair share of fine cigars and whiskey.

"I'm…"

"You're Brock Badd," he says, cutting me off.

"Yes, sir," I respond respectfully.

"You're in trouble," he says, more like a statement than a question.

"It seems so, sir."

I start to feel ashamed like I have failed my father.

"In a few words, tell me more," Stein says as if he's short on time.

Not wasting any time, I get right to the point.

"The Ranch has been ambushed. My entire family is being held hostage, and I don't know how much longer they have. I need an army—a strong one, and I need this to happen quick."

Stein goes silent, and my heart races while waiting on his response. I debate the reason for his instant silence. *Is he deciding if he can help me, or is he judging me for allowing this to happen? Maybe he thinks I'm weak compared to my father.*

As the seconds turn to minutes, his guy doesn't as much lower his elbow to rest his arm. He continues to hold the phone extended like it is his sacred mission. I look up at Tony, who I can tell is comfortable by the way he is staring off into space. It's like he has forgotten why we are here. I open my mouth to say something, anything to get Stein to talk. But I stop myself. Instead, I practice patience and wait. Then the phone beeps, alerting the man that he received a text message. He quickly lowers his arm, flips the phone to read the text, and then holds the phone back up using the same arm.

"I'll be in touch," Stein says and ends the call like my situation isn't an emergency.

The man lowers his arm and places the phone back in the briefcase. Before closing it, he pulls out a second phone and holds it out for me to grab. I take the phone and place it on my desk.

"When will he call?" I ask the man, trying my best not to sound as frustrated as I feel.

Of course, the man says nothing. He locks the briefcase and darts up like I don't exist.

"Can you tell him that this is urgent?" I request as the man makes his way towards the door.

Tony snaps back when he sees the guy heading in his direction. This time, he smartens up and opens the door wide for him to exit. I rush from behind my desk and grab the man by the arm before he reaches the door.

"Hey!" I yell.

As if someone pushed his pause button, he instantly stops and then looks down at my hand, which is squeezing his arm like it's a foreign object. He doesn't resist or try to pull away. He's standing still as a doorknob, beaming down at my hand. I release him just as quickly as I grabbed him, and he continues to walk towards the door like nothing happened.

"Just let him know we don't have much time. Please, man."

I never thought I would ever be in a position where I had to beg, but here I am. I'm worried about Mona and Vinchi more than anything. I haven't heard from Mona since I last saw her at the Ranch. For all I know, they all could be dead.

"Just let me know!" I yell again, but he is already walking down the hallway.

2

Mona Badd

I STEP OUTSIDE THE big house for a moment to get some fresh air and can't believe my fucking eyes. The Ranch is like Fort Knox, with trucks coming in and out, dropping off men. Kong is hauling them in every hour. He has about a dozen armed guards at each post, and his paranoia is showing. It bothers him that he doesn't have Brock on lockdown. He knows Brock ain't gonna take this shit lying down, so he's over-preparing for whatever Brock has planned. I don't know how Brock intends to get us out of this situation, but he better move fast, or it might not happen at all.

Kong has some tall, bony white man walking around with a clipboard and camera. With his thick-rimmed glasses and curly hair, the man looks like a banker. He is taking notes and snapping pictures like he's appraising the place. Four guards surround him, protecting his every move as he turns to face the big house while holding his camera steady. When I flip him off, he takes a deep breath like he's nervous, but after looking up at one of the guards, he exhales before snapping the shot and jotting down more notes.

I think Kong is planning on reopening the Ranch for business, because trucks with long trailers are bringing in supplies. Most of the trucks are heading towards the casino, the others towards the hospital and morgue. The thick fog of black smoke coming from the crematory lets me know at least one of the trucks was packed with bodies. The burning hasn't stopped since Kong's gotten here, and he has burned at least three hundred bodies this week alone. I haven't seen him since we were at the cemetery, but I know he's here. I just don't know where that fat fuck is hiding. Kong likes to be seen, so he's hiding for a reason. I don't know what the fuck he's up to, but I'm sure he has a lot up his sleeve.

As I turn to walk back inside the house, I am met by my sister, Nicchi. She is blocking the front door, and even worse, she is wearing my red leather jumpsuit. The one I had custom made to fit my body. The one I wear for our special functions. *This bitch got a lot of nerve.* Her attire tells me that Kong is hosting some kind of event tonight. This is humiliating. Inviting people here to the Ranch to broadcast our takedown. *He got a lot of nerve.* He ain't wasting no time trying to run this place.

"What the fuck does your trifling ass want?" I ask Nicchi.

She laughs like I made a joke. Then she sighs and rolls her big eyes before swinging the blonde ponytail that grazes the crack of her fat ass. She pops her gum while looking me up and down like I'm the hired help.

"I talked to Kong." She pauses to give me time to feel her authority. "We're making a lot of changes around here—starting with this house," she continues, then looks over her shoulder toward the foyer.

"Changes? What the fuck are you talking about?"

I'm getting heated because Nicchi is being vindictive. Out of all the places on this Ranch where she could lay her head, she chose my house.

"Yes, changes," she repeats sarcastically. "For starters, this shit in here is tacky as fuck, so I'm getting rid of all the furniture. I got a designer coming in, and we're gonna paint the walls, change these dumb-ass floors, and everything."

"Bitch, you're the tackiest thing about this house. Standing here wearing my shit with your bum ass," I snap.

Nicchi sucks her teeth and jerks her neck back like she's appalled.

Then she rolls her eyes toward the ceiling like she can't tolerate me anymore and snaps her fingers three times. On-demand, three guards come charging toward her like her life is in danger. She points at me with her long yellow fingernail before placing both of her hands on her ample hips. Then she waits. The guards grab me, two gripping my arms while the other points a gun in my back. Nicchi is smirking the whole time. I refuse to give her the pleasure of seeing me sweat, so I don't resist.

"Are you gonna behave?" Nicchi asks me while playing with her nails.

I don't respond. Instead, I keep my eyes fixed on Nicchi, giving her that look she knows all too well. When this is all over, I'm gonna fuck her up, and she knows it.

"Let her go," she says and waves her hand at the guards, shooing them away.

I take a deep breath and try to regain my composure. You can't tell by looking at me, but my blood is boiling. However, I can't let my anger get the best of me. If I'm going to help Brock take this Ranch back, I got to be wise. I have to stay calm and play the game, no matter how much it kills me.

"I don't know why Kong got you loose, but I'm gonna talk to him tonight and let him know I think you should be put up like the rest of them," Nicchi says, referring to me like I'm a dog.

"I need to see him," I tell her, ignoring her comment.

"See who?" she asks, playing dumb.

Nicchi spits her gum on the foyer floor and snaps her fingers at one of the servers to pick it up. As she turns to walk down the hall, I follow behind her.

"I need to see Kong," I say.

I have to talk to Kong. The closer I get to Kong, the closer I get to the safe. Brock gave me the code that will override Vinchi's code. If I put the safe on lockdown, Kong won't have all this power, and he won't be throwing money around like he is.

"Well, he don't want to see you," Nicchi says without turning around to face me.

She continues walking down the hall, her slew feet dragging in the dollar store flip-flops she's wearing.

"Kong's gonna be real pissed when he finds out I asked to see him, and you denied me."

Nicchi stops walking, and with one hand now on her hip, she turns around to face me.

"You can't tell by now that he don't give a fuck about you," Nicchi says, then throws her hands in the air.

Although she is shaking her head while staring at me, I know she is considering what I said. She won't admit it, but she knows how Kong feels about me.

"This ain't personal. It's about business," I tell her.

"Kong ain't got no business with the Badds anymore," Nicchi states in a firm tone.

"Well, he can't just hold us hostage. I need to know what's his plan for me and the rest of my family."

"Your family?" Nicchi scoffs and shakes her head at me like I'm stupid. "You know he ain't letting them niggas live. He might spare you because y'all grew up together, but your so-called brothers are dead, and you know it," Nicchi said matter-of-factly.

"It ain't got to go down like that." My voice is more desperate than I mean for it to sound. "Don't nobody got to die."

"You really think it's wise to let them live?" Nicchi looks at me as if she's trying to keep it real. "This takeover isn't in the works. It's actually happening. Y'all lost, Mona. The Ranch is ours now."

She pulls a picture off the wall before turning her nose up at it.

"Would your husband let us live?" Nicchi continues. "How many people has he killed to protect this place? You know how shit works, so I don't know why you're acting surprised. You need to prepare yourself 'cause he's gonna kill them all, starting with that crazy-ass Brip first.

He's too much of a liability," Nicchi stated like it's a done deal. "White walls, Mona? Really?"

Nicchi does a 360 in the hallway and throws up her hands in a gesture that says she's baffled by my décor. She goes from talking about killing my family to changing the wall color in a moment's time like it's all the same to her. The bitch is heartless.

"What about the wives? Is he planning to kill them, too?" I inquire.

Nicchi shrugs. "I don't know. He hasn't mentioned them. I guess because they ain't a threat."

"What about Vinchi?" I blurt out.

It's been days since I've seen Vinchi. I figure he's been dodging me because he's ashamed of what he's done. Plus, with all this nonsense going on with Mamma Badd, he's probably taking it hard. They were very close. But, if Kong is planning to kill Bobby, Billy, and Brip, he might add Vinchi to that list, too, since he's made himself just as much of a threat.

"I don't know," Nicchi replies quickly like she's hiding something.

"You don't know?" I repeat and step closer to her. "You're gonna let Kong kill your nephew—your flesh and blood?" I say, reminding her that Vinchi isn't just a Badd; he's blood.

"Oh, now he's my nephew?" Nicchi takes a step towards me with her arms folded across her chest.

"What's that supposed to mean?"

I'm offended. Nicchi and I ain't never been close, but I've always looked out for her.

"I can count on my right hand the number of times I saw Vinchi. You kept him away from me like he was too good to be around us in the projects. Now I'm supposed to have this maternal auntie instinct for him? Vinchi is just as much a stranger to me as your husband and the rest of your bougie family."

"You can say what you want, but I've been good to you."

I point at her and walk in even closer. Nicchi takes a step back.

"I looked out for you once I left the East Meadows projects. Kept you in a new Benz almost every year. Sent you stacks of money like it was toilet paper. And this is how you repay me?"

Unable to handle the truth, Nicchi turns her head. She can't look at me because she knows everything she's allowing to happen is dead wrong.

"It's out of my hands," Nicchi says, throwing her hands in the air like she has nothing do with any of this. "I don't make these decisions, you know. You can't blame me."

"Let me talk to Kong. I got to protect my son."

"I already told you that he don't want to see you," Nicchi replies, barely looking me in the eye.

"Tell me where he is, Nicchi," I plead.

Making eye contact with me, she shakes her head sorrowfully and sighs like she's debating whether or not she should tell me where Kong is. Just when she's about to part her thick lips to speak, a van pulls up in the circular driveway and honks twice. Nicchi's eyes light up, and her lips stretch into a wide smile.

"They're here!" she says before jogging towards the front door while clapping.

"Nicchi, wait." I follow behind her. "What about Kong? What about Vinchi?"

She waves an annoyed hand my way, silencing me.

"Not now, Mona. I got business to tend to."

Nicchi transitions back to her selfish self. Whoever is in the van seems to be more important to her than Vinchi. *This bitch is lowdown.*

When we get outside, Nicchi spreads her fat arms in a grand welcoming gesture and smiles as she hurries to the van with her flip-flops slapping against the pavement. A middle-aged black guy hops out the car wearing a cheap suit that is two sizes too big for him. As soon as his feet touch the ground, his eyes widen with amazement, and he twists his neck to look around.

"I can't believe I'm really here. I'm actually on the Badd Ranch," he says in awe.

"It ain't called that no more," Nicchi tells him and gives me a side-eye.

Stepping away from the car, the man takes in the big house as he pulls his pants over his pot belly, only from them to fall back down under his waist. Then he cleans his teeth with his tongue and adjusts the bright yellow pimp hat on his head. When his eyes finally escape the wonder of the Ranch and land on me, he stops in his tracks. His dream suddenly feels like a nightmare, especially with the look I'm giving him. He hesitates and cuts his eyes at Nicchi.

"You good, Alonzo?" Nicchi says and waves him over to her.

Nicchi screeches and hugs his neck like he is her long-lost friend.

"Welcome to my home," Nicchi boldly says.

"All this is you?" he says, looking at the house's double doors like they are the gates to heaven.

"Yep," Nicchi responds like she worked all her life for this very moment.

The bitch is shameless.

"I'm sure glad to be here, Miss Nicchi," the man says in a thick southern accent.

He pulls up his pants again and walks to the side of the van.

"What you got for me?" Nicchi asks, excited.

"Da best of da best," he says before sliding open the van's door.

Nicchi screams like a fat kid in a candy store when about ten sleazy-looking women jump out of the van. Alonzo claps his hands and orders the women to line up so Nicchi can take a better look at them. As Nicchi walks around them, she pulls on their hair, lifts their skirts, and feels their boobs like a female pimp.

"These tricks gonna make me some good money tonight," Nicchi says, looking at the women like they are made of gold.

To me, they look gold-plated. The women are busted as hell with their ashy knees, skinny legs, nappy weaves, and beer bellies. They all look a hot mess.

"Mona…" Nicchi turns to me, looking desperate. "I can't get in your breeding quarters. Why is that?"

"Because I closed it off, that's why," I respond with my arms folded across my chest.

"Well, I need you to open the door so I can set my girls up. That's where they're gonna be staying, and I got more coming tonight. Right, Alonzo?"

She gives Alonzo a quick look, and he nods.

"No," I tell her.

Nicchi starts breathing heavily.

"I ain't got time for this shit, Mona. Give me the key."

Nicchi holds out her hand like I have the key stuffed in my bra.

"You give me what I want first," I say, trying to bargain with her.

"Okay," she replies quickly, not putting up much of a fight. "But, even if I tell you where he is, I doubt security will let you through. He don't want to see you," she emphasized.

"Tell me anyway," I demand.

SECURITY ESCORTS ME to the crematory where Kong has set up his office. With all the activity going on there, I should have known this is where he would be. On my walk there, I pass by Billy's house and see someone looking at me through the curtains. After the discovery at the cemetery, Kong had everybody escorted back to their mansions. He doubled the security and cut the phone lines. All of them are prisoners, except me. At least that's what they think. The fact that I'm seemingly walking freely around the Ranch makes me look less trustworthy to them. I wish Kong would let me speak to them, but he won't. None of us can talk to each other.

I wonder where he's keeping Ace and, more importantly, Vinchi. He has us all separated. If there's one thing I know about Kong, he is a man of his word. If he promised the Badd men that he would let them kill Ace, he will. On the other hand, if what Nicchi says is true about him going to kill the Badd men, that shit is true, too. That's why I'm confused. Why let them kill Ace just to kill them all in the end? What type of twisted fate is that?

I didn't know what to think when I saw Mamma Badd's casket was empty. At first, I thought my eyes were playing tricks on me, but I knew my eyes were seeing right from the look on everybody's faces. I thought it meant she could still be alive, but then, I had to remind myself about Brock's revelation. I tried hard to forget him confessing to me that he killed his mother, and the moment I saw the empty casket, I almost did, thinking this is just some trickery going on between Ace and Kong. But where the fuck is her body? How did they get it off the Ranch without us knowing? This shit just doesn't make any sense.

It's sad the brothers have to go through this shit. It's obvious Kong is trying to break them down before he kills them. This shit is definitely a strategy. I have to play my part to make sure everybody stays alive and until the Ranch is back under our control. I know they don't trust me right now, but they'll thank me later. I just don't know how the fuck I'm going to pull this shit off. I can't take a piss without two guards following me to the toilet. Kong has this place on lockdown, and security is getting tighter every day. I have to figure something out.

We arrive at the crematory, and another guard stops us.

"What y'all need?" the man asks and holds out his hand.

"She says she wants to see Kong," replies one of the guards escorting me.

Most of these men who Kong has recruited from the East Meadows and other projects are all muscle and no brain. In other words, none of them are trained. I doubt half of them know how to shoot a pistol, but they outnumber us ten to one.

"Kong ain't seeing nobody."

The man gives me a piercing look. He knows who I am, and he already knows not to trust me. However, it seems he doesn't consider me to be a threat, because he lays his semi-automatic down in the grass and pulls a cigarette from behind his ears before sitting down on the curb. He lights the cigarette and relaxes as he takes a puff. He's waiting for me to protest.

"You sure about that, soldier?" I ask, causing him to second-guess himself.

"Yeah, I'm sure," he says, then jumps up and puts out the cigarette while keeping his eyes on me. "You trying to say I don't know my job?"

He walks towards me slowly. He's trying to intimidate me, but I don't feel it. I could take his skinny ass out with one hit and then shoot him with his own gun, but I keep my cool.

"All I'm saying is when I do see him, and I will, I will let him know that you refused to let me talk to him," I say and turn to walk away.

The guards who escorted me there follow behind me like they are glued to my side.

"Wait," the guard calls out before I can take two good steps.

"I'm gonna do you a favor and go holla at him, but only because I'm in a good mood," he says while pulling out another cigarette.

I nod my head. Kong's guards don't have the wit of a snail. Playing them is going to be easy, but shooting them all will be a challenge. I have to figure out how to move around them to get what I want, especially once I finally get to the safe. But, right now, that seems impossible, just like Mamma Badd's empty casket.

My two guards start kicking around an empty beer can to amuse themselves while waiting for the other guard to return. I look around the Ranch and shake my head in disappointment. The place is filthy. It's starting to look like the projects I left years ago. Empty beer bottles and cigarette butts litter the streets. Candy wrappers and Cheetos bags accompany them. Wads of spit are on the asphalt, and I just witnessed a guy piss on the curb. Kong is running this place into the ground. His guards are decorated with guns and two-ways, but they know nothing about the art of security. They are treating this like it's a block party. Watching his back is the last thing on their minds. They are too busy smoking weed and drinking beer like they are at a festival. Now Nicchi got whores here to entertain them. I can't believe the way this place is falling apart.

I look up, and the guard that went to talk to Kong is waving his lanky arm in our direction. My guards don't even notice him. They're too occupied with entertaining themselves with a can. When I start walking towards the crematory, they smarten up and try to catch up to me, grabbing my arm to keep me from moving too fast.

"He's in the basement," the guard says in between puffs, then rolls his eyes at me and walks back to his post.

As we walk through the hall to get to the basement, I have to cover my nose from the stench of the dead bodies lying everywhere. Some still have fresh blood on them. Kong is a real fool. No wonder he never evolved out of the East Meadows projects. Doesn't he know this ain't the way to do this? Hell, he'll kill everybody from the smell of these rotting corpses before Brock even gets here. I guess he thinks by burning so many bodies, he is flaunting his power and will gain respect.

I stop to stare at the body of a man lying on a gurney. He has a look of terror in his eyes—like he saw the devil right before he took his last breath. There is a bullet hole right between his eyes. The shot is so clean that I would swear Brip did it if he wasn't being held prisoner in his house.

"Keep walking," one guard orders me, grabbing my arm to move me along.

We walk down the stairs to the basement, and the smell of rotting and burning bodies hits so hard that I gag.

"Man, shit smells like roses compared to this. I can't wait to get the fuck out of here. Thank God we ain't stationed here," one guard comments before pushing me and saying, "Hurry the fuck up."

Not wanting to be here either, I pick up my pace.

When we get to the basement, Kong is sitting facing the door like he's been waiting on me. He stands and smiles, revealing his bite-sized yellow teeth that look like rotten corn kernels.

"Nothing like the smell of death in the morning," Kong says and inhales the toxic fumes like it's aromatherapy.

He smiles at the horrified look on my face as I try to shield my nose from the nauseating smell.

"Mona," he says, his heavy voice bouncing off the walls and beating against our eardrums.

For some reason, Kong looks bigger than the last time I saw him. He outstretches his arms for a hug, and I decide to go with the flow, wrapping my arms around his body. Of course, my arms barely stretch around his full waist. Seeming surprised by my embrace, he squeezes me into his musty body even tighter. His moist t-shirt smells like a bag of spoiled onions, and just being near him makes me want to bathe. As Kong kisses the top of my head, I feel the spit from his wet lips settling on my crown. Although I badly want to wipe his saliva from my hair, I play it cool. With his sweaty palms, he cups my face and strokes my cheeks with thick, dirt-laced thumbs.

"Are you okay?" he asks me.

Kong finally steps back and gives me room to breathe, but there is no fresh air. I continue to hold my breath the best I can to avoid inhaling the smell that's starting to make me sick.

"This ain't how you do things, Kong. All these bodies—"

Kong chuckles.

"I know what I'm doing. Now that the Ranch is mine, it's important for me to build my clientele. I'm burning these bodies for free—on good faith of a prosperous working relationship. You smell death, but I smell money. I smell a future."

"I trusted you, Kong. You're betraying me, you know? As far back as we go, and you do this shit?"

"I'm doing this for us," he quickly replies.

Trying to get a feel for where his mind is, I pause and take in what he's saying.

"This don't feel like it has shit to do with me, Kong. You're holding my family and me hostage here."

"You aren't being held hostage. I'm only trying to protect you, Mona. And them niggas ain't your family. I am!"

Kong pounds his chest, and something flies off his shirt and lands on my cheek. I wipe my face and step back.

"They'll never know you like I do. They don't have our history."

"What are you planning to do? Why won't you let me see them?" I ask.

"I'm rearranging things around here. The Ranch is mine now!" Kong replies, then looks down at me like he dares me to challenge him.

"Nicchi said you were going to kill them."

"Nicchi talks too fucking much!" Kong hisses. "But, yes, they got to die, Mona. You know that."

While trying not to look too shocked, I take a deep breath to stay calm, but my heart sinks.

"Where's the man you call your husband? If he surrenders, they might get to live. He's the face of this place. The others are just weak links. Brock's death will seal the deal."

"If you let me move around a little bit, I can try to find him."

"You sure you don't know where he is?"

Kong lifts my chin with his forefinger and penetrates my eyes with an evil stare.

"No," I say, and it's the truth.

"Well, I know where he's hiding. I could send for him, but I want him to come to me. He ain't no threat no more. At least not now. Too many of my people are here."

"Kong, nobody has to die."

"Everybody has to die," Kong says to me matter-of-factly.

"What about my son? Where is Vinchi?"

"Vinchi is fine," Kong quickly replies.

"Where is he?" I ask again, this time calmer.

"I said he was fine," Kong repeats, sounding annoyed.

"What about Ace? You promised them you would let them decide what to do with him."

"Well, there's been a change of plans," Kong admits.

"What does that mean?"

Kong looks at me and laughs. He knows I'm prying.

"Mona…" He grabs my face again. "…you ain't got to worry about nothing. No one is going to hurt you." He strokes my cheek and gives me a flirty look before planting his two large wet lips on my forehead. I can feel speckles of his saliva popping against my skin.

"Can I see them?"

"Why? You want to deliver the message that I'm going to kill them?"

I take a deep breath and search the room with my eyes. There is nothing I can do to change Kong's mind.

"What about the women? The wives?"

"I ain't thought that far ahead yet, but you know how much a nigga will pay to fuck one of them? Hundreds and thousands. I may have them auctioned."

"Do you even hear what you are saying?" I snap.

Kong looks at me like he doesn't appreciate my tone.

"I know exactly what I'm doing, Mona!" he yells.

Kong doesn't like to be challenged. Again, I take a deep breath in an attempt to keep my composure.

"When is all this going down?" I ask, my voice trailing off into a faint whisper.

"Sooner rather than later," Kong says and searches my face for a reaction. "I figure I'll start with Brip first. My people want to see him dead. It will bring them great pleasure to see him bleed, and I'll gain their loyalty."

"Was that always the plan?"

"Yes," Kong admits.

"So, you were playing Vinchi?"

"Vinchi played himself," Kong says through a chuckle. "If he was our son, he wouldn't be so dumb," he adds, taunting me.

I ball up my fist and control my anger by biting down on my bottom lip. Then I exhale.

"What did you do with Mamma Badd's body?" I inquire, having to know.

"I don't know what you're talking about. If she ain't in her final resting place, then maybe she ain't fucking dead. None of that shit matters to me, though. I got more important shit to think about. As long as she don't show up claiming this place, I don't give a fuck."

My face drops, and my shoulders slump in defeat. I can barely hold my head up. This shit is really happening. It's over.

"Please let me see them before you do it," I beg him.

Kong stares at me like my sadness is bringing him both pleasure and pain.

"I'm opening the Ranch back up tonight. I'm making my takeover official by throwing a big-ass party, and all of my people from the East Meadows projects are welcome. I need my people to know that I have arrived, and just as promised, I'm bringing them with me. They're gonna spread the word. This is the type of shit you got to see to believe," Kong proudly states. "It's going to be a real nice shindig."

He pinches the bottom of his double chin and grins. Then he stares back at me, giving me a considerate look.

"Why don't you put on something nice and join me at the casino as my guest? I want you by my side."

Kong takes a slow step towards me. So, I take a quick step back. I know what he's getting at; he's still in love with me. Although the idea of that sickens me, it may be our way out of this.

"What about Nicchi?" I ask, faking like I'm jealous.

Kong smiles at me like he's flattered.

"Don't worry about Nicchi. She's just a substitute for the real thing. Besides, she's your sister. I thought you would be happy to have her around."

His statement shows just how much he doesn't know about me.

Kong's hands travel from the sides of my face, down to my breasts, and then to my ass. He pulls me into what he thinks is a sensual embrace, and I try my best not to pull away. He massages the back of my neck, trying to comfort me, but it feels like he's choking me. His hands are rough and heavy.

"It's all going to work out the way it should have, Mona. You'll see."

I have to find a way to get them off the Ranch. Otherwise, they're dead.

3

Brip Badd

"SAY IT AGAIN!" the guard shouts, daring me to speak.
As I lean up, he strikes me in the gut with the back of his shotgun, knocking the wind out of me. I double over and gag, coughing up a wad of spit and blood. Before I can regain my composure, the guard's partner sucker punches me in the jaw, and I fall back to the floor. I hear Taffy scream my name.

"Brip, please! Please!"

Taffy tries running to my aid, but his partner snatches her away from me, pulling her into his grip. Taffy struggles to free herself from his grasp. She could knock his ass out if she wanted to, but she's being careful because she doesn't want anything to happen to me. She's trying to protect me, and I'm trying to protect her. From the corner of my eye, I watch him touching my wife, and my temperature starts to boil. Seeing his hands swiftly moving over her body and coping a feel wherever he can are all the permission I need to do what I'm planning to do to both of them.

"Go ahead, nigga." He pokes me hard in the back of my head with the barrel of his pistol. His finger is on the trigger. He wants to pull it so bad that his whole body is trembling. I know that feeling. "Say that shit again!"

These niggas are beyond foul. I can't believe the way shit is going down on this Ranch. My legacy. My home. My business. It's all fucked up. First, they dig up my mother's grave and steal her precious body from her coffin, and now, they want to fuck with my wife. Taffy is where I draw the fucking line. My mother, too. My mother was resting in peace before these fuck niggas got to her. The shit they did is disgusting—an abomination of the worst kind. They're gonna pay for their sins. It's judgement day, and all of these motherfuckers are 'bout to reap.

I roll over onto my stomach before leaning up on all fours. The guard kicks me in the back, and my body plops back down to the floor, belly first. Using my forearms, I push my weight up and take another deep breath. My head is hanging low. I'm trying to get the ringing in my ear to stop so I can think straight. I'm getting dizzy and feel like I'm gonna pass out. So, I take two quick breaths and squeeze my eyes shut for two split seconds before reopening them, trying to regain my focus. These niggas have been beating my ass every chance they get, but I ain't backing down. It's open season on a nigga. All of them are thirsty for my blood, but I'm only gonna take so much before I bite back. And, today, my fangs are coming out. It's do or die. I'll choose death before I go down like this, especially after that nigga tried my wife. Nobody touches my wife and lives to talk about it. No fucking body. I'm killing his ass today, even if that means we'll take our last breath together.

"Bitch-ass," he says to me as I stumble to my feet.

"Please, leave him alone," Taffy pleads.

She frees herself from his partner's grip and puts herself in between the guards and me.

Pissed, I push her away. I told her not to intervene. Protecting me ain't her fucking job. Taffy is carrying my child. Even if the baby ain't mine, it's still mine 'cause she's mine. I got a family to protect, and if I have to give up my life doing it, then so be it. If I had my right mind during Ace's attack, that shit would've never happened. At least not the way it did. I got to keep them safe now.

I move Taffy behind me and pull her into my back, shielding her body with mine. While wiping the blood from my mouth, I look at both niggas like they're already dead. They're holding their guns in my face, but I can tell they are amateurs from the way they're holding them. All I need is the right moment, and I'm grabbing one of those guns and making them both eat bullets. That's what their last meal is gonna be—hot steel washed down with a cup of their blood. I hope these niggas are ready to feast.

"Please, Brip. Just leave it alone," Taffy whispers in my ear.

I can feel her body trembling behind me, her heart pounds against my back. Taffy reads my mind; she knows what's coming next. She knows their deaths are inevitable at this point, but she pleads with me anyway. Taffy is thinking about tomorrow, but tomorrow ain't promised to none of us on this Ranch. So, I'm living for today. And, today, they will fucking die. She's been through so much already, and I hate I have to add this shit to her paranoia. But there's no way around it. If I don't kill them, they're gonna kill us.

"When you gonna understand that we're entitled to everything in this motherfucker?" the guard snarls and looks over my shoulder at my wife. "Don't you see what's going on? This Ranch is ours! If I want to fuck your wife, then that's my right!" he yells in my face.

I can smell the rum on his tongue. He and his partner have been drinking all day. I guess the liquor got them bold. That and the fact that it seems Kong is hauling in more muscle every hour. They are feeling mighty powerful, but everything they're doing is showing me that they're weak. I don't know where Kong is finding all these niggas, but it makes his ass look desperate and afraid, making *me* feel powerful. Powerful enough to start taking these niggas down one by one.

Before I can respond with a "fuck you", he rams his pistol in my mouth and sticks it so far down my throat that I gag. It's so deep in my mouth that I can practically taste the bullets. Ironically, I always wondered what a gun tastes like since I made so many niggas swallow bullets as their last meal. I guess you can say I got curious over the years. Although this fucking gun is in my mouth, I have no plans to swallow a bullet tonight. While he's busy force-feeding me his steel, I plan my next move.

His drunk partner grabs Taffy from behind me and pulls her into his waist. I hear her pleading for my life, and that shit pisses me off. My wife doesn't have to beg a nigga for shit, not even my life. His partner pulls Taffy into a forceful embrace that she pulls away from. My blood is boiling, but I see the light at the end of the tunnel. Now they're about to see it, too.

I have been trained to get out of a situation like this. I spent plenty of nights hemmed up with Brock demonstrating different defense techniques on me, and he wouldn't let up until I got them right. When he told me that what he was teaching me may save my life one day, I thought he was exaggerating. I thought he was too intense. Too serious. Too mean. But, that nigga was right.

Without wasting any time manipulating my body a certain way, my knee hits his chest in a blow so heavy he gasps for air before he knows what's going on. A move that is so discreet and silent his partner doesn't even notice. Besides, he is too busy putting his hands where they don't belong on my wife. I use that split second Brock calls a life-or-death moment—a moment so quick that if you blink, you miss it—to penetrate the back of his neck in such a way that he becomes temporarily paralyzed, losing his mobility and his grip.

Pulling the pistol out of my mouth, I aim at his friend first. It's tricky with Taffy being right under him, but I'm the best shot in Atlanta. I never miss, and I don't miss this time. I get his ass right between the eyes. It's beautiful. A single line of blood trickles down his forehead like a tear escaping his eye. The shot was so clean and pure that the nigga might have made it to heaven.

I deliver the next shot to his partner—close range, right through his left temple. The bullet is in and out like a thief in the night, leaving a mess behind. Blood and brains splatter on my face, but I don't mind. I had a taste for blood tonight.

"Brip, what the fuck! They're gonna kill you! They're gonna kill both of us!"

Taffy is panicking, but I don't have time to calm her down. I have to clean up my mess, and I need her help. As I run out of the kitchen towards the back door, I slip on some blood and hit the marble floor hard.

"Fuck," I yell.

I hop up and look out the window to see if anyone heard the shots. With so much commotion going on tonight, I doubt anyone heard anything. Music is blasting, and horns are honking like it's a street party. These niggas picked the perfect night for me to put bullets in them.

From my back window, I can see Billy's house. I turn on the porch light to let him know there may be trouble.

"Go get that red lightbulb out the kitchen and replace it with the one from the back porch. I got to get the word out to Billy," I yell to Taffy.

Following my orders, Taffy runs back to the kitchen and then back to the porch, slipping and falling on the same blood pouring out that nigga's skull.

Once Billy sees my red light on, he will know what's going down and alert Bobby.

When Taffy comes back, she looks like she's about to throw up.

"I ain't gonna let nothing happen to you. How many times I got to tell you that shit?" I try to assure her, but she's about to snap at any moment. I can feel it.

"Go get the Clorox and some towels. I need this blood cleaned up. I'm gonna drag these bodies down to the basement and put them in the wine freezer. I need you cleaning up behind me, and we got to move quick. We don't know when the next nigga is gonna come barging in here."

Taffy falls to her knees and starts crying hysterically. Her shoulders are hunched, and her chest is heaving like she's hyperventilating. I want to console her, but I don't have time for that shit. So, I don't.

"Taffy, I need you to snap out of this shit and get your head in the game," I tell her.

"We gonna die. They're gonna kill us. It's over…" she says in between sobs.

It hurts me to see that she doesn't believe in me anymore. It sounds like she's giving up. I'm gonna prove to Taffy that I got her back, though. I don't know how the fuck I'm going to do it, but I'm gonna get us out of this shit.

I start dragging the first body down the basement stairs by his ankles. This nigga is heavy as fuck. Doing this shit feels like a full-blown workout. Sweat beads are popping off my forehead and dripping onto his bloody body. Every time his head hits the step, blood gushes from it, creating more of a mess.

"Fuck," I yell out of frustration. "Taffy!"

This time, I don't sound nice. I need her fucking help, or her worst nightmare will come true.

"Get your ass up. I need you!" I yell while continuing to pull this nigga down the steps.

I pause to catch my breath. When I look up, I see Taffy with a bucket of hot soapy water and bleach. She's scrubbing the blood off the floor and painting the steps with the Clorox like her life depends on it. *That's my fucking girl.* I continue to pull. When she sees the mess I'm making, she stops what she's doing and darts back up the steps. She's moving so fast that she falls when she gets to the landing.

"Be careful, baby," I say to her and continue to pull.

Taffy returns seconds later with a few five-gallon garbage bags. She throws them to me without saying a word and then gets back to scrubbing the steps. I don't have to ask the reason for the bags. I immediately open one and wrap it around this nigga's big-ass bleeding head. I look up at Taffy and smile, but she's too busy with her Molly the Maid swag.

I finally get to the bottom of the stairs and swing open the cooler to our wine cellar located inside a utility room in the back of our basement. Those dumb-ass niggas won't be able to find it unless they are looking hard, and even then, the ignorant motherfuckers won't know what it is. The way the door is designed makes it look like the entrance to a fancy closet.

I pull his body inside, and thanks to the garbage bag containing his blood, Taffy doesn't have to clean anymore. After throwing his ass inside the freezer, I realize it can hold at least two more bodies, maybe even more if I'm strategic about how I position them.

"What that fuck are you doing?" Taffy screams behind me as she starts running back up the stairs. "We have to get the other one," she says.

Her head is in the game. I like that.

I turn around and run up the steps behind her, leaping over five steps at a time. Once I'm at the top, I waste no time covering as much of his body as I can with the garbage bag while Taffy is on her knees, scrubbing the floor. I got the second body down the steps even quicker.

"We need a lock," I tell Taffy after closing the freezer door. "Run to the garage and look in my toolbox. Find me something to secure this door."

Taffy darts back up the steps, and in record time, she returns with a padlock and a zip tie. The zip tie will be too obvious, so I grab the lock. When I notice I have nothing to attach it to, I dash to the garage.

"Where are you going?" Taffy yells. "We have to lock this door, Brip, or they're gonna find them."

I don't have time to respond. I can hear in her voice that she's starting to panic again. I know she wants this whole thing to be over. She's ready to get back to being held a hostage. That feels safer to her than fighting back.

When I get to the garage, I empty my toolbox and try to find something I can use to secure the padlock. I dump out the contents of two boxes before finding the perfect tool—an actual door latch. It's still brand new in the bag.

I peek out the garage door window. I don't see any activity, but I hear it. It sounds like it's hundreds of people on the Ranch drinking and celebrating their seeming victory. Grabbing my electric drill, I race back to the basement.

"Hold this," I tell Taffy, handing her the latch while I pull out my drill. I pray the batteries ain't dead. "Open the bag," I say.

Taffy hands me the latch, and I drill it into the door. Then I hold out my hand for her to give me the padlock. After securing the door, I discard the drill in the trash, grab Taffy's hand and the zip tie, and dart back up the stairs.

"I got to get this blood off my body. We both do," I say, looking at the speckles of blood on Taffy's neck. Some are even smeared across her forehead.

Taffy looks at the front door and then back at me. Her expression says she doesn't think we have time. Running to the door, I lock it.

"They're gonna know. We're not allowed to lock doors, remember?"

Taffy's eyes bulge with fear. She's panicking again. I grab her, pull her into a quick kiss, and lead her upstairs. We jump in the shower, not caring how hot or cold the water is, and begin to wash each other. Taffy is cleaning behind my ears and scrubbing my back like she did the floors. I take the washrag and wipe around her neck. We spent many nights fucking in this same shower. We made love in here with the same intensity that we are wiping each other down. Everything we do together is intense, including the way we love each other. I move the soapy rag down her body until it lands on her stomach. I see a little bulge and notice how hard it is. Suddenly, I remember she's carrying life in her.

"I'm sorry," I say, holding her stomach.

She places her hand on top of mine and nods, sniffing as she holds back a tear. Then she turns me back around and gives me one last scrub down. We don't have any time to waste. Not even for apologies. We get ourselves clean in less than three minutes, jump out the shower, and throw on sweats and t-shirts.

Before we can get back downstairs, we hear guards aggressively banging on the door and turning the knob. It won't be long before they blow the door open. Taffy gives me a wide-eyed stare like it's all over, but I reassure her with a "be cool" look. I point to the zip tie she left on the kitchen bar.

"Open this fucking door," someone on the other side of the door yells.

Taffy and I jump when we hear glass break. They're trying to get in through the window.

"Go swing open the back porch door, and leave it open," I say to her. "Quick!" I yell when I hear more glass breaking.

After Taffy pushes the door open, I hand her the zip tie.

"Tie me up," I say, holding out my hands like I'm surrendering to arrest.

Taffy looks confused but does what she's asked. More glass breaks, and the knocking on the door becomes kicking.

"Follow my lead," I say to her, and then with my hands tied in front of me, I run towards the living room and take a seat on the floor.

"Go open the door. If they ask you why the door was locked, tell them the guards did it."

"Brip, I can't. I can't—"

"You can. Baby, I got you," I say to her calm. "It's okay."

Taffy gives me a hesitant nod before taking a deep breath. The sound of breaking glass breaking and the door being kicked causes her to flinch and duck down like someone is throwing something at her. She keeps moving towards the door, though. Then she stops, takes a deep breath, and unlocks it.

4

Taffy Badd

FUCK, FUCK, FUCK! I can't do this shit anymore. I can't, I think to myself while trying to stay calm. Terror is written all over my face. I look like the poster child for an accessory to a crime. They're gonna take one good look at me and know Brip killed those two guards and that I helped get rid of the bodies. They're gonna kill us all—me, Brip, and the baby. We're all dying tonight.

I take a deep breath, and right when I place my hand on the knob, a brick comes flying through the window. I jump back and scream. My heart is racing so fast it feels like I just finished running a marathon. A lean down and place my weight on my knees to keep myself from hyperventilating. The kicking. The cursing. The popping of fireworks. The random gunfire. The banging on the door. The bodies. The blood. This fucking Ranch. It's all too much. I just can't take it anymore. I just can't.

"Open the door, Taffy," I hear Brip say from behind me.

I turn my head and look down the hall, searching for his voice with my eyes. I can't move. My body is going into shock.

"What the fuck is going on in there?" yells one of the guards.

I twist the lock and place my hand on the knob, but as soon as the guards hear the click, they kick the door. It crashes open, the force knocking me to the floor, and I land on my ass on the marble tiles. After quickly hopping up, I hold my hands in the air, surrendering.

"Why was the fucking door locked?" the lead guard asks.

"Your guy locked it. I swear." I wave my trembling hands in the air.

He looks at me like he can see the lies written on my face. I take slow steps backwards, making sure to keep my hands in the air. Two other guards storm through the doorway and stand by his side. They are holding guns the size of shotguns. The other's weapon is as small as the handguns I carry. It's not the size of the guns that intimidate me, though. It's the bullets they carry.

"Where is your husband?" the lead guard asks before cocking his gun.

All three of them rush past me in pursuit of Brip, knocking me to the floor again. I'm not the threat. Leaning up on my knees, I try to motivate myself to get up, but I just want to stay down. With my front door wide open, I get a notion to run. To run and never look back. I want to leave it all. Brip. The Ranch. All of it. But, I'm too paralyzed with fear. Too much has happened. Where would I go? And how far would I get before I'm caught and killed?

So much is going on outside. It's like Gotham City out there. Fireworks are lighting up the sky, and gunpowder is polluting the air. Plus, there's that god-awful smell that's fogging the Ranch, and it's getting stronger every day. It smells like a mixture of death, fear, betrayal, and everything else evil. I cover my nose to keep from gasping and pull myself to my feet. Then I take a slow step towards the door. When the air hits my face, despite the stench, I feel revived. Strong enough to make my escape, but one of the guards stops me.

"Where the fuck you think you going, bitch?" I hear him cock his gun.

I stop dead in my tracks, and while holding my hands, I slowly turn around.

"I'm just going to close the door."

It was a lie and the truth. Honestly, I didn't know what I was going to do once I got to the door.

"Well, you know the fucking rules. You don't touch any fucking doors. Now get back there," he says, giving me an evil stare.

I walk down the hall to the living room, where two guards have their guns pointing at Brip's head. I don't know how he can stay calm in all this chaos.

"I got to fucking piss! Untie me!" Brip yells, holding out his hands.

He could get an Academy Award with this performance. Meanwhile, I feel like I'm going to crack at any moment. I wonder if this is how Lera felt after she snapped. Am I going to lose it like Lera? All this time, I called her weak and crazy, but really, she'd just had enough. Now it's my turn. I take another deep breath to keep from fainting.

"Get this shit off of me! This ain't how it's supposed to go," Brip continues to rant like he has rights.

The guards seem relieved to see Brip tied up, but that doesn't stop them from keeping their guns on him. The fact that they are afraid of him is what scares me the most. How far will their fear lead them? Will their fear of Brip cause them to kill him? What will happen to me? What will happen to my baby if Brip isn't here to protect us?

"You don't make the fucking rules!" the lead guard yells and nudges Brip with his gun's barrel. "Where are my men?" he asks, looking around the room.

I try to keep a straight face. I pray he doesn't ask me. My knees feel like they are about to give out, and my entire body is trembling.

"I don't fucking know! They tied me up and left an hour ago. They said they would be back to untie me. They went out back, and now I got to fucking piss." Brip gestures towards the back porch with his head. "You gonna hold my dick while I piss?"

"Fuck you," the guard yells, then slaps Brip across the face with the butt of his pistol.

Blood trickles down Brip's face. He leans his head to the side, trying to shake off the pain. Then, he starts laughing like it's all a joke.

Pissed, the guard punches him in the mouth. Brip's head snaps back, and he grunts before sniffing hard and spitting out a wad of blood at the guard's feet.

"This ain't no way to treat a man in his own house," Brip says, his voice strained.

"You ain't heard? This ain't your shit no more," the guard snarls at Brip. "The only thing your name is on around here is the grave we're digging for you. That's it."

My entire body shudders as the guard chastises Brip.

The guard then looks at the other two men standing beside him. "Y'all post up here until the others get back," he demands.

"Nah, we supposed to be at the casino where the action is. That's probably where them two niggas at right now. That ain't right, man!" one of them complains.

"Look, I'll find them and send them back," he tells them. "Just do what I say."

"My post is almost up, and my girl and her friends are gonna be here soon for the party. I ain't staying here all night, man. So, I hope you find them niggas."

Brip starts to laugh, and the lead guard kicks him in the chin to silence him. Brip's body drops to the floor, his face bouncing against it when he lands.

"That's the last time I'm gonna tell you to shut the fuck up!" He looks at Brip like he wants to kill him, but obviously, there is a reason they are keeping him alive...at least for now. The lead guard turns his attention back to his comrades. "I'll send somebody to cover you if I can't find them."

He pulls out his two-way and says something into the speaker, but nobody replies. He sighs heavily before walking towards the door.

"Who's gonna untie me?"

He stops and looks at Brip; his expression says he can't take anymore complaining. So, gestures for one of his men to untie him. Brip gives me one of his "everything is going to be okay" looks, but it doesn't last long because I look away. I'm tired of false hope.

Our new guards have spent most of the night out on the back porch chain-smoking blunts and complaining. Every so often, they come inside to give us stern looks. I guess that's supposed to intimidate us. Brip is staying calm, but I see that look in his eyes. I know it's only a matter of time before he does something crazy.

We are sitting on the couch. He has me pulled so close to him that I may as well be in his lap. He's rubbing my shoulders, but it's more to calm his nerves than mine. He has an anxious look in his eyes. Everything is cool right now, but he just can't leave well enough alone. His ADHD ass craves conflict. I'm mentally keeping my fingers crossed, praying we get through the night.

Killing those two men has made Brip thirsty. Once he gets blood-thirsty, nothing other than more blood can quench his thirst. Killing those men gave him back some of his power. Brip was born into power. It's a part of his DNA; he can't function without it. I wish he wouldn't have done what he did. He's only digging a deeper hole for us, but you can't tell his arrogant, selfish ass nothing. He said he did that shit for me, but it was more for him. This shit has me wondering what I ever saw in a man like Brip in the first place. What's wrong with me to love a justified serial killer? What type of person does that make me? How could I have not seen him for who he is? Are money and love that blinding?

I sigh and lean up. I need air. Or at least a moment away from Brip. I stand up from the couch only to be pulled back down. I'm Brip's property. I'm a prisoner to two parties—first Brip and then our captives. I just want my life back.

"I need some air," I whisper to Brip.

He gives me an intense stare.

"Well, there ain't no air around here. You can breathe once I get us out of this shit, but until then, you got to keep holding your breath."

"I've been holding my breath our entire marriage. I'm suffocating, Brip," I snap.

Brip looks at me like he just got stung by a bee.

"You don't mean that," he arrogantly replies, then pulls me even closer to him. "This baby got you mean as hell," he says and rubs my stomach.

For some reason, him touching my stomach comforts me. I waited for so long for this moment, but I had no idea it would be this fucked up.

"I'm gonna take care of the both of you. Both of y'all are mine," he says in a loving but possessive way.

It's relieving that Brip will accept my child no matter what, but it doesn't change anything. I don't want this anymore. It's too much. Even if Brip manages to kill every guard walking the Ranch, I can't do it anymore. I can't be a Badd wife. I will never put my child in this kind of danger again.

I lower my head and move my eyes away from Brip's gaze. I can feel him looking at me. He's trying to figure out my mood. He wants to know what I'm thinking, but he will never ask. He's too arrogant. Or so I thought.

"You don't believe me, do you?" Brip says to me. "You don't believe I'm gonna get us out of this shit, huh?"

I move his hand from my stomach and twist my neck in his direction.

"Even if you do, then what?" I challenge him.

"What the fuck you mean?" Brip is frustrated.

"How many times are you supposed to get us out of this situation? I don't want my child around this shit, this life." Disgusted, I scoot my body away from him.

"That's them hormones talking," Brip says, dismissing me like he always does. "You don't mean that shit."

I sigh and lock eyes with him. Brip stares back at me, but he's not seeing me. He refuses. He's not seeing the weariness in my eyes; he's not seeing the fear and exhaustion. He only sees what he wants.

"I wish my brother Keno was here," I mumble under my breath.

"What you say?" Brip says although he heard me clear as day.

"I said I wish Keno was here," I repeat louder and more vexed.

"Why?" Brip sits up straight, fixes his eyes on me, and lowers his brows into an evil scowl.

"Because he would know what to do," I answer honestly.

Keno was the opposite of Brip. He wasn't moved by emotion but rather strategy and wisdom. He didn't just kill because he was good at it. He killed because it was necessary.

"Well, your brother ain't here," Brip replies with a heavy voice.

I look over my shoulders at the guards. I don't want anything to prompt their presence.

"You know that better than any of us," I snidely shoot back.

Brip takes a deep breath, sucking in whatever words he was about to say. Then he leans back and sweeps his hands over his head.

"Them damn hormones," he says again. "Now ain't the time for them."

Brip looks over at the guards and grits his teeth. He's getting that blood-thirsty look in his eyes again, and my heart starts to race.

"You ain't Keno's responsibility no more. You got me, and I'm gonna show you just how much I love you." Brip balls up his fist. "You see them two dumb-ass niggas out there shooting the breeze?" Brip's eyes never leave the doorway. "I'm gonna kill both them niggas tonight and make you a believer," he reveals.

Gasping, I jump up but am yanked right back down.

"No," I say in a loud whisper. "Are you crazy?"

Brip looks at me like I just asked a dumb question.

"I'm gonna slit their throats. Since the fireworks and gunfire have slowed down, that's the best way to do it. Nice and quiet. I got a razor hidden under that couch cushion where you're sitting. I got weapons hidden all over this house. These niggas don't stand a chance."

"Brip, you can't kill them *all*," I say in a level voice.

I'm talking to a crazy person, so I have to be calm to reason with him.

"Don't ever underestimate me, Taffy," Brip says and grabs my arm.

He pulls me off the couch, and I fall to my knees. Brip lifts the cushion, swiftly sticks his hand under it, and pulls out a small blade.

"You think I'm going to sit around and do nothing? I'd rather die than do that. These motherfuckers invade my home, touch my wife, and take my mother's body..." Brip bites down on his bottom lip.

He's barely mentioned the night at the cemetery, but his actions show it weighs on him. He doesn't believe his mother is alive. He thinks Ace and Kong are fucking with us. I think he's too afraid to hope that big. That night when they dug up her grave and found an empty coffin, something changed in Brip. It's like he activated his emergency "Fuck It" switch. He's not the same. He was silent most of that night, and when I tried to get him to talk about it, he just walked away. The next morning, he came downstairs like it never happened. From the way he's acting now, I know he is masking how he feels about it.

Brip places the razor in his mouth and fixes his eyes on me. He gestures with his finger for me to keep silent.

"Brip, please. You're going to get us killed," I whisper.

Again, he bites down on his bottom lip and then bucks at me like he wants to hit me, but he doesn't. Instead, he places two gentle hands on my shoulders and stands upright. He gestures with his hands for me to stay put and tip-toes towards the patio.

I close my eyes. I can't watch this. I can't watch Brip get us killed. I'm tired of seeing blood. I form fists with my hands so tightly that my nails break the skin. I can feel blood pooling in the palms of my hands. With my eyes still closed, I pray a silent prayer. I pray to vanish. To wake up from this nightmare, but that's not going to happen. When I open my eyes, there will be a whole other nightmare to deal with.

I hear a groan and thud. Then a stumble and another thud. Then I open my eyes.

Brip is facing me, standing over the two bodies with blood dripping from the razor.

"Get the bucket," he demands.

I can hear the frustration and arrogance in his voice.

I don't complain. I just do what he says. After all, I'm his prisoner.

5

Dalla Badd

I HAVE BEEN THROUGH a lot over the years. I've been beaten down like a dog, hunted like prey, and the two things that matter most to me snatched away. My hope has been slaughtered, and my emotions are bruised so badly my soul has scars that may never heal. My nerves are shot; paranoia is imprinted in my DNA. I know I'll never be the same again, but for some reason, I feel more at peace now than I ever did in the past. Oddly enough, this peaceful feeling scares me more than the chaos I know. Peace is new to me.

Billy, on the other hand, is the complete opposite. He's trying to keep it together, trying to be strong for me and BJ. He wants to carry the load for everyone, including his brothers, but it's too damn heavy. His back isn't that strong. Plus, he lost a piece of his spine when they dug up his mother and revealed her body was missing. Now his emotions are playing tricks on him. I can see in his eyes that he wishes he would've listened, and we just left that night. But we can't go back, and moving forward doesn't seem to be an option. We are stuck. But I have them; I'm not alone like I was before. I have my husband, and I'm holding my son in my arms right now. I have never felt more at peace. If we all die tonight, these moments with them will have been worth it.

I never knew that just holding my son could make me feel so

complete. To feel his skin against mine, smell his hair, and feel the weight of his tiny head against my chest feels like heaven. BJ holds me tight. He's missed my touch. Whenever I put him down, he cries because he doesn't want me to let him go. So, I carry him with me everywhere, even to the bathroom. When Billy tries to take him from me, he puts up a fight. BJ needs to feel our bond. He craves the nurture behind my touch. It gives him life; it gives me life. I wish I could be there for Billy more, but I can't give him my all. Not even half of me. BJ needs me. I can't let him down, and I won't.

I watch Billy pacing back and forth. The two guards assigned to our house are hanging out on the front porch drinking beer and rolling dice like they're on a street corner. I don't know if it's BJ's presence that keeps them from being so brut or Billy's down-to-earth personality and never-ending lure, but they make us feel comfortable. Billy has played poker with them, rolled their blunts, and treated them like guests in our home rather than invaders. I know why he's doing it. He wants to keep us safe. He's trying to keep us all alive, and the best way to do that is to keep the peace.

They have grown so accustomed to Billy that they give him daps in the morning. Billy just has that kind of effect on people, but I see the truth behind his eyes. He wants them dead…all of them. The guards treat Billy like he's a legend that they are being forced to take down. I can see the reluctance in their eyes when they march around the house with their weapons. They want to respect Billy, but they can't. It's not allowed. When the other guards come around, they have to pretend to be in charge. Billy knows it's an act, though.

The false kinship Billy has built with our guards has bought us some leeway. They don't feel the need for their guns while they're in the house, so they drop them at the door when they enter. Last night, they left for a party and didn't come back until the next morning. It was the first time they left us alone for an entire night. I tried to convince Billy it would have been a good time to escape, but he didn't think so. Sometimes they both leave for a few hours to go to the casino and even come back with food for us. Billy gives them poker tips, and they come back excited, flaunting all the money he helped them win. His winning them over is ingenious. It may be our way out of this house, but it won't get us off this Ranch. Not unless Billy can get us to Zone 5, but he knows that won't be easy.

Billy is a wreck right now. He's having a hard time keeping a straight face today. Last night, Brip's porch light went on. Something is up. I hate to admit that I don't care, but I don't. I don't dare tell Billy that, though. All I care about is us. Call me selfish, but my selfishness has kept us alive all these years.

"It's still on," Billy says, peeking out the blinds.

He's watching the front and back doors at the same time. He doesn't want the guards to see him.

"What the fuck is going on over there? If something happened to him or Taffy, they would have said something, right?" Billy loudly whispers to me.

Billy turns around and rubs both hands over his head. Then he inhales deeply and tilts his head up towards the ceiling to blow out a breath of hot air. He steps away from the porch, only to circle back around and peep through the blinds one last time. Nothing has changed. He shakes his head and walks towards me. When our eyes meet, he winks at me. He looks down at BJ, and a smile that doesn't seem too forced stretches across his face, but it fades quickly. Leaning down, he raises my chin so that our lips can meet in an official good morning kiss.

"You spoiling him too much, Dalla," Billy comments as he looks down at BJ and then at me before turning his back to both of us. "I got to get over there. I got to find out what's going on," he says with his back still facing me.

"No," I reply a little too quickly.

Billy spins around and faces me with a raised brow. He's questioning my loyalty to his family. He can sense I don't give a fuck, but he doesn't want to believe it. He can't right now because he needs me to care.

"It's too dangerous," I tell him.

"We're beyond too dangerous at this point," Billy says before walking back towards the couch and taking a seat next to me.

He plops down so hard that my weight shifts and causes BJ to stir a little. BJ opens his eyes and squints an aggravated eye like he's about to fuss, but then he quickly closes his lids and goes back to sleep. He's too comfortable in my arms to cry. Billy places his hand on my knee and massages it like it's a stress ball. He throws his head back, and it lands on the couch cushion.

"Maybe he found out something about Mamma?" Billy says under his breath.

I didn't want to be the one to tell Billy that Ace is fucking with him and that his mother is not alive. I can't kill that dream for him, but Billy can't afford a fantasy like this now. It's the reason we are still here, the reason we are in this situation. Ace is a twisted individual, and this psychological torment is right up his alley. I don't know how he managed to take Mamma Badd's body, but he did. Now, he's getting what he wants. Billy is back to being his prisoner, and he didn't even need chains to restrain him.

"You sure that's what it is?" I ask, trying to control my tone. I don't want Billy to think I'm chastising him about his theory.

"So you're saying they're dead?" Billy snaps.

He heard whatever I was trying to hide in my voice.

"Of course not." I place my hand on top of Billy's and kiss the top of BJ's head. "I'm just saying I don't think—"

"You don't think what, Dalla?"

Billy jumps up. He's accusing me of something. I don't even think he knows what it is yet.

"Baby, calm down. You don't want the guards to hear you," I whisper.

Billy gives me a considerate look and then turns to look over his shoulder.

"Sit back down," I say, patting the seat next to me, but Billy sits on the chair across from us.

He leans over, placing his elbows on his legs and tapping the top of his head with his fingers. He is thinking. When he leans back up, he stares right at me.

"I'm gonna find out what happened to my mother. I don't expect you to stick around for that, so you don't have to worry about me dragging you along. Nor do you have to pretend like you give a fuck about my family 'cause I know you don't. You never did, and I can't expect you to. However, I do expect you to respect them. I expect you to respect what the fuck is going on right now. I know BJ means the world to you," Billy adds, "but there is other shit going on around you that affects our son."

Billy darts up and penetrates me with dark eyes. He is angry. My heart drops, and suddenly the bubble I created to help me cope has burst. The last thing I want is for Billy to think I don't love him or that I don't support him. He's right. I don't care for his family; I never have. I blame them for all of this. But Billy loves them, and I have to respect that.

I lean over and gently place BJ's sleeping body on the couch. He stirs a little, but I put my hand on his back and soothe him back into a slumber before carefully rising from the sofa.

"Billy, you are my world." I take careful steps toward him. He is giving me an inquisitive look like he doesn't trust the motive behind my words. "I went through hell to get us to reunite, and I'll go through hell to keep us together." I cup his face with my hands and kiss the tip of his nose. "We're at rock bottom right now. I don't know how this is going to play out, but I want us to have peace before it all ends. We just reunited as a family, and yes, this family…" I point towards the floor. "…under this roof is all I care about right now. It's all I've ever cared about, and I'm not ashamed to admit that."

Billy catches a tear as it falls from my eyes before I even notice I'm crying.

"We're going to survive this. We didn't come this far to die. But I can't turn my back on my family, Dalla. I can't pretend that my mother's body wasn't in her casket. I can't just run off into the sunset with you and abandon my family, leaving them to die. If I did that, I would be as much a fuck nigga as Ace. I'm thinking that's the reason you love me. Because I got heart."

Everything he said was true. All the reasons I love him are tied to all the reasons I know he has to see this through.

I lean up on my toes and kiss Billy slowly. He pulls me into his chest and fists the back of my hair so sensually and tenderly that another tear escapes my eye. I love this man with all my heart, with everything I have in me. That means I have to love his cause. I've gotten myself out the lion's den one too many times to give up now. Together, Billy and I can turn this shit around. There is no other way around it if we are going to be together.

"Baby, I've got your back. We're gonna figure this out together," I assure him, and his entire mood changes.

I was going to get my happily-ever-after with Billy. I'm going to fight for it.

Smiling, I look up at him and say, "Maybe after this is all over, I'll finally get to meet your mother."

I said the magic words. I joined him in his fantasy. He knew I didn't believe what I was saying, but me saying it mattered to him. His eyes sparkle with love and hope, and he pulls me into his chest even tighter. He's gaining his strength back through me. He plants his lips on mine and devours my tongue like it's his last meal. I melt into his kiss and then into his body. Many nights, I dreamed of kissing my husband and holding my son, and now I have it. This situation is fucked up, but I can't help but be grateful for it.

We are so enthralled in one another's embrace that we don't notice the guards enter the room. One clears their throat in a jokingly way.

"How about we give you two some much-needed privacy, Mr...I mean, Billy," the guard says, quickly correcting himself.

Billy and I peel ourselves apart and face the guard. Blushing, I wipe Billy from my mouth.

"Yeah, now that y'all little man is sleep, might as well try and..." He clears his throat again. "...relax," he says and winks at Billy.

Billy nods at the young guards.

"I'd appreciate that. You heading to the casino?" Billy asks them like he is inquiring, but really, he is suggesting.

"Might as well. I want to see if that tip you gave me yesterday can win me a grip," one of the guards says.

"I promise if y'all do like I told you, you can win two grand," Billy tells them before walking their way and clapping hands with them both.

The guards look honored to be smacking hands and shooting the breeze with Billy Badd.

"Hell, yeah," the guard says anxiously. "We got about an hour or two before Kevin checks back in," he states, referring to the head guy. Then he looks at his partner with a raised brow.

"Fuck it," his partner says. "Let's do it. We're making more money in that casino than we are here!"

"Hell, yeah," the other guard agrees. "We'll back soon. Y'all want anything?" he asks before turning to leave.

"You can bring another burger and fries," Billy replies just to play the role, but he hasn't eaten since the night at the cemetery.

"Cool. What about your wife?"

"I'm okay," I respond, forcing a smile.

Billy looks at me, and I can already see the plot in his eyes. He's going to use this time to make a move.

Being as discreet as possible, the guards rush out the front door.

I was hoping when Billy heard the door slam, he would carry me upstairs and give me something to hope for, but instead, he ran towards the back door.

"I'm going over there," he says while throwing on his shoes.

"No, wait!"

I look over at BJ, who is still resting soundly. I try to pull Billy back, but I only get the hem of his shirt.

"What about Brip's guards? They may not worship you the way

ours do. You can't just go storming over there, Billy. You have to think this thing through."

"I won't go in. I'm just going to peep around a bit, check things out. He may know something about Mamma," Billy says, a desperate look fogging his eyes.

"You will get caught before you get out of the yard. Besides, you're forgetting there is a big-ass lake dividing the houses. You gonna swim?" Sarcasm floods my tone.

"No. I'm taking the canoe."

I scoff. "They're gonna fucking see you!"

Billy gives me a sharp look. He's wondering what happened to all that hope I was feeding him earlier.

"Not if I stay close to the shoreline," Billy responds like he has it all figured out. "I'll stop halfway and cut through the woods on foot."

Billy swings open the door and rushes out, only to stop dead in his tracks. He turns around, grabs me by the neck, and pulls me into another deep kiss. This one feels like a goodbye kiss. When he pulls away, I don't let go of him. I can't. Billy peels my hands from around his neck and gently pushes me back towards the door.

"Go look after our son," he says, reminding me of BJ. He's trying to distract me from having a breakdown.

I take a deep breath and step back inside the house, but I don't go all the way in. Billy stares back at me like he's wondering if I'm right… if maybe he's making a rushed decision. I speak to him with my eyes. I'm begging him to reconsider and figure things out another way, but he turns away from me. Just as he takes a step forward to walk away, a small pebble is lunged our way and taps the glass patio door. Startled, we both jump. I step back further into the house. Billy holds up his hand for me to be calm and squints his eyes, searching the backyard.

"What was—"

My question is interrupted by another pebble. This one hits against the glass and falls at my feet. I lean down to pick it up, and it is much like the rocks that decorate the lake.

"It's coming from the lake," I say to Billy, holding up the rock.

Another rock comes flying our way. I dodge it, but Billy rushes off towards the lake to find out who's trying to get our attention.

"Billy, wait," I plead, but he keeps going.

It could be a setup, or it could be a random guard warning us to get back inside. But Billy goes anyway. I watch him until he disappears into the shrubs that divide our backyard from the lake.

My heart starts to race again. In the heat of panic, I think of BJ. I run back in the house to find my son still resting peacefully on the couch. I rush over to him and gently kiss him on the forehead, making sure not to wake him. Then I spin back around and rush towards the patio door. Before I get there, I see Billy running in my direction with Taffy in his arms.

What the fuck is going on?

6

Billy Badd

WHEN TAFFY SEES Dalla, she breaks away from me and leaps into Dalla's arms, embracing her. She buries her face in Dalla's chest and sobs so hard that her knees get weak. With tears in her eyes, Dalla looks up at me for answers, but I don't know what's going on. She pulls Taffy into the house, and I follow behind them.

"She was hiding in the bushes," I tell Dalla.

Dalla is picking plant leaves from Taffy's hair and dusting the dirt off her clothes.

"Taffy, where is Brip?" I try to be calm, but I can't control my fucking anxiety. *Is that what the light was about? Is my little brother dead?*

Taffy keeps crying. She doesn't acknowledge that I'm talking to her. Dalla pulls her to the couch and sits her down.

"Get her some water," Dalla says, and I rush to the kitchen.

When I get back, Taffy is drying her eyes and taking deep breaths. She's trying to calm down. She sniffs hard and looks up at Dalla.

"They..." Her voice cracks, and she starts to sob again.

I shove the water in her face like it has a magic elixir to stop her from being emotional, but she pushes it away.

"It's okay, Taffy," Dalla calmly says.

She cares about Taffy. I can see it in the way she's consoling her. It's genuine. I believe Dalla cares about all my family. She just loves herself and BJ more. Dalla has been through a lot, and trials never seem to stop following her. But she's able to stand strong. She hasn't broken like Lera or Taffy yet, and she's been through a lot more. It's why I love her. It's why I have to give her a happy ending—the happy ending she's been dreaming of. But, first, I got to save my family. I have to find out what the fuck is going on with my mother.

Taffy drops her head so fast it looks like it's going to fall off her neck. Her entire body is trembling. Dalla takes the water from my hand and gently places the rim of the glass against her lips.

"Take a sip, Taffy."

Taffy follows Dalla's instructions. She takes two small sips and swallows the water down hard like it's liquor.

"Good. Now take a deep breath," Dalla tells her.

Her maternal instincts are spinning. They haven't stopped since she reunited with BJ. Seeing her with my son makes me feel complete, and there is nothing I want more than a life with the two of them. When I was in prison, my mind flooded with thoughts about the three of us. This was before I knew it was real. Back then, it was just a fantasy of mine. Now, I know it's real, and I will do anything to keep us together. But, I can't just walk away from this Ranch so easily. Dalla doesn't understand that, and I don't waste time trying to convince her because she will never understand the deep bond that binds me here. It's like part of my soul is anchored here in chains.

When my mother's empty casket was pulled from the dirt, it was like burying her all over again…only worse. I couldn't keep her safe when she was alive, and now I feel like I can't even keep her safe in death. My brothers and I didn't have that long to talk afterwards because Kong had us separated and locked in our homes shortly after. Now all I have are theories as to how. But, none of it makes sense. It doesn't seem possible. I would like to believe she's alive. We all would, but that sounds too impossible.

None of us saw her body. My mother requested a close casket, and of course, we honored her wishes. There was so much drama with the autopsy report that we don't know what's real or fake. If Mamma's dead, where the fuck is her body? And if she's alive, where the fuck is she? Does she need help? Is she hurt? All of the unanswered questions haunt me every day. I feel suffocated by them. This mystery is so perplexing that I almost forget what the fuck is going on around here. I forget that my wife and my son's lives are in danger. I forget that I don't know what the fuck is going on with my brothers. I don't know if they're alive or dead. If we don't make it out of this situation alive, I will never know what happened to our mother. I have to figure something out quick, but first, Dalla has to get Taffy to talk, even though I'm not sure I'm ready to hear what she has to say.

Taffy takes another deep breath. Tears fill her eyes again, but she closes them tightly and reopens them before exhaling air full of panic. She leans over, resting her elbows on her knees, and lowers her head. She covers her face and shakes her head like she's trying to wake up from a nightmare. Dalla places a gentle hand on her back and rubs in a circular motion.

"It's okay," Dalla says patiently.

But, her patience and Taffy's emotions are frustrating me. We don't have time for this shit.

"Taffy, where is Brip? Is my brother dead?" I ask, sounding more annoyed than intended.

Dalla cuts a sharp eye at me.

"He killed..." Taffy tries to speak but chokes on her tears.

I kneel in front of her and turn her face in my direction.

"Billy, stop!" Dalla yells, waking BJ.

She jumps up and scoops him from the couch. I don't let go of Taffy's face.

"Is he dead?" I continue. When she doesn't answer, I start shaking her. "Is my fucking brother dead? Tell me!"

I don't notice how rough I'm being until I see Taffy clam up in my hands, frozen with fear. I let her go and jump up, surprised by my actions. Dalla is looking at me like I'm possessed.

"Billy," Dalla condemns me.

"I'm sorry, Taffy," I say and throw my hands in the air.

Taffy doesn't move. She's staring off into space like nothing can surprise her anymore.

Dalla looks at me like I'm going to shatter into pieces at any moment. She thinks Brip's dead. I can see it in her eyes. She's holding back her tears for me. Turning her back to me, she lowers her head like she's already mourning Brip. My heart drops.

They killed my brother. They killed him.

My body falls back onto the couch. Everything inside me begins to sink.

I couldn't protect my mother, and I couldn't protect my brother. This shit is really happening. We're going to die.

"Billy," Dalla says and sits next to me with BJ on her hip. She wraps her free arm around my neck and tries to pull me into a hug. "Baby, it's going to be okay. We just have to leave. We have to leave tonight."

"Take me with you." Taffy jumps up from the sofa before kneeling on her knees. "Please take me with you. Please don't leave me here," she pleads. Tears roll down her face in messy streams as her bottom lip trembles. "He's going to get me killed. Brip is going to get us all killed," she blurts out and then buries her face in her hands, filling them with tears.

"He's alive?" I bolt up so quick that I knock her over. "My brother ain't dead?"

"Not yet," Taffy says, her voice strained.

"What do you mean? Do they have him?" I ask.

"No." Taffy shakes her head hard. "He's killing them. He keeps killing them," Taffy says before sobbing again.

"What?" Dalla says, confused. "How?"

I turn my head, stare at the back patio for a second, and smile. Brip is fighting back. This is the hope I've been looking for. My little brother ain't no fucking punk. He got a heart of steel that can only be penetrated with love, not fear.

Without looking back, I rush out the door. I have to talk to Brip.

When I get to Brip's back porch, he rushes outside with a blood-soaked machete.

"Brip, it's me," I say, holding my hands up. "Billy."

Brip has that crazy look in his eyes. I can see the rage behind his dilated pupils. His chest is heaving up and down with anxiety that only blood can cure. When Brip sees me, his entire face lights up. He drops his weapon and pulls me into a quick hug, then picks his knife back up and looks over my shoulders protectively.

"Taffy's gone," Brip says. Concern echoes throughout his entire body.

"She's okay," I tell him. "She's at my place with Dalla. She made it."

Brip looks up at me, relieved. He shakes his head and waves me into his house. I follow him to the kitchen. There is a trail of blood on his floor. He pulls a dish towel from a drawer and wipes his knife clean. That crazy look in his eyes is back. There is no talking him out of this killing spree, but hopefully, I can bring some order.

"What's going on, man?" I ask, allowing Brip to follow my eyes to the trail of blood.

"What the fuck does it look like?" Brip shoots back while sharpening his knife. "I'm protecting my house, protecting my wife," he says and places the knife under the sink.

He reaches for a bucket of water and pours bleach inside. His entire house smells like bleach. He dunks the blood-soaked dishrag inside and starts wiping up blood. He scrubs the same spot of blood long after it's gone.

"Where are you putting the bodies? The lake?" I inquire, although he could get away with burning them since this entire Ranch reeks with the smell of burning flesh. No one would know the difference.

"No, but that's a good idea. I'll do that once I run out of room. For now, they're in my wine freezer."

I hesitate before asking, "How many?"

"Six so far," Brip responds casually. "Just killed the last two before Taffy ran out of here frantic. One of them was the lead guy, so they may come looking for him," Brip adds like he's not nervous. "That's why Taffy left. She don't trust me. She don't believe I can protect her."

Brip stops scrubbing, and his head lowers. He takes a deep breath and exhales his frustration before dunking the rag back in the now bloody bucket of water. He takes his frustration out on the floor.

"What's your plan?"

I ask this question knowing he didn't have one. Brip got more heart than he does brains. He acts off emotion, not strategy.

"To kill the niggas that come looking for him," Brip says like that's the only plan he needs.

"I don't blame you for what you're doing, but they're gonna get suspicious after a while. We got to get more strategic with this shit."

"We?" Brip stops scrubbing the floor and looks up at me. "You put some niggas down, too?" he asks, surprised.

He knows killing ain't my style, but I'll do what I have to do.

"No, not yet," I say to him, hinting that I got his back. "I'm handling things a little differently at my house. It's keeping us going."

"Taffy says I can't kill all of them." He turns his attention back to the floor. "I guess she's right."

"We may not have to," I tell him.

Brip leans up on his knees and throws the rag in the bucket. He wipes the sweat from his brow, and a streak of blood from his hand smears across his forehead. After jumping to his feet, he sighs like he's exhausted from the day's events. I pray it means he doesn't kill anyone else.

"How the fuck did we get here, man?" Brip looks up at me for answers.

I can see the weariness hiding behind the rage in his eyes.

"I don't know," I say and lower my head.

It's been nonstop drama since the Ace attack, and for me, even before then. It started with Ace feeding me bullshit about Brock killing our mother. Now, I don't care if she's dead or alive.

"How are you holding up, though?" I ask Brip.

When he sees the look in my eyes, he knows I'm referring to Mamma. He shrugs his shoulders, then picks up the bucket of water and carries it to the bathroom. I can tell he doesn't want to talk about it. Brip can only handle so much.

"Where the fuck is Brock?"

He twists his head and shoots me a sharp look from over his shoulder. He needs someone to blame for all of this. Blaming Brock is easy because he ain't here. It's my turn to shrug my shoulders. The plan was for Brock to sneak back on the Ranch and kill Kong. But, that was two weeks ago, and before Kong started bringing in thirty guards a day. It was before the cemetery when we thought Vinchi was in charge. None of us expected this.

"Last I heard, he was supposed to call Mona when he was going to make a move," I tell Brip.

"Fuck Mona!" Spit flies from his mouth and lands on my forehead as he speaks. "Fuck Vinchi, too. They're both snakes. You seen her? I saw her from the window. She's walking around here free. This whole thing was a fucking setup. If she cared about us, she would have come by here. She would have got Brock in. I won't be surprised if Brock is dead," Brip says as he pours the dirty water down the toilet.

"I feel you, but we don't know what's going on. And Brock ain't dead," I assure him, although I never considered that Brip might be right.

"How the fuck you figure that?" Brip shoots back.

"Cause Brock Badd ain't no easy kill. Brock got more brains than all of us. You know that."

The tension in Brip's shoulders eases a bit. He stares at his reflection in the mirror as if this might be the last time he will see himself. It's almost like he's saying goodbye to himself. He lifts his eyes and stares at me through the mirror.

"If I see Mona...she's dead."

Brip isn't warning me. He's informing me.

"We can't make hasty decisions," I say, trying to talk him out of killing Mona. For all I know, Brip could be right. Mona could be in on this, but right now, we need to focus on the main enemies—Kong and Ace. They go before anybody else.

"Fuck that!" Brip spins around and penetrates my eyes with an evil stare. "She's the reason Mamma's body is gone. She helped them get rid of it." Brip starts to tremble. The tension is back in his shoulder, and a pulsating snake-like vein wraps around his neck. "How the fuck else can I explain it?"

Brip spins back around and turns on the faucet. Bending over the sink, he splashes water on his face. Then he picks up a bar of soap and scrubs his face clean with it. The bar becomes saturated with blood. Brip moves the bar from his face to his neck, wiping the blood clean like he's cleansing himself of his sins. I hesitate before responding. What Brip is saying makes more sense than my theory, but something inside of me can't let go of the idea that our mother is alive.

"How, if she's not dead?" I mumble under my breath.

My voice cracks, and my eyes immediately drop away from Brip's gaze. I don't want him to see how vulnerable I am, how hopeful I feel. I feel silly thinking it. Just like a kid believing in Santa Claus after puberty, I believe she's still alive.

Brip stops washing his face and turns to face me. Soap-suds pop against his cheek.

"She's dead, man." Brip's response is quick and assertive like he's not feeding into any more of my bullshit. "The whole thing was a ploy between Mona, Kong, and Ace. Why?" Brip keeps his eyes fixed on me. "I don't know," he says, answering his own question.

I shake my head in disagreement. No words can do my theory any justice. I can't believe she's dead; I won't allow myself to believe it. If she's still alive, she may be in danger. She might be held hostage. She could be hurting, and we're just sitting here stuck. I couldn't save her before, but now I can, and I won't let her down.

"We got to talk to Ace. He knows more than—"

Brip spins around and pushes me so hard that I fall through the door.

"Fuck Ace! That nigga already had his last words. He's dead!" With a hysterical look in his eye, Brip points a deadly finger at me.

"Think what the fuck you want, but Mamma is still alive! I know it," I say and charge back towards Brip. I'm not gonna let him dismiss me because he's not emotionally stable enough to accept the idea that she's alive. "We've got to talk to Brock. He may know more. Why else did he want to keep Ace alive? Why else—"

Brip suckers me in the jaw before I can finish my sentence. Bloody soap and water slide down my face. I fall against the doorframe and grab my jaw.

"Shut…the…fuck…up!" Brip hisses at me with his fist balled tight, ready to strike again. "We don't have time for this bullshit. I got a pregnant wife to protect. You got a wife and a baby! Stop! Just fucking stop, man! Why can't you ever fucking stop!" Brip yells, then punches a hole in the wall instead of striking me again.

I leap towards Brip, grabbing his shirt collar and pulling him into me.

"Okay," I say to him. "Okay," I repeat, pulling him into a hug.

Brip hesitates at first but then wraps his arms around me, embracing me. I can feel the weight of his burdens against my shoulders. He can't handle this. It's too much.

"Brip!" Taffy screams and leaps up from the couch when she sees Brip and me walking through the back door.

Taffy wraps her arms around Brip like she never thought she would see him again. Dalla gives me a wide-eyed stare like I killed us. She hesitates but gets up from the couch to save face. She keeps her eyes on Brip like he's a bomb waiting to detonate. At any moment, she's expecting Brip to explode, killing us all. Her eyes instantly go to BJ, who is still asleep on the sofa. She leans down and swiftly pulls him off the couch and into the safety of her arms.

"I'm going to put him down," Dalla says, looking at me. "Billy, can you help me upstairs?"

I nod and look back at Brip. He and Taffy are still embracing. I give him my best "be cool" look, and he gets my drift. He nods at me in agreement.

When I get upstairs, Dalla already has BJ in his crib.

"What the fuck are you thinking bringing him here?"

"Watch your tone," I whisper loudly. "Everything is going to be okay. I got a plan."

"What fucking plan?" Dalla says in a low voice. "He's going to get us all killed. Is that the plan?" Dalla folds her arms against her chest and lowers her head sorrowfully. "I know you love your brother," she continues in a soft voice, "but what about your son? Our son?"

Dalla turns to BJ and then shoots me another sad look. She's afraid.

"I love you." I take two steps towards her, grabbing her face and cupping it in my hands. "I love our son. I need you to trust that I'm going to protect our family."

I look her directly in the eyes and pause. I need her not only to believe what I'm saying but to feel it. She tries to look away, but I turn her head back in my direction so her sights are fixed on me. I feel her start to melt in my arms.

"Do you trust me?" I ask her.

Dalla looks up at me without speaking. I can see in her eyes that she wants to trust me, but her life experiences have taught her otherwise.

Her eyes mist with tears, and her bottom lip trembles as she fights off emotions. Dalla has learned to treat vulnerability like a luxury she can't afford. She saves up all her emotions, investing in strength instead. It's why I love her, but it's also why we're always on different pages.

I gently squeeze her face with my hands and lean in closer to her.

"Do you trust me?" I ask her again, but this time firmer and more desperate.

I need her to trust me. I need her by my side for this to work. Otherwise, she's right. We're all dead. Dalla tries to move my hands from her face, but I won't let her.

"Do you?" I say to her.

The mist that floods Dalla's eyes becomes a full rain of tears. Every last tear falls into my hands, creating a pond of sadness and fear. Dalla takes a breath so deep that she sucks in some of my air, and I feel like I can't breathe.

"I trust you," she says before falling into my arms, using my chest as a blanket to quiet her sobs.

Wrapping my arms around her, I squeeze tight. I kiss the top of her head and finger the hairs on her lower neckline.

"We're gonna get out of this alive. I promise. I'm going to give you that life you dreamed of." I kiss her again, and her sobs fade. "We're going to move far from here. Maybe to Spain. We're going to live on a beach. BJ's going to speak two languages and be free. You're going to cook Spanish food for me. I'm going to buy you new dresses every week, and on the weekends, we're going to go dancing all night."

As I stroke her hair, Dalla's sobs come to a hard stop. She's listening to every word I say, and she believes me.

"We're going to give BJ a sister."

When I say this, she looks up at me and smiles.

"A girl?" she says like she never thought of it.

"Yeah, a baby girl with your eyes and smile." I kiss her softly on the lips before whispering, "Then, we're going to give BJ's sister another brother."

Dalla looks up at me and penetrates my eyes with a loving gaze. I can feel hope radiating off her body. I can see my vision of the family we're going to build shining behind her beautiful eyes. She leans up on her toes and parts my lips with her tongue. She kisses me like she's saying hello and goodbye at the same time.

"I trust you," she says and smiles.

I wink at her, and as I turn to walk away, I hear the front door open. The guards are back twenty minutes earlier than expected. Dalla looks at me with pure terror in her eyes. In an instant, she sells the fantasy I sold her for fear.

"Be cool. I got this," I tell her. "Stay here."

Before I can get to the stairway, I hear Brip aggressively challenging the guards. Taffy screams. I charge down the steps so fast that I feel like I'm flying. When I get to the landing, Brip has one of the guards in a chokehold, and his partner is pointing his pistol at Brip.

"Let him go, Brip," I say with a heavy tone.

"Fuck that! You already know what time it is," Brip says and squeezes tighter.

Taffy has her hands covering her ears, waiting for shots to be fired.

"I said let him go," I yell, this time with more authority.

Brip looks up at me and then back at the guard. Then he does what I say. He pushes the guard to the ground, and I rush to step in between them.

"What the fuck is going on, Mr. Badd? I thought we could trust you?" the guard says while still pointing his pistol at Brip.

When he turns the gun on me, I throw my hands in the air. Then he immediately turns and points it back at Brip. His partner is still on the ground, trying to catch his breath as he massages where Brip had a tight grip on his neck. Brip is giving both the guards vicious stares, and Taffy still has her ears covered and eyes closed tight.

"You can trust me," I say.

With my hands still in the air, I slowly approach him, but he backs up. His partner jumps to his feet and draws his gun on me.

"Back up," he warns me.

Brip gets anxious, but I give him a look that tells him to stay calm. I stop walking.

"I know this looks fucked up, but both of you know I ain't been on no fuck shit. I respect you men. I respect your position, and most of all, I respect how you've been handling my wife and me."

"Why is he here?" asks the one with the gun pointed at Brip. He keeps his aim steady, but I can tell he's nervous as hell because he's trembling. The look Brip is giving him doesn't help.

"Let's talk like men," As I lower my hands, I keep my eyes fixed on them both. "Let his wife go upstairs with my wife. Ain't no sense in putting her through all of this."

They both give Taffy a considerate look. Taffy's eyes are glued shut, and she's shaking her head.

"Please, man. She's been through enough. She's carrying his child. I'm only asking you because you two got respect," I say, letting them know I appreciate them.

"Okay," one of them says.

But, Taffy doesn't move. So, I walk up to her and gently place my hand on her shoulder.

"Taffy…" When I remove her hands from her ears, she gives me a hesitant look. "Go upstairs. Everything is going to be okay. I promise," I say and kiss her on the cheek.

Taffy walks upstairs slow and steady like someone has a gun aimed at her back. She doesn't make any sudden movements. Once she turns the corner and walks down the hall, I face the guards again.

"We don't need to talk with all this commotion," I say while looking at the guns. "Let's be cool. Let's be men."

The first guard lowers his gun and moves away from Brip, but the second guard keeps his firearm aimed at him.

"It's cool, man," his partner tells him.

The guard finally lowers his gun like it weighs a ton but keeps a firm grip on the handle. He doesn't trust Brip, and I don't blame him.

"Why is he here?" he asks me.

"I went and got him after you left. I brought him here because I thought I could trust the two of you," I admit.

"If they find out, we're both dead!" one yells.

"That won't happen," I say with an even tone. "So, how much you boys win at the casino?"

"Twenty-eight hundred dollars," one of them blurts out, smiling as he reaches inside his pocket and pulls out a wad of cash. "You're good at that poker shit. We could've emptied more pockets than that, but we had to get back. It's getting a little hot out there. One of the head guys is missing, and everybody is going on lockdown."

Brip cuts his eyes at me. My heart races from what's about to go down.

"Cool, but twenty-eight hundred ain't shit compared to the money you could make," I tell them.

"What you mean? You got more tricks?" the guard asks, stuffing the money back in his pocket. "We ain't getting back to the casino for a while because it's getting tight around here. Too many guards have been fucking off. Kong is paying us good money to be here," he says.

"Is he paying you twenty-eight hundred?" I quickly ask.

"Fuck no," the other replies. "Not even half of that."

"I got fifty grand for both of you," I say.

Their eyes widen so big they almost pop out of their head.

"Bullshit," the one says. He cannot fathom having that amount of money in his possession.

"I know you ain't been around me that long, but both of you should know by now that I don't bullshit." I look them both in the eyes. "You boys ready to talk business?"

I take a seat on the couch, and they eagerly follow behind me, sitting on the sofa in front of me. Brip looks at me and smiles. He doesn't move. He stands very still as not to freak them out. He knows I don't have access to a dime, but that ain't the point. I'm buying their loyalty with imaginary money. Sometimes dropping dollars provides more protection than dropping bodies.

Leaning back in my seat, I feed these two dumb-ass thirsty niggas a plate full of bullshit. By the time I am done with them, they are licking the bottom of that plate. These niggas are so hungry that they don't know they're eating an imaginary meal. Unfortunately, it might be their last meal. But, that's just the way shit has to go for me to protect what's mine.

7

Mona Badd

"I HIRED YOU TO keep order around here," Kong says and pounds the table so hard the entire room shakes. "What the fuck is going on?" he asks, huffing like he's out of breath.

I place my hand on his back and try to get him to calm down. He turns his neck and gives me a weird look. It's the third time I've touched him this week, and by the look he's giving me, I'm not the only one counting. I learned that the more I touch him, the more he keeps me around. We've been inseparable for two days now. I'm getting closer to the safe. Plus, I hear everything.

I snap my fingers at one of the maids, and she comes running to me.

"Yes, Mrs. Badd."

Kong cuts his eyes at her and then back at me. He doesn't like her referring to me as Mrs. Badd. He doesn't want to be reminded that I'm married to Brock. He also doesn't want to be reminded that he doesn't know what the hell he is doing. He can't run this Ranch like Brock. He can't even keep his men in order.

"Get him some water," I tell her. "And it's Mona," I add.

Kong looks at me like he's pleased, then leans into me so close I can feel his large wet lips against my earlobe.

"I want Kool-Aid. I don't drink water," he demands.

I look at him and nod, then stop the maid before she leaves the room.

"Wait. Bring the Kool-Aid you made earlier—the cherry kind. Bring the entire pitcher and two grilled cheese sandwiches," I say without asking Kong if he's hungry.

Kong flashes me a secret smile with his beady eyes instead of his lips. He doesn't want his guards to see him smiling. That makes him look weak.

Some things never change. Kong is still fat as fuck, so I just guessed his ass is still on a hood diet of Kool-Aid, fried bologna sandwiches, and grilled cheese. He's also still ruthless as hell and putty in my hands. He needs guidance—always has—and that's what I'm here to do. Guide this big, dumb fuck in whatever direction I need him to go to get us out of this mess. The guards are running around partying like rockstars, eating, drinking, and fucking the women Nicchi's dumb ass is hauling in here every hour. The guards ain't here to put in work; they're here to play. This is a fucking vacation for these niggas. It's like Disneyland meets Gotham City.

We're in the conference room at the casino. It's where Kong has all his major meetings. All twenty of his lead guards are also in the office. He used to have twenty-one, but one of them is missing.

Kong is seated in the chair at the head of the table. As I pull out my notepad and pretend to take notes, Kong looks at me like this shit is official. He's such a fucking fool. I don't see how he got this far, but the fact that he has keeps me cautious. Even dumb niggas wise up. I just have to play the game right.

"Honestly, the last time I saw him, he was in the casino hitting them slot machines hard," one of the leads tells Kong. "He got a problem with gambling. He only took this job to pay off some debt. I think he hit big and took his ass home."

Kong leans back in his chair with flared nostrils. His nostrils are open wide enough to steal the air from all of us. He balls up his fist tight and then relaxes. Then he turns to me like he wants to say something but changes his mind.

"You put out the word that I got a twenty-five-thousand-dollar bounty on that nigga's head," Kong says, scanning the room with slanted eyes. "We got to tighten up around here. Let these niggas know I ain't playing no games," he snarls, looking like a growling Rottweiler. "I want each of you to kill one of your guards and make that shit public. That way, they'll know playtime is over."

"Come on, man. Don't you think that shit's kinda harsh? I mean—"

Kong pounds the table and jumps up. His broad body towers over us all, hoovering over the light and bringing a dim shade to the entire room.

"What did you say?" Kong asks, his nostrils flaring. "Come here." He gestures with his thick finger for the man to come closer to him.

Hesitantly, the man walks towards Kong, trembling all the way, and stops a few feet in front of him.

"Closer!" Kong demands.

The man takes a few more steps towards Kong, but that still isn't good enough. At that moment, the server returns with Kong's Kool-Aid and grilled cheese sandwich. Although the sandwich is cut in half, a fork and table knife lay inside a neatly-folded napkin next to it. Kong reaches for the silverware, lifting the napkin and emptying the contents on the table. Then he picks up the knife.

"Closer," he says again, this time more enraged.

The man looks down at the knife and then back at Kong. He doesn't move. He knows what's about to happen. Kong opens his mouth to order him again, but one of the other lead guards, looking for brownie points, grabs the man by the back of his neck and pushes him close enough for Kong to grab him. Kong grabs him by the throat and shoves the knife through his neck, twisting it. The sight is so gruesome I had to turn my head. Blood squirts from the man's neck like a fountain and gurgles from his mouth.

"You don't challenge me," Kong says, his voice strained. "No one challenges me." He pushes the knife deeper into the man's neck as if sending a message to the others.

When the man stopped choking on his blood, Kong pushed him to the side, and his body fell to the ground at my feet. Everybody in the room is still. They are afraid to blink.

Kong sits back down. A gush of wind from the cushion hits against my leg, and I jump like I've been stabbed. Kong looks at me. I can't read the look he's giving me. It's like he is warning me not to cross him and showing me that he has my back at the same time. It takes all I have to keep my eyes fixed on him without showing any emotion. He holds his gaze with me for what feels like hours before looking away and setting his sight on his food. He scoots his chair closer to the table, leans over, and grabs half of the sandwich. It has the guard's blood speckled across the top of it, but Kong doesn't care. He wipes the sandwich clean by rubbing it against his shirt and then takes two big bites until it is gone. Next, he reaches for the pitcher of Kool-Aid and drinks directly from the jar until it is all gone, as well. He lets out a loud burp that echoes through the room, crashing into every wall. The smell is so foul that I almost vomit. Kong is disgusting and brut. Nothing like my husband.

"Do you have anything you want to add?" Kong looks at me while leaning in to devour the second half of his blood-coated sandwich.

Distracted by everything that is happening, I have to take a deep breath to get my head back in the game. Kong isn't wondering what I think; he needs my opinion. He respects my expertise.

"Yeah," I say and lean in closer to the table.

I don't know what I am going to say, but this is my shot at securing whatever position Kong is giving me. However, this could also be a test to see how in I am. If I say the wrong thing, I could fuck up my plan, but if I don't say the right thing, I will lose his trust.

I look at Kong and then the guards. Opening my notebook, I read over a bunch of scribble scratch, pretending to gather my thoughts. I buy myself some time before clearing my throat.

"Once y'all down your guard, be sure to take them to the crematory right away. Don't just leave their bodies to rot. Kong has a lot of professionals coming in and out of the Ranch, and we want to be sure the Ranch keeps its integrity. Otherwise, the real money people gonna walk," I say and look at Kong.

He gives me a considerate look like he didn't think to see things the way I do.

"This ain't the East Meadows projects," I continue. "All that pissing and spitting on Ranch grounds needs to be over today. The next time you see one of your men pissing or shitting in the bushes, off them. And the casino is not an all-you-can-eat buffet or open bar. Start docking their checks for everything they eat or drink."

When I finish, I lean back in my seat. Kong's expression tells me that he's pleased. I'm offering him structure that he wouldn't have thought of himself.

"She's right. This place is my fucking investment." He stabs his finger in his chest. "No more free rides. This is my fucking house, and I want you to respect it. Keep it clean, or else you're gonna end up like this motherfucker." He points to the floor with his thumb without ever looking at the dead guard. "Is everything understood?" Kong says.

They all respond with a quick, uneasy yes.

"Now, on to the second order of business." Kong moves close to the table again. "It's time to start shedding some blood. Next week, I got a very important guest visiting the Ranch. He ain't gonna make a move unless he knows I'm serious. So, I got to show him how serious I am," Kong says. Then, he looks at me with a piercing stare that is so evil my entire body shudders. "The first Badd dies next week," Kong adds with his eyes still fixed on me.

I try my best not to flinch, but it feels like someone has snatched the air from my lungs. My stomach plunges to the bottom of my asshole, and my heartbeat slows. I feel like I'm having a stroke. Everything in my body goes numb. I grip my pen to try and control the panic that wraps around my entire body and squeezes me like a python. Kong keeps staring at me, waiting for me to oppose. But I'm not stupid. I need to breathe. I need him to look away so I can breathe. Otherwise,

I'm going to pass out right on top of the guard's bloody body. My knee starts to jerk, and my eyes blink at Kong uncontrollably.

"After this meeting ends, I need two of you to go get him and bring him to me. He'll stay under my watch until he dies. Understood?" Kong asks and finally looks away from me, turning his gaze to the guards.

I steal this moment to take a deep breath, but it doesn't help. I'm still suffocating inside. I sip in small bits of air and straighten my posture.

"Yes, sir," they respond in unison.

Kong leans back in his chair and smiles. Then he waves his hand in the air, dismissing them. They scurry off to fulfill their assignments. Once they're gone, Kong places his hand on top of mine. It feels heavy like a weight. Almost like he's smashing my hand with a hammer. I don't pull away, though. I can feel him looking at me, but I can't look up at him. If I do, he'll see how terrified I am.

"I like how you presented yourself today at this meeting," he has the nerve to say to me. "I missed our partnership."

Kong presses down even harder on my hand. I continue to avoid eye contact with him as he starts to rub my hand slowly. His skin feels like sandpaper against my flesh.

"I have something special planned for us tonight. Wear something nice," he says and pushes his chair back from the table.

I finally get the nerve to look him in the eye, and he blows a kiss at me before stepping over the dead body like it's trash. When he walks out the door, I double over and gag. I have to get in contact with Brock. I have to let him know what's going on. I can't let Brip die.

Before I step out of the casino, Nicchi comes charging at me. When I don't flinch, she stops dead in her tracks. She sees that look in my eye and knows not to fuck with me. Today ain't the day for her foolishness.

Instead of hitting me like she wants to, she points an accusing finger at me, her free hand sporting a balled fist.

"You're pathetic as fuck. You don't think I know what you're up too, trying to take my man? Just because your man is a coward and done left your ass for dead, you think you got the right to take mine?"

I don't waste time responding to her, but hearing her talk about Brock like that strikes a nerve. I grab her by the throat with one hand and squeeze. I pull her into my face so we are nose to nose. Using both hands, she tries her best to free herself from my grip, but she can't. Her arm flails in the air, trying to throw punches, but her fist mostly hits the air.

"You don't speak on my man," I say and squeeze even tighter. "Ever!"

I let her go, pushing her back, and she falls butt first on to the concrete.

She's looking at me with evil eyes while spit bubbles foam in the corners of her mouth. My guards help her. It takes two of them to pull her big ass from the ground. Nicchi looks around to see who's watching. I can tell she's embarrassed as she brushes the dirt off her ass. She is wearing shorts so short and tight they look like bikini bottoms. She pulls the shorts from her ass and adjusts the crop top, pulling it down like it was made to cover all her fat rolls. She then checks her earrings and notices that she is missing one extra-large gold-plated hoop. While holding her naked ear, she searches the concrete for it.

I lost my cool, but it felt good to blow off some steam. Nicchi throwing Brock's absence in my face makes me feel abandoned. All this shit that's going on, and he ain't here yet. With all the connections that he has, what's taking him so fucking long to get here? It's been two weeks already.

Thinking about Brock shifts my mind to Vinchi. I still haven't seen him. Kong won't let me know where he is, but he assures me that he's safe. I don't trust Kong, though. He ain't right in the head. And I damn sure don't want his ass, so Nicchi can calm all the way down with her noise.

"You're trying to turn him against me. I haven't seen him in days. You're so greedy, Mona. You just want it all," Nicchi says.

Finally spotting her earring, she leans her big ass over to pick it up. She blows the dirt off of it before sticking it back in her ear.

"You got me fucked up," I say and step towards her.

The guards step away from me as if to give me space. They have been respecting me a lot more after the meeting, but they're still on my ass like white on rice.

"You need to control your emotions. How many times do I have to tell you that?"

Nicchi pulls in air through her teeth and rolls her eyes. She folds her fat arms across her chest and pouts.

"We need to talk," I whisper to her, then look at the guards. "In private."

"What we got to talk about?" Nicchi snaps.

"About your dumb-ass future," I say to her in a matter-of-fact tone. "Kong is two seconds from putting you off this Ranch. I can make that happen tonight if I want to, but you're my sister, my blood. Although you're stupid as hell, I'm still gonna have your back just like always."

Concern floods Nicchi's eyes. Then she takes a deep breath and shrugs her shoulders. She knows without Kong, she's nothing, but without me, she really ain't shit.

"Let's go to the Big House," Nicchi says like she owns the place. "I will have the maids make us some lunch."

Swallowing my pride, I follow behind her.

NICCHI PURPOSELY TAKES a seat at the head of my table. Sitting at this table being served by our staff reminds me of when everything was good. Brock would be in front of me. Business was flowing. Brip trusted me. I thought my life was perfect, and then all this shit happened. It makes me wonder if everything was only an illusion, and nothing was ever perfect. Even if we do make it out of this, nothing will ever be the same again, especially me and Brock's relationship. There are some things time just can't heal.

"Roberta, I asked for my steak cooked medium rare," Nicchi says to the maid with her nose twisted.

She says medium rare like it's a new word she's trying out. Her hood ass don't know shit about steak nor how to ask for it cooked. She's acting brand new.

Using her fork, Nicchi lifts her steak and flips it over. "This shit is bleeding like it's still alive. Fix my shit right," Nicchi says, pushing the plate aside so hard that it falls on the floor. Then she leans back in her chair like she's a boss. "And clean up this mess," she adds, pointing to the floor.

Nicchi cuts an eye at me. She's showing off in front of me, but I ignore her simple ass. At least she got the guards to give us some privacy. She still has a little power but don't know it.

"How's your food?" she asks, looking at my plate.

I haven't touched my food because I ain't hungry. I ain't here to eat. I'm here 'cause I need her on my side. I have to get in contact with Brock and get to the safe before they kill Brip. She may be able to help me do that if I can convince her. I can't trust her as far as I can throw her, and I ain't no heavy lifter, but she's all I got right now.

"It's fine," I say and pick at my food to please her.

"So what's this all about?" Nicchi flips her wrist before folding her arms across her chest. She has her defenses up.

"I'm here to look out for you," I say, leaning into the table.

"By fucking my man?"

"We ain't fucked yet, but he wants to," I reply honestly.

Nicchi gets so upset that she picks up her glass of soda and throws it at me. Luckily, I'm too far away to get drenched by it.

"You need to grow the fuck up," I tell her like she's my misbehaving teenage daughter. "We're family. We are always gonna be family. So, stop with all this competition shit. Kong ain't nothing but another nigga that's gonna screw you over, and you're gonna let that happen because you can't control your emotions."

Pouting, Nicchi says, "All I got is Kong."

"No, bitch, all you got is me. Kong don't give a fuck about you. He don't give a fuck about me either."

Nicchi looks at me like she knows I'm telling the truth, but she still wants to be mad.

"What the fuck has he done for you besides give you dick? It's been me stuffing your pockets all these years, not him. You gonna cut off the one hand that feeds you? That's stupid, Nicchi. I taught you better than that." I shake my head like I'm ashamed of her. "You really think you and Kong are about to run this Ranch? Once he gets what he wants, you're out of here. He was talking about sending you home the other day," I lied.

"That ain't true," Nicchi says, pushing back from her chair and jumping to her feet. Her chair crashes to the floor.

I'm silent for a while. I'm giving her a straight face, hoping it helps her buy into my bullshit. But, in reality, Kong will get rid of her dumb ass with the snap of his fingers.

"You know how long I've been knowing Kong?" I ask her. "Way longer than you. I know that nigga inside and out. He's selfish and greedy. He's cutthroat, too. You know he ain't keeping you around. You don't serve any purpose to him. When you go back to the projects, what you gonna have besides that Benz I bought you? How you gonna feed yourself, your kids? Keep your weave fly?"

Nicchi sits back down. She doesn't want to hear what I'm saying because she knows it's true.

"What the fuck are you trying to say, Mona?"

"I need your help," I blurt out.

"How can I help you?" she says like I've knocked her back to down to size. "You're right. Kong got me here for show, but I ain't serving no real purpose. I can't go back to the projects with nothing. All them bitches are expecting me to come back with nothing. They all gonna be laughing at me."

"If you help me, I can make sure you're set for life. I'll put you in a position where you don't need Kong or me. You can fend for your own, Nicchi. Be independent. Start another salon like you're always talking about."

"You remember that?" Nicchi says with hope sparkling behind her eyes.

"Of course, I remember. You're my baby sister. I know we ain't as close as we should be, but we're all each other got. We had it tough growing up, but we survived. We can survive this shit, too. It's time for you to start looking out for yourself, Nicchi poo," I say, calling her by the pet name I hadn't used in over thirty years.

Nicchi folds like putty in my hands

"That's what I want—to be a boss and not need nobody," Nicchi whines.

"Well then, act like it. Help me out, and I promise your payout will be big."

"How? If Kong finds out, he's gonna kill me," Nicchi responds, considering Kong's wrath.

"You're way smarter than Kong. He's big and brut, but he ain't got no brains. If you follow my instructions, I'll make sure you stay two steps ahead of him. I ain't gonna let nothing happen to you, girl. I promise," I say, penetrating her eyes with a sincere look.

Nicchi nods and smiles at me. Roberta returns with her steak.

"I hope they cooked this shit this time," Nicchi says, and we both laugh.

The laugh we share almost feels genuine.

8

Lera Badd

How did this happen? All of it. How? How did Ace happen? How did what Bobby did to me happen? How did Brock happen? How is this happening right now? As soon as I try to control a situation, I am reminded I have no control. Everything I'm doing right now proves how weak I am. I want my strength back, but it seems to be buried somewhere deep inside of me covered by the suffocating emotions of fear, paranoia, and weakness. No matter how much I plow through my soul, I can't find my strength. Maybe it's gone forever. Maybe I killed myself. I feel like the living dead. Just a shell of leftover parts of myself. Remnants of the person I was once.

I pull away from his kiss, although my body yearns for more. Too much thinking has snatched the gift of desire away from me. The scrambled thoughts come together, forming a reality I can't handle. The person I've become isn't who I am. The stranger that has invaded my soul starts to question me again. Why did Ace happen? Why did Bobby do what he did to me? Why did I come at Brock like that? Why do I have feelings for him? I have all the answers for why, but I'm just not ready to answer them yet. I can't accept it. Not yet. Not now. Not right now.

He pulls me back in, and I part his lips with my tongue, pushing it deep in his mouth like I'm trying to kiss his soul. I close my eyes tight, allowing myself to get lost in him. I inhale deep, and lust is pulled into my body, possessing all of my inner parts. Lust swarms within me like a tsunami, drowning all my negative thoughts and effortlessly breaking through the resistance. I feel my panties sticking to me. Wet. Warm. Ready. His hands slide up my thigh. He becomes stiffer as his fingers slide around the moisture that's running down my leg. He presses his body against mine, pinning me deeper into the wall. I can feel his swelling against my pelvis. His kiss is long and full of passion. It's causing me to melt from the inside out. He's setting my soul on fire, burning all my inner fears. My insecurities are becoming ashes.

He sweeps his hand under my shirt and cups my breast. He sensually massages my nipples with his tongue, and my back arches in such ecstasy that I feel like I'm going to snap in half. My head falls back, hitting the wall. I spread my legs and allow his fingers to go deeper inside of me. He plays with my clit with his thumb while two fingers gently slide in and out of me with a rhythm so precise I almost explode. I push down on his hand, allowing him to penetrate me deeper. Grabbing my neck, he pulls me into another kiss. His breath against my neck teases me; the smell of his skin intoxicates me. I want more. I need more of the life he is giving me. His touch is resurrecting me.

In one single movement, he falls to his knees and pulls my legs over his shoulders. He snatches off my panties, throwing them over his shoulder like they are trash—something I no longer need. He buries his face in between my legs and gently pulls my clit into his mouth, taking small delicate sips of me. I place my hands on top of his head and push him deeper against me. His entire face from the tip of his nose to the bottom of his chin is drowning in my love. He stiffens his tongue and dives inside me, swimming deep enough to find my spot. My legs tremble with ecstasy. My body tenses with unbearable pleasure as he pokes at my g-spot with the tip of his tongue, using perfect timing and pressure. I cry out while digging my nails into his shoulders like I am clinging on to him for dear life. This moment is saving my life and giving me life all at the same time. And I don't want to let go.

As he continues to plunge into me, bumping against my spot, he ventures off to my ass, spreading my cheeks and toying with my ass with his knuckles. My entire face winces with desire in the most beautiful, ugly way before my body erupts with pleasure. I jerk like a bolt of lightning has struck me from the inside out. Then I slid down the wall like mush. I can't feel any of my limbs. The pleasure was so intense from our lovemaking that it has numbed all my other senses. Before my ass can hit the floor, he scoops me up and cradles me in his arms like I am delicate. Before I have time to wonder where he is taking me, I am already on a bed. I don't even know what room I am in. I don't care either.

He gently lays me across the bed, and while leaning over me, he pulls his shirt over his head and rips off his boxers. He looks down at me, admiring the bliss of my body. Desire beams through his eyes brighter than sun rays. His look almost blinds me. He leans down and places his body on top of mine. The weight of his body feels healing. He squeezes me tight, hugging me before coating my mouth with his lips. I wrap my arms around him and squeeze him tight. Pulling him deep into me, it feels like our souls are touching.

He pries my legs apart in a sexy, domineering way like he's breaking the lock of a vault he owns. My body squirms in anticipation, ready for what he is about to give me. The fitted sheet pops from the mattress and curls up towards my body. I grab a pillow and squeeze it, trying to release the pressure while waiting for him to part my legs with his dick. I can feel it against my thighs. It's ready. He's ready. Instead, he leans up. When the weight of his body rises from mine, a cold gush of air covers me, sending a chill up my spine. I raise up on my elbows and spread my legs, letting him know I am ready without saying a word. He looks down at me like he's dying of thirst and I'm the river that will surely hydrate him. But he walks away.

My eyes follow his perfectly-built body as he goes over to the nightstand and pulls out a box of condoms, ripping it open. My senses heighten as the chill covers my body in another gush. I hear rattling inside the cardboard box, the ripping of sharp plastic, and then the squish of the condom being rolled onto his dick. I even smell it. I close my legs as he walks back towards me, and I cover my naked body with the sheets. I feel exposed. I feel vulnerable again as the question returns. *Why?*

He looks down at me, confused. His penis deflates with every second that passes. He lowers his brow and squints his eyes. Then he opens his mouth to say something but doesn't speak. Making a dress from the bedsheets, I stand to face him.

"You use condoms with whores, not your fake wife," I say with a tone filled with contempt.

I feel cheap and used, just like that night with Ace. How dare him! Who does he think I am? Someone he needs to protect himself from? Or is he protecting that half-dead bitch, Tara? Fuck him for trying to place a barrier between the last bit of love we have left for each other.

Bobby doesn't try to stop me when I walk out of the room. *What the fuck was I thinking?* I rush to the shower to wash my body clean of the dangerous fantasy I toyed with today. *This was a mistake. Everything about Bobby Badd was a mistake.*

I LET THE hot water pour down on my body. At first, it felt scolding against my skin, but now it just feels healing. The burn is melting away my sins and getting the gunk of other people's energy off my flesh. I scrub my body so hard my skin feels rug burned. The steam fills the room so heavily, I can't make anything out. I feel like I'm in another world. If only I can stay here.

I know Bobby won't bother me. He's been good at giving me my space. He gave up on trying to get me to talk to him weeks ago. But, when we were passing each other in the hallway this morning, something happened. I felt the spark. Our bodies crashed into each other like a stellar collision, and I couldn't pull away. Feeling his body against mine was the closest I've felt to being my old self since all of this shit went down. It was like getting a glimpse of my old life. I couldn't pull away from that if I tried, because deep down inside, it's what I want. I want everything to go back to the way it was, even where I didn't know Tara. Truth hurts is an understatement. The truth kills you, and lies keep you alive. Lies provide more protection than the truth ever can.

What happened today between Bobby and me is proof that I still love him and almost want it to work. How can you love someone that you hate? Why would I love someone who hurt me that way? He left me for dead, and I let him touch my body like it's his. Weakness floods my body, and I grab the shower walls to keep from falling. There's a knot in my chest, and my stomach aches with grief.

I'm weak, so fucking weak.

I grab the rag and wipe around my neck where his lips were only minutes ago. No matter how hard I scrub, I still feel him. I can still smell him, too. I bend over and turn the shower knob. I need the water hotter, but I already have it turned up to its max. Switching gears, I set the knob to cold. I jump when the icy water hits my warm flesh like shards of glass, but I take the agony. Anything is better than the feeling of Bobby's touch. I treat the cold water like it's my penance. I push myself further into the stream. My entire body shudders, but I force myself to stay put. I just want this pain to go away. Crossing my arms around my body, I try to control the shiver.

The warm water causes me to think about Bobby, but the cold water pushes Ace in my mind. I close my eyes to try and drive away the memory of that night. But when I reopen them, it's still there. I see him on top of me with his hand on my neck. I feel him pushing himself inside of me, forcing me to look him in the eye while it's happening. The control. The fear. The constraint. I brought it all on myself. The realization causes the cold water to feel like sharp daggers; it cuts through my flesh like a thousand knives. I was only trying to protect myself, but I got caught in the same trap that I set. I thought I had everything under control. I thought I would be able to save us all, but I was wrong. I couldn't even rescue myself. I haven't had control of my life since the day I fell in love with Bobby Badd. If Bobby was the first foolish mistake I made, then thinking I could fuck Ace into submission was the second stupid mistake—the worst mistake of them all.

When the cold water doesn't feel like enough punishment, my eyes land on a razor, and for a split second, I think about slitting my wrist. Not necessarily to die but to stop the pain. Then again, maybe death is the only way to stop this pain. I pick up the shaving razor and run my finger over the sharp blade. I finesse it. I flirt with it. *Can I really do this?*

I close my eyes and grip the handle tighter. *Does Bobby think I'm a whore? Is that all I am to him?* The two thoughts collide, and I feel pathetic and weak. The cold water feels room temperature now. The brisk sharpness can't compete with this razor. This razor can end it all for me; cure me of my pain and mistakes. Death may be a fresh start. Anything is better than this.

I press the razor into my wrist and hold it there. At this point, I don't know what's stopping me. I'm so deep in thought that I don't notice when Bobby snatches the shower door open and slaps the razor out of my hand like I am a five-year-old playing with a knife—like I don't have the sense to know what I'm doing. The razor falls to my feet, pricking my big toe on its way down.

"What the fuck are you doing, Lera?"

I look up at him, and I just want to hide. He's staring back with those penetrating eyes; they are saying so much all at once. While he's screaming at me, I see judgment behind his glare. I also see guilt, annoyance, and shame. I feel so vulnerable under his presence that I wish I could vanish into thin air. I feel violated with him looking at my naked body, seeing all of me, even things I want to hide. But I keep a straight face. I have to. I can't crack under pressure. Not in front of him. Not like this. My pride is all I have left in this world. I take a deep breath and swallow air like it's a shot of whiskey. I blink hard serval times, hoping that Bobby will be gone each time I reopen my eyes. But he's still here, staring at me like I'm a wounded little puppy.

Bobby leans into the shower and turns off the water. Then he turns around, pulls a towel off the rack, and opens it, ready to wrap me up in it. He's holding the towel like it's a straightjacket—like I need to be restrained.

"Get out," he demands.

I try to look up at him, but I can't. Instead, I lower my chin in shame. My eyes mist with tears that I forbid to fall. *I'm not going to do it,* I say to myself. Or was I? I question my intentions.

When I don't move, Bobby grabs my arm and gently but forcefully pulls me out of the shower. My wet body falls into his chest, and he wraps the towel around my body, embracing me for a few seconds before letting me go. For a moment, I allow myself to get lost in the cocoon he has me wrapped in. I feel safe. I feel loved. I feel normal. Bobby plants a delicate kiss on top of my head. His lips linger a few seconds longer than we both expect. A comforting surge of energy is injected in my body, pushing its way down from the top of my head where his lips rest to the tip of my toes where the razor nicked me. After he finally pulls away, I straighten my posture like I wasn't in need of his embrace. My pride is all I have.

"Get dressed, quick," he tells me, his tone serious.

Relieved that there are bigger problems to distract him from what he just witnessed, I look up at him with curious eyes.

"Something's going down, and I need you to be ready just in case. So, put on some tennis shoes and meet me downstairs," he says before turning and rushing out the bathroom.

What the fuck is going on? I mumble, then rush to my room located on the opposite end of the hall. I'm as far away from Bobby as I can get. Bobby hates that I'm not close to him. He doesn't trust the guards. One night, I woke up and tripped over his body. He was sleeping outside my door with a small pillow and blanket. My pride didn't allow me to thank him, nor did I look at him. But I did feel something that I pushed away instantly, burying it with the rest of my emotions.

I open the dresser drawer and pull out a pair of jogging pants and a sweater. The fabric clings to my wet body because I didn't have time to dry off. I put on shoes without socks and then run down the steps like the house is on fire.

Immediately, I start thinking about Brock. I don't know why I think about him so much. I'm not sure if I'm rebelling or vindicating myself for the shit Bobby did to me, but Brock runs through my mind daily. It's complicated to explain how I feel about it. My feelings fall somewhere in between brotherly love and romantic. I saw a different side of him when we were together. Brock didn't make me feel like I was a victim. He twisted all my weaknesses and showed me that they are strengths. With him, I felt like I was evolving into somebody I could learn to love and respect again. He protected me and allowed me to protect myself. Brock trusted me. I wonder if this is about him. *Is he back? Is he here to save us?*

When I get to the bottom of the stairs, Bobby comes out of nowhere and grabs me, pulling me into a protective hold. *Pop!* The sound of four gunshots ring out so loud and close that it sounds like it's coming from our living room. Then another few pops follow. I jump and bury my face deep into Bobby's chest for safety. He covers my ears with his large hands. Starting to feel weak under his embrace, I pull away. My pride is all I have left.

"Is it Brock?" I ask with too much anticipation in my voice.

Bobby pulls away and gives me a look that I can't read. Bobby talks with his eyes, but sometimes it's a language no one can understand. Grabbing my arm, he quickly leads me into the kitchen.

"Get down," he says, moving one of the dining room chairs and pushing me underneath the table.

When he turns to leave, I panic. Maybe it's not Brock. Maybe they're killing us all. More gunfire rattles the house.

"Where are you going?" I yell from under the table, concern slipping from my lips.

Bobby stops and turns to face me. He knows I still care about him.

"I'll be back," he says matter-of-factly.

"But, Bobby…" Fear covers my voice. Finally, no pride.

"I mean what I say," he says, cutting me off before jogging towards the front door.

9

Bobby Badd

OUTSIDE, IT'S ORGANIZED chaos. At that moment, I know what I'm witnessing ain't got shit to do with Brock. This ain't his style. I wonder if Lera is gonna be disappointed to learn that Brock, her self-prescribed savior, ain't back yet. It's mindboggling trying to understand the sudden feelings she has for my brother. If I had time to consider it all, I would have questions for her, but I ain't got time for bullshit. Besides, I trust my brother, although he don't deserve it.

I blame myself for everything Lera has done to herself and others up to this point. That's all on me. I even take the blame for what she did to Tara. I thank God that I made the moves I did and got them off this Ranch before the takeover. But the way shit is going now, that don't necessarily mean they're safe. I trust Jayson to care for my family. He loves his sister and Blake, but the love between us has been lost. Him deciding he has the power to take my family away from me is an issue I'll deal with once all this shit passes. I'm hopeful that we all are going to pull through this and come out on top. This shit is just a phase that we all are gonna learn from and make right. But, until then, I got to make sure Lera survives. I got to survive, too. Otherwise, my son will have no one.

"Mr. Badd," a guard calls to me from behind the bushes near my front porch.

His voice is faint but loud enough to draw my attention. I can hear the fear in it.

"What's going on out here?" I respond without bringing too much attention to myself.

"They're killing us. They just killed my partner. Shot him straight in the head, execution-style. They're cold, man." His voice trembles. "That man got six kids. He only came here for the money they offered. That dude wasn't no killer. None of us are. Shit, half of us can't even hold a fucking gun right. Now they're slaughtering us like fucking sheep. Please help me. I'll do anything," he pleads.

I turn away from the sound of his voice. I have no sympathy for a man who evaded my home with pointed guns, taking shit that didn't belong to them. I despise thieves. They're worse than murderers because they're weak. They ain't got no heart. But I could use his little ass. I just don't know how yet.

I look out into the street and watch as the lead guards put these men on their knees before blowing their brains out. The ones that run off are gunned down with a shot to their back. The thud of a body follows every pop of a gun. Blood is running down the street like a river. Grown men are crying and begging for their lives; some are fighting back. *What the fuck is Kong doing?*

One of the shooters sets their sights on me. He squints his eyes and lowers his brow at me. He thinks he's intimidating me, but I don't scare easily. When I don't look away from him, he gets pissed and starts walking towards me. Before he can get to me, he shoots two more runaway guards. One takes a bullet in the chest and the other in the leg. He steps over the body like it's a speed bump that's slowing him down.

"Please, man. Pleaasse help me," the guard whispers from the bushes.

"Get back in the house," the shooter says to me.

I don't flinch. I keep my eyes fixed on him. He's holding the gun;

however, the closer he gets to me, the more nervous he becomes. I give him a blank stare and fold my arms defiantly across my chest. I ain't in the mood to be fucked with today. Not on my own front porch.

"You heard what the fuck I said!" he yells and aims his gun at me.

I still don't flinch.

"Do you know where you're aiming that gun?" I respond, using a level tone.

Nothing he's doing makes me nervous, and he knows it. He lowers the gun a little but immediately lifts it back in my direction.

"I'll kill your cocky ass right now!" he threatens, fixing his aim.

"Kill me?" I point to my chest. "Kill yourself." I point back at him. "Kill your daughter. Kill your lady. Kill your whole bloodline."

The man swallows hard and trembles. I don't move. Instead, I stand with my arms still folded over my chest and my chin raised. I'm ready for whatever he's got. I'm not afraid. For some reason, I know I can dodge his bullet if I have to.

"Where's the other guard? There were two of them."

I don't respond to his question. I just look at him. I don't blink; I don't flinch. He sees that look in my eyes. He knows today ain't the day to fuck with me, and I make him feel that shit in his bones. He finally relents and lowers his gun.

"I got to take a look around your house," he tells me like it's an order, but I know it's really a question. So, I answer him.

"No," I reply firmly.

He swallows hard, then looks over his shoulder before turning around and aiming his gun at another guard trying to run. He shoots him in the back, and the guard's body falls on top of another one laying in the street. The shooter knows he can't kill me, so he takes the easy way out to ease the anxiety my presence is causing him. He turns back around and looks at me.

"If you see him, send him straight to me," he says again like it's an order, but really, it's a question. This time, I don't respond.

He walks back to the chaos in the streets with his tail between his legs. *All these niggas out here know I mean what I say. My voice echoes even when I'm not speaking.* I watch as he aims his gun and starts shooting at random guards. He makes a mistake and shoots a lead, causing his body to fly back in the grass. *These niggas are dumb as fuck out here.* I turn to face the bushes.

"Get in the house," I say to the guard in hiding.

He crawls out from behind the shrubs and runs to my front door as if his life depends on it.

"Why is he here?" Lera points at the guard like I just rescued an abandoned puppy.

"I don't know yet," I tell her and then look at the young man who's crouched down in the corner. He's trembling uncontrollably.

"If they find him here—"

"Hey," I say, shooting her a sharp look, "I got it under control."

I tell her this not fulling knowing myself what that means.

Lera sweeps her hands over her head. Her hair is growing back in beautifully. The short cut brings out the beautiful features of her high cheekbones and full lips that shine radiantly on her face. She walks in circles before looking out the front window and grimacing at the disgusting sight of dead bodies in the streets.

"I don't understand. Why are they killing each other?"

Lera looks to me for answers, but I don't have any. However, this tells me that she's starting to trust me again. I can even see glimpses of the old Lera behind her eyes. The light is dull, but it's there. She's still there, and so is her love for me. The love I don't deserve but still crave. Something about her energy gives me strength. Lera makes me feel like a man in ways that Tara can't.

"Aye," I say to the guard.

He looks up at me, barely able to hold his head up. The kid is spazzing out.

"Come," I tell him, pointing to in front of me.

Lera looks at me and then back at the guard, who is cowering against the wall. She places her hands in the back pockets of her jogging pants and stands still. She's waiting for my next move. The way she trusts my judgement without ever questioning me is so attractive. But, I can't get caught up in all that emotion. Not today. Today, I got to figure out how to get us out of here.

The guard tries to stand to his feet but is so shell-shocked, he falls against the wall and covers his ears like gunfire is still erupting. It's quieting down outside. Now they're trying to clean up the mess they made. Trucks from the morgue are picking up the bodies from the street.

"Man up," I say to him, using a stern tone. "It's over now. You survived so far."

The man grabs the wall and uses it as a crutch to pull himself up. With weak, trembling legs, he walks my way. Lera looks at the boy and empathizes with him. She tries to hide it, but I see the sorrow she has for him in her eyes.

"What's your name, kid?"

"Fre…" The words get stuck in his throat as he tries to avoid eye contact with me. "Freddie," he finally answers, pushing it out of his mouth like it took all the energy he has.

"How old are you?"

"I'll be twenty next week," he says and drops his head. "If I live that long."

"Hopefully, you'll live to see your fiftieth birthday, but you got to be smart."

I tap my finger against his temple. He jumps and ducks after I touch him before falling back.

"Get up," I say, disgusted by the timid man. His fear will kill him quicker than any bullet.

Freddie gets up slowly from the ground. He's taking so long that I lean down and yank him up by his shirt collar. Then I pull him to me and look at him. He trembles and flinches like I'm about to hit him. If I could knock some heart into him, I would, but I can't. You either got heart or you don't. And he ain't got it, so I don't waste my time.

"If I'm gonna help you, you need to get your mind right. Otherwise, I'm putting your ass out on them streets to get slaughtered with the rest of your friends."

"Please don't," Freddie begs.

"Stop fucking begging," I tell her.

Annoyed, I ball up my fist. I want to sucker him in his jaw, but I taught myself not to act out in anger. That's what weak men do. Instead, I let him go and push him away from me like his bitch-ass-ness is contagious.

I look up at Lera, who's staring at me hard. I don't know what she's thinking.

"Lock him in the basement...in the sauna," she says after walking over to me. "They won't find him in there."

She gives Freddie a compassionate look. When she sees I notice it, she wipes it from her face, replacing the look with a blank stare.

"Get up," I order Freddie.

This time, he jumps to his feet quickly.

I look at Lera and nod. Her face lights up. She seems honored that I trust her judgement. I've earned a bit more of her respect, but I still have a long way to go.

"I got a little brother out there," Freddie states, looking me directly in the eye.

"What the fuck that got to do with me?" I respond coldly, an emotionless stare glazing over my eyes.

"His name is Donnie," he continues. "He's only seventeen, and we only came 'cause they said we could earn enough money to move our mother and little sisters out the East Meadows projects. They promised us five G's a piece. That's enough for a down payment on a house to rent." Freddie's eyes lower. "I hope he ain't dead. I promised Mama I would protect him."

Breathing in hard, Lera covers her mouth and turns her back to us.

"I'm gonna let you hang out in my sauna to keep you safe. I don't know shit about your brother, man, and I can't concern myself with all that."

"Yes, sir," Freddie says and sniffs, fighting to hold back his tears.

Without another word, I lead him to the basement.

WHEN I GET back upstairs, Lera is in the kitchen, pouring herself a glass of Scotch. I walk over to her and snatch the glass from her hand, emptying the liquor into the sink. Lera snaps her neck, turning to me, and gives me a snide look. Reaching over my head, she grabs another glass before leaning over towards the half-empty bottle of Scotch. I've watched her drink enough, and I'm not gonna have her drowning her sorrows in liquor because of me. This ain't the way for her to handle her grief. When all this shit is over, I'm gonna make sure that she gets some real help, but I got to play warden for now. I snatch the bottle from her and break it against the floor.

"Enough!" I yell.

She jumps at the sound of the glass cracking against the tile. Spinning around, she looks at the busted bottle of Scotch with her mouth open. It's like I got rid of her lifeline and pulled the plug on her oxygen. She turns back towards me and pounds her two delicate fists against my chest. I take her punches like a man. I deserve them. I deserve more.

"Who do you think you are?" she says in one exasperated breath.

She stares at me and waits for me to respond, although she knows I don't answer questions like that. She inhales deeply and shakes her head at me before walking to the pantry to pull out a broom. She carefully sweeps up the glass. Cleaning eases her nerves. The other day, I walked in on her scrubbing the bathroom tub with a toothbrush. Then she vacuumed the rug over a dozen times. Her cleaning I don't mind, but the drinking has to go. I won't let her destroy herself. Not anymore.

Lera walks past me and empties the dustpan in the trash. Then she heads back to the pantry to get the mop. I grab her arm, pulling her back to me. Cupping her face in my hands, I stare into her eyes. I need to know that she's okay. It takes a few seconds, but she resists my touch, pushing me off her and disappearing into the pantry. I stare at the door, waiting for her to return. A few minutes go by, and when she walks back out, she sweeps the mop over the liquor, soaking it up. After a few moments, she stops and turns to me.

"Why did you save him?" she asks, referring to Freddie.

"Because it felt right."

"Did putting me off the Ranch feel right, too?" Lera shoots back.

Now she's going deep. Deeper than I'm ready to go, but she deserves answers. She deserves the truth.

"No," I quickly answer. "But I felt it was my only option."

Lera rolls her neck and exaggerates an eye roll before lifting her head to the ceiling in disbelief.

"You know I mean what I say, girl," I remind her.

"No, you mean what you do," she says, dropping the broom and pointing a convicting finger at me.

She steps over the rest of the liquor and pushes past me. I try to snatch her back, but she dodges my attempt.

"Aye," I say, but she ignores me.

I chase behind her. Before she can get up the stairs, I leap towards her, pulling her into me and holding her put.

"Calm down," I whisper in her ear. "We need to talk about this. No more running away."

"What can you possibly have to say?" She breaks away from my grasp, spins around, and gives me a look of contempt.

"What I did was fucked up. It was beyond fucked up, but I love you. That shit hasn't changed, and it never will."

Lera rolls her eyes again.

"This ain't the time for lies or games, Lera. You either believe me or you don't."

"You love your wife, Tara."

"Tara ain't my wife. You are." I grab both her arms and force her to look at me. "Our wedding in Vegas was real, Lera. It wasn't no fucking ploy. So much shit went down that I fucked up and reacted off my emotions. I wasn't in my right mind, and I let you get hurt. I ain't gonna let that happen again."

"I don't need you to protect me, Bobby. You can't!"

"I can and I will," I say, shaking her a little. "Look at me," I demand, but Lera's eyes land everywhere but on who's in front of her. "Look at me," I say again sternly.

Lera's eyes flicker. She's using her long lashes to stave off the tears. When she finally looks up at me, her eyes melt into mine.

"I love you," I slowly express, pulling the words straight from my heart.

Lera starts to sob like I'm murdering her.

"I love you," I say again and pull her into my chest.

She cries so hard that she depletes all her energy and falls into my arms, barely able to hold her weight.

"I don't believe you," she says through her tears. "No, you don't. You can't love me. You can't."

She lifts her hand to beat against my chest, but she's too weak. I hate how much I have hurt her, but I can't go back. I'm the kind of nigga that never looks back. I set my sights ahead, seeing far enough ahead to even see around corners. I don't know what else to do to convince Lera other than showing her. My words don't mean shit to her right now. They're just fucking words, and I have to respect that. I don't blame her. I was on some real fuck-nigga shit with her, but I got to make it right. I have to show her that I love her.

I lift her chin with my finger and part her lips with my tongue. At first, she fights me, but then, she gives in, allowing her body to relax in my arms.

Pulling away from her, I whisper the words "I love you" again and plant more kisses on her lips. Then her nose. Then her forehead and the bottom of her chin. Lera sniffs and shakes her head. She's still fighting me. She doesn't want to believe I love her, because then, she will be forced to accept that she still loves me, and for her, that shit is forbidden. Her loving me is like turning against herself. It's genocide—an abomination of the worst kind. But it's real.

I finger her short, curly hair before gently guiding her neck back to my face. I kiss her even deeper. So deep that she moans with ecstasy.

Hearing her sultry, soft whimpers cause me to swell. I think about this morning and how her body made me forget everything. Her skin against mine was just what I needed to get through the day, but then I fucked it up. I was too much in my head. I shouldn't have put on the condom, but I'm too fucking rationale not to. Ace Lucky violated her. Being violated in that way may have caused her to act out, using the very thing he took from her as a weapon. I don't know where Lera has been while I was at Tara's bedside, and I don't even want my mind to go there. But whatever she got, if she does have something, I deserve it.

Scooping Lera up, I carry her to the couch while we're still engaged in a kiss. She wraps her arms around my neck tight, being sure not to break away from the kiss.

I gently place her on the couch and pull her sweats down, but a knock at the door causes both of us to freeze. Whoever is at the door could have just walked in, but they knocked for a reason. I pull myself off Lera, and she props her body up on her elbows with curiosity and fear in her eyes. Another knock follows the first one. We look at each other, speaking only with our eyes. I hold my hand out, gesturing for her to stay put. She shakes her head at me and leans up. She's so fucking stubborn. She gets up, and after adjusting her pants back on her waist, she follows behind me.

"Stay here," I whisper, stopping her at the foyer.

This time, Lera listens and watches me tip-toe towards the door.

When I look through the peephole, I'm stunned by who's on the other side of the door. I turn and face Lera to let her know everything is okay. She holds out her upturned hands, asking who is at the door without saying a word. When I swing it open, Lera sighs and twists her face in disappointment. That's my exact sentiment.

10

Mona Badd

BOBBY IS LOOKING at me like he sees a ghost. I guess I am a ghost to them. I haven't seen any of them since that day at the cemetery. I'm starting to think Kong set it up that way so they won't trust me. It breaks our bond. I look at Bobby and then over my shoulder at all the chaos happening in the streets, hinting for him to let me inside. But he's just standing there looking dumbfounded. You never know what Bobby is thinking.

Kong is a fucking fool to order the killing of one guard per post. All it did was cause mayhem. So much mayhem that he lost over half his muscle in under an hour. He even lost a few leads. The men he hired are dumb as a rock, but they ain't stupid enough to sit down and take a bullet. Now, they don't trust him, and the ones that were able to escape the Ranch are gonna spread the word. Ain't nobody going to be rushing here to work for Kong no matter what he offers them. But, this shit works in our favor. With half the guards either dead, on the run, or wounded, I have fewer eyes on me. This gives me a window of opportunity to meet with everybody to develop a plan to get us out of this shit and to warn Brip about tonight. The guards were supposed to send for him hours ago, but when hell broke loose, the shit got delayed. Thank God!

I still have blood on the back of my shoes from the walk here. Bodies are everywhere. The ones that are still alive are lying in the streets waiting to die. Kong ain't sending no help for them. This is a perfect example of why he can't run this Ranch. He ain't no leader. Not by far. He's just a bloodthirsty tyrant. Being a leader means you gain respect before you do fear. Kong just wants people to fear him. He don't know shit about respect.

I rub my bloodstained tennis shoes against Bobby's welcome mat and look up at him. He still ain't ready to let me in, but I'm not waiting any longer for his stuck-up ass to invite me inside. I don't have time for this shit. Pushing past him, I step into the house. The first person I see is Lera's crazy ass. She's staring at me with her arms folded across her chest like she wants to fight. If the bitch wants to go, we can go, but I ain't here for all that. I'm here to save her ass. I'm here to save them all, so they better start respecting me.

"We need to talk," I say, rolling my eyes at Lera as I turn to face Bobby. He still holding the door open like he's seeing me out.

"Talk about what?" Lera asks sternly while slowly walking towards me.

I don't know when this bitch got so bold, but I ain't here for her. Ignoring her, I stare at Bobby. When he finally takes the time to notice the urgency in my eyes, he closes the door, and I show myself to their living room. As I walk towards Lera, she's blocking my way. I guess she thinks her scrawny ass is enough to stop me. I move right past her, knocking her in the shoulder kind of on purpose but mainly by accident. Not even two seconds later, I feel someone jump on my back. It's that crazy bitch. She's cursing and spitting like a rabid dog.

"What the fuck?" I yell and swing her around, attempting to get her off of me.

Leaning down, I run towards the wall, slamming her head against it.

"Lera, calm down!" Bobby says, pulling her off of me.

The bitch has her nails in me so tight that she breaks skin as Bobby rips her away from me. I look down at the bloody scratches on my arm and then back at Bobby. *This bitch is fucking nuts.*

"I don't want that bitch here! I don't trust her, Bobby. Make her leave."

"Shut the fuck up!" I yell, pointing at her. "Bobby, I'm trying to be nice, but this bitch is trying my patience. We don't have time for this foolishness," I say, staring at Lera with squinted eyes. I want to knock the bitch out so bad my knuckles are throbbing.

Bobby has his arms wrapped around Lera, restraining her from behind and whispering something in her ear. Tears are streaming down her cheeks, and she is breathing like she's about to hyperventilate. What the fuck did I ever do to her ass besides try to help her? I really owe her an ass whooping for all the speculations about her and Brock.

"Where's Brock? She probably killed him, Bobby. Brock would've been here by now," Lera yells while trying to twist out of Bobby's grip.

I squeeze both my fists. This bitch done struck a nerve.

"Let her go," I demand of Bobby, but he's nobody's fool.

"Both of y'all need to calm down."

"What does this bitch know about my husband?" I hiss.

"I know you don't deserve him," Lera shoots back.

On that note, I charge towards her quicker than I remember, because before Lera even has a chance to take her next breath, we're nose to nose. Bobby protectively swings her around out of my reach and holds out his hand to calm me down.

"Be cool, Mona," Bobby calmly says.

"Ask her what the fuck is she talking about, Bobby?" I'm so upset that spit is flying out my mouth like venom. "Ask her did she fuck my husband, your brother." The words roll off my tongue like tumbleweed.

It's what I've been waiting to ask her since she got here. By the look in Bobby's eyes, so has he. Bobby gives Lera a serious look but doesn't say anything. He's a bitch. He doesn't want to know the truth. After what he did to her, she deserved to fuck another man. Just not my fucking husband.

"Is that what you want to know?" Lera says to Bobby.

Bobby still doesn't respond. He lets her go, and she shoots a bird at me before circling around Bobby and heading towards the stairs. Once she reaches the top of the stairs, she slams a door like a teenager having a temper tantrum.

"She's gonna get us killed," I look at Bobby and say. "Her little ass needs some fucking help."

"We all need fucking help right now," Bobby snaps at me.

"Well, why the fuck you think I'm here? To have tea?"

Bobby sweeps his hands over his head and exhales. He looks at me like he wants to say something but changes his mind.

"Say it," I challenge him.

"Why you think she fucked Brock?" Bobby spits out like the thought never crossed his mind.

"The same reason you think it," I say, and he shakes his head, disagreeing with me.

"Why are you here, Mona?" Bobby swings his hands in the air. "Shouldn't you be out running your new empire?"

"Fuck you for that," I say, stabbing my finger at him.

Bobby gives me an apologetic look. He can see in my eyes that he hurt me. I know they don't trust me. They all came to their conclusions that I'm in on this shit with Kong. I stopped by Brip's house first, but neither he nor Taffy opened the door. Brip not trusting me stings worse than a needle. I love Brip like my own flesh and blood. When I tried Billy, they ignored me the same way. Bobby was my last resort because he's such an asshole, but he's more levelheaded than all of them. Just like me, he can control his emotions. If I sat in my feelings for too long, I wouldn't have the heart to help them. I would just let them all die, but I ain't that type of bitch. I own my fucking emotions. I know how to control them. I'll never have a weak-ass mind like Lera, spilling emotions every moment I get.

"Why are you here?" Bobby asks again before taking a deep breath.

"I would have come sooner, but they've been watching me like a hawk. Thank God Kong decided to fuck up and kill his men 'cause that gives us leeway to do what we got to do."

"Which is?" Bobby says snidely.

"Get Brip the fuck out of here. They're gonna kill him next week. Kong's men are coming for him tonight."

Bobby's eyes widen with anger and fear. "How the fuck you know that?"

The disbelieving look that he's giving me makes me believe he is accusing me of being an accomplice.

"I overheard it. Kong is letting me in. I've been playing my cards right and risking my life for the sake of all of us. If I was in on this shit, wouldn't I just let it happen?"

Bobby gives me a considerate look before taking a step back. He's debating on whether or not he should trust me. He knows he should, but his pride is telling him otherwise.

"We don't have that much time, Bobby. We have to get him the fuck out of here, and I got to get a hold of Brock because, after Brip, you and Billy are next," I reveal.

"What do you suppose we do?"

"Get him to Zone 5. With all this chaos going on, we might be able to pull it off. They will never find him there. Maybe Brip can help us get in contact with Brock."

"I don't know, Mona." Hesitance fogs Bobby's voice. He sweeps another hand over his head and down his face. "That shit sounds risky."

"It is, but it's our only option, Bobby. I don't know where Brock is, but we can't wait around on him any longer."

Bobby takes a deep breath and nods his head a few times like he's convincing himself that my plan could work.

"Where do you think he is?" Bobby asks me, referring to Brock.

I can tell by his tone that he already has his suspicions. He thinks Brock is dead.

"I don't know, but I know he's around. Brock can dig his way out of fire and dirt. Why he hasn't come yet is beyond me, but I'm sure he's got a good explanation."

"If we get Brip out, we need to get the other wives out, too. This is too much for them."

"I agree, but you know they all ain't gonna agree to go."

"Well, they don't have a choice." Bobby looks at me and pauses. "Did you hear anything about…" He hesitates before continuing. "… about Mamma? Her body?"

I shake my head. "Kong says he ain't got nothing to do with it. He acts like it's a surprise to him, too."

"What about Ace? What role does he play in all this?"

I shrug my shoulders. "Ace was just a pawn for Kong. He got him on lockdown somewhere. He got Vinchi, too." My voice drops, and I lower my head.

Bobby doesn't say anything to comfort me, which makes me wonder if he thinks Vinchi deserves what he's getting. My heart starts to swell with fear. I immediately shake it off, squeezing my fist and taking deep, rib-stretching breaths.

"Does Brip know?" Bobby asks.

"I stopped by there first, but he didn't answer," I say, breaking my gaze with Bobby. "Neither did Billy. You have a short window of time, but you need to get over there and warn them. I can try to distract Kong for about two hours, but that's all the time I have. And even that's pushing it."

"You think you can get me to Billy's? His house is closer."

"Yeah, but let's take the back way," I tell him. "If we get stopped, let me do the talking. But we got to go now, and you need to leave Lera here. She's a liability," I add.

"I ain't leaving her again," Bobby firmly says.

Disapproving, I shake my head. Lera needs help. She's likely to get us all killed.

"Well, that's your call," I say and wave my hands in the air, surrendering to his poor decision. "Before we go, I need something."

"What?" Bobby asks, raising a curious brow at me.

"You got any cash?"

Bobby gives me an incriminating look that he doesn't think I caught, but I ignore it. I need all the cash I can get, and knowing Bobby, he got a stash somewhere in this house for moments like this. I promised Nicchi money. I need to grease her hands with a few grand to keep her on my side. If it's one thing Nicchi loves more than power, it's money. I already got her questioning Kong. I just need the money to seal the deal, and her simple ass is bought. Depending on how much cash Bobby has, I might be able to buy us a guard or two. Kong ain't paying them what they're worth, and he's killing them. My proposition may be just the break they're looking for.

"I may have a few grand buried in the backyard near the pool," Bobby says without asking me why.

"Get the shovel," I tell him.

"WHERE HAVE YOU been?" Kong asks, giving me a skeptical look.

I try not to hesitate so that I don't arouse his suspicions.

"Where have I been?" I repeat his question and look at him like I'm confused.

Kong isn't smart, but he's also not dumb. He's been trying to hide it, but he's been paranoid ever since he got here. He knows he's been fucking up and that he is in over his head. He doesn't have any leads on Brock, which means any moment now his little party will come to a very humiliating, bloody end. Every day, he loses a piece of confidence. I can see right through that mask he's wearing.

"A few of my lead men said they hadn't seen you." Kong squints his eyes at me. "I sent for you hours ago."

"Well, if you haven't noticed, your lead guards done fucked up," I say while pulling out a menu from the nightstand.

I try to distract him, and food is a good distraction for Kong.

We are at his penthouse suite in the casino. All that redecorating Nicchi did to the big house, and Kong hasn't stepped foot inside. He doesn't plan to either. I got to figure out how to get him to leave so I can get to the safe. But the safe comes second to Brip's life.

I was able to get Bobby and Lera to Billy's without anyone stopping us. I wanted to go inside to see everyone, but I felt it would be best not to rouse any of them up with my presence. They need a clear head if they're gonna pull off saving Brip.

Before I left, Bobby gave me a bag that felt like it had at least twenty grand in it. He told me that he never counted the money, so he couldn't tell me how much was inside. Even if it's fifteen hundred dollars, I plan to make that shit stretch just like Jesus did with the fish. When I'm determined, nothing can stop me. Nicchi is so simple that all I have to give her ass is about five grand, and she's gonna be walking around like she's nigga rich doing whatever I ask with the promise of more.

This is my first time in Kong's suite. I've been avoiding it until I couldn't anymore. I know what he wants, and I know what I'm going to have to do to keep myself in the know. The idea of him touching me makes my skin crawl, and my stomach turns flips. If I fuck him, he's gonna be stupid enough to think that he and I are real. I'll fuck him for Brip's life. I'll fuck him for this Ranch, too. But it ain't gonna be easy or pleasant for me.

Kong grabs my arm. His hands feel rough and dirty like he's been rubbing them against piss-stained concrete. My natural reaction is to pull away from his touch, but I take a deep breath and stay put. I hate every second of his skin touching mine. His touch freezes me. I try not to move so that I don't entice him to venture further than my wrist. To my dismay, he pulls me into the bed where he is laying. Kong had a custom-size mattress made to hold his massive body, but the bed is still too small.

"Why you so tense, Mona?"

"You see what's going on out there?" I reply and gently try to pull away from him, but he doesn't let me go.

"Tonight, I want you to relax," he says, rubbing my arm. His skin is so dry that it scratches my arm.

"Okay." I turn to him and half-smile, then reach back for the menu.

Kong snatches the menu out of my hand and tosses it to the side.

"I got something special planned for us tonight," he leans in and whispers in my ear.

I can feel his hot breath against my neck. His lips are so close to my skin that I can feel their moisture.

"This is like old times, isn't it?"

I nod and force a smile. Now Kong is massaging the sides and back of my neck. His touch stiffens my entire body. I know what I have to do tonight, but I ain't ready.

"You want a drink?" I ask, leaning up. "I need a drink."

Avoiding eye contact with him, I break away from his touch. I can feel him staring at me like I'm a piece of meat he's been waiting to devour.

"I bought something for you to wear. It's in the bathroom. Go put it on," Kong demands.

I turn and give him a fake surprised look.

"Really?" I try to control my voice from shaking.

Kong doesn't respond. He pushes his weight against the headboard and pulls his shirt over his head. His body has more ripples and waves than the ocean, and his chest hangs down towards his belly like he's breastfed an entire village. I try not to gag. He sticks his hand in his pants and plays with himself, then points to the bathroom, ordering me to go put on what he bought. When his penis bursts through his sweats, I spin around and head towards the bathroom. On the way, I grab a bottle of Jack Daniels and chug it. I got to flood my thoughts for this. Shit, if I had a crack pipe, I might take a hit—anything to escape the reality of what's coming.

When I walk into the bathroom, I'm so shocked by what I see hanging on the shower door that I drop the bottle, cracking it on the floor. My mouth flies open, and my heart skips a few beats. How could he? The audacity of this motherfucker! It's my wedding dress. The very dress I wore when I exchanged vows with Brock. This tells me that Nicchi is involved in this bullshit. I hope she sees that this nigga ain't shit. Kong got me all the way fucked up if he thinks I'm about to fuck him in my wedding dress.

I ball up my fist and turn to charge at him, but I stop myself. I remember Brip and realize just how much I love him. I'll do anything for him, even this shit. I swallow gulps of air to settle the stirring in my gut.

"Hurry up now," Kong yells from the bedroom. I can hear the eagerness in his voice.

Slipping the dress off the hanger, I hold it in my arms like it's a baby. Then I smell it, and my mind floods with memories of Brock and me. The early days. I was so grateful that he chose me to be his wife out of all the women he could have. Brock made me feel valuable. Sexy. He loves me. I start thinking about how he would feel about what I'm about to do and how I'm about to do it. Fucking Kong is already disrespectful enough, but him thinking I would do it while wearing my wedding dress takes the cake. I can't do this. If Kong wants me, it has to be on my terms.

I put the dress back on the hanger, then stare at myself in the mirror. I can barely look myself in the eye. Brock lied to me for years about Goldie and their love child. For all I know, there could be more Goldies out there. So, me fucking Kong should be vindication, especially with all the weirdness going on between Brock and Lera. Did he really fuck Lera? I can't imagine him doing that. Fucking Lera wouldn't just be him screwing me over but his brother, as well. Brock loves his brothers more than he loves himself. They just don't see it.

I splash some water on my face, and my mascara drips down my cheeks like black tears. Fucking Kong is going to be like crying black tears. I don't even try to fix my face or freshen up. I pull my shirt over my head so that I'm down to nothing but my bra and panties. I'm wearing a set that doesn't match, and a white bra of all things. You can't get any less sexy than that. My panties are made of cotton. I wear them for comfort, so they are oversized. They're pulled to my belly button. I could use some lotion on my legs and feet and a few squirts of perfume, but I don't bother. Kong is going to get me, but not the way he wants me.

I walk out of the bathroom like I have molasses stuck to my feet. I'm so hesitant that I can barely lift my legs. As I get closer to the bedroom, I hear Kong grunting and moaning. When I appear before him, his eyes widen with arousal and then disappointment.

"Where's the dress I wanted you to wear?" he asks, barely leaning up.

While I was in the bathroom, he pulled off his boxers and was stroking his snack-sized dick. Veins pop from the tip, making it look like an oversized mushroom cap—mold and all. I want no parts of him, but what choice do I have? I always liked to consider myself a woman who got by based on my brain and not my body, but there ain't no way around this shit. Most of it is my fault. I trusted Kong, and that's why we're all in this position right now. I owe it to them. I owe it to the Ranch. I've never fucked another man outside of Brock, but this ain't the first time I whored myself out for the Ranch. I've been doing that shit for years. I got so good at it that I never had to drop my panties, but obviously, times have changed.

"I ain't wearing it," I sternly reply.

Kong smiles, and with a curved finger, he motions for me to come towards him. He repositions himself on the bed so that he is sitting upright and puts his dick in a chokehold. His eyes are penetrating mine with lust. Kong licks his thick lips and a glaze of saliva slimes over his mouth. He moans as he squeezes his dick.

"I've been waiting a long time for this. You know how much I dreamed of this day?" he says to me through squinted eyes. "Come," he demands.

I walk over to the side of the bed and try my best to stare at him without seeing him. I try to take my mind someplace else, but I'm stuck here, trapped in his purgatory of lust and power. Kong forcefully grabs my hand. He knows I don't want this, but he doesn't care. He places my hand on his dick and moans in ecstasy.

"Can you feel how much I missed you?" he moans.

"You sure you want this? We're partners, right? Maybe we shouldn't be fucking each other…" I try to talk my way out of it, but it's too late.

"We're more than that," Kong says and looks me directly in the eye. "This is the way it should be."

Kong pulls me onto the mattress and starts fondling my breasts. He removes my bra straps one at a time until my breasts fall out, springing into his face.

"Come sit on my lap," he says, his eyes glued to my chest.

Reluctantly, I climb on top of him while trying my best to keep his dick from touching my thighs, but that was impossible. I immediately feel it swell a few more inches against me. Kong grabs my hips and pushes me closer to him. Then he grabs my breast and leans up, licking around my nipples like he's sucking sugar from a cane. I want to scream. I want to punch him. Spit on his face and leave, but I don't. Instead, I close my eyes real tight and try to think of Brock, but I can't see him. I can't see my husband. Is that what my life has come to?

Kong reaches underneath me and grabs his dick.

"You ready?" he asks, although he couldn't care less if I was or not.

Just wanting to get this shit over with, I keep my eyes glued shut. I can feel his penis scraping against my inner thigh, making its way to my pussy, and my entire body goes tense. I don't want this.

"Mmm," he moans. "Just relax," he says with a stiff hand on my back to keep me still.

Just when he's about to shove his dick inside of me, someone busts through the door.

"Kong!" one of his lead guards yells.

Kong leans up and looks over my shoulder. My eyes are still shut. I'm so relieved for the interruption that I'm afraid if I open my eyes, it will all go away.

"You don't knock?" Kong booms, his voice so loud it echoes off the walls.

I can feel the tension and annoyance in Kong's voice. His entire body tenses up underneath me, and the swelling against my thigh goes down. *Thank God.*

"I'm sorry, sir." The guard's voice is shaky. "But this is important."

"Nothing is this important." Spit flies from Kong's mouth and lands on my neck. His breath feels like steam from a sauna.

"It's about Brip, sir," the guard reluctantly says.

Kong's grip on me grows tighter. I can feel him staring at me, but I don't look at him. I have to play it cool.

"What about him?" he yells over my shoulder with his eyes fixed on me.

"He's gone."

"What?" Kong yells. His voice is full of fury.

Kong forcefully pushes me off him. I roll to the other side of the bed and have to grab the nightstand to keep from falling off the mattress.

"What the fuck do you mean he's gone?" Kong pounds against the mattress, and I swear it feels like my body jolts through the air.

He snaps his neck in my direction and flares his nostrils like he's about to charge at me.

"Sir..." The guard's voice shakes as he holds up his hand and takes a few steps back. "They're all gone. All of them."

Kong grabs my arm and pulls me into him.

"What the fuck did you do?"

I try my best not to smile. *They got away. They did it.*

11

Brock Badd

"**K**ENO SAYS THAT'S poison. It turns brains to foam and mush," Tony says as he hands me the coke.

Tony talks about Keno every day. His brother sounds like he was a wise man—a man I would've loved to have on my team. Having Tony is second best, though. This man is a true soldier in every sense of the word. When I get the Ranch back, I'm keeping him by my side and crowning him as my lieutenant. He's loyal, fearless, and hard as fuck. They don't make men like Tony anymore. With the right training, I'll get his mind back right. I know I can, but first things first. I got to use this truth elixir and get what I've been waiting on. I don't know how he did it, but he found it for me after being gone for three days. At first, I thought he wasn't coming back, but he returned with more than what I asked for—at least a brick of coke and the money I gave him to cop it. He's a real soldier. He doesn't need cash or guns to get what he wants—just muscle and strategy.

"Sometimes poisoning a person's mind is the only way to get the truth," I respond, taking the coke from him.

"Are we getting Taffy today?" Tony asks, sounding hopeful.

I take a deep breath and look down at my phone. I have the ringer on and the volume turned up high, but that doesn't stop me from checking it every hour. I still haven't heard from Stein. It's been a week. I tried calling the number I called before, but no one is answering. I don't understand it. Why would he just leave me hanging? My father told me that I could rely on him. What the fuck is this about? I'll give it another few days, but if I don't hear anything by then, Tony and I will have to come up with a way to take the Ranch on our own.

One of my connects has been telling me crazy shit, saying the Ranch is a bloodbath and that people are getting killed on the streets. Pimp and whores walking the beat, and bodies burned by the second. I can't imagine any of the things he's saying, and I don't want to. If all that shit is going down, where the fuck does that leave my family? Mona still hasn't called. That ain't good. But if I focus too much on that, I'm gonna get weak, and I can't get weak. Not now. Not ever.

I turn to walk back to the basement. Before I open the door, I pull the cell phone out of my pocket that Stein left me and look down at it. It's on, but still no calls. I sigh and shove the phone back in my pocket. Stein got me out here like a fucking kid waiting on Santa. I'm starting to think the motherfucker *is* Santa 'cause the shit ain't feeling real no more. I turn to face Tony, who is about to follow me downstairs. I stop him. I know he won't pay attention to any of the shit Lady L says, but I still don't want him around. This is a private matter.

"Watch the house. I'll be back." I place my hand on his shoulder, and he nods.

Tony spins around and marches down the hallway like a solider on duty. I watch him until he disappears around the corner. Then I open the door and make my way downstairs. From the stairway, I can hear Lady L stirring and making a fuss. Angelo is trying to calm her down. She tries to get her to eat and drink, but Lady L refuses. Their relationship seems complicated. They definitely on some love-hate type shit. Angelo is concerned about her mother. I can see the concern drowning out the shine of greed behind her eyes. Angelo doesn't want partnership or money anymore. She wants her mother alive. Bloodstains don't wash off your hands as easily when it's family. I know that all too well.

"Don't fucking touch me, you bitch!" Lady L is fighting with Angelo.

When I see the drama going on in front of me, I second-guess my decision to untie Lady L. No one is watching, but she's causing a scene. The woman's veins pump more drama than they do blood.

"You're one stupid bitch!" Angelo fusses back at her mother while dodging her weak punches. "This is how you want to die? I swear to God once you're dead, I'm gonna bury you looking just like this. No makeup, no wig. The whole world is gonna look at you and laugh," Angelo taunts her.

The thought of dying naked causes Lady L to calm down a little.

"Now, take a sip." Angelo shoves the water into Lady L's mouth, and she swallows hard like she's pushing rocks down her throat.

"I got something I think she may like," I say, interrupting them.

Startled by my presence, they both jump. When I hold up the brick of coke, Lady L's eyes light up like she sees heaven's gates. She tries to stand up and lean towards me but falls back down. Her knees are too weak. Her legs are so skinny, I don't see how she ever stood on them. Angelo catches her and wraps her arm around her.

"Take another sip first." She places the bottle back to her mother's lips but gentler this time.

Lady L takes a big sip while keeping her eyes fixed on me and the coke.

"You gonna try to eat something?" Angelo asks her mother, using a parental tone.

"I need to build up an appetite first," Lady L replies and licks her cracked lips.

Both Angelo and Lady L look up at me like I'm Jesus holding the gift of life in my hands. My stomach turns at how pathetic they are. I shake my head in judgement and hold the bag of coke in the air.

"This is a gift," I remind them both. "The way this gift exchange is going to work is I'm gonna gift you something, and you're gonna gift me something." I pause, allowing my words to sink in.

Staring at the bag, Lady L is foaming at the mouth and practically wagging her tail like a dog waiting for a treat. I'm not even sure she's listening to me. Her eyes are bulging like a fiend straight out of rehab. I look past her at Angelo, and Angelo nods. She gets my drift.

I pull out a knife, slit the bag open, and sprinkle a little of the powder on a book. Then I slide it over to Lady L. She dives nose first into the book like she's thirsty for knowledge, but knowledge ain't what she wants. It's what I want. Before she can take a drag, I slide the book from underneath her as she inhales dust from the carpet and then hisses at me like a snake. I place my finger under her wrinkled chin and lift her face until her eyes meet mine.

"You in the mood to talk?"

"I will be," she says, then breaks away from my gaze and fixes her eyes on the coke.

"If you don't talk, I'm gonna make you watch while I flush this shit down the toilet. Then I'm gonna let you die." My eyes move from Lady L to Angelo.

Angelo gives me a stiff nod and looks at her mother like she's praying that she cooperates.

"She'll talk," Angelo says with a reassuring nod.

I slide the book back in front of Lady L, and she dives back in, sniffing like she's in search of oxygen. When she's done with her line, she falls back against the wall like nirvana just exploded inside of her. Then she darts back up, snapping her fingers for another line. I look at Angelo, and she gives me a nod of approval. So, I sprinkle a little more of the truth elixir onto the book and watch as Lady L indulges.

"You good?" I ask Angelo, looking at the bag.

"That's the last thing I need right now," Angelo says and turns her face to look at her mother, who is now leaning against the wall and looking like she's counting falling stars.

Lady L has a sinister smile plastered across her face. Her entire body is so relaxed it's like her bones turned to putty. She's mumbling something under her breath. I look at Angelo like she's Lady L's interpreter, but Angelo just rolls her eyes and frowns. She's looking at her mother like she's a spectacle, and she is.

I kneel before Lady L and wave my hand in front of her face to see if she's coherent. Her eyes don't flinch, and I start to feel like I made a mistake. *This woman is gone.* I snap my fingers, but she still doesn't move. Her mouth is moving, but I don't know what she's saying. She's whispering her thoughts.

"She can talk," Angelo says and shoots her mother a quick stare.

I look at Angelo and then back at Lady L, who looks like she is taking a mental break and won't be back for months. I decide to try and probe her anyway. I don't have time to wonder anymore.

"Lady L, how did you get the letters?"

"What letters?" she responds.

I wasn't expecting her voice to be so clear. It almost startled me. Lady L continues to stare off into space like she's watching a play. She's smiling and frowning at the same time.

"The letters my mother wrote."

"I found them. He was trying to hide them from me. They both were," she says, then mumbles something else under her breath.

I lean my ear in closer to her mouth.

"I know everything he's done. He tried to keep secrets from me, but I know everything. He doesn't know my secrets, though," Lady L states and pushes out a vindicated laugh.

She laughs so hard that her body falls over. Angelo hikes her back up against the wall.

Deciding to go straight for the gold, I ask, "Was my mother and your husband having an affair?"

"He told me that he loved her. He said that was never going to change." Lady L balls up her fist. "She always thought she was better than me. He told me that they forced him to marry me. He never loved me. He loved her. His secret love. I have a secret, too, though." Lady L chuckles. "I wasn't going to let him get away with it. Not after all these years. Mr. Badd invited me over to talk, but we didn't talk." A flirtatious smile stretches her lips, cracking them. Specks of blood pop from them. "He always watched me when I walked away. I could feel him," she says and smiles again. "We wasn't going to let them get away with their little plan. Not ever…"

"What plan?" I ask.

"He thought he was going to take it all and vanish like a ghost. Both of them, but I didn't let that happen. Me and Mr. Badd tried to stop them."

"Tried?" I was confused. "My father killed Carlo Lucky? You had him do it?"

"He vanished like a ghost."

Lady L's voice cracks and dry coughs erupt from her mouth. Then her entire face drops into a scowl as she squints her eyes. Angelo grabs the bottle of water, but Lady L smacks it out of her hands and points to the coke. I look at Angelo, and again, she nods. I quickly form another line on the book and hand it to her. Anything to keep her talking. She leans over and inhales it all in one sniff.

"What happened to your husband? What happened to Carlo Lucky?"

"They got away. They took it all and vanished like ghosts. She stole everything from me. My love, my money, my life."

"Is Carlo Lucky still alive? Is your husband still alive?"

Lady L starts to laugh uncontrollably. So much that she chokes on her saliva. Angelo places a gentle hand on her back and pats. I can see the detail of every bone in her spine. Her long, wrinkled neck is hunched over like it's broken.

"Give her some water," I order.

"She ain't gonna take it," Angelo snaps like she's tired of hearing this shit.

"You know what she's talking about?" I question her.

"I don't know what the fuck she's saying. I just know she hates your mom and my dad. They obviously was fucking all those years, and she still feels some type of way about it."

"Is he alive?" I ask Angelo, desperate. "Is your father still alive?"

"I ain't never seen the nigga," Angelo snaps.

I reach for Lady L's face and turn it my way.

"Is Carlo Lucky still alive?"

Lady L looks up at me and smiles.

"You can't kill a ghost," she says and falls over onto Angelo's lap.

"Wake her up," I demand.

Looking up at me, Angelo says, "She ain't getting up, not for hours."

I notice the hurt behind her eyes. This topic bothers her. I guess she does look like the poster child for a girl with daddy issues.

"Is he still alive?" I ask her again, this time more sternly. I got a feeling she knows more than what she's saying.

Angelo looks up at me and then quickly looks away. I've interrogated so many people that I know when someone is hiding something, and Angelo is definitely withholding information.

"If you want to make it out of here alive, you'll answer my question."

Angelo grabs the water she's been force-feeding her mother and takes a swig. Then she sweeps her hands over her face and shrugs her shoulders.

"I don't know no facts. All this shit is rumors. Hearsay. That's what you want?"

"There is truth in every lie," I say back to her. "What do you know?"

"It's not what I know. It's what I've heard."

"Tell me!" I yell, and Angelo jumps.

"They think he's still alive. Before he left, he robbed your father blind."

"Impossible." I chuckle, amused.

No one stole from my father and lived to talk about it. Then again, I remember my father burning him alive, or at least that's what they said.

"You asked me to tell you what I heard, so I'm doing that. Is any of this shit true?" Angelo holds up her hands. "I don't fucking know, and I don't fucking care. That nigga is always gonna be dead to me, even if he *is* alive. Who could leave their child with a woman like her?"

Angelo's eyes glare down at Lady L, who is snoring on her lap. "Over some fucking pussy at that," Angelo scoffs.

I lean up and take a few steps back. I consider everything I heard and what I read, but I still don't know what to believe or why it matters to me. Could Carlo Lucky be our father? Was Mamma planning to escape the day I... I can't even bring myself to confess what I did to her that day. If all this is true, I did more than just kill my mother. I killed her dreams. I took everything she'd been waiting for away from her.

Just when this shit starts to hit heavy, and my chest begins to swell with anxiety, I feel my phone vibrating. I jump like I got stung by a bee and pull the phone out my pocket. I'm so anxious for some good news that my hand is trembling.

I quickly glance over at Angelo and Lady L. Angelo is staring at the ceiling battling unwanted emotions, and Lady L is sound asleep. I decide I received enough info for one day. I don't know what any of it means, but other pressing matters distract me. The Ranch is my priority. I've been waiting on this call for days. After grabbing the coke, I run up the stairs to take Stein's call in privacy.

I CLEAR MY throat, trying to curb my anxiety. I don't want Stein to know how desperate I am for his help, although I must have called him over a dozen times, following each call with a text message since he doesn't have his voicemail set up. A desperate man shows like a weak man. Stein can't see me as weak. It destroys our family brands and keeps him in control. Despite my heart racing, I answer the phone as even-tempered as I can, and I bite down on my bottom lip to control the speed of my words.

"Hello," I say and hold my breath.

Stein doesn't respond, but I hear him breathing on the phone. It's almost like he's trying to listen to what's going on in the background.

"Hello," I say again, this time a little louder.

I'm beginning to think Stein is a bullshitter. I don't understand the reasoning behind why he does things.

Stein clears his throat. In my mind, I see him taking a seat and getting comfortable. I hear a flickering sound. I can't see him, but I can almost swear this motherfucker just lit a cigarette or a cigar. My entire life is falling apart, and this nigga is somewhere living in a ghost town chilling.

"You still need my help?" he asks matter-of-factly.

"Yes. I needed it yesterday. I need it now," I respond quickly in one breath, then try to calm myself down.

"Who has the Ranch?"

Stein stops beating around the bush. I told Stein before that the Ranch got taken, but I didn't tell him who because I didn't think it mattered, and I still don't. I hesitate, and Stein waits.

"A long-time enemy," I finally respond.

"Who has the Ranch?" Stein repeats his question with the same tone and tempo as he did the first time.

"He goes by Kong," I say with hesitance resting on my lips. "And…"

I stop myself from saying more. I don't want him to know about Ace. Mostly because I'm embarrassed, but mainly because it shouldn't fucking matter.

"And?" Stein catches me.

"Ace Lucky," I reveal.

"Ace Lucky?" he says in a tone that throws me off.

There's emotion behind his voice. Does he know Ace? I know he may know of him, but the way he said his name was weird—almost like he's concerned. I don't respond right away. I want him to know that I hear what he's saying even though he ain't telling me. I clear my throat.

Ignoring his question, I clear my throat and say, "Time is running out. If you can't help me, just let me know."

"I asked you a question," Stein replies in a heavy tone, his voice full of authority. It's almost parental.

"And I answered your question," I respond like a defiant teenager.

"I'll help you, but I'm not killing Ace," he tells me like that's where he draws the line.

It's on the tip of my tongue to ask him why, to probe him for more information. Who the fuck is Ace Lucky to him?

"Ace has invaded my land and is holding my family hostage. He wants my entire family killed. He's already had my father killed. So, he's going to die either way."

"Then I can't help you," Stein says before hanging up.

I look down at the phone, wondering if he hung up on purpose or if it was an accident. Stein owes this to my family. Why is he putting Ace Lucky before my father? His loyalty should lie with the Badds. I immediately call Stein back. I don't expect him to answer, but I call anyway. To my surprise, he answers the phone without saying hello.

"Stein?"

"I'm here," he responds short.

"If he lives, he's always going to be a threat to my family. I can't justify keeping him around."

Stein pauses. For a while, I didn't hear anything. No breathing. No background noise. Just silence. Silence so loud it causes my ears to ring. I almost thought he hung up again, but then he clears his throat.

"I don't break promises. I promised someone years ago that I would protect him. This was before your father and I's agreement."

He had to be talking about Carlo Lucky, Ace's father. Who else would give a fuck about protecting him?

"Carlo Lucky? A father protecting his son even in death."

Stein chuckles, and my heart skips a beat. I heard the truth behind his laugh. The idea of Carlo Lucky being dead is comical to him. He's still alive and protecting Ace. Is he trying to take the Ranch with his son?

"Carlo Lucky is the type of man that will die for his family. I promised him and his wife that I would protect his family as long as I have air in my lungs. And that's just what I plan to do. Protect them all. If I help you, Ace lives."

My mind immediately goes to Angelo and Lady L. If he knew I had them tied up in my basement, what would he do? Put a hit out on me? Trying to play it cool, I swallow hard and clear my throat.

"Ace's mother is quite the character," I mumble. "She needs more than protection."

"I said I promised his wife," Stein says, correcting me without using words. "Your mother was quite the character, too, in her younger days. I've never met a woman with more beauty and grace than Beverly."

"Yes, she was," I say under my breath. "Her death shook us all."

Stein chuckles again. That same comical laugh, but this time, my heart stops. There is something so revealing behind his laugh that it sends a jolt of curiosity up my spine. My head starts to spin in so many directions that I don't know where this conversation is going anymore. My mind flashes back to the words he used early. *His wife*. *His promise* to them. Then the words my mother used in the letters are pulled to the front of my mind. I start putting pieces together like a puzzle, but my mind is not ready to receive the result my conscience is trying to give me. It doesn't make sense. Is Stein trying to let me know that he knows what I did? Does he know I killed her? Or is he trying to say she's alive? That they're both alive and well.

"A woman like Beverly can't die. She just simply moves on to something better," Stein says in a telling voice.

We are both silent for a while. Stein is giving me time to process everything he's not saying to me, but my mind won't allow me to receive any of it. It can't. He starts to laugh under his breath.

"How did you know my mother?" I ask, breaking the silence.

Stein stops laughing and takes a deep breath.

After a moment of silence, he responds, "When you're ready to ask me the right questions, I'll have answers. In the meantime, I'll help you take back your Ranch, but my terms don't change. Understood?"

My mind is so stuck on his last words that I don't even know I agree to his terms until I hear myself say, "Yes, sir."

"Look for me. I'll be there sooner than you expect."

12

Billy Badd

It's a miracle we all made it to Zone 5 in one piece. Now we just got to figure out how the fuck to get off this Ranch without being seen. Six of us sharing less than a thousand square feet underground is already causing tension. I designed this place for temporary situations, nothing long term. We got about two weeks max before we'll be ready to kill each other. We're halfway there now.

Lera is looking at Dalla like she got a taste for her blood, and Brip hates everybody, especially the two guards that got us here. If it wasn't for them stealing one of the vans from the morgue used to pick up bodies, we wouldn't be here. It turns out Bobby's guard and my guard are brothers. They killed his little gambling buddy. The shit they did to them young dudes is sickening. If they can execute their own men like that, then we're just as good as dead. At first, it was just about getting Brip and the wives to safety, but Brip refused to go without Bobby and me. We all squeezed into the back of that van and played dead. Dalla had to give BJ something to put him to sleep so he didn't wake up crying, blowing our cover. The shit was tense. I can still see the strain in her eyes. She was holding BJ so tight it was like she was trying to put him back inside of her where he was safe, but it's over now.

Taffy hasn't said more than two words since she got here, and Brip is just ready to kill somebody. He's eyeballing our guards now, making them uneasy.

"I don't know why the fuck they're still here. This place ain't big enough for all of us," Brip says with his eyes on the two young brothers, Freddie and Donnie.

"They saved us," Taffy expresses, defending them.

"Fuck them. I saved us," Brip shoots back since the whole thing was his idea.

"If we let them go, there's a good chance they will rat us out. You want that?" Bobby calmly asks, being the voice of reason.

"I didn't say let them go. We need to off they asses." Brip grimaces at them, and the young boys try to avoid eye contact with him.

"Nobody is killing anybody!" Taffy screams.

Brip grabs her hand, pulling her into his lap.

Leaning up from my chair, I tell them, "We all need to calm down."

I look down at Dalla, who is sitting on the edge of a worn wooden chair and clutching BJ in her arms like she is his lifeline. I apologize to her with my eyes, but I can tell by the look she's giving me that being here ain't enough for her. She wants out. This is no place for a baby. The few blankets here smell like mold, and there is only enough water to last about a month, or maybe two weeks with all of us. I have military meals of powdered chicken, rice, and other canned foods. Good thing none of us have an appetite. This place is moist and drafty. It's not the best breathing conditions, but we're all alive. Our homes were comfortable, but there, we were held hostage. Here, we're free and together. Now we just have to get on one accord to think our way out of this situation.

"What's the plan?" Bobby asks me, and everyone looks at me like I got all the answers.

"The plan is to get the fuck out of here, but we need to lay low for a few days. They're probably out looking for us now."

"What if they find us?" Taffy asks, panicked by the thought.

Brip drapes his arm around her shoulders and pulls her into his chest.

"They won't find us here. It's impossible," I tell her.

"You sure about that?" Bobby asks.

Dalla rolls concerned eyes my way like she's wondering the same thing.

"There's no way," I say, confident.

Unless Mona gives us up, ain't nobody finding us, but we can't stay here forever. This place ain't made for that.

"Yeah, this shit is like something out of a movie, man. I can't believe this place even exists. We're under a fucking tree," Donnie says, amused.

Brip jumps up, and Taffy has to catch herself from falling to the floor. Before I can stop him, he charges at Donnie and grabs him by the throat.

"Nigga, is this shit a game to you?"

"Let him go, Brip," Bobby calmly says.

Donnie's brother Freddie, who is squeezing his fists tight, is trying to stay calm but watching Brip like a hawk. He's ready to die for his brother today, and the last thing we need is two dead bodies rotting in here.

"Nigga, you ain't even here. You don't see shit. You don't say shit," Brip says and pushes him to the ground.

Freddie lifts his brother to his feet and pats him on his back while whispering something in his ear.

"We got to get out of here," I say to Bobby. He knows Brip is like a ticking time bomb. "We're gonna have to go in pairs, starting with the women first."

"I agree," Bobby says and looks at Lera.

Lera has her arms folded defensively across her chest. She is swaying her body from side to side, fidgeting her bad nerves away. She looks at Bobby, and he nods at her.

"How am I going to pull this off with a baby? I'm not going anywhere without you, Billy," Dalla says to me and kisses BJ on top of the head.

I kneel on one knee and scratch the bottom of my chin. I take a deep breath. I have to figure this shit out. I look up at Brip and then back at Bobby. He already knows what I'm thinking. We have to get Brip out first.

"Brip," I say, and Bobby nods his head. "And both the guards."

Brip knows the Ranch like the back of his hand, and he's ruthless enough to get the women out without a scratch. I don't know if he's wise enough, though. The guards are just extra protection—two extra niggas that can take a bullet for us. I hope that doesn't happen, but if it does, I'll be grateful it was them and not my brother or my wife. Besides, there is no way Brip is going to let them make it out of this alive.

"Yeah," Bobby says, nodding his head and walking my way. "They can follow that route to the other lake and take the boat across. That'll bring them to the main road behind that gas station."

"Yeah, but once they get there, where are they gonna go?"

Bobby sighs. We're stuck again.

"I can call my older brother and get us a ride," Donnie offers.

Brip jumps up, and I hold my hand out to calm him down. Once we're off this Ranch, these niggas can't be trusted, but we need a car to get them the fuck out of here.

"No," Dalla says, cutting an eye at Donnie. "I don't trust his plan."

"You got a better idea?" Lera snaps.

Dalla ignores Lera and looks at me, shaking her head.

"These niggas proved they will do anything for money. How do we know that once we're out, they don't take us straight back to the Ranch for a promised fifteen hundred dollars?" Dalla says.

She has a point, but we got to take a risk if we're gonna get out of here.

"That's not gonna happen," Donnie interrupts. "The way they

killed us on the street, we don't trust them either. When my brother finds out what Kong did, he's gonna be gunning for that nigga."

"Who the fuck is your brother to step to Kong?" Brip yells, silencing Donnie. "Dalla's right. I don't trust these niggas. Plus, I ain't got my fucking gun. All I got are these." He balls up his fists and forcefully rams them into each other. "I hit hard but only got two fucking hands. My gun holds fifteen bullets. Do the math." Brip looks at Bobby and me while pointing to the side of his head. "Think," he adds.

"I got a pistol for you," I say reluctantly, and Bobby cuts his eyes at me.

Letting Brip know about the gun I have stashed under the bathroom sink is a bad idea, but he's going to need it. Brip's eyes light up before landing on the two guards.

"But we ain't got no bullets to waste," I tell him.

Brip gets my point and shakes his head.

"If I got a gun, I got us a car. Guaranteed," Brip assures me.

"Let's say Brip gets them out, and he's got the car. Where the fuck are they going then? The second Ranch?" Bobby asks.

"No. My lake house will be the safest place for them. Dalla knows how to get there." I look at Dalla, and she gives me a hesitant nod.

She's rocking BJ, although he has been sleeping for an hour now. Her legs are trembling. Surviving was easier before when she was alone. Now that she's reunited with BJ, her instincts are off.

"You guys post up there and wait for us as long as you can," I tell them.

"As long as we can? What does that mean?" Dalla asks, her voice full of fear.

"It means I'm coming for you, baby. That's what it means," I assure her.

I stroke the side of her face, and she buries her cheek into my hand.

"I'm not leaving without you," she says to me.

"You have to," I let her know.

Dalla bites down on her bottom lip and tightly closes her eyes before reopening them, revealing misty eyes. Pinching her lips together, she breathes through her nose. She gives me one last pleading look that I dismiss with my eyes. She's been through enough. Keeping her and BJ alive is my priority. My life comes second.

"Well, unless somebody has a better plan, it sounds like a go?" Bobby looks around the room at each of us.

"What about Brock? Shouldn't we wait here for him," Lera adds, and everybody snaps their head in her direction.

"Why don't you wait here for him," Taffy snaps and starts walking in circles, frustrated. "I'm not waiting. I want off this Ranch for good," Taffy reveals.

"What the fuck is that supposed to mean?" Brip asks while jumping up to grab Taffy's hand, but she pulls away.

"It means I'm not waiting at no lake house. I'm finding my mother, and I'm getting as far away from this place as I can," Taffy's voice fumes with frustration. "And I'm not coming back," she adds with her eyes fixed on Brip.

Brip looks like all the bones in his body broke at once. His entire body slumps with disappointment. As he falls back into his seat and buries his hands in his face, Taffy continues to pace around the room with her hands on her stomach, rubbing it in small circles. Dalla hands me BJ and gets up to place a supportive hand on Taffy's shoulder, but Taffy pushes her away. Dalla looks at me with eyes full of sympathy.

"We can't make her stay at the lake house. I can't make any of them stay," Dalla says, looking at me and then Bobby.

Brip leans up, sweeping his head over his face. Then he glances over at Taffy and nods his head in defeat.

"If Taffy wants to leave, let her go," Brip says with a broken voice.

Taffy falls to her knees and starts sobbing uncontrollably. Dalla runs to her side, wrapping her arms around Taffy and pulling her into a nurturing hug.

"Y'all just let me know when it's time to go, and I'm gonna do my part. Then I'm coming back for both of y'all," Brip says, looking at Bobby and me before walking down the short hallway and locking himself in the bathroom.

When Taffy hears the door slam behind him, she sobs harder.

13

Mona Badd

"**Y**OU THINK I'M a joke?" Kong says softly and pulls me into his chest.

He's so upset that he exhales, and hot air flies up into my nose like steam. His face is twisted in anger. One brow is dipping down, and his beady eyes are sunken into his face.

"Where the fuck are they?" He balls up his fist and throws it in the air, swaying it above my head.

He hasn't hit me yet. At first, I didn't think he would, but now, I don't know. He's pissed and embarrassed. I guess his little crush on me is over.

Kong lets go of my arm before shoving me to the floor. Before I can get up, he dives to the floor and straddles me like a straightjacket. I can't move. I can't breathe. I can't even think. He's suffocating me. He places his hands on my neck and squeezes tight. I grab his hands and dig my nails into him so deep I can feel the skin pop before it breaks, but Kong doesn't flinch. I feel like my eyes are about to pop out of their sockets. My entire head feels like it's about to explode before he lets go. I cough while trying to take in as much air as possible, but I still can't breathe with him on top of me. *This nigga is gonna kill me. He wants me dead.* I can see it behind his eyes.

When I start hyperventilating, Kong rolls off me and stands to his feet. His vast body creates a dark cloud that hovers over me like the angel of death. I roll over onto my side and try to catch my breath, but I can't. It's like Kong snatched the air from my body. I try to calm down by slowing my breathing and sipping up small doses of air until my heart rate drops. When I get my stride back, I fall to the floor and let the threat of death wear off my body. I have never been this close to death; I've never felt this weak before. I've always been able to protect myself, even before Brock and the Badds. But something has changed. I'm weaker.

The entire time I'm sitting here struggling not to let each breath be my last, I'm thinking about my husband. *Where is Brock? Can he feel me dying?* I keep hoping Brock is gonna burst through the door at any minute and put Kong on his back, but he is nowhere to be found.

My throat feels like I've consumed a set of knives. Sharp pains cut through my esophagus, and I can barely swallow my spit. I can still feel Kong's hands around my neck like a noose. My nostrils feel like somebody has sewed them shut. But I manage to roll my body over and lean my weight on my knees. I look up at Kong as he stares at me with his wide arms crossed over his broad chest. His jaw is clutched tight, and his nostrils are so flared that I can see the thoughts in his brain. He's watching me squirm around on the floor like a fish out of water, waiting for me to get up so he can knock me back down.

"I thought you were the one person I can trust, Mona," Kong says in a somber tone like he almost feels guilty about what he's doing to me. "But you go and fuck me like this?"

I can see the anger filling his chest like helium filling a balloon. Kong walks closer and looks down at me. Then he slowly walks circles around my body like a lion hunting prey.

"I'm gonna give you one more chance to tell me where they are," Kong says in a calm but angry voice. "If you can't do that, I'm gonna have to treat your ass like a bitch on the street."

He stops and faces my back. For some reason, I'm still looking at the door, waiting for Brock. At this point, I need to be looking up at the sky, because only Jesus can get me out of this mess.

"WHERE ARE THEY!" Kong yells so loud the entire room shakes, and I almost lose my balance. I place my hands on the carpet to keep myself from falling over.

I try to take a deep breath, but my nostrils are so swollen that only a few strands of air slip in. I tighten my fist and straighten my back. My neck aches from the grip Kong had around my throat, but I gather enough strength to turn and look over my shoulder, fixing my eyes on him. Kong may be roaring at me like an angry lion, but he's forgotten something. I'm not just a lioness but a pack of lioness all in one. If I want to, I can rip him to shreds in one bite.

I push my dry lips into my mouth to moisten them and clear the lump out of my throat so he can hear my voice clearly as I yell, "Fuck you," with all the strength I can muster.

I see the shadow of his hand rise, or maybe it's his foot. But, shortly after that, I feel an intense pain pierce the back of my skull. The pain is sharp and sudden, and my eyes cross before my vision blurs. Whatever he hit me with was heavy. The crack against my skull echoes against my eardrums, and I get so dizzy that I feel nauseous. The last thing I remember is falling.

ICE COLD WATER is dumped on my face; the feeling is so startling it shocks me like I am being electrocuted. My entire body jolts up, and my eyes shoot open for a few seconds. Whenever I try to reopen my eyes, my lids close like someone has sewn anchors to my lashes. They feel so heavy that opening them feels permanently impossible. *Did this nigga drug me?* My head throbs with pain, and dry blood stains the skin on my neck and shoulders.

"Momma," I hear somebody say.

It sounds like Vinchi, but I could be dreaming. I could even be dead. I don't have my sight, but I can smell. I smell the floor I lay on and the air. It smells familiar. The smell of mold and dust fills my nostrils. If I had the energy, I would sneeze. But, underneath that smell is another familiar aroma that I remember. The scent of Brock's cologne lingers in the air. I can almost see him. I know where I am, but I'm just too tired to remember it. I guess this means I'm not dead, but is Brock here? I can smell him. I can feel him.

"She's lost too much blood. She ain't gonna make it," another voice says.

This voice sounds both familiar and strange. For some reason, just hearing the voice makes me uneasy, and I feel myself getting upset.

More water is dumped on my face, and my eyes pop open again. This time, I am able to make out a silhouette leaning over me, but my vision is still blurred. I can't confirm that it is Vinchi no more than I can deny that I am hallucinating. I feel a hand tapping against my cheek.

"Stay with me. Stay with me," the person encourages me. "I'm so sorry. This is my fault. I'm gonna fix it. I promise," they continue as my eyes slowly roll back into my head until I can't hear anything else.

As SOON AS I open my eyes, an unbearable pain greets me. My entire body feels like a Mack truck has hit it. I try to lean up, but a dizzy spell sends me right back to the ground. The room is dark, but the glare from the single bulb hanging from the ceiling splits through my head like an ax. The light seems to beam straight through my eyes, frying my brain. My head spins in agony. I groan and grab my temple. That's when I feel the gauze taped around my entire head. It's soaked with my blood. I try to use my hands to shield my eyes, but the dim light shines right through my fingers. I groan some more before rolling over on the concrete. The floor is cold and wet. The rough, rocky texture scrapes against my skin.

Where the fuck am I? I slowly open my eyes, making sure not to rush my sight. Little by little, everything starts to look clearer. That's when I realize where I am. I am in a holding cell in Brock's dungeon. When I'm able to open my eyes wide enough, I see Ace Lucky staring at me and smiling like my pain is amusing him. Instantly, I go into defensive mode.

Ace is sitting with his back against the brick wall and his arms resting on his knees. His clothes look torn, and he looks frail. He looks a lot smaller than I remember from the night at the cemetery, but the evil behind his eyes hasn't changed. *Kong put me down here with Ace? I guess he's going to leave him to kill me.*

I try to stand up only to fall back down. I let the wall behind me break my fall before my body lands back to the floor. Ace isn't restrained. No handcuffs. No rope tying his hands and legs together. If he wanted to kill me, I would be an easy target. But, I can't just lay down and die, although a part of me already feels dead.

"If I was you, I wouldn't move," Ace says in a tone between "I don't give a fuck" and "I feel sorry for you."

"Fu..." I try to speak, but my words get stuck in my throat.

I rub my neck. Feeling the swelling in my throat, I try to massage away the pain. I manage to lean up enough and scoot my body against the wall so that I am facing Ace. The wall barely holds my weight up, but there is no way I am lying with my back to Ace. I watch him through blurred vision. He is still smiling at me.

"You're lucky to be alive," he says to me in that tone again. "Vinchi was able to convince Kong to let one of your doctors treat you. They gave you some meds and wrapped you up, but you still got a lot of bleeding that they can't stop. You may die tonight," Ace states with a smile.

"You..." I try to speak, but my voice is strained. It feels like I'm force-feeding myself acid. The sharp pains burn. "You gon di..." I try my best to express what I am thinking, but the words sit stubbornly in my throat. I want to tell Ace that he is a dead man—more dead than me, more dead than Kong. But I can't speak.

Ace knows what I'm trying to say. I can see it from the amused look he is giving me. This shit is all a game to him.

I look around the room for Vinchi, but I don't see him. Maybe my eyes are failing me. Ace said he was here, and I remember him pouring water on my face. It was his cologne that I smelled. It reminded me of Brock. They wear the same cologne, and it smells the same on their skin.

Where is he now? And what kind of prisoner wears cologne? I'm confused and afraid. *My poor son. This is where Kong has been hiding him. Locking him in this dungeon with a psychopath is beyond evil. Vinchi doesn't deserve any of this.*

"Looking for your boy?" Ace asks. "He ain't here."

"Where…" I try to inquire about Vinchi.

"He comes and goes," Ace informs me.

Now I'm confused. *Is Kong not holding Vinchi hostage?* That didn't make any sense to me. If he had free rein on the Ranch, I would have seen him by now. He would be trying to help us. Whatever Kong cracked my skull with must have been hard if I'm starting to believe anything this sociopath has to say.

"If you give him what he wants, he might let you live. You probably know more than anybody that Kong is more emotional than logical. He wants your husband. He wants Brock dead. But will he die for you?" Ace snidely says.

I wish I could tell him to shut the fuck up, but I can't.

"I'm surprised he's not here yet, but I can just imagine all the shit that's keeping him busy." Ace laughs. "How do you think he's going to take the news about his mother? Do you think he'll be relieved to find out he didn't actually do what he thinks he did?" Ace laughs again. "Brock ain't coming back for y'all. He's out there searching for answers that only I have. Your husband don't give a fuck about you. He don't care about this Ranch either. He ain't never coming…"

Ace fires words at me like emotional bullets that penetrate my spirit, causing my soul to bleed. I don't know I'm screaming until I start coughing up blood. My throat throbs with pain, but I need him to shut the fuck up. He's saying too much all at once. *What the fuck is he talking about? What is he trying to say about Brock and Mamma Badd?*

I can't bear this shit. I can't bear much else. If it's my time to die, then at least let me die in peace.

Ace stands to his feet and takes slow, calculated steps towards me. I press my back against the wall even harder like I'm trying to move it. Ace kneels in front of me until we are nose to nose. A big grin stretches across his face as he places his hands on my bandage. The blood soaks through and stains his fingers. He rubs his fingers together, playing with my blood like it's dirt in his hands.

"I'm gonna outlive all of you. Watch and see," Ace whispers loudly. "I'm Ace Lucky. I always win," he says and strokes the side of my face. "I don't like many people, but for a moment, I liked your son, my nephew. He reminded me of myself, but now, I've changed my mind. I'm gonna make him pay. Maybe I'll make him the first Badd that dies," Ace says in my ear.

I ball up my fist and raise my elbow only for it to fall to my side. Ace doesn't flinch. Instead, he pulls me forward and then pushes me back into the wall.

"Save your energy. You got a few more funerals to go to before you die."

Ace fingers his overgrown beard while staring back at me, emotionless. I can see the hate behind his eyes. He really believes he is going to survive this.

"I can kill you right now if I wanted to. All I have to do is this," he says, then places his hand over my mouth and nose.

I can't breathe, and I am too weak to fight. Maybe I want to die. I know he is just trying to scare me, but when he doesn't let me go after a few seconds, I start to think maybe this was Kong's plan—to have Ace finish me off.

When my eyes start rolling back in my head, I believe it's over for me, but then I hear footsteps. Ace quickly removes his hand from my face, and a puff of air is pushed into my nostrils. My chest heaves from my heavy breathing. Ace pushes me to the floor and leans over my body. When I hear the cell door open, he waves someone inside.

"I think she's coming to," Ace says, his tone changed.

"Momma."

I hear Vinchi's voice before I see him. Footsteps rush my way. Ace steps aside, and Vinchi takes his place. The sight of my son's sweet face fuels me with life.

"Momma," Vinchi says, relieved as he gently places my head in his lap. "Can you talk?" he asks while stroking the sides of my face.

"She ain't talking good yet. Did you ask him?" Ace says.

I try to speak. I try to warn Vinchi about Kong, but I only choke on my saliva.

"Calm down, Momma. Get her some water," Vinchi yells over his shoulder.

If he can order someone to get me water, why can't he get me the fuck out of here?

"She has to call your father. If he hears her voice, he will come. That's the only way Kong is gonna keep her alive. Let him take the bullet for all of us," Ace says, convincing Vinchi.

"I found her phone. I'm calling him now." Vinchi looks over his shoulder at me. "Momma, I need you to talk to Daddy. Tell him to get here. Can you talk?"

One of the guards comes back and hands Ace a bottle of water. I nod my head. I need Brock. Brock can fix this, but I can't let him walk into a setup. I have to warn him.

"If you get Dad to come, Kong agreed to let everybody go, including me," Vinchi adds, his voice shaking from fear.

I try to reach for the phone, but Vinchi pulls it away from me.

"I'll call him now."

I watch him scroll through the burner phone that Brock gave me, searching for his father's number. I can see the hesitance in his eyes, but to him, this is the only way he can fix this situation. He's trying to make all of this mess right. He'll sacrifice Brock for all of us, but he doesn't know that Kong and Ace are liars. They both are playing him. Vinchi is so damn gullible.

"Found it," Vinchi says, then looks down at me with a weak smile to reassure me.

He presses the call button, and I hear the phone ringing. However, before Brock can answer, a ruckus breaks out in the hallway. We hear scuffling, followed by a crashing sound. Feet are dragging, and the sound of fists crushing bones echoes off the walls.

"Fuck all y'all niggas," a voice yells. "All y'all dead."

Stunned, Vinchi drops the phone and jumps up. It falls beside my ear. I hear when Brock picks up, but I'm too distracted to say anything and too weak to speak.

As the voice grows louder the closer the person gets to the cell, Ace slowly walks back to his corner with his tail between his legs. We all know that voice. To everybody else, it sounds like terror, but to me, it sounds like a savior. It's Brip. I bet Ace ain't gonna have shit to say for the rest of the night. He ain't gonna be able to talk once Brip knocks his teeth out.

Not long after Brip is pushed into the cell with us, I hear another voice—a voice that re-energizes me. It is Brock, my husband. Just hearing his voice is like God himself breathing air back into my lungs. Brock calls my name several times, but I can't answer him. My tongue is too swollen to speak. I try to turn my face towards the receiver, but my head feels too heavy. Sharp pains dig into my temples with every move I make. Brock goes silent, but he doesn't hang up. I know he's still on the line because I hear him breathing. He's listening, seeing with his ears. He hears Brip ranting. He hears the terror in Brip's voice when he screams my name.

After a few more seconds of silence, he says, "I'm on my way."

He knows I need him. I heard the urgency in his voice. The authority. The power. The redemption. The love. He revealed it all in one breath.

Ease falls over my body that is so strong it feels like my first breath of air after being pulled from the bottom of the ocean. It feels like I've been given CPR and revived. The throbbing in my head stops, and the aches in my body cease. I almost feel numb. Everything is going to be okay. Brip is here, and Brock is on his way.

As I feel my eyes roll back into my head, I don't fight the heavily sedated sleep that wraps around my body like a python, squeezing me into submission and forcing me to let everything go. I just let it happen. I allow my eyes to close, and I pray all of this shit will be over when I reopen them.

14

Brip Badd

"Get me some fucking help!" I scream over my shoulder.

I stand over Vinchi as he holds Mona's bleeding head in his lap. Her eyes look like they are glued shut, and her face is swollen. Mona looks dead. She looks fucking dead.

"I swear to God all y'all niggas dead. Every last one of you. You all fucking dead!"

I reach down and grab the back of Vinchi's neck, yanking him away from Mona. He doesn't deserve to be touching her. For all I know, he is responsible for what was done to her.

Vinchi flies back but regains his balance, jumping to his feet and stumbling on his heels. He bucks at me, and I buck back, looking him dead in his eyes. I don't give a fuck if this little nigga is blood. If I have to, I'll snap his fucking neck right here, right now. First, the nigga tries to kill me. Then he helps these motherfuckers take over the Ranch, and now this.

I stare down at Mona. Blood is dripping from the gauze around her head and onto the concrete. Seeing Mona like this is hard. I've never seen her look so weak; I didn't think it was possible. Grief starts to flood my body, and I can barely stand up straight. When I feel my body begin to fall, I stop myself and land on one knee instead of two. I can't let myself fall apart. I have to get us out of here. I got to get Mona help.

I can't help but blame myself for this shit. When she came to Billy's place, I told Billy not to let her in. I told them that I didn't give a fuck about her, but I was wrong. This shit is my fault. She risked her life to save me, and look what happened to her.

Dropping to both knees, I move closer to Mona and lean over to see if she's still breathing, but I can't tell if she is or not. Her skin looks pasty, and she's changing colors. If Mona dies, all this shit ends. There will be no more Ranch. *Where the fuck is Brock?*

"I'm going to get her help," Vinchi yells over my shoulder.

I don't even turn to acknowledge his bitch ass.

"Uncle Brip, I swear—"

I turn to face that motherfucker so fast that my neck pops.

"Don't you ever fucking call me that!" I point my finger at him like it's my Glock.

Vinchi holds up his hands, surrendering as if I have a gun, and backs up. That's when I notice something I didn't see before. Motherfucking Ace!

"What the fuck!" I yell so hard that I feel the vibrations in my bones. Quickly, I jump up, and before I even realize what I'm doing, I'm squeezing that motherfucker's throat with no plans of letting go.

"Uncle Brip, let him go!" I hear Vinchi's bitch ass scream from behind me. "Let him go! You're gonna kill him. We can't kill him."

Vinchi grabs me from behind, but I maintain my grip on the nigga. I can't let go. Not until he's dead. I can feel him dying in my hands. His eyes are bulging, and his lips stretch across his face, desperately seeking the air that I'm stealing from him. I stare this nigga dead in his eyes and watch as his eyes turn colors and change shape. His brows dip and rise in desperation. He can feel his final hour nearing; he can smell the Reaper as he approaches.

Just when this nigga's head is about to collapse onto his shoulder, I feel a sharp pain against my back. It hits me hard—so hard that I let go and fall over Ace. When my body hits the floor, I roll over like it's on fire. I look up and see Vinchi standing with one of the guards. The guard is holding a baton. That shit put me on my back, but it wasn't permanent. Ignoring the ache in my back, I jump to my feet and wrestle the guard to the ground. I break that nigga's wrist. I hear it crack, and shortly after that, I hear the sound of the metal baton as it clanks against the concrete. I pick it up and strick that nigga's skull with two ruthless blows. *Pop! Pop!* First came the noise and then the splatter. Looking down at the baton, I wonder if it's what one of these niggas used to take Mona out.

I look over at her body. She looks stiff. Lifeless. My heart falls into my stomach, and I take a deep breath, pulling it back into my chest before charging at Ace with the baton.

I raise my hands, but before I can whale on the nigga, Vinchi uses his body to cover Ace's. He's protecting that nigga like he's his blood. I don't know why I don't crack Vinchi's skull. It's in me to do it, but I don't because I see something in his eyes. I look past the terror and see desperation. I lower the baton to my side but squeeze it tightly in my hand.

"Don't," Vinchi pleads with me through squinted eyes, then flinches like I'm swinging at him. "He knows where Grandma is. He knows, Uncle Brip."

I shake my head. He sounds just like Billy, and I ain't got time for this shit they on. These niggas out here believing in fairytales while our lives are at stake. Vinchi shakes Ace, trying to get him to regain consciousness. Ace starts coughing, and Vinchi guides his body up with a gentle hand to his back. When Ace sees me, he freezes. I squeeze the baton even tighter. Ace's eyes look toward the bleeding guard and back to me. Then he smiles. Vinchi immediately puts himself between Ace and me. He knows what's up.

"If you kill him, we'll never find her," Vinchi says.

"You mean find her body?" I correct Vinchi, letting him know I'm not buying into the bullshit.

"No." Vinchi gives me a serious stare. "He knows things, Uncle Brip. He knows," he repeats.

"Is that why you let him do this shit to your momma?"

"It wasn't him. It was Kong, and I'm trying to play this shit smart."

"That's not what this shit looks like to me." I shake my head and look back at Mona.

"I'm going to get her help," he tells me.

"How?"

"Kong needs me," Vinchi admits.

"Why?"

"Because he can't get into the safe without my dad or me," Vinchi says.

Shaking my head, I glare at Vinchi. I don't believe shit he says. He already gave Kong the code. He already fucked up.

"Naw, you're lying, nigga!" I point the baton at him, warning him. "You've been doing a lot of lying, and I'm sick of the shit." I walk towards Vinchi.

"You don't think I learned from my father? He taught me a lot, and I listened. I watched his every move. Why do you think we're still alive? Kong threatened to kill you because he's trying to lure Dad here. He doesn't know I changed the code. He thinks it's some shit Dad did remotely."

"And who gave you that plan?" I ask.

"I did," Ace grunts. "You should listen to our nephew. He's not as dumb as you think," he adds, his voice strained.

Just hearing his voice sparks my anger and ignites hatred in my soul. I charge towards him swinging the baton in the air, while Vinchi pleads for me not to kill him. Instead of hitting Ace, I hit the wall. Concrete dust crumbles and falls from the wall, creating a slight powder that causes Ace to choke and cough.

"I know you don't like it, Uncle Brip, but we need him. He's been helping me survive this shit."

"He put you in this shit," I yell down at Vinchi before yanking him up. "What the fuck is wrong with you?" I smush him in the head, and his neck jolts back.

"You don't understand. You don't understand reasoning. You just react," Vinchi says to me, sounding exactly like Brock.

For some reason, his words calm me down as if they came directly from my brother's mouth.

"You may not like any of this, but this is the situation right now, Uncle Brip. All of our lives are in danger. Not only is Ace helping to keep us alive, but he has information about Grandma that we all deserve to hear and consider. He's our only ally right now."

Shaking my head again, I take slow steps away from Vinchi. I sweep my hands over my head and down towards my face. I don't know why, but suddenly this motherfucker is starting to make sense. I begin to feel weak, defeated even. I guess that's what reasoning feels like. I don't like it, but I accept it for now. At least for a little bit.

"You better listen to him." Ace clears his throat and looks at me. "If you don't want to believe what he's saying, then believe what you see. You trust your sight, don't you?"

I don't know why, but I'm clinging to every word that comes out of Ace's mouth.

"Yeah, use that sight of yours," Ace says as I glance around the room. "What do you see? We're all in the same fucked-up situation. Yeah, I came to take the Ranch. I wanted all of you dead, but I also had an obligation."

"What obligation?" I hear myself ask before my mind even makes the connection that I am speaking.

"The obligation to tell the truth. To let you know what the fuck is going on with your mother." Ace pauses, giving his words time to sink in. "Kong fucked me over, too. That's why I'm down here and not up there." He raises his head to the ceiling. "I've been here for weeks. He plans to kill me once he gets to the safe. I ain't too keen on keeping any of you alive, but if it means saving my ass, then so be it," Ace curtly states.

"Who are you obligated to?" I ask Ace.

He gives me a sinister half-smile that I want to wipe off his face with my fist.

"More like *what* I'm obligated to?" he replies, teasing me with hidden information.

"Where's my mother's body?"

Ace looks me directly in the eyes. His stare is evil, but he smiles to balance the menacing look he's giving me. He can give two shits about my mother, and it shows. Yet, for some reason, he's invested, and it's more than this Ranch and money.

"Her body's around, still protecting the soul that lives inside of it." Ace smiles at me with his eyes.

"She's alive, Uncle Brip. I know she is—"

"You don't know shit," I say with my heart pounding against my chest. My mind is racing. "You saw her die. You said you saw your father…" I couldn't finish my sentence.

"I don't know what I saw," Vinchi says in a low voice. "I saw him rush out of the room, and I saw what I thought was her body covered with a sheet. Did you see her? Did you see Grandma's body?" Vinchi challenges me.

I close my eyes, remembering the beautiful casket that was supposed to contain my mother. I remember her last wishes. Not to be seen. We all honored them. I shake off the awful memory. The sting of her death is something I numbed over the years through violence and anger, but now, it's burning again. I don't want to believe my mother is alive, because then, I will feel abandoned by her. Betrayed. None of this shit makes sense.

"How? Why?" I feel the words roll off my tongue before I remember speaking them.

"Because of the man I called father," Ace says.

"My father killed your father years ago. Everyone knows that!"

"Really?" Ace replies with a sarcastic chuckle. "Did you see his body?" he asks, mocking Vinchi's voice.

I swallow hard before turning back to him. It's the only way I can control myself from cracking his skull. I set my sights back on Mona. If my mother's dead or alive, she doesn't need my help right now, but Mona does. Mona has been more than a sister-in-law to me; she's been a second mother. I grit my teeth and clutch my fist at the sight of her dying body. Then I turn and grimace at Vinchi. He's worried about his grandmother while his mother is dying, and he's just letting the shit happen.

"Get her some help," I demand.

Before Vinchi can respond, I hear the sound of heavy footsteps pounding against the concrete floor. Each step heavier than the next. Before I can turn to face him, Kong calls my name.

"Welcome," he says and spreads his arms wide before flashing a conniving grin. "I see you couldn't hide from me."

"Hide? You got me fucked up. I came to you. You ain't send for me," I scoffed.

Kong squints at me and asks, "You ready to die?"

"No, but I'm ready to kill," I reply and squeeze the baton. "I'm gonna get what I came for," I warn him.

Kong gives me an amused look, but I don't flinch. This gorilla-ass nigga doesn't intimidate me at all. Trees were made to be fucking cut. And with the right ambition, you can move mountains. Kong ain't shit but his size. That's it. I can get around that—all of that. I ain't going down without a fight.

Vinchi jumps up and steps in between us.

"Wait," he says, holding up his hands, "remember our deal?"

"No," Kong answers without looking at Vinchi.

I move Vinchi out the way, pushing him to my side.

"You sure this is what you want?" I stand firm.

Kong doesn't respond. He just looks at me and smiles before taking slow steps towards me. His armed guards are standing behind him, aiming at me, but I still won't budge. That nigga don't move me.

"If you kill him, you will never get into the safe," Vinchi says, desperate.

"Some things money can't buy," Kong says as he continues walking my way with clutched fists.

I lift my chin, standing tall. I can't wait to break this nigga's skull in half. He just needs to get a little closer, and I'm gonna put this nigga on his back. I hear Vinchi in the background pleading for my life like a little bitch. What he doesn't know is I got Kong right where I want him. A few more steps in my direction and this nigga is done.

I stretch the kinks out of my neck and flex my shoulders like a ballplayer ready to hit a home run. I plant my feet and fix my stance so that I'm unmovable. I don't break eye contact with him. I'm gonna send this gorilla back to his zoo in a fucking body bag. My heart doesn't skip a beat. I'm calm. Balanced. Ready. Kong knows this, but he's pretending not to see me. He knows he can't move me. He knows I don't bend or break. He keeps walking. Slow stepping. Dragging his fucking feet. *Bring it on, nigga.* If he really wanted this, he would have taken it by now, but I can feel his hesitation in every step. He ain't too sure what the fuck he's gonna get or how it's gonna come once he stops in front of me. But, I know. I'm ending all this shit tonight. I'm tired of being a fucking hostage. This shit is over. It ends now.

Kong is now close enough to me that I can smell his filth. Motherfucker smells like a farm animal. The funk is oozing from his pores. I like his stink, though. It motivates me. It reminds me of how dirty I can get. *Yeah, bring it on, nigga.*

"You promised," Vinchi cries from beside me.

"Shut the fuck up, nigga," I say while keeping my eyes fixed on Kong. "Man up. Bitch don't run through your veins," I remind him.

Kong looks at Vinchi and smiles with his eyes.

"You sure about this, Kong?" I hear Ace ask. "Did you come here to kill or to conquer?"

"Fuck you. You next," Kong huffs.

"I'm just saying. Brock is on his way. He called his dad and told him to come like you asked. I heard him."

Kong stops walking and gives Ace a considerate look.

"He told him about his momma. That nigga is coming. He'll probably be here tonight. Then when he gets here, you can kill two birds with one stone. Get the code to the safe and then off all of them. But, if you let this muthafucka force you to be impatient, you're gonna fuck it all up and return to the East Meadows project with nothing but blood when you need money."

"I need both." Kong forces the words from his mouth, and spit flies out like aerosol spray.

"You can have both, but you got to be patient. That nigga gonna die. But don't nothing go with blood like money," Ace calmly states before walking back to his wall and scooting down to take a seat on the floor.

Kong looks at me and then Ace and then Mona. I guess his peanut-ass brain is working overtime. He must get tired of thinking for himself and replaces his thoughts with Ace's because he stops just a few inches away from me.

"You dead," he says, pointing a fat finger in my face before turning around.

"What about my mother?" Vinchi asks.

Kong stops and looks at Mona for a minute too long.

"Leave her," he says and throws up his hands, dismissing Mona's dying body. "She dug her own grave," he adds, then walks out the cell.

"You a bitch!" My words hit him in the back, bringing him to a halt.

Kong spins around slowly to face me. He squeezes his fist and is biting down on his thick lip like a growling dog. *Yeah, bring your ass back here*, I think to myself. Then he looks over my shoulder at Ace, I assume. He takes a deep breath and shakes his head before chuckling at me.

"Don't worry. I'll be sure to bury you next to her," he says with laughter.

"FUCK YOU!" I scream, throwing the baton at him. I miss him by a few inches.

Ignoring me, Kong laughs before walking down the hall like he has one up on me. The sound of his laughter echoing off the walls taunts and stabs me like daggers to my chest.

I rush to Mona's side and then turn to Vinchi. "She's gonna die if we don't get her help soon."

15

Taffy Badd

"WHERE THE FUCK are we?" I complain as I stumble over broken tree branches and thick bushes.

It feels like we've been walking for hours, although it's only been a few hours since Brip left. I'm so over this whole life I can scream. I hold my belly, protecting my baby from the inside, and step over a puddle only to land feet first in a sinkhole full of mud. The mud pulls me in by my ankles.

"Fuck!" I yell. "I need help," I demand as my body sinks lower into the pit.

Lera comes and extends her left hand for me to grab while balancing herself on a branch. Reluctantly, I grab her hand and free myself from the pit. I look down at my tired, aching legs that are covered with mud and burst into tears. As soon as I start crying, BJ starts to cry, too.

"We got to keep moving, Taffy," Dalla yells down at me, annoyed.

She's balancing BJ on her back. He is tied to her using an old t-shirt. She rocks him to soothe his frustration, but he only cries louder. Gunshots pop in the air, and we all jump before ducking. This is too much.

"She's right," Lera calmly says.

To my surprise, Lera is acting pretty normal, but I still don't trust her ass. I don't trust any of them, not even Brip. The last time all three of us were together, it was a disaster. Dalla betrayed us all. Lera ran off with Tony, and I was forced to put my life and my unborn child's life in danger. Yet, here we are right back where we left off. Stuck and abandoned by these fucking Badd men.

I jump up and sniff while still holding my ears. My ears are ringing so loudly that I can barely hear anything else. The smell of gunpowder is making me nauseous. I look at Dalla, then behind me and all around me. *What direction does she want us to keep moving? There is nowhere to go. We are wandering around lost in this wilderness like Hebrew slaves.* The sun is going to set soon, so we all need to accept that we will be spending the night out here if we don't turn around and go back.

I know they blame me for us being in this situation. I can see it in their eyes, although they haven't verbally said it. But I don't give a fuck. Both of them are being extra careful not to upset me. If I gave a fuck about either of them, I would think it was sweet. But fuck both of them. My baby and I don't need their fake-ass sympathy. We don't need them to lead the way either. *I'm out of here.*

I turn around to walk in the opposite direction. I'm moving so quickly that I hit my foot on a tree stump and fall face-first into a mound of dirty, wet leaves.

"Fuck!" I scream and slowly lean up.

With my knees supporting my weight, I wipe the mud from my face. Another round of gunfire erupts, and my spirit jumps out of my body. I grab my belly to let my baby know it's okay.

"It sounds like it's getting closer," Lera tells Dalla.

Dalla's voice floods with concern as she looks off into the distance and responds, "I know."

"We need to keep moving. If she wants to go back, let her," Lera says to Dalla like I'm not even here.

"We're not leaving her. Just like we didn't leave you," she states, reminding Lera of her breakdown.

When I feel Dalla's footsteps coming towards me, I look up at her with tears in my eyes. Her body shades the sun. I know what she's about to say. She inhales deeply and blows the air out from her teeth. Then she reaches behind her and pats BJ on his back.

"I'm not leaving you. And you can't go back!" Dalla says calmly at first but ends with anger. "Be reasonable. We are all in this fucked-up situation together. Look at me." She turns and flashes BJ in my face, "My son is in this shit, while your child is in your belly! Now is not the time to pick sides or be pissed off."

Another round of gunfire erupts, and we all fall to our knees.

"If we don't get the fuck out of here, we are all dead, my son and your unborn child included. Is that what you want?"

"No," I say through an exasperated breath.

"Well, get the fuck up!" Dalla yells.

"We have to go back! If we don't, we're dead anyway," I argue.

"No, there is a way out," Dalla says, trying to convince me. "There has to be."

Stepping in front of Dalla, Lera leans over and grabs my arm, attempting to yank me up. This bitch got me fucked up. I leap up and push her off of me. She falls back and trips over the same stump that sent me flying into the bed of wet leaves. When her body hits the ground ass first, she jumps back up and bucks at me but stops herself. Her eyes land on my belly. Then she turns her back to me, cursing under her breath.

"Be cool, Lera," Dalla says to her in a calm tone.

"Fuck her! She's going to get us killed. She's going to get your son killed. If she wants to die, let her!" Lera yells in one breath and wipes off the leaves stuck to her butt. "She's the reason we are in this fucking situation. If she hadn't sent Brip away, we would've been out of here by now."

"Fuck you!" I yell at her. Now she's getting too personal.

Brip didn't leave because of me. He left because he's a blood-thirsty tyrant. All that man cares about is himself. If he cared about us, he wouldn't have killed the two brothers who were there to help us. He shot them in cold blood and left them there to die. His gunfire attracted the attention of some guards that were hunting for us in the woods. Instead of running away from the shooting, they ran towards it, looking for trouble. After he shot those guards, I told him that I didn't trust him and that it was over. Brip looked at me like I had just shot him. I don't know what hurt him most—me saying I didn't trust him or that it was over. After that, he told me that he was going to prove to me that he could be trusted. He was going to show that he would protect me. I told him to prove it, and he did exactly what I expected him to do. He ran off. He gave Dalla rushed directions on how to get us out of here and ran back towards the Ranch, towards the gunfire.

I don't know why the sight of Brip disturbs my peace, but his presence has become nails on a chalkboard. Maybe it's the hormones from the baby, or perhaps it's years of built-up frustration all coming out at once. I wanted him to leave. I wanted him gone. I didn't want him checking on me, placing his hand on my shoulder, or continuously reassuring me that everything would be okay. I just wanted him gone. But, then, I regretted the moment I saw him disappear into the woods. I panicked, but I hid it from Lera and Dalla. Every gunshot that pops, I pray it's not him getting hit. That's why I want to go back, but I can't admit it. I can't admit that I fucked up. So, I pretend not to give a fuck, and I plan to fake it to the end.

"Fuck, Brip!" This time, my voice cracks, and my words get trapped in my throat. "We need to go back, or we're going to die here. We have to go back."

"He's probably dead," Lera coldly says with squinted eyes and dipped brows.

On that note, I rush her and sock her dead in the jaw. Lera flies back, landing in the same bed of leaves, and gasps. She is shocked by my assault. She didn't know I can hit so fucking hard. Dalla moves to stand in between us.

"Y'all bitches really fighting right now?" Dalla says to us like the disapproving older sister. "If y'all want to die, then you're gonna do it alone. BJ and I got too much to live for. I'm out of here," Dalla says, then turns to walk away.

Lera and I look at each other, apologizing with our eyes before following behind her.

"WE GOT ABOUT another hour before the sun sets," Lera tells us before laying back in the car's seat.

She takes a swig of water and stuffs a few chips in her mouth. We packed a few supplies before we left, mostly junk food and water. Dalla and I are sitting in the front seat of the abandoned car with our chairs reclined. She's feeding BJ, and I'm fighting off morning sickness and stress.

"You sure you don't want any?" Lera asks, holding the bag of chips in my face.

The smell alone makes me want to gag.

"No," I answer and slap the bag out of my face.

"You have to eat something," Dalla says to me in a maternal voice.

It is the calmest we've been all day. We walked another two miles and came across the red box Chevy that Brip told Dalla about; it was our landmark. Wherever we are, we're close to getting out of here. We don't have time on our hands, so it looks like we're going to have to spend the night here. The gunfire has stopped. I guess they gave up looking for us for the night, but Dalla says we have to leave before the sun rises to keep them off our tracks. Once we get off the Ranch, we are back at square one again, but Dalla doesn't seem concerned. She never is.

I think of Brip. That may have been the last time I ever see him. The words I spoke to him may have been my last words. Tears stream down my face, but I wipe them away before anyone can see them. I don't know why I'm ashamed to miss him. Sitting here makes me feel trapped in my emotions. I just want to keep moving. I want this to be over, but I have no idea what the end looks like for me. I just want a fresh start. I want my child to be safe, and the only way that can happen is if he or she is far away from this life.

"Did you guys know about Tara?" Lera asks.

Her tough-girl façade is vanishing. What Bobby did to her was more fucked up than all of this, but she's still here—strong. I overlooked that side of her. I can tell she's still hurt, though. Who wouldn't be? To be betrayed twice by the man you gave your all to is devastating.

"I never saw her," I say, turning to face her.

"I knew of her," Dalla admits, "but I didn't know it was that serious. The marriage and the baby wasn't something any of us knew about."

"She's the one who said they were married, but he said they weren't," Lera states like she is trying to determine how to feel about Bobby.

"Do you think you can forgive him?" I ask.

If Lera can forgive Bobby, then maybe I don't hate Brip as much as I think I do.

"No," Lera answers, disappointed.

We all were silent for a while.

"I'm sorry about what Ace did to you," Dalla expresses genuinely. "I endured years of violence from that man before..." She pauses and sniffs back tears, then looks down at BJ's sleeping face and smiles. "... before Billy saved me. I never thought I would experience real love or have a family. Everything I've done has been for them. I'm going to get my happily-ever-after, and I hope you guys do, too."

Besides the sound of crickets and the occasional unidentified rustling in the leaves, there is more silence.

"I thought I killed her," Lera utters in a low voice. She leans up and places her back against the door. Resting her hands on her shaking knees, she takes a deep breath. "I blame myself for Tara," Lera shares and laughs under her breath, "but that wasn't on me."

Dalla squirms in her seat. If anyone was to blame for Tara, it was her, but Ace did it all.

"Taffy was tied up and hysterical, and Brip was bleeding and dying.

I just wanted to make it right. When Ace called me, I was going to use the last thing I had to protect us."

Lera sighed like the words rolling off her tongue were attached to anchors. They were heavy and burdened her soul. Speaking them was giving her relief.

"My body. I was going to fuck him into submission." She laughs sarcastically this time. "But, by the time I realized what I was doing, I told him to stop." She shook her head. "I told him to stop like he was just going to get up and let me go. Nope. Instead, he pinned me down and went harder. Longer. Faster. Is that even rape? I don't know what the fuck it was, but it took something from me that I can never get back."

"It was rape," Dalla immediately interjects and places her hand on top of Lera's. "That's not your fault. None of you knew how sadistic Ace was, and you *can* take back what you lost. I'm a living testament of that."

Lera wipes tears from her eyes, then sniffs and straightens her back, placing her tough girl mask back on.

"I'm just confused," Lera says.

"About what?" Dalla asks. "What he did to you?"

"No, how it makes me feel. I feel like…" Lera pauses. "I feel like I lost so much of myself. Being around Tony helped me feel more balanced. But Brock made me feel…" She pauses again.

Dalla and I go silent, wondering about the words dangling from her tongue. No doubt something is going on between her and Brock, and it is weird and awkward timing. I don't get it.

"He made me feel like I was strong," Lera continues. "Like I was myself again—the woman I was before I met Bobby. I didn't know I missed that part about myself until Brock brought it out of me. Then, all of a sudden, I felt like I was back in control. Like I had options. Then it just happened…" She was admitting something.

Another awkward silence followed. We both wanted to know what she meant. I'm sure Mona would die to know what happened.

"None of us are perfect. I'm probably the most imperfect person in the world, but I know my heart," Dalla tells her. "The love I have for my son and husband is the most perfect part about me."

"That's what I used to want," I say while looking at Dalla cradling BJ.

I remember a time when all I wanted was a baby to complete our family. Now it's hitting me that I have the baby, but I don't have the family, and everything has changed.

"I don't even know if this baby is Brips," I admit.

They didn't gasp, but I could feel the shock my revelation caused.

"Sick of the cheating and the dictating, I did what you did, Lera." I turn and look her in the eyes. "I took matters into my own hands. Brip killed him." My voice drops. "I got an innocent man killed. The possible father of my child."

"Brip knows?" Lera asked, stunned.

"Yes, he knows."

"And he still loves you?" She says it like she's trying to get me to see something that I wasn't seeing. "You and Brip's love is stronger than all of this. I always envied that about you two."

I smile and consider Lera's words. Only time will tell if it's strong enough to outlast all of this.

"GET UP. SOMEBODY'S out there," Dalla whispers while shaking us both.

Popping my head up, I wipe the sleep from my eyes. We've only been sleeping for a few hours. Dalla must've stayed awake to keep watch. I look through the darkness, and it was pitch black. I didn't hear or see anything.

"Who's out there?" Lera whispers loudly.

"Shhh," Dalla says and points behind us.

We turn our heads and see a small light coming towards the car.

Someone is holding a flashlight. When they spot the vehicle, they shine the flashlight in our direction. We all duck, but as soon as the light hits BJ, he wakes up screaming.

"Fuck," Dalla whispers.

Fear floods her voice as she frantically tries to calm BJ down. She covers his mouth to silence his screams, but that only makes it worse. Besides, it's too late. They caught us.

Lera kicks and screams as they pull open the car's back door.

16

Vinchi Badd

OCUS. BREATHE. THINK. Make a move. I keep repeating these words. His words. Dad always told me that if I ever find myself in a bind, all I have to do is focus, breathe, think, and then make a move. Mediate. It's what I've been doing all day. Trying to think my way out of this fucking bind. I fucked up. I fucked up bad, but I gotta make a move. I gotta focus. I gotta think. I gotta save Mom. Uncle Brip says if we don't get her help tonight, she ain't gonna make it. He's putting everything on me. He looks at me like I'm a murderer. Like I'm a cold-blooded killer that would ambush my own family and allow my mother to die. I look like all those things, but if there's anything I've learned so far, it's that nothing is as it seems. I'm going to get us out of this situation because it's the right thing to do. I just don't know how yet. I have to think. I have to breathe. All the weight has fallen on my shoulders, and now I'm starting to second-guess how strong I am.

"You know who I am?" she asks me, but I can barely hear because I'm trying to focus. "You probably don't even remember me." She sucks in air through her teeth and rolls her eyes.

She's distracting me. I'm meeting with Kong soon, and I have to be focused. The racing of my heart is distracting, too. I have to calm down; I have to believe in myself. Dad says if I don't believe in myself, I'm fucked, and everyone who needs me is fucked.

She walks over to the kitchen and opens the refrigerator, only to slam it closed seconds later. Now she's opening and closing cabinets and popping her gum. All of her noise is distracting me.

"You want a drink?"

She reopens the cabinet, pulls out a glass, and holds it in the air towards me. I don't respond.

"Are you even old enough to drink?" She plays with her hair before flipping it back over her shoulder and looking up in the air, pondering. "Naw, nigga, you ain't old enough, but I guess that shit don't matter now. You the man today," she says, then slams the glass on the countertop.

The sound distracts me, and a thought flees my mind. I try to grab it, but it escapes. I close my eyes and breathe. Then think.

"I heard your momma done got herself in a heap of trouble fucking around with Kong." She turns and stares at me like she's probing me for information. "They say she may not make it through the night. Hmmm," she scoffs under her breath and rolls her eyes again.

Now she's popping her gum again. She pours herself a drink, sits down in front of me, and snaps her finger.

"Boy, you in there?" she asks, giving me a strange look. "It ain't my fault, you know. None of this shit is. Your momma thinks she rules the world, is all. I don't want her to die. I mean…"

She sighs and takes a sip of her drink. She swallows so quickly that she chokes a bit. After clearing her throat, she continues.

"She brought all this shit on herself. She thinks everybody is supposed to do what she says. She thinks she runs the fucking world, but now you see she don't. She thought she had Kong wrapped around her finger. She actually thought fucking him was going to eliminate her problems. Like he's that thirsty for pussy that he's just gonna let all the foul shit she did slide."

She watches me out the corner of her eye and takes another sip of her drink. This time, it's a bigger sip than the first one. She smacks her lips and sucks her teeth. The noise she makes is very distracting, and her conversation is throwing me off my game. What does she mean by Mom had sex with Kong? She would never do that. She's making my mother out to be weak, but she's the strongest person I know, male or female, and that strength is in me. I just have to focus.

"I tried to tell her just to let shit be—that the shit is over for y'all. But, naw, she can't lose. She just can't. She never could."

She gets up from the chair and walks back to the bar while humming and snapping her fingers to a song playing in her head. She opens and closes another cabinet. The sound of the wooden doors slamming against the panel is distracting. She scrapes her glass across the granite countertop and pours another drink. She places ice in the glass, and it chimes. More lip smacking. More tongue sucking. More humming. Less silence. I need to focus. She sighs heavily before returning to her chair. Her feet are heavy; she drags them when she walks. She sits on the leather chair, and it whistles. She spills a little of the drink from the glass onto her feet and exaggerates a squeal like it's hot water.

"You know, I didn't even know Mona had you until you were two years old. That's fucked up." She sucks her teeth again and sips. "I was excited about being an auntie. I was excited about Mona joining the Badd family, but then she left all of us in the East Meadow projects like we wasn't shit—like she was too good for us. She would come back once a month, giving out food like she was some type of fucking missionary. Folks were bowing down to her and practically kissing her hand like she was the fucking pope."

She stands up and points her finger in the air.

"All that power went straight to her head. Now look at her," she says and flops back down. "Head is fucked up now." She shakes her head and lowers her eyes.

"What he hit her with?" she asks, looking at me, but I still don't respond. "You're a weird-ass kid. What, your momma told you not to talk to me?" She sucks her teeth again. "Kong cut your fucking tongue out, too? He loves doing that shit. I guess it does keep niggas quiet."

She takes her last sip and sighs.

"You know I'm your auntie, your flesh and blood. But you don't have to talk to me. Go ahead and listen to her." She dismisses me with a wave of her hand. "I'm the only person that can help you," she informs me, and finally, I start to think.

I look up at her, and our eyes meet. I'm seeing her a little differently now. She looks like Momma. They have the same eyes and forehead, but she doesn't carry herself like my momma. She doesn't hold her head up like Momma. She doesn't walk with her back straight like Momma, and her eyes don't tell the same story as Momma's. They are just shaped the same.

"Your momma did buy me a new Benz every year. She sent money for me to start my salon and kept me in all the fly gear. Nobody in the East Meadows projects fucked with me. I could cut through a crowd like butter because of her stuck-up ass. We had a little talk before she went and fucked Kong—my fucking man." She leans closer to me, resting her elbows on her knees. "But niggas come and go, and if Kong can do her like that, ain't no telling what he's gonna do to me."

She leans back in her seat, and I see the concern she's been hiding come up from behind her eyes.

"What the fuck is gonna happen to me if Mona dies?" she selfishly asks, then leans in closer to me again. "If it wasn't for your family, Kong and the East Meadows projects wouldn't be shit," she whispers loudly and looks over her shoulders. "Kong is fucking everything up for everybody. He's killing his own and shit. Ain't nobody gonna respect him after this. Without y'all, we're back to government cheese. And what's gonna happen to my shop?"

She looks at me as if waiting for me to respond. What does she want me to tell her? What can I tell her? I have to think. I have to make a move.

She looks over her shoulder twice before leaning closer to me. "Before your momma went and got her head knocked in, we had a plan," she whispers.

It's time for me to make a move.

"What kind of plan?"

She widens her eyes like she's shocked to hear my voice. She looks back over her shoulders and swallows hard. She leans in to say something else but then leans back in her chair again like she's having second thoughts. I look at her and nod. She leans back forward.

"To get rid of Kong," she whispers as if she just revealed a deadly secret.

Pushing her body back against the chair, she nods. What does that nod mean? Does it mean she can help me?

"What was the plan?" I need her to give me more, but she just shrugs.

"She already gave me one payment and promised me more." She held her long fingernail in my face. "Can you get me the other half, because this shit is risky for me? If Kong did that to her, he will do worse to me, and I need security."

"Yes," is all I say to her. But I don't know what I'm agreeing to, and neither does she.

"Where you gonna get the money?" she asks.

By questioning me, I know she doesn't believe me.

"I have the code to the safe, remember?"

She looks at me and smiles so wide that her cheeks cover her ears, her two gold fronts gleaming underneath the light.

"I knew you was smart. My price goes up, though. The stakes are higher now," she says, looking over her shoulder before standing up. "Just let me know what you need me to do, and I'll do it. I promise. I'm gonna make him pay for what he did to my sister, even though she shouldn't have fucked him."

"How do I know I can trust you?"

She turns her head my way so quickly that her neck pops.

"Shit, how do I know I can trust your little ass? You ain't got no experience, and it don't seem like you got much heart. But what you do have is the code to that safe. That makes up for everything else," she says, looking back at the door. "Shit, that's the only reason any of you are still alive. All he cares about is that safe." She curls her long weave around her fingers. "Might as well bury him there. He'll be happy. Just lock his ass in there," she says, waving her hand in the air and laughing.

I look at her before jumping to my feet. *Think. Breathe. Make a move.* It feels like someone just flipped my switch. If I can get to the safe, I can lock him inside and hold him there until I figure this shit out. Maybe this will work. It's a simple solution to a big problem, but perhaps it will work.

"Auntie Nicchi…"

She smiles when I say her name.

"…I think you might be on to something."

Happy to have a part in the master plan, she nods her head, and as we both sit back down, I whisper in her ear, "It's time to make a move."

KONG STARES AT me, waiting for me to speak. He's squeezing his massive fist and clenching his jaw. His eyes are penetrating me with evil. He looks like he wants to break me in half, and by the size of his hands, I don't doubt that he can, but he won't. Not without the code. Not without me delivering my father to him for him to burn on the stake. But, as Auntie Nicchi said, I hold all the cards. It's time I start playing them right.

"My mother needs medical attention right now," I demand.

My heart is racing, but I pretend that it's not. I keep a straight face. Kong himself doesn't scare me. If his strength matched his wit, then I would be afraid, but it doesn't. He's just muscle—nothing else.

"No," he says and bites down on his bottom lip.

"Now!" I yell.

He grimaces before leaning up and towering over me. He's trying to intimidate me.

"If she dies, you'll never get the code, but if you get her to the clinic now, I'll open the safe for you today," I bargain with him.

Kong sits back down.

"What about your father? I want him, too. Just as bad as I want inside of that safe."

"I told you that he's on his way. You'll get everything you want, but my mother has to live."

Kong looks at me through beady eyes. He's considering my request. His balls his hands into a fist and releases them. Then he feathers the bottom of his chin with his thumb and breathes in deeply.

"I don't trust your father, and I don't trust you."

"We don't trust each other," I reply. "That's a given. We never will, but we both need each other right now. The millions that are in that safe…" I make sure to entice him with a dollar amount, and his eyes widen with greed. "…isn't worth my mother's life," I continue. "Your friend's life," I add.

"She's a snake." He pounds against the chair with his fist, and the arm breaks off.

The sudden snapping of the wood startles me, but I keep myself from jumping. I maintain my straight face and focus. I breathe, then think. Now it's time for Kong to make a move.

"She's your only way into the safe," I say and sit up straight, making sure not to break eye contact with him. "When my dad gets here, he's all yours. I told you that," I lie. "He has to pay for what he did to my grandmother. I want his blood, but not on my hands."

Kong smiles like he's admiring the way I think.

I don't know if my dad will show up or not, and hopefully, that won't matter because Kong will be locked in the safe. I wanted my father dead for killing my grandmother, but now, all of that has changed. No one believes Ace, but I do. I know my grandmother is alive. I can feel it. I don't know what my father was doing in her room that day or what he planned to do, but he didn't kill her. Maybe he knows more about it than we do. We have to find her. We have to let her know Grandpa is dead and that it's safe for her to come home. I dream about her face every night, about being in her arms again and smelling her sweet rose scent. But, first, I have to get this Ranch back in a safe place. That way, she can come home. It's the only reason Ace is still alive. He told me a lot, and I believe him. He shared things with me that my family is going to have a hard time accepting, but the truth is the truth. Good or Badd.

"I'll send her to the clinic and make sure they look after her. Now take me to the safe," Kong orders me.

"No, I want her out of prison and under medical care first. When I know she's safe, then I'll take you," I tell him.

"Fine, but I'm still killing your uncles and your dad. Brip first!"

Taking a deep breath, I nod my head and say, "My main concern is my mother."

He laughs and stands up. "Okay. Well, let's go get her."

It's time to make a move. My heart races as I follow behind Kong. We pass Auntie Nicchi on our way.

"It was nice seeing you, Auntie N," I say.

Kong shoots a weird look at me, and Auntie Nicchi gives me a half nod and a smile.

"You just stay out of trouble, and everything will be alright. Kong got this place *locked up*. If you respect that, then you will live," Auntie Nicchi responds.

We are talking in code. I see the curiosity behind Kong's eyes, but he's too full of greed and arrogance to catch any of it. Our plan is on. I just hope I'm not fucking up by trusting Nicchi, but I have to take the risk. It's my only option. It's time to make a move.

17

Billy Badd

I WATCH AS BOBBY does a full set of pushups. Sweat slides down his body and forms a puddle underneath him. The breaths he pushes out are full of anxiety, but the air that he pulls in seems more settled. Bobby does a good job of keeping it all together. Not one part of him is out of place. His emotions are balanced and mood steady. I try to learn from him, but ever since Dalla walked out that door with BJ, I haven't been able to stop pacing. I pray I made the right decision. There was no other option. They couldn't stay—none of them.

After about ten sets of pushups, Bobby finally leans up and pulls his shirt off a chair, using it to wipe the sweat pouring from his body. He exhales, and his shoulders relax. Looking at me with a raised brow, he takes a swig of water from his bottle.

"After all this is over, you should put a gym down here," Bobby says jokingly.

Half-smiling, I nod my head. "Hopefully, after all this is over, we won't have a need for this place. Hopefully, we can plan better."

"As long we Badds and have this Ranch, we will always have a need for this place. That's the harsh reality of all this shit. It can happen again, and it probably will," Bobby says before taking a seat.

Bobby leans over, resting his elbows on his knees, and tries to control his breathing. He wipes sweat from his brow and looks up at me to see how I'm taking what he said. I know what he's saying. He's over this shit, and I feel him. I am, too.

"What you thinking?" I ask him.

Bobby moves his shirt from his left shoulder to his right and leans back, stretching his legs. He throws back his head and chugs the remaining water like it's the last sip of water he'll ever have before speaking.

"I know y'all took it personal when I didn't tell you about Blake. This very shit we're in right now is why I needed to protect him." Bobby leans back and sighs.

I nod at him. I completely understand. All I'm thinking about is BJ and Dalla. Dalla is right. We can't stay here. My family ain't worth all this shit. I have to protect them, and if that means leaving the Ranch and everything associated with it behind, then so be it. At this point, I don't even give a fuck about the money.

"I get it, man. I wish I was as smart as you," I admit.

Bobby looks at me with compassion blazing behind his eyes. "You did what you thought was right. Your family is safe, man. If Brip can't keep them safe, nobody can," he says with a smile.

We both share a brief chuckle at the expense of our crazy-ass brother, who is also hard as rocks. He would give his life for all of us. Brip is the type to have your back no matter what, and he's fearless.

"Yeah. Brip is a whole fucking goon through and through," I say, laughing. "But I think I'm done. When we get out of this, I'm walking away, man."

"Me, too," Bobby admits. "I just don't know what direction I'm going in. I have to find Tara and Blake, but I also got to try to work things out with Lera. I know I fucked that up. The chances of us getting back together are slim, but I got to at least try. Give her the chance to turn me down. I still love her."

"But you love Tara, too. You know you can't have them both. What you gonna do if Lera happens to forgive you?"

Bobby sweeps his hands over his face and pushes out an anxious breath. He massages the back of his neck before leaning up to stand.

"I don't fucking know. Tara and Blake are my family. They always have been, but Tara and I ain't been on no romantic type shit in a while. At least not until recently. I don't know what I was thinking, but all that shit about you, Mamma, and Brock had me all messed up in the head. Tara was my person. Over the years, she's been my haven. I could vent to her. Lera is new to all this shit. I couldn't unload how fucked up our family is on her, so I went to Tara like I always did. She understands this shit. She's been a part of it almost as long as I have. Tara's like my fucking rock, man, but Lera is my heart."

Bobby places anxious hands on top of his head before letting them fall from his face. He sighs and then takes a deep breath while straightening his posture.

"When I was in prison, all I thought about was Dalla and our child. I gave myself time to hate her for all the fucked-up shit she did to survive and keep me alive. Then, I forgave her and fell madly in love with her. All I thought about was the family she's spent a year fighting for. I started to respect her then. I can't be without her, man. I got to protect them, and I will. I'll leave this place, but the break ain't gonna be that easy. Not for either of us. There are a lot of loose ends to tie up." I look Bobby in the eye, but he looks away.

He knows what I'm getting at. I plan to leave all this shit behind me when I go, but we owe it to Mamma to find out what fuck happened to her, dead or alive. We need to know her story because it's as much a part of our Badd history as this Ranch. I don't plan to let this shit go, nor am I going to let my brothers ignore this shit. I don't care if they think I'm crazy, we're gonna get to the bottom of this shit.

Bobby sits down and crosses his ankle over his knee. He leans back in the half-broken wooden chair, clasping his hands together and giving me a considerate look.

"What do you think happened, Billy?" he asks while staring at me. "You think she's alive?"

Bobby's eyes are penetrating mine with what I feel is sarcasm, but he's willing to hear me out. That's just Bobby. He always keeps the balance between us four. No sides chosen. He's on everybody's side.

"Yes," I admit, then turn my back to him.

I'm not sure why embarrassment is flooding me. Maybe it's the crazy look he's giving me.

I pace back and forth for a while, walking off my bad nerves. Then I turn back to face him. I hate the way he's looking at me. His brow is raised like questions are stuck at the tip of his tongue. Bobby clears his throat and readjusts his position on the chair, placing both feet firmly on the ground. He breathes in like he's preparing himself to talk some sense into me.

"You spent years speculating that Mamma was murdered. Not by just anyone but our own brother. Now…" He pauses, giving his words time to sink in. "…you think somehow she's alive. Help me understand you, man, because I can't right now." Bobby throws his hands in the air. "You got a beautiful family, man," Bobby says with sincerity. "Don't let this bullshit keep you from them."

"It ain't bullshit!" I yell louder than I intended.

My mood swing doesn't move Bobby, though. He gives me the floor to explain myself.

"If there is a chance that Mamma is alive, we owe it to ourselves to find her. How, if she's hurt or being held hostage somewhere?" Almost choking on my last words, I stop to take a deep breath. I pace back and forth for a while, trying to walk off the stress of my theories being true.

"We didn't protect her, man," I say, turning back to face Bobby.

My last words cause him to shift in his seat. He knows I'm spitting truth.

"We all saw it, but we chose to ignore what he was doing to her. We sat back and did nothing while the light behind her eyes become dimmer every year. We saw her trying to cover the welts around her neck with expensive scarfs; we saw her face caked with makeup more days than others. We knew what she was hiding, and we let her hide it. He was killing her every day, and we just ignored it."

Bobby's shoulders stiffen. He leans up from the chair and turns his back to me. This ain't easy to hear, but it's the truth. We let our mother suffer because we were too afraid to challenge our father. We didn't respect her like we respected him.

"I was just a kid, man," Bobby says with his back still turned to me. "We all were," he adds and finally faces me.

"Naw, man. We were just kids, and then we became men. Nothing changed," I say to him. "We just got older and more accustomed to what he was doing to her. The shit became normal. That should have never happened! Ever!" I slice through the air with my hand.

Bobby walks in circles around the small chair like he is playing musical chairs. He tightens his fists and then releases them before blowing out breaths of air full of sorrow and anger.

"Is that what this is about?" Bobby stops pacing and faces me. Almost challenging me. "You trying to ease your guilt?"

"No, it's about doing the right thing by our mother. We can't just ignore that she wasn't in that fucking casket. How would they have taken her body? When would they have had the time to dig her up? She never was in there. Never!"

Bobby holds up his hands. "Okay, man. Just calm down. We're gonna get to the bottom of this."

The tone of desperation in Bobby's voice only pisses me off more. This isn't a game to me. I need answers. We need answers. Him trying to calm me down only feels like he's nullifying what I feel, what I know to be true. My mother is alive. *Our* mother. I sigh and roll my eyes. Shrugging my shoulders, I dismiss him.

"If I have to go this journey alone, I will, but I know I owe this to her," I say, stabbing myself in the chest with my finger. "And when this is all over, I'll sleep good at night."

Bobby stares at me for a second without saying anything. Then he silently nods his head. The compassionate look is back in his eyes.

"I got you, man. Whatever you need, however I can help, I got you." Bobby walks towards me and places his hand on my shoulder. "You're right. We sat back and watched him kill her."

"Thank goodness she was strong enough to save herself," I added. "Mamma is a survivor. She's always been. You faked your death, remember?" I reminded Bobby, and his eyes flashed at me like a lightbulb had just gone off in his head.

I watch him reprocessing everything I just told him.

"I did, didn't I?" he says under his breath like it was all making sense now.

"We gonna find her, man. She's out there. I can feel her."

Bobby swallows hard and looks at me through tear-glazed eyes. He opens his mouth to speak, but before he can get a word out, someone bursts through the door. Startled, we both jump but then quickly get into position, ready to fight 'til death to protect each other.

DALLA BURIES HER face in my chest and sobs. I wrap my arms around her and BJ, squeezing them tightly. I close my eyes, and an image of what could have happened to them flashes in my mind, causing my heart to race. They were safe now. Or at least safer than they were before. Dalla raises her face towards mine, and I wipe the tears from her eyes with my thumb before kissing her long and deep. When I pull away, she pulls me back into another kiss. I can feel the fear stirring inside of her. I had put her in harm's way. I failed my family.

"I'm sorry," I whisper to her, and she dismisses my apology with a sweet smile.

"Don't do that. Don't blame yourself." She places a delicate hand on my chest, relieving me of the anxiety that was building up inside of me.

I pull BJ from her arms, and he falls into my nook with ease. I kiss the top of his head and inhale the innocence of his scent. His love intoxicates me, giving me a temporary high. In this moment, I am able to find gratitude. Dalla and BJ could have died, but they didn't. They were rescued by Brock instead. *Thank God.*

"Brip's not here?" Taffy asks, her voice shaky. "He didn't come back?"

Tony rushes to her side and wraps his arms possessively around her, but she gently pushes him away and hugs her trembling body.

"Brip is okay," Brock assures her, although he didn't know for sure himself. "There are people in the world that just don't get caught slipping, and Brip is one of them," he tells Taffy.

"Just like you," Lera says in a tone that causes all of our eyes to bulge, starting with Bobby. She stares at Brock like he is her hero.

Brock looks at Bobby, giving him a blank stare before looking back at Lera.

"Like all of us," Brock says to Lera and then dismisses her by turning his back.

Bobby keeps his eyes on Brock, but of course, no one can read his look.

Taffy starts to panic. "We got to find him. He's in trouble. I know it."

"We will. It's all set up," Brock tells her, then nods at Bobby and me. "We're taking this Ranch back tonight.

"We're outnumbered almost ten to one," Bobby informs Brock. "We can't take them out on our own. That's why we're here." Bobby is agitated for more than one reason.

Brock's lips curve up into a smile as he replies, "Not anymore," then gives us a confident look. "I got backup coming. We're gonna make it out on top—all of us. I didn't abandon any of you."

His gaze meets all of our eyes individually. When Brock looks at Lera, Bobby studies their reactions.

"When all of this is over," Brock continues, "we got a lot to discuss. For now, Bobby and Billy, I need you to get in position, because any minute now, we're marching off to war."

I LIFT DALLA's body, placing her on the sink. She wraps her long legs around my waist as I fist her hair and pull her into a deep kiss. This is how I'm positioning myself for war—making love to my wife. Brock is confident we will make it out without a scratch, but I'm not taking a chance on not being able to feel my wife one last time. I gave BJ to Bobby before Dalla and I locked ourselves in the bathroom.

Dalla pulls her shirt over her head, and I unsnap her bra. Her breasts spring out, her hard nipples pointing at me like two missiles ready to launch. There is so much passion in our touch. I wrap my hands around her breasts; her skin slides in between my fingers like silk. I caress her nipples with my thumb before diving into them, pulling them into my mouth, sucking and tracing my tongue around her areolae like they are made of chocolate. Dalla yanks my shirt from over my head, and her hands melt into my chest. She ventures everywhere on my body before her hands land in my boxers. She pulls out the swollen member like it's her lifeline. Her hands passively grip my shaft while her fingers massage around my swollen head, her touch sending bolts of passion straight through my dick. With every stroke, I grow bigger and bigger. A few anxious drops drip from my penis, and Dalla kisses me deeper when she feels the inside of her hand moisten.

I help her as she unbuttons her pants, pulling them off her body. Not wanting to waste any more time undressing, I rip her panties straight from her body. Dalla arches her back, and it curves perfectly like the letter C. As she spreads her legs, breaths of ecstasy and desire hiss through her teeth. I feel the heat of her insides drawing me into her like a magnet. When I push inside her, she exhales like she had been holding her breath, then wraps her arms tighter around my neck and squeezes my body with her thick thighs. Each thrust is more passionate than the next. Her wetness drowns me, sucking me into her deeper.

Dalla calls out my name with a voice so sultry I almost nut off her harmony alone. I silence her love moans by burying my tongue in her mouth. The kiss we share causes her pot to boil over. I'm ready to explode, but at the same time, I don't want it to end. So, I take a deep breath and control my passion, extending the pleasure for as long as possible. Dalla squeezes and rocks with me in perfect synchronization.

"Oh, baby, I'm coming," Dalla moans with ecstasy. "I'm coming," she screeches and squeezes my neck tighter.

I feel her insides contract, wrapping around me until life is literally squeezed out of me.

"Shit." I sigh and hold onto the wall to keep my weight stable. My knees weaken, but I am still planted firmly inside my wife.

Dalla stares at me with blissful eyes. Her body becomes putty in my hands before her head falls onto my shoulder.

I kiss the side of her neck and whisper, *"I love you, girl,"* in her ear.

18

Vinchi Badd

WHEN I WALK into the prison with Kong, Brip is holding Momma's head in his lap, and it looks like he's been crying. Ace is in a corner, far away from Brip. One of his eyes is swollen shut, and blood is dripping from the corner of his busted mouth. I don't have to guess what happened. Brip's eyes dart up at me and then at Kong. His brows lower into an evil grimace. If he wasn't holding Momma so delicately, he would have jumped up ready to fight. The harsh look in his eyes softens when he sees the medics behind us with a stretcher. Brip looks at me and nods his head in approval. I just hope he approves of my plan.

As the medics roll the stretcher towards Momma, Brip reluctantly steps back and watches them like a hawk. When they lean down to pick up Momma's body, he starts to fuss.

"Be careful," Brip demands, "and watch her fucking head, nigga!"

Kong looks at Brip through squinted eyes. They are both thirsty for each other's blood, but Kong has other plans right now. He wants in the safe, and I'm going to give him just what he wants. Brip looks back at me, and I try to speak to him with my eyes. I give him a reassuring look, letting him know to be easy.

"They're taking her to the clinic?" Brip asks.

"Yes," I respond, nodding my head.

My eyes go from him to Momma and then to Ace, who is in the corner giving me a weird look. His silent stare gives me an eerie feeling. He seems upset.

"I'm going to make sure they take care of her," I add.

"You do that, because if something happens to her…"

"Fuck you and her," Kong says in one breath, interrupting Brip.

Brip bucks at Kong, but Kong stands his ground, ready to strike. Brip's nostrils flare, and he tightens his fist, slowly swinging it back in preparation to deliver a punch. I hold up my hand and give Brip another look to be cool. He has to be chill if any of this is going to work. Now is not the time for him to be emotional.

The medics place Momma's motionless body on the stretcher. Blood soaks through her gauze and drips on the floor. Her skin is discolored, and there are swollen dark circles under her eyes. Her lips look dry, and her mouth is slightly open, revealing part of her idle tongue. I've never seen her look so weak. It's scary to see her in this state. I have to make Momma proud. I have to finish what she started and get the Ranch back. Then I'm gonna deal with Kong for what he did to her.

I place my hand on Momma's swollen face, and Brip rests a supportive hand on my back.

"This is tough. She's gonna pull through, nephew," Brip says to me.

Kong lets out a sarcastic chuckle that causes Brip's hand to feel heavier on my back, but he doesn't react. He knows Momma comes first.

After I watch the stretcher roll out with Momma, Kong gestures with his head for me to follow him. Brip doesn't let me go. He keeps his eyes fixed on Kong. Uncle Brip is pissed at me. He doesn't trust me, but I can feel the protection in his touch. He doesn't want to let me go, but he has to. As I walk away, Brip's hand slides off my back.

"Watch your back, nephew," Brip yells as I walk out behind Kong.

When I turn to look at him, he gives me a supportive nod.

KONG AND I watch from behind the window while the doctors work on Momma. She's hooked up to a bunch of machines, and they are carefully cutting the gauze off her head. There is so much blood dripping onto the ground that I fear she will never recover. I don't want to watch, but I'm not giving Kong shit until I know they have her stable.

"What did you hit her with?" I ask Kong without taking my eyes off Momma.

Kong laughs. His laugh is sinister and sounds like he's choking and wheezing.

"I don't remember," he replies, amused. "But it worked," he adds. "Everyone thought Mona Badd was unstoppable, but now we all see that anyone can be stopped."

I turn and look him dead in the eyes. His eyes are still lit with amusement. When he sees the look I am giving him, they become evil. Now he's challenging me.

"It's time to go," Kong says and bites down on his bottom lip.

"Not yet," I reply, turning away from his gaze. Every second that passes, I feel angrier while I'm standing here watching my mother fighting to live.

"Now, or I tell them to cut the cord," Kong says through a chuckle. "I want inside that safe."

"The deal is after she's stable," I tell him, not moving an inch.

"I call the shots. I make the fucking deals, and I can break the fucking deals. Now let's go."

Kong turns to walk away but not before yanking me by the neck and pushing me in front of him. I stumble over my feet but regain my balance to keep from falling. I look up at Kong like I want to spit in his face, and I start imagining all the ways he will die.

"Don't make me hurt you." Kong points a stiff finger at me.

I swallow all of my emotions. They slide down my throat like a bag of rocks, resting uncomfortably in my gut. I pray that enough time has passed for Nicchi to do her part. I'm so anxious to end this shit that I don't know what to do. I turn around, looking over my shoulder back at Momma. Something is going on in there. The doctors are quickly moving around the operating room. There are so many hands on her body that I can barely see her now. I try to run back, but Kong grabs me again. This time, I hit the floor when he pushes me down.

"You want to be next on that table?"

He yanks me up from the floor and pushes me towards the door. Before he has time to grab me again, I rush out the door. He follows behind me; he's on my ass like white on rice.

"Slow down," he says, grabbing me by the collar. "If you try anything funny, I'll break your neck with my bare hands," he threatens after pulling me under his chin, blowing hot air in my ear.

I try to pull away from his grip, but it's too tight. He holds me by the back of my neck all the way to the safe. We cut through the crowds of guards with ease. When they see Kong, they all step aside. The closer we get to the safe, the tighter security is. Kong has the safe surrounded. When I see how many armed men are protecting the vault, my heart sinks. There is no way Nicchi got through all of this.

We turn the corner and walk down the hall. I smell Nicchi's cheap perfume before I see her. That's when I realize I fucked up. As soon as we turn the corner, I see Nicchi standing in front of the guards with her arms folded. When Kong sees her, he stops in his tracks. He cuts his eyes at me and then back at her.

"What the fuck is going on?" Kong asks and pushes me back to the ground only to pull me back up. He slams me against the wall and lifts my entire body by my throat. "You playing games with me, boy? What I tell you I was gonna do to ya? Huh? What I tell ya?"

Kong squeezes my throat so tight it feels like he's going to rip my head from my neck. My legs dangle in the air as my body climbs the wall, trying to escape him, but it's impossible. I hear Nicchi's heels clicking my way. Her steps are slow and cautious. When they stop, Kong lets me go and turns to grab her, but she dodges him.

"Baby, what are you doing?" she screams.

"Don't fuck with me, Nicchi. I'll fucking crack your face open," he says, taking slow steps towards her.

Nicchi holds out her hands while walking backwards, trying to calm him down.

"Baby, I'm not the enemy. Why do you think I'm here?"

"Why are you here?" The words shoot out of Kong's mouth like missiles.

"He was trying to set you up!" Nicchi screams.

Auntie Nicchi turned on me. I fucked up. I didn't think. I made a move too soon. I just killed my whole family.

"But I got his ass. You gonna be proud of me, baby. You don't need him. You can kill them all, baby, 'cause I got him to give me the code to the safe," Nicchi reveals in a panicked breath.

It's all over. I stumble to my feet and rest my back against the wall. I try to make eye contact with Nicchi, but she avoids me. I was foolish to give her the code. The plan was for her to lock herself inside the safe. Then, when I opened the safe, Nicchi was going to scream, catching him off guard, and I was going to push his ass inside and close the door. It wasn't the best plan, but it was all I had. Nicchi told me not to worry about the guards. She said she grew up with most of them. She played Spades with them and had even let them borrow money when they were down and out. So, she felt like they would be more loyal to her than Kong. But she played me. She played me bad.

Kong turns to look at me and gives me a wicked smile.

"Grab him," Kong orders, and a guard charges at me. "You got the code?" he asks Nicchi with a smile spread across his face.

"Yes, baby," she replies and stands on her tip-toes to kiss Kong on the lips.

But Kong pushes her off of him. Turning her around, he nudges her towards the vault.

"Open it," he demands.

The excitement disappears from Kong's eyes. Now, he's looking like it's all too good to be true.

"Okay, baby. I'm gonna make you proud. You gonna see," Nicchi says and walks towards the keypad.

Kong is on her back like a magnet.

"Baby, give me some room," Nicchi asks politely, but Kong doesn't let up.

My heart races as I watch Nicchi press each number with her long yellow fingernail. It feels like everything is moving in slow motion. The guard grips my arm tighter, but he doesn't have to worry. I'm not gonna run. I'm gonna take my death like a man. At least I tried to save them. That has to count for something.

Nicchi presses the last button and the asterisk sign, and the safe clicks as the door automatically unlocks and beeps. Kong pushes Nicchi aside and places his big hand on the door handle, laughing a laugh so full of evil and pride that it feels like the ground is shaking. He's finally getting what he wanted. He turns the knob, and the door clicks again before he pulls it open.

"See, baby, I told you I had your back," Nicchi says to Kong but turns to look at me.

I watch her pull something out of her bra. When Kong opens the door, he takes one step inside, stretches his arms wide, and inhales the smell of the money like it's oxygen he's been lacking. He laughs a hearty laugh, and just as he turns around to thank Nicchi, she drenches his face with what I assume is pepper spray. Caught off guard, Kong stumbles back. That's when one of the guards hits him in the stomach, causing Kong to fall to the floor. Nicchi reaches for the door and closes it. As soon as the door clicks shut, she drops to her knees, hyperventilating like she's having an asthma attack. The guard lets go of my arm. When I look up at him, he nods, and I run to her.

"You did it," I say, surprised.

"Boy, I told you I was gonna help. Damn! I can't believe I pulled that shit off. Is he really in there?" Nicchi turns around to make sure the door is closed.

"His bitch ass is in there," one of the guards confirms. "Y'all should've let me kill him like he killed my brother."

I turn to the guard and nod before helping Nicchi off the ground. Wrapping my arms around her, I hug her. Her body feels like my mother's.

"Thanks," I tell her.

Cupping my face in her hands, she replies, "We family boy."

"Everybody is going to be compensated," I assure all three of them with a sincere nod. "My father is going to appreciate this. You gonna be set for life, I promise."

They all smile.

As I walk towards the vault's keypad, Nicchi gets anxious.

"What you doing?" she asks, nervous.

"Changing the code," I say.

I have to be smart. I can only trust Nicchi and her friendly guards so far.

I strain my ears trying to listen to what is going on behind the door, but the iron is so thick I can't hear a thing. When I'm about to override the code, the Ranch's emergency siren goes off. The sharp sound shoots through the air so loud it brings us to our knees. We cover our ears.

"Is it Kong? Did he get out? What the fuck is going on?" Nicchi shoots questions at me back to back.

I rush down the hall and look out the window to see army trucks muscling their way through the roads. Professional guards dressed in combat gear and toting semi-automatics crowd the streets. Everyone is scattering like roaches, running for safety, but they can't hide. Walking in front of the trucks, leading the pack, is my father. He isn't armed, and he isn't wearing a bulletproof vest. He walks the streets confident and powerful like he owns them, because he does. Brock "The Rock" Badd is back. Now it's time for everybody to pay.

"Stay here," I tell them.

"But Vinchi…" Nicchi complained.

"Just trust me," I say to Nicchi and run out the door to join my father.

19

Brip Badd

"**YOU HEAR THAT?**" I say to his bitch ass. "That ain't the sound of heaven's bells ringing, welcoming you in." I kick at his feet, and he glares back at me. "That's not even the sound of hell's gates opening. It's much worse than that." I laugh down at him. "That's the sound of the chickens coming home to roost, nigga."

I walk backwards away from Ace. I don't trust this nigga enough to have my back turned to him.

The piercing sound of sirens makes the prison feel like it's shaking. It's like the walls are cracking and about to tumble down. Excited, I clap my hands. I can't stop smiling. The sirens are the sound of victory. The war is over. Brock came back. Brock "The Rock" Badd is back on the Ranch, and he ain't here to fight for this place. He's just taking it.

I stare down at the dried bloodstain on the concrete. I hope Mona hears the sirens. I hope the sound of the horns opens her eyes and vibrates in her bones so much that she gets up and walks out of that hospital.

"It's over, Ace." I take a few steps towards him. "I was going to give myself the pleasure of killing you tonight. I had already decided that you breathed enough of my air—that it was time for your bitch ass to die. But…" I hold up my hands, surrendering to my motivation. "…I'm gonna leave you to Mr. Badd."

I snicker at the thought of all the horrible things Brock is going to do to Ace.

"He may burn you alive, or maybe he'll drown you," I continue. "Or maybe he'll feed your ass to them weak-ass gators you threatened my wife with."

I clench my fist and raise my hand in the air. Before I know it, I'm whaling on his ass. He falls over and spits out blood. I yank him up by his shirt collar.

"I told you that you were gonna pay for what you did to my wife. I'm gonna make sure your death is long and miserable."

I push him back to the ground, but he uses his hand to catch himself before his face pounds against the concrete.

Using the cinder block wall to hold his weight, Ace stumbles to feet. He's hunched over, holding his rib cage and grimacing in pain. The little shit I just did to him ain't nothing compared to how he's going to die.

"Killing me ain't gonna be as easy as you think," Ace says and grins, his teeth coated in his blood. "Hell, I'll probably outlive you."

Ace is one cocky motherfucker, but his words don't bother me anymore. The shit is over. All his ass got is talk right now, and I'm gonna let him have it. Ace is on ice right now, but soon enough, he's gonna be in fire.

"You're finished, nigga, and I ain't wasting my time convincing you."

I walk towards the cell's gate and grab the bars. I'm so anxious to get out of here that I feel like I can bust a hole straight through these bars.

"I can't wait to see your face when it's all over," Ace says from behind me.

I turn my head slightly and look back at him from over my shoulder. "Nigga, how you gonna see with no eyes? Huh?"

I chuckle and stretch my neck to try to look around the corner. When I spot a guard, I scream out to him.

"Aye!" I yell. "Let me the fuck out of here, or you're gonna be the first to burn," I threaten.

Two guards hesitantly run my way. When they see me, they surrender, dropping their weapons and holding out their hands.

"Please, Mr. Badd. You have to understand that we were forced. We were—"

"Shut the fuck up and let me out," I demand and take a step back, giving them room to unlock the cell.

I have no mercy for not one of these motherfuckers, and I ain't the forgiving type of nigga. They're all gonna pay. I'm gonna see to it that their whole bloodline pays for this shit. I don't give a fuck. Every man, woman, and child in their bloodline is dead. These niggas are gonna see how dark I am. Lucifer ain't got shit on me.

"I'm gonna get you out of here, sir," one of the guards says, stepping towards the gate.

His hands shake as he fumbles to find the right key. I keep my eyes fixed on him. I watch his lips moving and his body trembling as he babbles something, but I'm not listening to a word he's saying. After finally finding the key, he shoves it in the lock. His friend sees the look in my eyes and takes off running before his partner opens the cell. He's a smart man.

"I'll see you soon, Brip," Ace says to me and laughs. "I can't wait…" he struggles to say through pained, shallow breaths. "I can't wait to see your face."

I don't even give that nigga the pleasure in turning around to address him. When the guard slides the cell open, I walk out and take a deep breath, inhaling my lost freedom. The guard steps back. The siren is still ringing loud. The guard follows my eyes as I look down at his gun. He takes cautious steps backwards until his back is against the wall. Leaning over, I scoop up the rifle, and he holds his hands out, surrendering.

"Please, sir. Please. You don't understand." He stretches his fingers in a stop gesture as I aim at him. "Please, don't…"

Before he can finish his sentence, I put a bullet bullseye in his forehead. His brain hits the brick wall before it catches his body. When I look down at him, his eyes are still bulging and glazed with fear. I admire my work—so beautiful, so clean. A trail of blood stretches towards my feet, but I don't move. I let his blood stain my white sneakers. I'm gonna wear this nigga's death like a badge of honor. Blood gives me strength; it fuels me the same as it does a vampire. When I turn around, I aim the gun at Ace, who smiles at me and then frowns when he sees that I'm serious.

"You don't want to kill me before you learn the truth. If you kill me, your mother's secret dies with me."

I smell the fear exuding from his body. It's pouring out of his pores like steam, but this arrogant nigga is still trying to play it cool like he doesn't have a care in the world. Using his lies as insurance to live ain't gonna fly with me. I ain't my brothers. Regardless of what they decide, I'm killing this nigga. They're just gonna have to forgive me later. Luckily for his ass, now ain't the time for him to die, but I'm gonna give this nigga a bullet. He's owed a few, and today is payday.

Ace holds out his hands and closes his eyes. He knows he's about to catch one. He just doesn't know where.

"You're making a big mistake. I can tell you where she is," he blurts out, his tone desperate.

Just to let him know how much I don't give a fuck about the shit he's saying, I let him take one in the leg. I hear him scream, but I turn away before his body falls. I throw the rifle over my shoulder and prepare myself to join the battle. It ain't Halloween, but today, I'm wearing the mask of the Grim Reaper. *It's payday, motherfuckers.*

As soon as I step foot outside of the casino, my trigger finger is on autopilot. I'm shooting everything moving, knocking these niggas down like bowling pins. They're falling hard, too. Everywhere I look, a nigga is getting blazed up. They try to run but ain't nowhere to hide. They're scattering like roaches now that we've flicked the light. I got my sights set on one nigga, though—Kong. I would love the honor of killing him, but I don't see him. He ain't the type of nigga you can miss.

The distinct smell of blood and gun smoke in the air gets me high. I fire my last round, knocking down about ten niggas, and then throw the gun to the side. Snatching a gun from a body, I fire another round. I use this pistol to cut through the crowd like butter.

There is so much smoke is in the air that I can barely see my target. Army trucks and niggas dressed in black suits and carrying semi-automatics are lighting dude up. Whoever they are, they're on some real James Bond type shit. Brock really outdid himself. For a minute, I thought we wasn't going to get out of this shit, but that was just me being weak and underestimating my brother. Brock didn't show up when we wanted him, but he showed up with a bang.

I squint my eyes and try to see through the thick fog of smoke that clouds the air. I'm looking for my brother, but I don't see him, and I probably won't see him until all of this is over.

We haven't connected since the first attack with Ace. We got a lot of shit to fix and a lot to recover, but I strongly feel that it can happen. If it's one thing this experience has taught me, it's that I need to be more involved with the Ranch's operations. The fact that something like this could happen right under our noses is fucked up, and I want to make sure it never happens again. Brock has to promote me to head of security, and I ain't asking him. I'm telling him. I got more to offer than bullets and muscle. Besides, knocking heads in is getting old, and if I don't stop, my wife will leave me. So, it's time I get a seat at the table with my brothers. It's not just Taffy and me anymore. When the baby comes, we'll be a family. As that child grows in her belly, I can feel myself changing more every day.

Taffy has lost hope in me, and that feels worse than when I caught her with ole boy. Worse than when she told me that she doesn't know who's the father of this baby. I need my wife to at least trust me. If she can't do that, then we ain't shit. She needs to see me in a different light—something other than reckless and foolish. That means getting off the streets. Maybe I'll put on a suit and tie every day like Bobby. Polish myself up a bit to show her that I have another side in me, too. Show her that I'm more than just a goon but a businessman. I can learn to be that for her and the baby.

The sound of bodies dropping is starting to die down, and the smoke is clearing up. I can see a little better now. While walking towards the casino, I spot Vinchi.

"Aye!" I yell to him.

When he sees me, he starts running my way. I drop my weapon and wrap my arms around my nephew. While holding his face in my hands, I look him dead in the eye and yell, "I'm proud of you," my voice competing with the sirens.

"I'm sorry," he says and sniffs, then chokes on the smoke.

"Man up," I say. "Where's your father?"

"Last I saw him, he was walking towards the crematory. I think he's looking for Kong," Vinchi replies.

"What about your momma?" I ask, my eyes darting from him to the chaos. Now isn't the time to chat, but I have to know about Mona. "How is she? Did Kong get her help?"

"Yes," Vinchi says with a head nod. "The last I saw her, they were working on her."

His eyes drop. I know he's blaming himself, but I don't console him because he needs to feel every ounce of the guilt suffocating him.

"Let's find your father," I say, handing my gun to him. Then I lean over and take one from a dead body since they won't be needing it anymore.

Vinchi is just as good a shooter. We both learned from the same teacher. We run into the chaos, covering each other. Our shooting style is flawless; we don't miss one shot. Vinchi and I are like poetry in motion—our shots precise and purposeful. We don't shoot based off of our emotions but strategy. I got beef with Vinchi, but he's blood. After today, I need to squash the shit. Family is all we got.

When we get to the crematory, I kick down the door and rush inside. The stench of rotting bodies turns my stomach, but that don't stop me from creating new smells. These niggas are so desperate that they're hiding underneath dead bodies to stay alive. Vinchi and I shoot through the dead bodies, killing them twice and hitting a new target. When we get to the basement door, I hold out my hand to stop Vinchi. I lean in and listen before shooting down the stairs. I don't want to take a chance and hit Brock.

"Y'all niggas better run," I yell down the stairway, but I don't hear anything.

After gesturing for Vinchi to cover me, I slowly walk down the steps, ready to expect anything. When we get to the bottom of the stairs, I notice that the room is empty.

"Where the fuck is that fat motherfucker hiding?" I say, referring to Kong. "You ain't seen him?" I ask Vinchi.

He swallows hard and shakes his head no. I can see the anxiety building up inside of him.

"It's okay, man," I say, trying to calm him down. "That nigga ain't hurting you. It's over," I assure him, and he gives me a hesitant nod. "It don't look like Brock is here either. We got to find him," I say, still trying to compete with the sirens.

"Let's try the big house," Vinchi yells back. "Maybe he went ther—"

Before Vinchi can finish his sentence, the sirens stop.

That can only mean one thing. The war is over. Vinchi and I both look at each other. My ears are still ringing, and my trigger finger is itching for more, but it's over.

"Let's go," I say, running up the steps.

Vinchi follows behind me.

20

Mona Badd

Y HEAD FEELS like it's split right down the center. It's throbbing like somebody is using my brain as a basketball, slam-dunking it against my skull's inner corners. I feel my eyes flinching to blink, but opening them is hard. Somebody is calling my name, but I don't know if I'm dreaming or not. I've been having all types of crazy dreams these past few days. They've been nightmares that I can't wake up from.

"Mona," I hear him say.

It sounds like Brock, but it can't be him. I haven't seen him since the day of the last attack, but he did tell me that he was coming. I remember him saying, *I'm on my way,* but I could've been dreaming then, too. Maybe it's Brip. Last time my eyes worked, I saw him standing over me in the prison. I remember the floor feeling cold and wet. It doesn't feel like that anymore. It's warm in here, and something soft is laying over my body.

"Open your eyes," they say again.

Maybe it's Vinchi. When I do open my eyes, he has a lot of explaining to do. What the fuck is he doing running around with Kong? Nobody trusts him. *I got to get up from here to save him. I got to*

*save this Ranch. Kong is going to kill them all. This ain't no time to sleep.
I have to get up.*

I feel myself lean up and swing my feet from off the bed, but when
I don't feel the floor underneath, I know I'm still dreaming. My eyes
are still flickering. I'm trying my best to open them, but I'm just too
tired. I have to get up. I got to convince Kong to let us go. He can have
this Ranch. I'll give him the code in exchange for letting us all live. *The
safe.* I have to get to the safe and override the code like Brock asked me
to do. I have to warn Brock not to come because Kong is going to kill
him on the spot.

"That's it, baby," the voice says. "Open your eyes."

*Baby? Who the fuck is calling me baby? Is it Kong? I don't want that
nigga nowhere near me. If that's the case, I'll stay sleep.*

I feel a hand on top of mine, and a surge of energy sparks through
my body. The hand strokes my skin; it feels heavy and gentle at the
same time. I know that touch. It feels like my husband; it feels like
Brock. *But how?*

"Come on, Mona. I need you," the voice says. "It's all over. We
survived, baby. We got the Ranch back. Now, I just need you to wake
up for me," he says.

I feel warm lips on top of my forehead. Brock holds them there for
a while, allowing the love from his kiss to marinate on my skin. When
he leans closer to me, I can smell him. His scent. The fragrance of his
body when he sweats. My husband is back. He saved us. My eyes start
flickering again and then open, but the light is so blinding that I close
them shut.

"Come back to me, baby." Brock squeezes my hand. "I'm so sorry,
Mona. I'll never leave you again. I won't lie to you anymore. You are
my whole life, woman. You are my heartbeat. You're the air in my lungs
and the blood in my veins. If you die, I die, and we got too much to
live for. We got such a bright future ahead of us. Together. Forever."

Brock kisses the palm of my hand, and his touch gives me life. I
start feeling tingling all over my body. His words make me want to
jump off this bed. I wish it was that easy, but I have to get up. We got a

lot to celebrate. A lot to repair. A lot to look forward to. I have to open my eyes to let him know that I accept his apology and ask him to please accept mine. It's time for us to start over. I'm ready.

I open my eyes, and this time, I let the light burn right through my pupils. I don't close them. Instead, I take a deep breath and open them as wide as I can. I can't see anything right away—just brightness. Then the brightness passes, and a blur of white fills the room. I blink a little, and with every blink, the room becomes clearer. Now, I can see the form standing over my bedside. Standing 6'3" with a build like a Greek God, it could only be one person. My husband. It's Brock. He lowers his face close to mine, and I can feel his breath.

"Come on, baby. Wake up. We got to put back on our crowns and clean up this mess, but I can't do shit without my queen. I won't make a move without you, baby."

I open my eyes wider, and the image of him fills in until he is fully formed.

"Bro…" My strained voice cracks. "Brock," I force out of my mouth as loud as I can, but my voice hits the air like a faint whisper.

"Shhh," Brock says and kisses my dry lips. "Save your energy."

He grabs my hand, and I squeeze his. It's the only way I can communicate with him.

"Get her some water," he demands over his shoulder.

My sight zooms in behind him, and it's Vinchi. My son is alive. *We survived. We made it.* I exhale a therapeutic breath and look up at Brock with tears glazing my eyes. He looks down at me with his eyes fixed on mine and gives me a reassuring nod.

Moments later, Vinchi returns with a cup of water. When I look in his eyes, I see something that wasn't there before. He almost looks shell-shocked. His eyes are covered in guilt and fear. His back is hunched over, and he's standing there like he doesn't deserve to be in our presence.

"Here you go, Momma," Vinchi says with a wounded voice.

I muster up enough strength to drink the water from the glass he is holding. He needs me. With every sip, the pain in my throat feels soothed. I drink the entire glass. Brock looks down at me and smiles. I try to lean up, but Brock gently pushes me back down.

"Slow down," he says, then adjusts the hospital bed so that I'm sitting upright and places a pillow behind my back.

"Th…" I take a deep breath and swallow hard. I motion for Vinchi to get me more water. "The others," I say, forcing the words from my tired throat.

Brock looks at me and nods. "They're okay," he tells me and grabs my hand. "You kept them alive. You kept all of them alive," he says like I'm the hero.

A tear falls from my eye, and Brock catches it before it can roll down to my lips. They thought I betrayed them. They didn't understand the sacrifices I made for them. But, Brock does. He understands everything I've done up until this point, and he's praising me for it. I didn't do it alone, though. Vinchi had some tough decisions to make, too.

"Vinchi…" I say to Brock.

Before I can finish, Brock interrupts me. "Vinchi and I are gonna be alright. We're all gonna be okay. We're gonna get stronger from this. I got a lot to discuss with you all, but not until you are feeling better. I'm going to get a cleanup crew out here to fix all this mess. I want this place sparkling like it's brand new. It's a lot of blood in the streets. A lot of bodies. More than the crematory can burn."

"What about Kong?" I ask, clearer than I expected.

Brock looks down at me and sweeps his hand over my forehead. I pray Brock killed him or at least has him locked up somewhere awaiting trial. All these years, I thought I knew Kong, but I didn't. I thought I could control him. I thought I could take advantage of Kong because of how he felt about me, but I was wrong. Kong is a bigger enemy to this family than Ace. We shouldn't wait to kill him. He needs to die tonight if he isn't already dead.

"I'll find him," Brock says, and a wave of concern floods my body.

"He got away?" I yell with a chest full of air. "How is that possible?"

Vinchi walks in holding my glass of water. When he hears us talking about Kong, he stops like he's interrupting a private conversation. I wave him inside with my hand. Vinchi has earned his seat at the table. After today, Brock needs to give him an official position. I don't give a fuck what the rest of them say. My son is the real hero.

"I looked everywhere for him," he says and turns to Vinchi to grab the glass. He places it up to my lips, and I take small sips of the water, swallowing them like hard liquor. "He must've had an escape plan. I ambushed every building he could've been hiding in, but he wasn't there, and that nigga ain't hard to miss in a crowd."

I look over at Vinchi, waiting for him to add what he knows about where Kong could be, but as soon as my eyes lock with his, he looks away. I know my son. I gave birth to him. Something ain't right.

Vinchi slowly starts to back out of the room, but Brock stops him when he turns and notices him leaving.

"It's okay, son. You can stay." He motions him back into the room with a nod of his head.

"I-I have to...I need to go help-help Uncle Brip," Vinchi says, tripping over his words.

Brock looks at him and nods. "Okay, son. We'll catch up later. Don't go too far," he says and smiles proudly at his son.

Brock doesn't see what I'm seeing. Vinchi is hiding something, but why? Is he still trying to set up Brock? After all of this, does he still want his father dead? If he knows where Kong is, he needs to let us know, or we're gonna end up right back in the same boat. We're all at risk, and who says Brock will be around to save us next time.

I look at Brock. It's at the tip of my tongue to out Vinchi, but I can't. I need to meet with him one-on-one and find out what the fuck is going on. Brock loves Vinchi, but he ain't as forgiving as me. He doesn't understand him the way I do. Besides, the others are already on the fence with him. If they find out he had something to do with helping Kong escape, they might just exile him, and I can't let that happen to my son. I will protect him with my last breath.

"I'm proud of him," Brock says, looking over his shoulder like

Vinchi is still in the room. Then he turns back to me and places his hand on top of mine. "He didn't crack under pressure. He survived. Brip says he's the one who made sure Kong got you some help. I don't know how he convinced him to do that other than strategy and good tactics. If it wasn't for our son…"

Brock looks away, directing his eyes toward the floor. He's fighting away tears and grief. He takes a deep breath, pushing away his emotions like they're poisonous, and looks back at me.

"They say you wouldn't have made it. You would've bled out. Vinchi got you help right in time," Brock says and squeezes my hand.

The intensity in Brock's stare makes me feel needed. The last conversations we had left me feeling obsolete, disrespected, and replaceable. Not now, though. I can feel how much Brock needs me in his touch alone.

"That nigga can't hide forever." Brock sniffs and sweeps his hand over his face. When he exhales, his shoulders drop from the release of the tension. "We got a lot of work to do, Mona. We got to rebuild this place in seven days. I need everything cleaned up and open for business."

"You don't think it's too soon?" I ask.

"I don't think it's soon enough," Brock responds, giving me an anxious look. "Once this place is cleaned up, I'm going to spend two days meeting with all of our top clients. I'm going to invite them to spend a night at the Ranch just to dispel the rumors. I want them to know their taxes are still doing the job. I'm gonna have to cut some checks, too. I got to make it to the safe so I can count how much cash we have on reserve. It will be better to take it from the safe than our account."

"Why give them money?"

I'm not sure I agree with Brock giving away money like it's Christmas. Besides, the cleanup and renovations that he's planning to do are going to set us back.

"Think of it as a stimulus plan. The same money I hand them is going to buy back our trust, then end up right back in our hands," Brock explains.

This man is brilliant! I see where he's going with this now.

"I'm gonna wait a few months for this to blow over—give everybody a chance to forget or become distracted by the next scandal. Then, I'm gonna raise taxes." Brock smiles at me. "That's gonna buy back our respect."

"Sounds like a lot of work. I have to get out of this bed and get back to the big house to set up camp. Nicchi 'bout tore the whole place down," I say, leaning up.

Brock places his hand on my shoulder, stopping me.

I lean back and sigh. Then, I dart back up when I think about my sister. *Did she make it out okay?*

"Nicchi," I say and grab Brock's hand. "Is she…" I choke on my words.

My sister and I haven't been close in years, but it was always my job to protect her. Brock briefly looks away like he's trying to hide something. He blinks and looks back at me, lowering his head.

"Please don't tell me she's dead!" I start to panic.

Brock places his hand on top of mine to calm me down.

"I don't know yet. We're making a record of all the dead through photos. I'm going to send them out to the East Meadows projects so people can know they lost family members and what Kong did to them. I'll be sure to send you the photos of the females so you can look through them, but I haven't seen her. The place is clear," Brock says like he's warning me. "You need to rest."

I let out a breath full of anxiety and say a silent prayer. I pray Nicchi wasn't foolish enough to get herself killed. I feel so burdened that I just want to go back to sleep, but there is too much to do.

"I can rest when I'm dead. Besides, working gives me strength. You know that. I got to make sure the cleaners are doing their job and—"

"Not now," Brock says firmly, cutting me off. "We got a lot of personal shit to work out before you get back out there. Once you're in work mode, you get to going, and before you know it, we both forget things that should've been addressed. We have to talk about Goldie," he says and drops his head.

My entire spirit drops thinking about the bitch he fucked and had a son with. Kong let her and the boy go the night he took over the Ranch. She's the last person I want to talk about, but I know Brock feels the need to apologize so we can officially move on.

"I don't care about—"

Brock holds out his hand for me to calm down, interrupting me yet again.

"Lera, too," he adds.

It feels like Kong hit me in the head with another ax or whatever the fuck he used to hit me. My whole spirit drops. I don't care to talk about Goldie, but Lera I need to know about, although I don't want to know. She's family. If he fucked her, that will affect our relationship and break the brothers' bond.

I feel Brock's eyes on me, but I can't allow myself to look at him. I don't want him to see the fear and hurt in my eyes. Him fucking Goldie was one thing, partially my fault. She was a stray breeder, but Lera? I will never understand that, but something happened between them. I know it. Lera is in love with him. I can see it in her eyes. But does Brock love her? Is that what he wants to talk to me about? The thought alone turns my stomach.

Brock places his finger under my chin and raises my face until our eyes meet.

"We're gonna get past this. I swear." He gives me a reassuring nod and then says, "I'm gonna let you get some rest."

Brock leans down and kisses me on the forehead, then turns to walk out of the room.

21
Bobby Badd

L ERA'S BEEN WALKING around beaming like a lovesick puppy ever since Brock *rescued* the day. He was about two weeks too long if you ask me, but I'm happy we all made it out okay. I heard Mona got badly hurt, but that type of shit can happen when you're sleeping with the enemy. I got a right mind to walk away and leave all this shit behind me, but I won't get far without cash. I have Tara and my son to think about. I would add Lera to that equation, but it ain't looking good for us. Besides, I need to know what happened between her and Brock. If I can't get it from her mouth, then I need to talk to my brother man to man. I don't even know if I'm ready to hear the truth. Too much shit is already on my plate, but this will continue to eat at me until I know.

My brothers and I have had our fair share of disagreements and have even come to blows at times, but we never cut each other this deep before. That's why I halfway can't believe it's true. Brock wouldn't just up and fuck my wife. It ain't him. Or is it? The nigga does think he's a god, and most gods think they are entitled to everything because they believe they created everything. But Brock ain't have shit to do with building me and Lera's love. I created all that beauty before I fucked it up.

I shake away the thought and set my attention back on finding my son and Tara. All this shit has been one big distraction. I still got obligations. And I'm thinking about bringing Jayson in for treason. His taking Tara and Blake away like a thief in the night doesn't sit well with me, although his decision kept them safe from all this madness. Still, that's not how shit works, and he knows that.

I pick up the phone and redial his number. It rings a few times. I almost think I'm gonna catch his voicemail, but he picks up.

"Yeah," he answers like I'm bothering him.

"You know who the fuck this is?"

"What you got going on, Bobby?" Jayson says with an attitude.

This nigga is really pushing it.

When I hear Blake laughing in the background, my nerves ease. He's taunting his uncles about beating him in a video game. Hearing the joy in his voice lets me know he ain't hurt, but I don't hear Tara. Jayson lowers the phone and sends my son away.

This nigga got a lot of fucking nerve. I appreciate the way he's protecting Blake, but the way he's doing it is foul.

"Put my son on the phone," I demand.

"No," Jayson responds firmly.

"You sure you want things to go this way?" I threaten.

Jayson hesitates for a moment like he's weighing his options and then replies, "Do what you got to do, man, but I ain't letting nothing happen to my family."

"Your family!"

Jayson ain't used to seeing me angry, but he is taking this shit too far.

"Yes, my motherfucking family," he boldly says. "You can talk to Blake once I know shit your way is safe. Otherwise, we good on all that."

Anger seeps through my veins, causing my heart to pound against my chest like a fist punching a brick wall. I breathe in through my nose and exhale silently. I can't lose my cool. My silence causes Jayson to stir.

I can hear him fidgeting around from the other end of the phone. He's wondering what I'm thinking, what I'm planning, how deep of a grave his words are digging for him. Right now, they got him six feet under, but I can always dig a little deeper.

"Hello?" Jayson asks, although I'm sure he can hear me breathing.

I don't respond. Sometimes silence is all you need to say.

I tighten my fist a few times to relieve some tension, then start pacing back and forth. If Jayson wants to pretend like he's got the power, I'll give him what he wants, but only for a while—only until I get what I want. My family.

"It's all good over here. The storm done passed, and now it's time for the calm," I humbly say.

"I don't know," Jayson says, being difficult.

"What don't you know?" I ask with a heavy tone, feeling myself getting angry again.

"I've been hearing all types of crazy shit about the Ranch. The streets are talking, man. Even if the storm did past, who's to say it's calm?"

"I mean what I say," I warn Jayson. "The Ranch is good, and we're all gonna remember who came through to help us during our trying times."

Jayson had been my right-hand man for years, and I paid him good money to stand by my side. I know he was looking out for Tara and Blake, but it's fucked up that he didn't try to lend a hand in helping my family and this Ranch.

"I ain't putting my nephew or my sister in harm's way," Jayson shoots back. "Give shit a few more weeks to blow over and then call me back. I'll let you know how I feel then," he says and prepares to hang up.

"Wait," I say, humble. If he mentioned Tara, that must mean she's still alive. I have to know how she's doing. "Tara," is all my mouth can say. Nothing more.

My heart punches against my chest again as I wait for Jayson to tell me the condition of Tara. I don't know which would be worse—Tara being alive but physically impaired or dead.

"She's right here," he tells me.

"Can she talk? Can she—"

"Like I said, I need a few weeks for all this shit to blow over. We'll talk then," he says before hanging up.

"Jayson!" I scream, although I know he isn't on the other end of the phone.

I try to call him back, but he has blocked my number. His lack of respect for me has made my decision to kill him an easy one.

Full of anger, I turn around and toss my phone in the air. It lands with a thud on the couch. When I look up, I see Lera standing in the corner with her arms folded across her chest. She heard my entire conversation. That's not what I wanted. I'm trying to protect them all—Tara, Blake, and her. Seeing the gloomy look in her eyes gives me mixed emotions. I can't hide my love for Tara and Blake from Lera, but at the same time, I can't make her feel disregarded. I don't know how to balance the two.

"What's up?" is all I manage to say.

"Bad news?" Lera shifts her body weight from one leg to the other and rolls her eyes a little.

I ignore her question. "How you feeling?"

She shrugs and sits down on the couch. Picking up the phone, she tosses it to me before relaxing back onto the cushion.

"How's your family?" she asks with sarcasm.

"I don't know," I answer honestly.

"Hmmm," she hums under her breath, then fixes her big brown eyes on me.

Her hair is growing back in nicely. Beautiful loose curls shape her oval face. Lera is stunning, but her inner beauty is even more breathtaking. She's hiding that from me, though.

"I can't just forget that I have a son, Lera," I tell her.

Lera sucks in air through her teeth and rolls her eyes. "Nobody is asking you to forget him. All I wanted was for you to be honest about your family."

"You're my family," I say to her.

She shakes her head and laughs. "No. I'm not. What will Tara think about you saying that?"

Lera studies my face for any hidden notions. I don't know how to respond to her question, so I don't. When I don't respond, Lera fills in the blanks. Her weight shifts on the couch, and she breaks her gaze with me.

"I know it don't make sense, but what I have with you is special, and it ain't got shit to do with them. I told you several times that this shit between you and me is real. What I did was fucked up, but I can't keep trying to convince you that I love you, especially if you don't want to be convinced."

Lera covers her mouth with her hand and looks away, shaking her head in disagreement. She ain't trying to hear me. She just wants to beat me down, and I get that. But either we move on from this shit or let it go. I'm gonna leave that up to her.

"Is she alive?" Lera asks, then looks away from me.

I can't tell if she is hoping that Tara is alive or dead.

"She's alive, but I don't know her condition," I respond with frustration in my voice.

Lera looks at me with sympathetic eyes. Her inner beauty is coming out of hiding. Even with all my betrayal, she finds the time to concern herself with how I feel. She swallows hard. Words of encouragement are on the tip of her tongue, but she doesn't betray her emotions by voicing them. Her eyes say it all, though.

"All this shit is over now. We're rebuilding. What does that mean for us?" I ask her.

The look in Lera's eyes changes. She's back to being agitated and cold.

"You need to answer that question for yourself. I'm not going to let you have two families, so who do you choose?" Lera stands up, demanding an immediate decision.

She oversimplifies her question. I can't simply choose between her and Tara. Tara comes with Blake. Tara has always been there for me, and she may need me to be there for her. Lera, on the other hand, is love. Carefree, worry-free love and beauty. I'm not sure I have time for such luxuries. I'm not even sure I deserve it. Lera wants to be chosen because, by choosing her, it will validate our entire relationship. It will make her feel like all this wasn't for nothing—like she isn't a fool. I get that, but it's not that simple. The shit is way beyond black and white; it's a gray area. Even then, there are thousands of shades of gray, and I don't know where we fall in all that. I just know I love her.

"If you want the divorce, I can give you that. I ain't gonna leave you high and dry either. I'll make sure you're set," I say, hinting that I got her covered financially.

"My severance package," she says through a chuckle and walks behind the couch. "How much am I worth?"

"There ain't no dollar amount to your worth," I sincerely state.

Her eyes brighten a bit. Then they go dull again because she doesn't want to believe me.

"If I say I want to stay and work things out, what does that mean for you and Tara?" Lera slowly walks towards me. "You can't have us both."

"Tara is always going to be a part of my life."

"Of course. She's Blake's mother, but she calls herself your wife."

"She's not," I say.

Lera is now close enough for me to grab, so I take her hand in mine.

"You're my only wife." My voice is soft and sincere.

Lera tries to pull away, but I don't let her.

"You've been through a lot on account of me. If we decide to work it out, you will be my one and only, but I can't abandon Tara. She may need long-term care. I might have to spend days with her, and you're gonna have to be okay with that and trust me. Tara is my best friend, and I have to protect her. I'm always gonna be committed to helping her in any way that I can, and that's never gonna change," I firmly say.

Lera snatches her hand away from me, and I let her go. If we decide to work things out, she needs to know she ain't gonna be able to dictate how I interact with Tara. Tara almost lost her life because of all of this shit. The very reason Tara and I aren't together is because she feared this very thing would happen. So, I have to be there to assure her that she and Blake will be safe. I got a lot of work to do with them, and I'm not sure Lera will understand that. I foresee a lot of unnecessary drama and resentment. Maybe Lera and I should go our separate ways. Perhaps it's for the best.

"I already trusted you once," Lera says like I used up all her trust.

I can't argue with that. Every man deserves a second chance, but under these circumstances, maybe that doesn't apply to me. I nod my head, surrendering to Lera's uncertainty. She confuses me with a disappointed look. She turns to walk away, but I stop her. I have something to ask her.

"Aye," I say to her back.

She turns around and gives me an exhausted look as if to say, *What now?*

"Is there anything I need to know about you and my brother? Anything you need to get off your chest?"

Lera's eyes look away like they always do when anybody mentions Brock. I don't expect her to answer my question, but I still had to ask.

"It's complicated," she says with a shrug before turning to walk away.

22

Dalla Badd

BILLY TRIES TO pull away from me, but I won't let him. I wrap my arms around his waist even tighter. He kisses the top of my head and squeezes me. We survived, and I'm grateful. But this is far from over. As long as we're on this Ranch, we will always be at risk.

"Dalla…" Billy whispers and plants two more kisses on top of my head, "…come on. We got a lot of stuff to figure out before we leave. We need to talk."

Prying my arms from around him, Billy grabs my hand and leads me to the couch. I wipe tears from my eyes and smile at him. The worst of it is over. We are so close to our happily-ever-after that I can smell it. I can smell the saltiness of the ocean that surrounds us. I can hear BJ laughing and splashing in the water. I can feel my head against Billy's chest as we lay in the sand. His heartbeats are rhythmic and calming. We are so close. I want to leave now. I don't want to wait any longer. We need to leave today.

After taking a seat on our couch, Billy grabs my hand and pats the space beside him. I sit down. He stares at me and winks before smiling.

"I told you everything was going to be okay," he says, then leans over and plants a kiss on my lips.

I savor every moment of the warmth and softness coming from his lips. Closing my eyes, I find myself back on the beach—back at our safe place. When he pulls away, my eyes open, and I am jolted back to reality.

"Do you trust me?"

It feels like a trick question. I trust Billy, but I do not trust the situation we are in.

I give him an inquisitive look but nod my head yes. Billy needs to know that I trust him. He deserves that much.

"Of course," I say, almost afraid of what he is going to say next.

Billy smiles at me and strokes my face with the side of his index finger.

"You're so beautiful," he says under his breath, speaking more to himself than me.

My entire soul beams, and my heart feels like it's going to burst with sunlight. I spent so much time waiting for this exact moment to reunite my family, and now it's here. I can feel the love that Billy has for me in his touch, and I see it in his gaze. Looking at him feels electromagnetic. Our eyes penetrate each other before our bodies crash into one another like a magnet. I grab his hand and kiss it.

"I need you to be patient," Billy says.

Disappointment instantly floods my body, but I hide it. Or at least I try to, but Billy can see right through me.

"Hey, just trust me," he says reassuringly. "We already got one foot out the door, but we got to settle things the right way."

"Okay, but what does that mean, and how much longer will we be here?"

When Billy doesn't respond right away, I instantly know he doesn't have the answer. He looks away, but I turn his face back to me.

"How much longer, Billy?"

Billy clears his throat. "A day, a week, a month," he says and shrugs.

I pull away from him only to be pulled back in.

"Hey, don't do that. We've come this far, right?"

"We can't keep gambling for luck. This Ranch isn't safe. I heard one of the guys saying they haven't found Kong, and Ace is still here. It's not safe for us here. You said before that you wish you had listened and left when we had a chance. Now we have that chance," I say with urgency in my tone.

Billy gives me the "you're right" eyes but straightens his posture, standing his ground.

"I know," he admits. "I'm going to send you and BJ to the lake house tonight."

"No." I jump up.

"It's already settled, Dalla," Billy says, firm. "We have a family meeting tonight," he tells me, using a softer tone. "I'm going to let Brock and the rest of the family know that I'm out. Then we're discussing Mamma. I'm going to need his approval to set up a task force to find her. If he approves it, I might be leaving with you all tonight." Billy gives me a hopeful look.

"And if he doesn't approve your task force?" I try not to sound cynical, but sarcasm slides off my tongue anyway.

Billy pauses and stares back at me for a second like he's wondering if I got his back.

"Then I stay a little longer until I can get things settled. I'm not walking away from this shit without answers."

"Fine," I say and walk towards him. "Then I'm staying, and that's settled."

Billy shakes his head like he doesn't know what to do with me. I don't want to stay, but I'm not separating our family again. I can't. If I stay, Billy will be motivated to leave the Ranch as soon as he can and not get caught up in all of Brock and Mona's bullshit.

"What time is the meeting?"

"This evening at eight," Billy answers and sits back down.

"I want to be there," I add.

"No," Billy quickly says.

"Ace is still on this Ranch. I deserve a say in what happens to him. I deserve a say in all of this. I'm not sitting on the sidelines anymore."

Billy tries to rub the frustration from his face. Then he squeezes the bridge of his nose and blows air out of his mouth.

"It's enough going on. If I have you with me, it's going to cause conflict."

"Will Mona be there?" I ask, folding my hands over my chest.

"Last I heard, Mona was still in the hospital. I don't think she's going to be there, Dalla. We don't have time for this shit. I don't even plan to stay long. I'm going to let the family know I'm out and that I plan to find Mamma with or without their help."

"As long as Ace Lucky's lies are keeping him alive, we will always be in danger," I say, and Billy jumps like pinched him.

"So you think he's lying? You think my mother just woke up and climbed out of her coffin? Or maybe Jesus raised her from the dead."

Billy is talking so fast that spit flies from his mouth. I don't want to argue with Billy because once he gets an idea in his head, there is no reasoning with him. He only listens to me once it's too late.

Ace is the problem. Wherever we end up, and no matter how far we go, we will never be safe with Ace alive. He'll always be hunting for us, lurking in the shadows and following our trails. He needs to die, and I'm going to make sure it happens whether Billy likes it or not. When I made the difficult decision to kill his father, it saved his life. I didn't need his permission to do that, and I don't need his permission to kill Ace. I'll kill Ace and ask for forgiveness later. Billy has to forgive me. After all, he loves me, and that's how love works.

"Whatever you say, Billy." I place my hand on his chest to calm him down. "I don't want to fight anymore."

Billy gives me a weird look like he knows I'm up to something. He's smart, but I'm smarter. I plan to kill Ace without lifting a finger.

I NEED SOME fresh air, but apparently stepping outside my house isn't the way to get it. The stench from burning bodies and gunpowder pollute the air. Heavy dust fog looms underneath the clouds. I cover my nose with my shirt. The blood of those killed stain the concrete, and bullet shells litter the ground. Shattered glass and tire marks lace the streets. I've never been a fan of the Ranch, but it was always a beautiful place. Not anymore, though. Beautiful landscapes and magazine-like building structures can no longer hide its true evil.

I jump over a pool of blood only to land on a piece of cracked glass. When I look up, my eyes see the person I was hoping to run into. Lera is slowly walking in my direction. Her arms are folded defensively across her chest, and she's looking at me through squinted eyes. She's not hiding the fact that she hates me. They all hate me, and that hate is only going to heighten once I do what I plan to do to end this madness once and for all.

"What are you doing out?" I ask her once she gets close enough to hear me.

"What? I need permission to take a walk?" Lera scoffs and rolls her eyes at me.

"Of course not. We're all free now, right?" I reply sarcastically.

Lera shrugs her shoulders and turns to look behind her like she's paranoid.

"It's over now," I tell her. "At least that's the word."

"Hmmm," she responds, sounding like Bobby.

"I'm surprised you're still here," I say.

She fixes her eyes on me and stares back at me silently. I can see it in her demeanor that she feels out of place, like a drifter. Now that we have the Ranch back, reality has set in, and she's still a victim of Ace and suffering betrayal by Bobby. Lera doesn't have a plan. She's just here.

"Why wouldn't I be here?" she asks, defensive.

"Why would you?" I say back, locking eyes with her. "I heard

Bobby may be going to get Tara and Blake," I add, using my words wisely.

At the mere mention of Tara and Blake's names, Lera's shoulders slump with disappointment. She doesn't respond right away. Instead, she takes a deep breath and puts back on her tough girl mask.

"He can do what he wants. I'll leave when I get my money."

"What money?" I ask, sarcasm dripping from my tone. "Look around you." I redirect my eyes from her towards the wreckage surrounding us. "Whatever money you thought you were going to get is going to be tied up in fixing all of this," I say, pointing at the streets.

"Brock wouldn't do that to me," Lera says, sounding confident.

What is it with her and Brock?

"Don't let Brock fool you like Bobby did," I say in a serious tone, and her eyes dart up like she just got shocked with the truth. "I'm not trying to get in your business, but whatever you had going on with Brock is over. He is back to only caring about this Ranch, his wife, and himself. He'll put this place over you in a heartbeat. You got to start looking out for yourself, especially now that they are keeping that murdering rapist Ace alive." I use my words purposely.

At the mention of Ace's name, Lera shifts her body weight from one leg to the other.

"What do you mean? They're definitely going to kill him."

"No, they're not," I inform her. "They believe his lies. They think he knows where their mother is, and that's going to buy Ace at least a few months. I know Ace. He's already plotting his escape. He's going to walk out of this place alive and well. He always wins," I warn her. "Once you leave this Ranch, he's going to make it his business to find you and…"

I stop and take a breath, giving my words time to sink in. When I look up, Lera's eyes are bulging with both anger and terror.

"Just take care of yourself, Lera. With Bobby making Tara and Blake a priority, who knows if he'll have the time to protect you."

Lera inhales a deep breath and turns her back to me. She stares off into space, considering my words. Then she slowly looks around at all the destruction that surrounds her. She's probably wondering if she could have survived this alone. Her and Bobby's relationship may be on the rocks, but if it wasn't for him, she wouldn't be alive. If Lera leaves this Ranch, she'll be worse off than me. I hate to play the devil's advocate, but Lera needs Ace dead as much as I do. And I believe that with my help, she can be the one to kill him.

Spinning around to face me, Lera says, "I can protect myself. I'm not like you and Taffy."

"But you *are* like us," I remind her. "Just as damaged and wounded by this lifestyle, but I can say that unlike us, you take matters into your own hands. You might be the strongest of the three of us. Hell, if any of us can achieve killing Ace, it's you. He's right in Brock's dungeon," I purposely say.

"Billy told me to stay away from him, Lera," I continue. "I'm just putting a bug in your ear. Things have changed, and you need to prepare yourself for your next step. Ace will escape. He's hunted me for years, and he's going to do you the same way."

"He'll never touch me again," Lera says, tightening her fists and expelling a hot, angry breath.

"Yeah, if he's dead, he won't, but alive…" I shrug my shoulders and raise my brow, warning her.

Lera lowers her brows and squints her eyes. I can almost read her mind. She knows what she has to do. She squeezes both her fists tightly and turns to walk away. I cross my fingers and pray she will do what I know she can do—kill that motherfucker. Unlike me, Lera has nothing to lose.

23

Vinchi Badd

WHEN I GET to the safe and see the door half-open, I take a deep breath but forget to exhale. I choke on the air trapped in my mouth. For a split second, I feel like such a failure that I don't try to breathe, thinking they all will be better off without me.

I slowly open the door, cautiously peeking my head inside. Kong is gone, and he grabbed all he could grab before leaving. The safe is damn near empty. I fucked up. I fucked up bad and need to tell my father. He needs to know what I did before it's too late. Kong could come back at any moment and catch us all off guard. *Why did I ever give Nicchi the code to the safe?*

I remember walking towards the safe to change the code, and then the sirens went off, distracting me. There was so much going on all at once. I told Auntie Nicchi to wait for me. I wonder how long she waited before unlocking the door. I wonder if it was fear or greed that got her to betray me. I guess it doesn't matter now.

When my father finds out what I did, he ain't gonna trust me, and especially now that he knows I tried to ambush him. He may put me off the Ranch. I thought I didn't care what my father thought of me, especially after thinking he killed my grandmother, but when he looked at me today, I saw something in his eyes that I never saw before. He was proud of me. I saw love behind his eyes—pure love. After being held in bondage by so much hate, his love is like a breath of fresh air. But his love for me is going to vanish once he learns the truth. *I fucked up.* Closing the door to the safe, I turn to walk away.

Wherever Kong is, he still plans to kill us all, starting with me. I made a fool of him, and I know he ain't taking being defeated well. If only I had waited, my father would have arrived, and Kong would be dead. I have to talk my way out of this. I have to think my way through this situation, but it's going to be hard to face my parents and let them know Kong got away with the money. They won't believe me. Nobody trusts anybody anymore. Especially me. Uncle Brip decided to trust me only recently, and I know that's not one hundred percent. If my father puts me off the Ranch, I'm as good as dead.

While approaching the stairway, I hear footsteps coming down. I turn to run. I need to hide, but where? My heart starts racing. *Could it be Kong? Maybe it's my father.* I don't know which is worse. *Breathe, Vinchi. Breathe.* I can tell by the soft steps that it's not Kong. He walks like he's trying to knock holes in the ground. I know these footsteps. Calm. Calculated, not forced. *It's my dad. He's going to wonder what I'm doing down here. What will I tell him? Think, Vinchi. Think!* I pound against my head with my fist, and without thinking, I start to run up the steps, crashing into him.

"Whoa," my father says and grabs me. "Vinchi?" He gives me a curious look.

"Dad?" I try to sound surprised, but to my surprise, he looks at me and smiles.

"You really have been running this place the way I taught you." He gives me a proud look, and my mind is relieved. But my heart sinks with guilt. "Checking on the safe," he says while patting me on the back as if to say, *Job well done.* "Everything good?"

I swallow hard and nod, giving a hesitant half-smile. I can't look him in the eye. At least not for too long. I curve around him and continue up the steps, but he gently grabs me.

"Son, wait."

I stop and turn around in slow motion, praying he doesn't see the beads of sweat popping up on my forehead.

"We got a family meeting starting in about an hour or so. I want you there," he informs me with a serious look. "You've earned your seat at the table, son."

"Dad…" My voice cracks.

He knows I'm hesitating but takes it as something else. He holds out his hand in an "*it's okay*" gesture.

"Son, I understand more than anyone the difficult choices you had to make under pressure. If you're worried about your uncles, let me handle them. I'm still sitting in the big chair, and they're gonna have to listen to what I say. Nothing's changed in that department. But my main focus right now is you and me getting back on track. You're my firstborn, Vinchi. For that alone, you'll always hold a special place in my heart."

My eyes mist with tears that I'm terrified to let fall in his presence. This is the most sentimental I've ever seen my father. He doesn't give compliments, and he never says I love you. This feels so genuine that I can't bear to be in his presence. The guilt is overwhelming. I was going to have him killed, and all this time, he loved me.

"I don't deserve your love," I say and look away from him.

I can't look him in the eyes. I just can't. Not at this moment.

"Son…" He exhales a remorseful breath and looks me in the eye. He is so strong. So confident. So focused. "You deserve more than my love, and I'm going to see to it that you get it."

A tear escapes my eye as he wraps his arms around me, embracing me so tight I think he will never let me go. He pats me on the back, and I feel encouraged. I feel strong. I feel like I'm him.

"Everything is going to be okay. We're going to get our relationship back on track. I love you, Vinchi," he says and squeezes me. "Don't think for one second that I'm upset with you. You make me proud every day. If it wasn't for you, this place wouldn't be standing."

He pulls away, and I quickly wipe away the tears, too embarrassed to let him see my tear-glossed cheeks. To my surprise, he's crying, too, but he's not hiding it. My father looks at me, smiles, and then nods. He holds up his fist, and I pound it. Then he beats against his chest and raises his chin.

"We're unstoppable, son," he says, standing strong like he's made of iron. The single tear he allowed to fall from his eye lingers on his cheek, evaporating as the air hits his face. "Let's go talk before the meeting starts. Later, you can help me count the money. We're gonna need it to clean up this mess. Thank goodness I keep a good stash."

He turns to walk up the steps, and I hesitantly follow behind him, still wiping away tears.

"YOUR FATHER TOLD me that the two of you had a heart-to-heart," Momma says while flipping through a photo album.

She's looking at pictures of dead women like she's shopping for curtains. When I don't respond, she looks up at me and stares hard.

I can hide from my father, but not her. Nothing gets past Momma. She's always been in tune with my every emotion; she can see the slightest change in my mood. I clear my throat and look at her. When she sees the look of sorrow, remorse, and guilt in my eyes, she looks away like it's burning her insides. She's disappointed in me and doesn't even know why. Yet, she pretends not to see what I'm showing her.

"Yeah," I respond and wipe the sweat from my forehead.

"He says he's going to give you an official title. That means you'll get a mansion and be on the payroll. You know what that means, don't you?" Momma warns me.

"I know it's serious," I respond, defensive.

"I hear you're joining us at the meeting tonight. Now that you got a seat at the table, you have to be strong. Your uncles may not like it, but you can't take any of that shit personally. It's business," she schools me, and I nod my head. "I'll be there tonight. You know I have your back," she hints to me.

I look at my mother, who still has the bandage covering her head. Her face is still swollen from the attack, but she plans to attend the meeting.

"You sure you should go?"

"Life goes on," she replies, fixing her eyes back on the photo album.

She stares hard at a photo and squints her eyes while holding the album closer to her face. Then she pushes it under my nose.

"Look at this for me. This doesn't look like Nicchi, does it?"

I look down at the photo intensely, almost praying it is Auntie Nicchi because that will eliminate most of my problems. But it doesn't look like her. At least it's not what she was wearing the last time I saw her. Her and this dead woman have the same body type and weave, but it isn't her.

"Nah," I say and push the photo out of my face. Looking at dead women is the last thing I want to do right now.

Momma sighs and places the album on her nightstand. She readjusts her weight on the hospital bed, grabbing on to the rails and propping herself up. When I lean in to help her, she pushes me away and starts to pick at her bandage like she's trying to remove it.

"I pray that girl wasn't stupid enough to get killed," she says with a sigh and an eye roll.

She's trying to hide how worried she is about Auntie Nicchi, but I can see it as plain as day, just like she can see what I'm hiding. Her bandage is too tight to remove, so she stops picking at it. She fixes her eyes on me.

"Brip told me that if it wasn't for you, I wouldn't be alive. You got Kong to agree to get me help," she says, her eyes lingering on me.

I break away from her gaze and shrug. "I-I guess," I reply, stumbling over my words.

"Kong ain't the man to be reasoned with. Once he makes up his mind about something, that pretty much is it. How did you convince him? That nigga ain't got a good bone in his body."

I swallow hard, my eyes searching every corner of the room, but Momma is hard to avoid. My silence creates an eerie tension in the room. It's so loud. Too loud. I finally get the courage to lock eyes with her, and when she sees me, she silently gasps. She doesn't know what I did, but she knows I fucked up. We both still play pretend, though.

"I-I just was…" I was at a loss for words. "I was firm, that's all."

"Kong doesn't like firm," she informs me. "What about Nicchi? When's the last time you seen her? Was she there when you talked to Kong? Were you around him when your father set the alarm?"

She fires questions at me back to back, giving me no time to make up a response. So I blurt out the truth in bits.

"I negotiated with him," I respond.

"How?" she asks.

"You for the…" I lower my eyes. "…for the safe," I say with my eyes still glued to the floor. "Auntie Nicchi helped me. I gave her the code."

Momma's body darts upward like she is trying to grab me, but when she gets close enough, she falls back, flooded with disappointment in me. She places both hands on top of her head and shakes it remorsefully.

"Where are they?" she calmly asks.

I look at her and shake my head, letting her know that I didn't know.

"I locked him in the safe seconds before the alarm sounded. Last I saw Auntie Nicchi, she was following my instructions and waiting for me."

"You didn't change the code?" Momma slowly says.

Her question makes me feel stupid. Looking at her, I shake my head no, my shoulders slumping over.

"When I went back to check the safe, they both were gone. They took the… The money is gone."

"Oh, Lord." Momma sigh again, and her body sinks deeper into her hospital bed.

She covers her face with her hands and slowly shakes her head like she's trying to wake up from a bad dream.

"Does your father know?"

"I tried to tell him, but he's acting so proud of me. I just..." My head lowers. "I can't face him. He's never been this proud of me. Once my uncles find out what I did, they're gonna put me off this Ranch. I'm already in the hot seat."

"That's not going to happen," Momma says, straightening her posture and giving me a firm look. "Let me handle your father. Don't say shit about this at the meeting. Understood?"

I look at her and nod. She leans back in her bed, covering her face like the light is blinding her. She then waves her hands at me, gesturing for me to leave. So, I do.

24
Brock Badd

LERA FOLLOWED ME to the casino. She's been trailing me for the last hour, being just as discreet as I taught her to be, but she forgets I have eyes in the back of my head and x-ray vision. I slow down on purpose, giving her time to catch up to me. I don't know what she wants from me, but this has to stop today. I'm remolding this Ranch, and things are slowly returning to normal. I don't need anything fucking this up.

What we did was irresponsible; it was a tiny moment we created in the heat of passion. Everything was imploding in our worlds, and all we had was each other to look to for comfort. But that's all it was—a moment—a small fragment in time. Like a speck of dust in the light, it shouldn't be visible. She has to let this shit go.

It isn't what she's trying to make it. Lera is just looking for something to cling on to; she needs something of her own because everything she had was stripped from her. This assumed love affair she has for me has nothing to do with love or respect, and everything to do with feeling like she's in control of her life.

I like Lera. I saw her with new eyes when we were together, but I won't lead her on or aide in her forcing herself to believe we had something. I want Lera to get help. She needs to snap out of this shit and take back control of her life. Stop needing people. She's enough on her own—with or without my brother.

I stop and turn around to face her. When our eyes meet, she stops walking and smiles at me.

"You knew I was here," she said, slowly walking towards me.

I opened the door to the casino and let her enter first. She walked through the door and stopped, waiting for me. She looked at me with pure admiration. It was the same look that brought us to this point. That night with Lera, I felt just as lost as she did. I was struggling to find my way again. I didn't have the respect and support from my wife, but Lera understood me. She clung to my every word and followed behind me blindly. She was so vulnerable and soft. So delicate, and she trusted me with her life. I needed someone to trust me. I was so confused, and Lera brought what I thought to be temporary support. Her support brought clarity back to my life.

"You've been tracking me for a while," I say, making sure my voice is emotionless. I don't want to confuse Lera in any way.

"I'm so happy I made it back," she says and leaps into my arms, hugging my neck.

I stand there stiff as a board, barely breathing while she embraces me. When she doesn't feel me hugging her, she lets go and takes a step back, watching me with a curious eye.

"Is everything okay?" she asks.

"It will be as soon as I get this place up and running again. I'm happy to see you're okay, Lera," I say genuinely and turn to walk away.

"Is that all?" Lera's words bounce off my back like a stone.

I turn around to face her again. Locking eyes with her, I rub my hand down my mouth. Then I pinch the bridge of my nose and sigh.

"What we did was a mistake," I whisper. "It was wrong," I add, giving her a stern look. "Let's move past it. We're family, and we're under a lot of pressure."

"Mistake?" Lera repeats, turning up her nose and folding her arms across her chest. She shifts her weight from one leg to the other. "What are you saying, Brock?"

I sweep my hands over my head and take a step toward her. I try not to look at her like she's crazy because I don't want to offend her, but she obviously has some issues she's dealing with.

"What do you want from me, Lera?" I stare back at her with a raised brow.

She's offended by my tone. I can tell by the way her neck is snapping.

"Respect!" she yells.

I look over my shoulder to be sure we are alone.

"I do respect you, but you are making it really hard right now. We shared a kiss. A moment that should have never happened."

"It was more than a kiss." She laughs through her anger and lets out a breath of hot air.

She was right. It was a little more than a kiss, but we didn't fuck. We came close, but I was strong enough to pull away before she did something I thought we both would regret. Lera had her pants off and her legs wrapped around my body when I pried my hands off her bare breasts and put my clothes back on. I left her lying there in the dark, and that's where our secret needs to stay.

"You've been through a lot, Lera," I say in a calm voice. "I'm going to see to it that you get help, but you and I are family. Nothing more." I slice through the air with my hand.

"That's not true," she yells and leaps towards me, wrapping her arms around my neck again.

I try to pry her arms away, but she only squeezes tighter.

"Something happened between us that night. Don't deny it."

"I'm not denying anything." I finally manage to yank her off of me and push her back. "We are nothing, Lera. Nothing!" I yell. "I had respect for you, but the way you're coming at me right now as my brother's wife…" I shake my head. "…you're about to make me lose respect for you. I hate what Ace did to you. It's fucked up, but I won't let you fuck up my family because you're damaged."

My words hit her like a bullet, and she has to catch herself from falling back. Her mouth drops open, and her eyes bulge with rage. I sigh, disappointed. I let my emotions get the best of me, but Lera is here to bring trouble. I'm done with trouble. I want peace.

"Look, I didn't mean that," I say, holding up my hands and surrendering myself with an apology. "I'm gonna talk to my wife."

I pause to let those words sink in. At the mention of Mona, Lera sucks her teeth and rolls her eyes.

"And then Bobby," I continue. "I'm gonna let them know the mistake we made and pray they forgive us, but we need to keep our distance until your mind gets clear because you're not thinking straight right now."

Before I can turn to walk away, Lera hurls two more words at my back.

"Fuck you!"

It hits me so hard that I stop in my tracks. I may have been too harsh with Lera, but I don't know how else to make her understand that she may be at the brink of a nervous breakdown. When I turn around to apologize, I only see the back of her head as she exits the door in tears.

WHILE ENTERING THE conference room, I notice the bloodstains on the floor before taking my seat at the head of the table. Today will be the last meeting I have here, but the room doesn't feel the same. It feels haunted. Shifting around in my chair, I try to make myself comfortable, but it's not happening. This chair feels stiffer than I remember, and the room seems a lot smaller.

Mona places a supportive hand on top of mine, and that familiar feeling returns. The warmth from her touch sends a surge of energy through my spine, and I feel stronger. There's going to be a lot of tough talk today. I just hope they receive what I have to say. Their support isn't needed, because I'm gonna do what I have to do regardless. But it would be nice to have it.

They're watching me, waiting for me to speak so they can decide how they are gonna react. I see the burdens weighing heavily on their shoulders and the exhaustion dulling the white of their eyes. We've all been through a lot, but we're gonna come out on top if we continue working together as a family.

I look over at my son, and my mind feels at ease. It feels good to have an heir to this all. I'm proud of him, but he won't receive it. Every time I look at him, he looks away. Is he that frightened of me? I guess I was scared of my dad, not wanting to be a disappointment to him. Disappointing him was worse than death. If he was here today, I wonder what he would have to say about all this. This Ranch has been here for over forty years, and we never once came close to an ambush. All this happened on my watch, but I can't look back. I can only look forward now. That's all any of us can do.

I clear my throat, and Mona immediately places a glass of water in front of me. This woman has treated me like a king for years, even when I didn't deserve it. I can live three lifetimes and never meet a woman that comes in a close second to Mona. I've been blessed to have her.

I thank Mona with a nod, take a sip of the water, and greet everyone individually with my eyes.

"Tough times," I begin and drop my head, but only for a moment. "But we're still here," I continue, using a firm tone.

Brip claps his hands and nods.

"Hell, yeah," he agrees, boosting the morale.

I take a deep breath and pull my chair closer to the table. I'm starting to get my wind back.

"We got a lot of work to do. I'm sure you all know that." I pause to look at all of them.

Bobby and Billy disconnect for a moment, but I choose not to address it. I don't have the time.

"All those years of paying Stein has paid off," I tell them.

"The Stein," Brip says, a smile stretching across his face.

I smile at him and nod. "Yes, The Stein. We got to make sure to give him a bonus because we never know when we're gonna need him again."

"This shit shouldn't happen again," Bobby comments.

"I agree, and I'm confident that after restructuring a few things, it won't. But we may need Stein for something else."

They all look at each other confused. Everybody except Billy. It's like he had a premonition about this very moment. I have to tell them about Mamma and Carlo Lucky. They deserve to know. Maybe then, they'll understand why I didn't come sooner.

I take a deep breath and exhale slowly before leaning back in my seat. I haven't even told Mona yet. I look at her, and she's giving me a curious look. They all are, Vinchi included. I clasp my hands together and hope they are ready to receive what I'm about to say. They really don't have a choice.

"While you all were stuck here, I was out there seeking answers." I give my words time to sink in. Billy leans closer to the table. "I don't know how you're gonna take this information I'm about to give you, but we all deserve to know the truth. The truth is going to help us move forward in building our legacy stronger and bigger than before, but it's also going to fucking hurt," I add. I clear my throat before continuing. "We all heard the stories about Mamma Badd and Carlo Lucky."

"Oh, shit," Brip whines, throwing up his hands and leaning back in his chair. "They done got to you too, Brock?"

"Let him finish," Billy yells and looks at me to proceed.

Finally, Billy and I are on the same page.

"Whether we want to believe it or not..." I look at Brip first and then everyone else. Billy nods his head at me. "...it's all true. They were in love. So in love that they may have had four kids together."

The room goes silent. I look over at Brip, who has his face buried in his hands. He is shaking his head in disbelief. It's only a matter of time before he snaps, so I have to hurry and get everything out.

"We thought Papa Badd killed Carlo Lucky, but…" I hesitate on this one. The more I speak, the more our lives sound like a tragic soap opera. "…he's still alive."

"I knew it!" Billy slams his hand down on the table and jumps up.

I look up at him, questioning what he knows. That's when I notice Bobby and Brip giving each other weird looks. I look at Mona, and she looks away from me. Vinchi still hasn't looked my way since I sat down.

"What's going on?" I ask, looking at Billy.

"Don't start with the bullshit," Brip says. "I'm tired of the fucking bullshit. Mamma is dead!" he yells, his nostrils flaring.

"Chill out," I yell at Brip. *What am I missing? What do they know?* "Somebody tell me what the fuck is going on," I say.

"The night Kong took over the Ranch, Ace had us dig up Mamma's grave. She wasn't in her coffin, man. Her body wasn't there," Billy shares with me.

I push my chair back and stand to my feet only to sit back down. I start putting together all the pieces of the letters that I read and the information Lady L told me. Then I remember what Stein insinuated about Carlo Lucky's wife.

Mamma is alive. I didn't kill her. She faked her death. It was planned. It's what she was trying to tell me that night.

"This is bullshit," Bobby says. "I'm not buying any of this shit until I get proof."

"What more proof do you need, man?" Billy says to Bobby.

I bang my fist against the table, bringing everybody back to order before things get too out of hand.

"The first thing we're going to do is take a DNA test—all of us," I say, letting them know this is an order and not a request. "Ace is still in my dungeon. I will have him take one, too. That will rule out the myth of the affair."

"What about Mamma's body?" Billy asks, desperate.

"We're gonna find her. Maybe Stein can help, but before we off Ace, we're gonna get all we can get out of him. He knows more than he's letting on. He knew that coffin was empty. Mamma's alive, and we're gonna find her."

As I give Billy a reassuring nod, I can see relief cover his entire body. I look at Brip, who is still shaking his head disapprovingly.

"Brip, I know this is hard for you to believe, but we owe it to Mamma to accept the truth and find her."

Brip takes a deep breath and sweeps his hands over his face.

"We've all been through a lot, and I know adding this to our plates is enough to send us over the edge. But we're all strong enough to handle it. We've proven that," I add. "That's why we need Ace alive. I'll get him to talk."

"I can help," Vinchi offers, finally speaking. "I spent a lot of time with him at the dungeon. He's crazy, but I believe him when he says he's family and that Grandma's alive. I believe him, Dad," Vinchi says like he's trying to convince me, but I don't need convincing.

"I know," I reply, giving him a reassuring nod.

With tears in her eyes, Mona grabs my hand. She's letting me know without words that I have her support, too.

Bobby clears his throat and leans in closer to the table.

"Whatever you guys need me to do in regards to Mamma is fine, but I got my own shit I have to handle. Tara and Blake are missing, and they come first. I'm leaving the Ranch to find them," he informs us.

"No one leaves." I look at Bobby, but I'm speaking to everyone. "It's too soon to be on the streets. I'll send someone to find them both and bring them here."

"With all due respect, Brock, you don't decide what happens to my family or when I come and go. I don't want to be a part of this shit anymore," he admits.

"I'm sorry, but that doesn't matter. We're in this shit for life—til death do us part," I say and stare back at him through squinted eyes. He takes what I'm saying personal, as he should.

"You threatening me?" Bobby asks.

"I'm giving you an order—all of you. No one leaves until I give the okay. The DNA test will be here by the end of the week. We got a lot more shit to discuss on the operations side, but I think we've said enough for one night. We'll meet back here after the test results are in. I expect to see everyone here," I say and look at Bobby before standing.

Then I grab Mona's hand, and we walk out the door together.

25

Bobby Badd

I CAREFULLY PLACE THE swab to the home DNA test Brock ordered securely in the bag. It was easier than I thought. All I had to do was rub a piece of cotton attached to a stick inside my mouth. No blood. No sting. I guess the sting is going to be a delayed response. I don't know how to feel about any of this shit. At this point, does it matter if Carlo Lucky is our father? I think this is all bullshit. Just another way for Brock and Mona to try and control us. This shit is over for me, though. I'm only doing this DNA test to keep the peace, but I'm packing my shit and leaving tonight. I don't need permission to find my family.

I already got one of my connects tracing Jayson's phone via the cell tower to locate him. He's calling me back tonight. As soon as I get the word, I'm out of here. Jayson knows I'm coming for him, and if I know him like I think I do, he has already packed up and left. But that's okay. He can only run so far before he falls into one of my traps.

I can't stop thinking about Tara. I didn't think she was going to make it. I could feel her blood on my hands. It weighed me down, but now, I feel lighter...more hopeful. Tara is strong. She is stronger than any woman I know. Even death can't stop her if she doesn't want to be stopped. That's the part about her that I admire the most. She's a fighter. She wasn't going to leave Blake. No way.

I don't know what I'm going to say when I see her. I said so much to her when she was in a coma. The thought of looking her in the eyes makes my chest tight. All the things she warned me about happened. Her biggest fear came to pass, and I couldn't protect her as I promised.

I'm just as scared to see her as I am excited because of the unknown. Can she walk? Can she talk? Is she scarred for life? Can she think straight, or is her brain all fucked up like Taffy's brother Tony? Whatever it is, I'm prepared to be there for her. 'Round the clock if I have to. But I have to realize that my being there for Tara means not being there for Lera. I'm at a crossroad with this shit, but I can't keep them both. Lera ain't exactly making my decision hard.

I have to face the fact that Lera ain't the same, but before I leave here, we need to talk. We got to settle things. I have to make sure she gets set up somewhere safe, though. I want to make sure she doesn't have to worry about a thing financially, but she needs to understand there is no coming back once we go our separate ways. It will officially be over for us. All I'll have left of Lera are the good memories and guilt of what I've done to her—how I hurt her and changed her forever. I wish I could make it right, but she won't let me. Even if she did, Tara and Blake ain't going nowhere. So, neither am I.

I pull a few t-shirts from my closet and place them on my bed. I'm packing light. Digging deep in my closet, I find my second stash of money. Sitting on the edge of my bed, I start counting it. I know once I tell Brock I'm leaving, he's gonna freeze all my accounts like he did with Billy. I don't want to fight with my brother, especially not over money. I'm too fucking exhausted. I got enough connects to make it out there on my own. My name is still gonna be my name regardless of who Mamma fucked, and the Badd name will always be as good as cash.

So far, I got about five grand spread out on the floor. I don't even remember where this money came from. We were raised to believe that value was always in our name, not money. That's why I never bothered counting it. But I was wise enough to know that rainy days come. Our name may be powerful, but it can't stop the rain. Look at this mess we're cleaning up now. The Ranch looks like little Vietnam.

I lean down to organize my bills, separating the fifties from the hundreds. When I look up, I see Lera standing in the doorway, staring at my luggage. She looks like she's been crying. I want to ask her what's wrong, but she'll never tell me. Besides, I can tell she tried to wipe away her tears before coming to confront me. She didn't want me to see her tears, so I'll pretend they ain't there. It breaks my heart to see how broken she is, though. This ain't the life I planned for us. But, if I ain't learned nothing else from all this back-to-back drama, I learned that shit never works out the way you plan it. Life happens. It's happening right now. Lera can see it.

Her eyes lead from my empty suitcase up to me. Locking eyes with me, she waits for me to respond to the questions she didn't ask.

"What's up?" I stare back at her.

She breaks her gaze and looks down at the money.

"You spring cleaning?" she asks, being sarcastic.

"Something like that," I say, scrapping the money off the floor and throwing it in my suitcase. "I'm leaving," I tell her and pause.

Lera stares back at me like she's at a loss for words. If I had asked her to come with me, she would've turned me down, but the fact that I didn't tears another hole in her soul. I can't win for losing with her. Besides, she ain't gonna want to see Tara no more than Tara wants to see her. This situation is awkward as hell.

"Where you going?" she asks and leans on the door like she's bracing herself for what I'm about to say.

"I got to find my son," I reply, purposely not mentioning Tara's name.

"And Tara," she adds.

"Yes," I answer short. I don't want to discuss Tara with her. No good or understanding will come out of it. "What's your plans, Lera?"

"What do you mean?" she snaps, giving me a confused look. "You putting me off the Ranch again?" She tilts her head to the side and raises her brow. "You dumping me for your family?"

I already know where this conversation is going, and I'm not in the mood for it. I stand into a stretch before sweeping my hands over my exhausted face. Then I look at Lera. The mist in her eyes thickens. I don't know what to do to make her feel better. You can't give somebody what they need if they don't know what they need themselves.

"I can apologize a million times to you about that, but you'll never understand," I calmly say. "You made it very clear that you don't want to be with me, and trust me, I understand why. But I don't know when or if I'll ever return once I leave here. So, where does that leave you?"

Lera avoids eye contact with me. It's sad. She doesn't know her next move. When I met her, she had it all together. She had a plan. A vision. A dream. Ambition. Then she fucked with a nigga like me. I have to help her. She has to let me.

"I think you should leave with me," I say, and she perks up. Her spirits lift. "But that ain't gonna work. So, I can make sure you get set up somewhere safe and—"

"Fuck you and your family!" Lera shouts with such discord her entire body trembles. "I don't need shit from you. I'm not some charity case to ease your conscience. I don't need your fucking handouts!"

"Well, what do you need!" I don't mean to yell, but Lera is doing nothing to relieve all the shit on my mind. She's adding to it. I wish she could just make things simpler. "How can I make things easier for you?" I ask in a calmer tone.

"Honestly…" Lera takes a step toward me. "…things would have been easier if that bitch would've just died."

Her words are so cold a chill shoots down my spine.

I look at Lera, stunned by her words. If Tara died, then being with me would be an easier decision for her. But she's alive, and unlike Lera, she needs me.

"I know you don't mean that," I lie, knowing she meant every word she said. "But I understand why you said it." I rub the bottom of my chin and give Lera a considerate look. "Let me ask you a question," I say and pause.

Lera flicks her eyes up at me and sniffs up her emotions.

"Do you want to stay married or not?"

Lera looks at me with the truth dancing on her tongue, but her anger burns right through the truth.

"If we stay married, I would have to forgive you," she responds calmly.

"Yes," I agree.

"Could you forgive me?"

"For what?" I ask, confused.

"For fucking your brother," she coldly states.

Lera keeps her eyes fixed on me, staring at me without blinking. She doesn't want to miss one single emotion that pains my face. Her words hit me so hard that I fall back to a sitting position on the bed. I shake my head in disbelief and bite down on my bottom lip to keep from losing control. Keeping calm was something I was good at doing, but now, I'm not so sure. I tighten my fists and force my chin up, looking at Lera as she smirks at me.

"Forgiveness ain't so easy, is it?" she says snidely and turns to walk away.

I BUST THROUGH the big house door, slamming it behind me so hard that the chandelier shakes. The first person I see rushing down the hall with terror in her eyes is Mona. When she sees me, she calms down a little but not much. Mona is still traumatized by all of this.

"Bobby, what's going on? Is everything okay? What's happening?"

Before I can respond, Brock appears behind her. When he sees the look in my eyes, he already knows why I'm here.

"Mona, go lay down." He places a gentle hand on her shoulder.

Confused, she looks up at him and back at me.

"No, let her stay. This shit involves her, too."

Brock looks at Mona and then at me before he nods apologetically.

"What's this about, Brock?" Mona asks him, but she's looking at me.

"Lera," he says and grabs her hand.

To my surprise, Mona gives Brock an understanding nod. She then squeezes his hand and turns to walk away.

"You sure you want to leave, Mona?" I say, beckoning her to stay.

Mona stops and turns to face me. She gives me a sympathetic look and shakes her head.

"You don't care that your husband fucked my wife?"

Mona's eyes widen, and Brock spins around to face her. He grabs her hand for her to stay. Mona looks confused. She looks at me for answers when she should be looking at Brock.

"That's not true," Brock says to Mona first and then me.

Mona nods at Brock, then looks at me like I should believe him.

"Bobby…" he calmly says to me. He releases Mona's hand and cautiously walks toward me. "I love you," he says, using his words like a magic elixir. "I've disrespected you in ways that you should never forgive, but I didn't fuck her. I swear I didn't."

Mona sighs hard, and Brock turns to her, giving her sympathetic eyes. Then he looks back at me.

"Saying sorry ain't enough. It's laughable. So, I won't say it, but I love you, man. I love you," he says again with emphasis. "Please forgive me."

"What am I forgiving you for?"

"For being selfish, for being weak, and for being inappropriate with Lera."

I don't know what the fuck he's admitting to, but forgiveness ain't an option. He crossed the line. All of this shit is just further confirmation I'm done with it all.

"Fuck you, man," I say, then dig deep in my pocket and pull out the DNA test, throwing it at him. "I'm out of here, and I ain't coming back."

Brock's shoulders drop, and he lowers his head. He nods at me, giving me the okay to leave.

26
Mona Badd

"**I**'M SORRY, MONA," Brock says and sits down on the bed beside me. He grabs my hand, kissing it before gently placing it in his lap. He stares at me, ready to react to whatever emotion I'm going to give him. I look up at him, and he looks so broken. His spirit looks like it has been shattered. I need Brock to be strong now more than ever because of all the work we have to do, but I don't have the energy to build him back up. When he told me about Goldie and his son, I was upset, but I took part in that blame being that she was a breeder, and I allowed that shit. But, when he told me about Lera, I was crushed. I still am, but now ain't the time to be weak. We all have big pills to swallow if we want to move past this and come out stronger.

I remove my hand from his. I need a minute to reprocess everything. Brock told me that he came close, but he claims he didn't sleep with Lera. Now I wonder how truthful he was being. Why would Bobby say he did? When he gave me a play-by-play of everything that happened, it didn't matter to me if he stuck his dick in her or not. It all hurts the same. He tried to get me to understand, and for a while, I hurt my head trying, and then I just stopped. I either could forgive him or walk away, and I chose to forgive my husband. I love Brock like I love my own skin.

For a moment, I thought I would never see Brock again. Infidelity seems trivial when faced with life or death. Besides, I told him about Kong and how I betrayed him, hoping to take back the Ranch. I told him about all the mistakes I made that led us to this point. That was a hard pill for him to swallow, too. But at the end of the day, our love conquered all, and we forgave each other. The shit still stings, though.

I take a deep breath but swallow the air as opposed to exhaling. I then turn to face Brock and nod.

"I know," I say and give him a half-smile. "You think he's really going to leave?" I ask him, referring to Bobby.

Brock sighs and leans over, placing his weight on his knees.

"Yes," he says remorsefully. "I ain't gonna try to stop him or hold him back. When he's ready to talk and forgive me, I'll be here." Brock stands to his feet and stretches. "I'm so blessed that I didn't lose you," Brock confesses. "Without you, I wouldn't be standing right now. You are my strength, Mona. My backbone. You always have been." He places his hand under my chin and raises my face towards his. "I promise, from here on out, I will never do anything to hurt you. I won't put you in harm's way, and the truth is all I'm going to give you. Nothing less," he says and plants a kiss on my lips.

My insides start to stir. My pot of emotion fills with lust, and relief starts to boil before I feel the tingling. I look up at Brock and can tell by the look he's giving me that he feels it, too.

"I don't know what I would do without you," I whisper to him as he lowers me onto the bed.

"You'll be strong," he says and kisses me on my neck.

He places his hand in between my thighs and slowly rubs upward.

"You'll keep being the glue that holds this place together."

He moves up my body and unbuttons my top before burying his nose in my cleavage. He pulls my breast from my bra and licks around my nipple while toying with my clit with his thumb. I spread my legs, making as much room for him as I can. I'm so eager to feel him inside of me that my head knocks against the headboard.

"Be careful," he whispers to me and gently pulls my panties to the side.

He pushes himself inside of me slowly, and I feel every place his thick head bumps against my insides. My toes curl with ecstasy, and I dig my nails into the bed while Brock gives me long, gentle strokes. It feels so good that I melt all over. My wetness drips down my legs and forms a messy puddle underneath us.

"You're my everything," he whispers in my ear.

His words have the same effect on me as his penis. They penetrate me deeply, creating warm moisture that lights up my body like a flame. I wrap my arms around his neck and pull him in closer to me. I never want him to stop touching me. It has been years since we made love. Slow. Sensual. Tender. Before, all we had time to do was fuck. It was all our egos allowed, but now, everything has changed.

Brock kisses me as he pushes himself deeper inside of me. I cherish every moment of his breathing, every moment of him filling up my swollen insides, and his heavy breathing on my neck. I squeeze him from the inside out, and when he can't take it anymore, he releases inside of me. The surge that comes out of him sprays like a hose. Brock's body shudders before he collapses on top of me, still feeling the ecstasy and savoring every moment of me.

He is careful when he rolls over beside me. "You okay?" he asks, lifting his head and looking in my direction.

"Yes, and thank you," I reply, and he smiles. "I needed that," I reveal. "Now that you've revved up the engine, I hope you plan on pressing the gas some more tonight," I say, hinting that I need more.

"I plan to press the gas every night," he responds, rubbing in between my legs.

Brock rolls from his side to his back and stares up at the ceiling. He blows out air.

"What are you thinking about now?" I ask.

"Too much shit," he says and sniffs. "I have to go to the safe and start the count. I want to make sure it's accurate. It's gonna cost to get things back up and running as quickly as we want," Brock states through a yawn.

My heart starts racing as I think about what Vinchi revealed to me. With everything that has happened since the meeting, I haven't had a chance to figure out how I can clear Vinchi. I'm tired of the lies, though. Lies have hurt us enough.

Brock wipes his face, then pushes his lips in his mouth. He's thinking too much, and now I'm about to add to his plate.

"Maybe we can train Vinchi to take Bobby's place," Brock suggests. "He can bring in a whole new clientele. A younger crowd can't hurt. These young boys out here making more money than the older hustlers. I got to replace Bobby immediately if we're gonna do this right. You think Vinchi can handle that?"

I swallow hard and nod my head, but I don't make eye contact with him.

"What's on your mind? You have something else in mind for Vinchi?" Brock leans up, planting his elbow on the bed and holding up his head with his hand. He looks at me, and I sigh hard. "Talk to me, baby. We're open books, right?" Brock reminds me.

"You ain't gonna like what I got to say, Mr. Badd."

I look at him and pause. I can see his whole mood change but only for a moment. He rolls out of bed and stands over me with his arms folded. He's arming himself with enough emotional strength to handle what I'm about to say to him. I lean up, pushing my back against the headboard.

"The safe is empty," I blurt out.

Brock is so used to bad news at this point that he doesn't even flinch. I'm shocked. I wait for him to react before I tell him the rest. He looks at me and nods for me to explain.

"Vinchi," I say through a sigh.

Brock unfolds his arms and closes his eyes to blink but doesn't reopen them. He turns his back to me for a split second and then spins back around to face me. Disappointment floods his face. He rubs the back of his neck and paces in circles.

"What he do?" he asks me, but really, he's talking to himself. "He took the money? He made a deal with Kong? He knows where that nigga is?"

Paranoia burns through Brock like fire.

"No," I say, answering all his questions. "It's not what you think. He thought he was doing the right thing to save me, to save this place. He gave the code to Nicchi."

"What the fuck he do that for?" Brock waves his hands in the air. "I taught him better than that."

"It made sense to him. He had Kong locked in there for a while, right before you came, but they escaped during all the chaos."

"Shit!" Brock says and kicks the air.

He stops and takes deep breaths to calm himself down.

"He had that nigga in the safe? Actually inside?" Brock says like it was the dumbest thing he ever said.

"He didn't know any better," I reply, defending Vinchi.

"He ain't as ready as I thought," Brock expresses.

"That's not fair, Brock. We all did some fucked-up shit to survive."

Brock looks at me and bites down on his bottom lip to keep from responding to what I said. He is beyond pissed, but he is handling it well. He tightens his fist and takes another deep breath.

"You're right," he forces himself to say. "He was only trying to help."

I'm shocked at the man Brock is becoming. All of this chaos has gifted him with forgiveness and understanding. Now I know for sure we're gonna come out of this on top. Brock is officially the perfect man—strong, wise, and forgiving.

"When you find Kong, you'll find the money."

"Money ain't shit," Brock reminds himself. "Not compared to you," he adds and walks towards me. He leans down and kisses me. "Vinchi saved your life. I don't give a fuck how he did it."

"He was afraid to tell you," I reveal.

"Well, that's got to change. My son has to be able to talk to me. I don't want him to fear me like I feared my father. You can't learn shit when you're in a constant state of fear and judgement. You can't think for yourself. All these years, I've been thinking like my father. It's time I start using *my* mind. Make my own decisions."

"I agree, baby." I smile at my husband in full admiration.

"We will make the money back. I ain't worried about it," Brock says and lets out a breath of relief. "I already got the streets looking for that nigga. His big ass can't hide for long. I got a bounty on his head the size of Texas. Somebody's gonna find him."

"What about Nicchi?"

"We're gonna find your sister, too. She was only acting out of fear, but she helped save you, and she's gonna be compensated for it." Brock grabs both of my hands. "We're gonna get over this. I promise."

He leans down and plants another kiss on my forehead.

"Ready for me to press on that gas again?" He gives me a lustful smile, and I lean back.

27

Taffy Badd

I HOLD MY BREATH as the doctor moves the ultrasound wand over my stomach area. I'm no stranger to losing babies. After all this stress, why would this child choose to live?

Brip is sitting next to me, watching the doctors every move. I wish it was our regular doctor, but he refuses to come to the Ranch after he heard about everything that went down. I can't blame him. I was surprised when I woke up this morning and learned Brip had planned this for me. Taking the lead to do things like this isn't like him. With everything that has happened, Brip is not the same anymore. Then again, none of us are.

My eyes switch from the ultrasound screen back to the doctor's face. With his eyes glued to the screen, he squints his eyes and lowers his brows.

What does he see? What does he not see?

"Ah," he says like he forgot something, then leans forward to push a button on the machine. That's when we hear the heartbeat, and I breathe. He's alive. Or she.

"What's that noise?" Brip says, naïve.

I open my mouth to speak, but the doctor beats me to the punch.

"That's the sound of a healthy heartbeat," he says and winks at me.

I can't help but smile. However, before my lips curve, a tear escapes my eye. *This is really happening. I'm really going to be a mother. Finally.*

Brip leans in to kiss me but stops and moves back, giving me my space. He looks like he wants to hug me, celebrate with me, but he's not sure if it's appropriate. So, instead, he nods his head at me and smiles. He's been distant with me ever since the day in the woods. It's almost like we are two strangers getting to know each other again. I regret what I said to him, but I'm not sure I don't mean it. I don't know if it's my maternal instinct or all the stress this year, but sometimes I want to walk away from this place and never look back. I know that's impossible, though. I'm in this thing for life regardless of what happens between Brip and me.

"Are you sure? How do we know that he…" I stop myself. "…or she is really okay? Does everything look normal?"

"Mrs. Badd, your baby is fine. I'm still going to run some tests, but I'm confident you'll have a healthy baby girl," the doctor reveals.

"Girl?" Brip and I say in unison.

The doctor looks at us and nods.

Brip looks at me with his eyes misting with tears. He's waiting for permission to be happy about this. He's waiting for me to give him the okay to be a part of it all. I hold out my hand, and Brip grabs it and kisses it three times.

"A girl?" he repeats. "I can't believe this. We don't have any girls. Mamma is going to be…" He stops himself and looks away, clearing his throat. "My mother would be so happy."

Brip wipes his eyes before any tears fall. Then he takes a deep breath and exhales through a smile.

"A girl," he mumbles under his breath. "A baby girl," he says again, still in shock.

"I'm going to give you two some privacy. I'll be back in a few to take some bloodwork?"

"What kind of bloodwork?" Brip snaps.

I know where the anger is coming from. He still doesn't know. *We* still don't know if this is his baby or not. Brip doesn't want to think about it. He wants to push it far back in his mind, but we have to discuss it at some point. We have to know the truth.

"Bloodwork is an extra precaution, Mr. Badd. It's normal at this stage in the pregnancy. In a few months, you both are going to have a healthy baby. But I want to be sure to dot all my i's and cross all my t's."

Brip sniffs and nods with pride. He avoids eye contact with me, looking at the blank ultrasound screen.

"Thanks, doctor," I say.

He nods at me and rushes out the door. Brip and I sit in silence for a while. We are both ignoring the obvious.

"I'm sorry, Taffy," Brip says, finally breaking the silence.

"For what?" I pretend not to know what he's upset about.

"I'm tripping. All this talk about blood tests and secrets just got me on edge," he admits, referring to the DNA test Brock made him take early this morning. "It's a lot, but I want to be here for you and the baby," he says sincerely. "If you let me."

I rub my stomach and lean up. Brip rushes to my side to assist me. Placing his hand on my back, he guides me up. His touch is gentle but full of hesitance. It breaks my heart to see us here. Afraid to touch each other. Afraid to smile together and have something to be hopeful for.

"All this time, and I didn't even notice how far along you are." Brip moves his hand towards my belly but stops midway. "Can I?" he asks like he's talking to a stranger.

I grab his hand and place it on top of my swollen stomach. His touch comforts me. I lean my head back in the hospital bed and cherish this moment before it passes.

"In three months, she's gonna be here. That's gonna change everything."

"I know," I agree and then ask, "What about us?"

Brip darts his eyes at me, surprised by my question.

"You know where I stand, Taffy," he says and rubs circles around my swollen belly. "I'm here for you regardless," he hints. "I love you like no other. So much has happened, but I don't want it to be the end of us. Things are going to change with me. No more headbanging and busting bullets in the streets. It's time for me to settle down and be there for my family—for both of you if you allow me."

As Brip continues to rub my stomach, I place my hand on top of his and smile at him. Brip lives for what he does, but the fact that he would give it all up for me and the baby, who might not even be his, means a lot. It says a lot. Maybe there is hope for us after all.

"What are you going to do?"

"I haven't talked to Brock yet, but he got to give me a new position. I want in on the operations side, and I need a salary increase and more days off to spend with you and the baby. Vacations three times a year. Long weekends. I want our baby to see the world. That's all that matters to me at this point. Nothing else."

"What if…" My voice cracks, and he knows what's coming next.

I clear my throat and take a deep breath. Brip moves his hand from my belly and fixes his eyes on me, waiting on me to say the words.

"What if she's not yours?"

"I don't want to hear you say that again," Brip says in the most serious tone I've ever heard him use. "She's mine, and that's final. I've already decided that, and I don't need no DNA test to prove it. Understood?"

I nod, but I know nothing is that simple. Plus, I want to know. The truth is the truth. Everything will mean more to me if we know the truth.

"I want you to take a DNA test."

"Why?" Brip takes a step back. "I just told you it doesn't matter."

"You're always going to wonder. You'll know and I'll know that you mean all these great things you are saying if we get the test."

Brip turns his back and sighs.

"Secrets have almost destroyed this family. No more secrets, Brip. The truth is the main part of forgiveness. I don't want to pretend. If we are moving forward with our lives together, a lot has to change on my end, too."

"Like what?"

"I have to be more than just your wife. I was more than that when I met you. I had dreams. Goals, Brip. I can't just sit around wearing a 'B' necklace, waiting for you to come home. That's not me anymore. I have more to offer you than that, and I don't want our little girl to grow up thinking all she has to offer a man is her hand in marriage and a pretty face."

"No one's going to objectify my daughter," Brip vows.

I smile at the thought that our child will have a protective man like him as her father, but she needs more than protecting.

"Well, don't do it to me, because she's going to have two eyes that see everything, especially us."

Brip drops his head. "I never looked at it like that before. I just thought I was being a good husband by protecting you and giving you the world. I didn't want you to have to work or worry about anything, but you're right. She deserves more than I gave you. You deserve more, too, Taffy." Brip walks back over to my bedside and places his hand on my belly again. He sighs and smiles. "Okay. Whatever you want. Whatever you need, I got you, Taffy. If you want that shop you've always been talking about, I got you. I'll do anything for the both of you, including taking that test. I just want my family."

"Well, you got us, baby," I say, then lean over and kiss him.

I WALK OUT of our mansion and head to the casino. Brip and I have been staying in the presidential suite because I can't stay in our house— not after everything that went down. The floor is stained with blood, and they haven't even removed the bodies that Brip has in the freezer.

After my doctor's appointment, I decided to put back on my 'B' necklace. It feels different than what I remember. Before, it felt heavy, but now, I feel like I can handle the weight. It feels new. I like the direction Brip and I are moving in. He even agreed to have my mother flown to the Ranch once everything settles down. I need my mother now more than ever.

Clutching my necklace, I cross the street. The cleanup crew is moving a lot faster than we all expected. They have already repaved half the roads, and the landscapers are planting new flowers and shrubs. When I look down at the blooming flowers, I smile, hopeful that we all will be okay.

"Scrappy," I hear Tony call from behind me.

I turn around, and he is running towards me like a quarterback.

I'm happy he bonded enough with Brock that he wants to keep him on the Ranch. Brock is going to pay him a full salary. The other day, he officially apologized to me about Keno and Tony. I was shocked. It was nice to have his apology, but I knew what dirty business my brothers were in.

I'm thankful Tony is still here. Brock is dedicated to getting him help; he believes he can get the old Tony back. He has already started him on memory sessions. Brock flew in the best neuroscientist in the country to work with Tony. I'm not sure my brother will ever be back to the way he was, and at this point, it doesn't matter to me. Yes, his mind changed, but his love for me hasn't changed a bit. That's all that matters. Tony's love is what makes him great to me, not his mind.

"You okay?"

"I think I'm okay," he responds, giving me a confused look.

"What's wrong, Tony?"

"I don't know. I think Lera is mad."

"When did you see Lera?" I ask.

"I don't know," Tony responds and looks behind him. "Are you okay?" He looks me over, inspecting me for damages.

I smile and place my hand on his arm.

"I'm fine, Tony. We both are going to be fine. It's all over now. You saved me," I tell him.

"I did," he responds proudly. "Yes, I did. He said to look out for Scrappy. Always look out for Scrappy." Tony blinks hard.

"Who are you talking about, Tony?"

"Keno." He pushed the word out of his mouth like it hurt to say his name.

"Keno would be very proud of you," I say. "Brock is going to help you remember more things."

Tony shakes his head. "I don't want to remember more things. I only want to remember enough." That's the wisest thing I've ever heard Tony say. "I wish I could remember why Lera is mad. She's real mad."

"Lera is going to be okay."

"Yeah, she should stay, too," Tony says. "But she doesn't want to remember either."

"Tony, did Lera tell you she was leaving?"

I haven't seen Lera since we were lost in the woods. I get sad when I think about her. I remember how in love she was with Bobby, how hopeful she was for their future. Now she's like a different person. She needs help, but until she sees that for herself, she's going to continue to suffer. I don't know what's next for her. Bobby has Blake and Tara. I have Brip. Dalla has Billy, and Mona has Brock. What does Lera have? She doesn't even have her sanity.

"Yes, 'cause she wants him dead," Tony says and then turns around, distracted by all the work going on. He fixes his eyes on the asphalt truck.

"Tony?" I fight for his attention, but he is already gone. "Tony!" I shake him.

When he turns back around towards me, he has already forgotten what he was talking about.

"Huh?" he says and scratches the back of his head.

"Who does Lera want dead?"

Tony blinks three times and closes his eyes tight on the fourth, trying to remember. Seconds later, he reopens them and smiles at me.

"I saved you," he says, only remembering what he wants to recall.

"That's right." I smile back at my brother. "Let's go get you something to eat," I tell him, and Tony follows behind me like a guard dog.

28

Billy Badd

I LOOK AT DALLA and pray she had nothing to do with any of this. Everything seems to be falling into place. I'm meeting with Brock today to discuss the task force we are putting together to find Mamma, and my family is finally safe. After all the family has been through, there's been an unspoken agreement to forgive Dalla for all the fucked-up shit she has done, but if she had something to do with Lera taking Ace and leaving the Ranch, I'm not so sure I'll be able to forgive her. The sirens went off this morning—a sound we hoped never to hear again. Then the phone rang, and Brock broke the news. Ace is gone, and so is Lera.

Dalla is humming in BJ's room and packing a small bag of his items. He doesn't have much, just a few things. She's wearing a long white dress that accentuates her hourglass figure. She looks beach-ready. Her skin is already glowing like it's been kissed by the sun. She looks so beautiful. It's been a while since I've seen her all dressed up and calm. Years even. Her sweet rose fragrant perfume lingers in the air.

Our passports came in the other day, and I got a nice place for us in Spain. If all goes well, we'll be leaving the Ranch by the end of the week. Brock is more understanding than ever. He agreed to finance our move, and he doesn't have a problem with me working offsite as long as I physically check in once a month. He even unfroze my account. Dalla and I are good to go, but I have to know that I can trust her first.

When Dalla sees me lurking in the doorway, she jumps, dropping one of BJ's toys, and then laughs. She's been on cloud nine all day.

"You scared me," she says while still smiling, then picks up BJ's toy and playfully throws it at me.

I catch it with one hand. When she notices I'm not smiling, she immediately breaks eye contact with me and spins back around to continue collecting BJ's things and humming. This time, her humming isn't so peaceful. It's more forced. It's a distraction. Seeing how she is reacting already answers my question. She did it. Somehow, she got Lera to escape with Ace. How could she be so fucking selfish?

"Dalla." I call her name, but she doesn't turn to face me. She keeps humming and folding small clothes. "Dalla," I say again, more forceful, and reluctantly, she turns around.

Guilt is written all over her face. She doesn't even try to hide it. It's funny how our connection is so strong we can almost read each other's minds. I just wish I caught this move before it happened.

"Where are they?" I ask, not wasting time.

Dalla continues to play dumb. She lowers her brow and squints her eyes like she doesn't understand my question, but the truth is hidden in plain sight. Guilt floods her eyes, and her hands are jittery. She drops one of BJ's socks, and when she bends down to reach for it, she clumsily hits her forehead on the chest. She stands upright, grabbing her head. She looks in the mirror, rubbing away the pain and inspecting herself for damages. Then she bites down on her bottom lip and turns back around like I didn't ask her a question.

"Aye, I asked you a question." She can hear the intolerance building up in my voice. "You're on some real disrespectful shit right now," I add.

On that note, she turns and faces me, giving me a sorrowful look. But I don't pity her. If she got Lera to do this shit, it's real fucked up, and if it gets out, the peace we're trying to rebuild as a family will be broken. They won't be able to move past this. Neither will I.

Dalla knows Ace is the key component in aiding us to find our mother. He knows the whole story. Without him, finding her will take years as opposed to months or even days. She knows how I feel about my mother. How could she take this from me? How could she take this from my brothers? It wasn't her decision to make, but Dalla only sees herself. I'm starting to see that now.

And Lera has been through enough. Now, she's on the run with the sociopathic serial killer who raped her. Dalla knows Lera isn't strong enough to handle Ace. When Bobby finds out this was Dalla's plan, I won't be able to defend her. Yet, here she is packing clothes and humming like she ain't got a care in the world. I never knew how damaged Dalla was until now.

"Wh-what?" As Dalla shakes her head, a curl escapes its pin and falls over her eye. She sweeps the loose hair from her face. *How can someone so beautiful be so vicious?*

"I know you had something to do with it."

"To do with what, Billy?" she screams back, annoyed.

She turns to me with both hands on her hip and her neck rolling.

"I've been here packing. That's all." She throws her hands in the air.

"Lera is gone, and so is Ace," I say to her, but she only shrugs her shoulders. "You hear what I said?" I snatch a piece of clothing out of her hand. "This shit is serious, Dalla!"

I grab her arm and shake her. When I look in her eyes, I see she is stunned by my anger. I let her go and back up. Dalla rubs her arm. I didn't mean to hurt her.

"He can kill her. You know that?"

"How do you know she won't kill him?" Dalla argues back. "He deserves to die, and Lera deserves to be the one who does it. She's not as weak as you all think, you know."

"Do you hear yourself!" I scream, causing her to jump. "Ace is dangerous. You know that more than any of us. Lera is weak. She's been through so much, and you get her to do your dirty work. What type of fucked-up pers—" I stop myself.

Dalla looks at me with wide eyes, shocked by the insult I almost gave her. I take a deep breath and clasp my hands together, calming myself down.

"Ace knows where my mother is. He's pivotal to this investigation."

"Even if he does know, he's not going to tell you," Dalla replies, dismissing me. "He's fucked your brain enough. Aren't you tired?"

"You don't get to decide these things. You don't decide how valuable Ace is to us. You don't decide who lives and who dies just because you think they're in your way."

Dalla laughs sarcastically under her breath.

"Isn't that what your family does? Kill those in their way. You're actually passing judgement on me?" Dalla pulls in air through her teeth and rolls her eyes at me.

"We got people out looking for both of them now. If Ace ends up dead, you'll be taking that trip to Spain alone. I know you don't give a fuck about anybody but yourself, but I thought you would care enough about me to support me in finding my mother. But you've already decided that my mother's whereabouts aren't important to you, and I can't roll with you like that."

Dalla's jaw drops. She finally stops folding clothes. Tears fill her eyes, but I don't wait to watch them fall. I'm too pissed.

"I love you, Billy. You know that!"

I turn to look at her, but I have no words. I just shake my head. I'm beyond disappointed. At least she could pretend to give a fuck.

"I'll make sure you get your passport."

"Billy!" she yells. I hear her from the hallway. "Billy, please don't do this," she begs through a sob.

I can hear her feet pounding against the hallway floor, but I'm already at the bottom step.

"I'm sorry. I'm sorry!"

She finally apologizes, but it's too late. I can't forgive her for this.

"WE GOT TO find him before it's too late," Brock says with both his hands resting on the desk. "He could know where she is, where they both are." He sighs and takes a seat. "All I needed was a few days with him in my dungeon, and that nigga would've been singing like a fucking canary."

"I know," I say and pull out the chair in front of his desk to take a seat. "But until then, we got to work with what we have. I don't want this to slow us down."

"How, if she doesn't want to be found?" Brock asks, his voice hesitant.

I shake my head, disagreeing.

"Naw, that's not the case," I say like I'm sure. "She may be afraid. She doesn't know Daddy is dead. She probably thinks she can't come back."

Brock looks at me and nods.

"Tell me more about this Stein guy," I say.

"I don't know much. That nigga probably lives in the heart of the Bermuda Triangle. Finding him ain't gonna be easy, but he knows more, too. I can hear it in his voice."

"And he won't take your calls?"

Brock shakes his head no.

"I'm gonna find him," I tell Brock.

We sit in silence for a while. Brock stares at me, and I try to guess what he's thinking. He wants to say something.

"All those years, we were fighting over nothing," Brock confesses. "We could have been working together. I'm sure the clues were there, but anger and pride blinded us. I'm done with all that, brother. I want to be there for you. I need you, man." he says while leaning in closer to the table.

I've never seen Brock so sentimental. He's the type that doesn't apologize because his god complex makes him feel he does no wrong. But, right now, he's being genuine. I can feel it.

"I love you, man, and I'm sorry," he adds.

"I love you, too, brother. All that shit that happened before is water under the bridge. We're moving forward. This time next year, we could be sitting with Mamma."

Brock lowers his head. His eyes shift from mine to the stack of papers on his desk. He stares down at them idly, then forces himself to raise his chin in my direction. He fixes his eyes back on me; his gaze is steady. He takes a deep breath but swallows the air. He pushes back in his seat and opens his mouth, but nothing comes out.

"I–" He hesitates.

I lean in closer to him, giving him a supportive nod. Opening up and being vulnerable isn't something Brock is used to doing, so I know this is tough for him.

"I have to tell you something," Brock says, struggling with his words.

I've never seen him so nervous, so anxious.

"Just say it, man." I nod at him. "It's okay."

"I-I thought that I did it."

I give Brock a confused stare, but he looks away from me. I already know where he's going with this. I'm not sure I want to hear him say it, but I have to let him get it off his chest.

"I thought I killed her that night," he blurts out, and his head drops so low I thought it was going to fall off his neck.

I feel like I've been stabbed in the chest. *Is he saying what I think he's saying? Did he try to kill Mamma? Naw, he's confused.* I want to get up and walk away. Leave him right where he is sitting, but I can't move. Something has me glued to this chair. I have to let him finish.

"She tried to tell me the truth about her and Carlo Lucky that night, but she was nervous and anxious. She only got out that one part—the part that made me feel like I had no other options. She told me that I wasn't her child, and I got up and ran. I had to fix it. I couldn't let our father know. He would have exiled me. All I ever wanted was to be like him, and he was a rotten son of a bitch."

Brock lets the words escape from his tongue like they had been trapped there for years.

"I came back that night. I was so fucking drunk," he admits.

It all makes sense to me. Brock stopped drinking the night we thought Mamma died.

"And I—"

"Stop," I say, interrupting him. I can't bear to hear anymore.

I look away from Brock. I can't look at his face. My heart races. A combination of anger and forgiveness stir inside of me. When I look up, tears are falling from Brock's eyes. I know my brother so well that I understand why he made the decision he made, but it doesn't make it less fucked up. If Mamma hadn't decided to fake her death, she would really be dead—murdered by her son. And for what? For him to sit in the very chair that he is in now. I don't get it. I never will.

"When we do find her..." His voice cracks. "...how do I tell her that I killed her? I don't deserve to see her. I don't deserve to be in her presence. What type of man does what I did? Who kills their flesh and blood? The woman who gave them life. I'm a monster, man. And, in time, I'm going to pay for what I did."

I take a deep breath, trying to contain my emotions. I want to knock Brock's ass out. At the same time, I want to hug him. I don't know which I want to do the most; both my emotions level out. The hate I feel for my brother is just as strong as the love I feel for him.

"It didn't happen, Brock. You didn't kill her."

"But I thought I did. That makes it real regardless if she's alive or not."

"I didn't kill Dad," I admit, and his eyes dart up at me, blinking away tears.

"I know she did it," Brock reveals, referring to Dalla. "I have a feeling your wife has something to do with Ace's disappearance, too, but I don't care anymore." Brock shrugs. "I just want us to start over.

I don't only want to rebuild this Ranch; I want to rebuild the relationships between us brothers. These days, family is more important than anything," Brock gives me a genuine look, tears still staining his cheeks. "I love y'all." Brock fights back his tears. "Bobby…" he says through a sigh. "Bobby may not be around for a while, and that's all on me," he confesses, then lowers his head.

My mind instantly runs on the suspicious surrounding him and Lera's relationship. Is there any truth in it? It showed in Lera's behavior, but I can't imagine Brock crossing that line. Then again, he did try to kill our mother. So, what's it to him to fuck Bobby's wife? It's at the tip of my tongue to probe him for more, but I leave it alone. Swallowing my emotions and curiosity, I nod my head. Brock is right. It's time for us to forgive and start fresh. We have more important things to look forward to. An actual bright future. The return of a queen. Mamma Badd. Or should I say, Mamma Lucky.

"And that's just what we're gonna do. When Mamma returns, she's going to be proud of us. She's going to be proud of you," I add.

Brock shakes his head, disagreeing with me. He feels like he doesn't deserve forgiveness, and he's right. But I have to forgive him. We all do.

He sniffs and wipes his face before straightening his posture.

"I'm gonna get you connected with Stein," Brock says, getting back to business. He stuffs papers in a folder before handing it to me. "This is all I have on him," he states through a sigh. "Ace may be MIA for now, but I'm gonna make sure we find him alive. Let me handle finding him and Lera. In the meantime, I got his mother and sister at the other Ranch. You may want to question them before you head out," he says with a half-smile, giving me his approval to leave and live happily ever after with my wife, who betrayed us all in her own way. The wife who I also love unconditionally. The wife who I understand like no other.

"I know if anybody can find her, it's you," Brock adds, giving me a confident look. "Bring her home, man."

"I promise I will."

29

Brock Badd

THE DNA TEST results are back quicker than I expected. I stare down at the torn envelope and wonder if I made a mistake. *Did we need this?* So much has gone down already. We're divided enough with Bobby gone; that's all on me. I'm trying my best to make things right, but I keep getting this unsettling feeling in my soul. Something ain't right, and this test confirms it. Still, there's more.

I woke up this morning with my chest tight and gasping for air. I've been feeling this tightening for two days now. Mona thinks it's a form of PTSD. She thinks I'm not sleeping because I feel like Kong or someone else will take over the Ranch again, but I ain't worried about that. The way I gunned down the invaders, no one is dumb enough to try us like that again. It will be like suicide. There is something else I'm worried about, though. I just don't know what it is yet. It's a weird feeling that comes and goes.

I take a deep breath and squeeze my fist tight until the pacing of my heart slows down. I wipe the sweat from my brow and massage the burning sensation out of the center of my chest. It almost feels like someone stabbed me. Maybe it's symbolic. This sharp pain could symbolize all the pain I've caused my family. Bobby. Mona. Lera. Billy. I hurt them all. I should have been more sympathetic to Lera. I know how fragile she is, but I barked at her and not only caused her to run but caused her to seek revenge. I pray she's okay. I've been trying to call Bobby all morning to let him know what's going on. He ain't taking my calls, though. I can't blame him, but I'm gonna keep calling him until he answers. He needs to know what's going on with his wife. We're supposed to be cleaning up the mess, not making more. But some dirt we'll never be able to clean.

Mona suggested that I write Bobby a letter since he won't hear me out. That shit sounded corny as hell to me until I picked up the pen and started writing. I pulled thoughts from my mind that I never knew existed until I wrote them on paper. When I finished, I felt purged. Empty. Healed even. But I won't fully feel at peace until Bobby reads them and finds understanding and, hopefully, forgiveness. I really fucked up.

"You're up early, Mr. Badd," I hear Mona say from behind me.

Turning around, I see my beautiful wife wearing a red satin robe. She gives me a flirtatious look. Lately, through all this chaos and cleaning up, Mona and I have found time to have what feels like a second honeymoon. Or should I say a first considering I never took her anywhere after we got married. We said "I do" and went straight to work building our legacy. We redefined romance. To us, romance was staying up all night planning our next move. We shared in the bliss of signing contracts, shaking hands, and depositing checks. Mona never complained. She didn't care about trivial things like flowers and chocolates. Deals and real estate turned her on. New opportunities are what got her pussy wet. Our success was our foreplay. But, now, I'm ready to slow down and enjoy her more. I'm ready to give her the flowers and chocolates. Vacations and lovemaking versus fucking. I'm prepared to show my wife just how much I appreciate her.

Mona walks behind me and places two delicate hands on my shoulders, massaging out the knots.

"You're thinking too hard again, Mr. Badd."

I lean into her. Mona knows just the right spot to touch. I don't have to coach her or guide her hands. She just knows. I lower my head and allow her to dig deeper into the tension of my shoulders. *What did*

I do to deserve a woman like this? No woman in the world can take care of me like Mona Badd. No one understands me better. I grab her hand and pull her around my desk so that she is facing me. I look up at her and smile before kissing her hands.

"The test results are back," I say, and her body tenses up.

"That soon?" she asks, spotting the open envelope on my desk.

I pick it up and look down at it like I can see through the paper. I already know the results, though. This is going to be a lot for us all to deal with. Luckily for me, I got some blood from Ace before Lera took him, and I didn't need a syringe and needle to get it if you know what I mean. Brip did a number on him, putting a bullet in Ace's pelvis, but his injuries were minor. I need Ace alive, so I sent him to the clinic. They were able to remove the bullet and stitch him back up. Now that the results are back, I see a lot of the shit Ace was saying is true, but some of it was bullshit. I got to find him. I need the truth. We all do.

"I was surprised by how quickly they came back, too, but it's better to rip the Band-Aid off fast instead of slowly."

I hand Mona the envelope, and she pulls it out of my hand like it's heavy. She gives me a reluctant look before pulling out the carbon copies. When she looks down at the results, the papers drop to the floor. She gasps and covers her mouth, hiding her shock. She then takes a step back and shakes her head sorrowfully.

"Are we sure this is accurate? Somebody could be fucking with us."

She tries to feed me an excuse, but I ain't got a taste for bullshit. The truth is the truth.

I lean down and pick up the paper that's resting at her feet. I look down at the results one more time to be sure I saw them right. Then I look up at Mona and nod my head.

"This ain't what my eyes wanted to see either, but it's the truth, and we need to deal with it to move on."

I fold up the results and place them in the envelope before dropping it on my desk. I hear the paper crashing onto my wood desk like it's made of metal. Mona walks in circles with both hands on her head. Her bandages are gone. She's fully recovered, but now, she has this shit to heal from. She stops pacing and turns to face me. She watches me in silence, mouthing something I can't understand under her breath. Her hands are trembling. So is her bottom lip. She covers her mouth like she's blocking a yawn, but she's actually holding back a scream.

"Brock," she says, and I look at her.

She doesn't say anything else. At least not for a while. She shakes her head in opposition.

"Don't. Don't do this." She pushes the words out of her mouth in a desperate plea. "We don't need this, Brock. None of us do," she begs me with her eyes. "We can fix this shit. We can tell them anything. They won't dispute it," Mona whispers loudly, then looks over her shoulder to make sure we're alone.

I can't say I didn't have the same thought as Mona. I can make all this shit go away if I want to. I can control the narrative like I've done in the past, but I ain't on that fuck-nigga shit no more. I'm a new man. I can feel the person I'm becoming brewing in my soul every day, and I like him. I don't know him yet, but he deserves a chance. Besides, this is our life I'm fucking with, and I don't have the right to make my brothers' choices anymore. And I damn sure can't hide something like this from them. So, I'm going to call an emergency meeting and share the results.

"No," I say, pushing back in my chair and standing to my feet.

"Brock, please," Mona begs, giving me her final plea.

"From here on out, we're gonna do the right thing. It ain't all about us no more, baby."

"We got to look at the bigger picture, Mr. Badd."

"I have," I respond quickly. "I looked at the bigger picture, and all I see is them. My family. My brothers. Us."

I reach out my hand for Mona to grab. She looks down at it like I'm holding a noose to hang us all, but she still grabs my hand. She's reluctant, but she still grabs it.

"You got my back, baby?" I ask her.

"Always," Mona says, her voice trembling.

30

Dalla Badd

BJ is sleeping in my arms, his tiny head resting on my shoulder. With all the noise going on outside, he's still sleeping solid. I tap on the door to Taffy and Brip's suite at the casino. I need a break. I need to collect my thoughts and figure out how I can get my husband back. The look he gave me burned a hole right through my soul. He doesn't trust me; he's not coming with us. I can't let this happen, but I don't know how to fix it.

Taffy opens the door and takes a step back when she sees me, grabbing her swollen belly like she's protecting her unborn child from a monster. Is that how they see me? Is that how Billy sees me? I force a smile. When I see her glowing skin and cute round belly, it's hard not to smile. My eyes lead to her 'B' necklace; it's sparkling. I'm happy for her and Brip. Taffy seems more relaxed now, more confident—at least before I knocked on her door unannounced.

"What do you want?"

"I need a favor," I say, and she rolls her eyes like my request is laughable.

My heart sinks a bit, but I take a deep breath and don't allow myself to get offended.

"Is that what Lera did for you? A favor?" Taffy says and shakes her head at me like I'm despicable.

Ashamed, I lower my head. The magnitude of my actions is only hitting me now. All the fucked-up shit I did is starting to come together, hitting me like a Mack truck.

"How could you? She could be dead. Hasn't she been through enough? What does she have? Who does she have?" Taffy shakes her head but keeps her eyes fixed on me. "I know it was you. This type of shit has your name written all over it. Did you try Tony first?"

When I don't respond, Taffy takes a defensive step towards me and waves her finger in my face. "Stay the fuck away from my brother. You hear me?"

I look up at her with tears in my eyes and nod.

Taffy seems surprised by my tears, but she doesn't let her guard down. I take a deep breath and apologize with my eyes—an apology Taffy won't accept.

"Can you watch BJ for me?" I ask and lean over, placing his sleeping body in her arms before she has a chance to respond.

Taffy grabs BJ and gives me a curious look.

"You're not coming back. are you? You're running again," she assumes.

"I'll never leave my son," I firmly reply. "I just need to fix something."

Taffy laughs sarcastically. "There's not enough time in this life to fix all the shit you created," she says while rocking BJ. "Maybe leaving him isn't such a bad idea. He deserves so much better," she adds and slams the door in my face.

Her words sting throughout my entire body like poison flowing through my veins. Mainly because I halfway believe her.

HOW AM I going to fix this shit? What was I thinking? Tears blur my vision. I wipe them away but only more fall. I'm facing Mamma Badd's grave, or lack of, and meditating on everything I've done to bring myself to this point. *Why am I so fucked up?* I can't get the way Billy looked at me out of my mind. It was almost like he didn't know me—like I'm a dangerous stranger that he can't trust. I never considered all the things that I've done to be selfish, but being on the outside looking, I see it now.

I look at the empty hole in the ground where Billy's mother's coffin once was buried. I remember the look on his face that night, too. It was full of both hope and fear. When I first met Billy, his mother had just died, and he was hurting bad. He carried so much guilt. All he needed was my support. He needed me to have his back, but I was too afraid that supporting him would mean never getting our happily-ever-after. If his mother faked her death, she doesn't want to be found. Why doesn't he get that? Why can't we just move on with our lives?

When I planned for Lera to kill Ace, I had no idea she would escape with him. That wasn't my plan. I thought she would put a bullet in his brain, which he deserves. With Ace alive, we're all in danger. Why can't they see that? They can't understand how big of a mind-fuck Ace is. When it comes to a person's mind, Ace fucks hard. Raw. Uncut. He rapes minds. I guess that's how he got Lera to get him off the Ranch. I didn't think this would happen. Now Billy doesn't want me.

I sniff hard, wiping the mixture of snot and tears from my face. I've come too far for it to end like this. Billy and I had both feet out the door. *Why couldn't I just leave it alone?* I stare at his mother's grave and wonder if she's really alive. If she is, maybe we're similar. What pushed her to leave her children? Her life? I wonder if Mamma Badd made mistakes that she couldn't escape. Was faking her death the only way to fix her mistakes?

I walk over to the gaping hole in the ground, and for a split second, I think about jumping inside and burying myself. Then an image of my son flashes through my mind, and I take a few steps back. I've already buried myself in so much deception and lies that I don't need her empty grave to house me. But, just like her, I can't stay buried for much longer. I have to find a way to dig myself out of this hole. I'm tired. I don't have much fight left in me, but I have to give my family one last shot. If only I knew where Lera was, maybe I could find them and bring them back to the Ranch…if Lera survives Ace. Taffy's right. Lera has endured so much already. *Why would I do this to her? What type of person am I?*

On that note, I take slow steps towards the grave until my feet are at the hole's edge. Taking a deep breath, I lean over to see how deep it is. I'm halfway hoping I mistakenly fall in. The other half of me is clutching the dirt with my feet, protecting myself. When I see the distorted body lying at the bottom, I think my eyes are playing tricks on me. I jump back and rub my eyes, then take another step forward for a closer look. *Is that her? Is it Mamma Badd?*

I squint my eyes and look down in the hole. Then I pull my cell phone out of my pocket and turn on the flashlight, shining it inside. It's definitely a woman's body, but it's not Mamma Badd. For one, the body doesn't look like it has been there long. The woman lying face down in the dirt, with her torso twisted like her neck is broken, looks just like Mona. But it can't be. Wades of cash surround her body. My heart starts to race, and when I take two careful steps back to run, someone grabs me from behind and plants their hand over my mouth.

I yell for help, but my screams are muted. I can feel his body behind me. His hand is covering my nose, and I can barely breathe. As he lifts my body from the ground, my feet kick in the air as I desperately try to free myself, but there is no hope. *Is this Ace? Is this finally it for me?*

"Stop squirming, or I'm going to snap your fucking neck," the voice whispers in my ear. "You want to live?"

I try to nod my head, but I can't move. His grip is too tight. All I can think about is getting back to BJ. So, I do as he says, and the man finally puts me down. When my feet hit the ground, my legs are so weak with fear that I can hardly stand. My entire body trembles as I turn around and face Kong. His shirt is covered in dirt and blood, and he smells like a farm animal. His eyes are bloodshot red. He looks paranoid and angry. His large lips are cracked and dry.

"Take me to Brock, or you're dead," he threatens, pulling a gun out of his waistband and pressing it against my forehead.

I quickly nod, and he slowly removes the gun. Then he grips the back of my neck, guiding me out of the cemetery.

31

Bobby Badd

I PREDICTED HOW JAYSON was gonna move. The cell towers placed him in Florida, but now the nigga is in South Carolina. He got my son and Tara posted up in some raggedy-ass trailer home in the woods. This shit doesn't look safe, nor does it look sanitary. The trailer is rusted, the porch is lopsided, and several windows are broken and patched with newspaper.

This is how he got my family living? This is the better life he's providing them? Jayson is full of shit.

I've been watching his paranoid ass from behind this oak tree for twenty minutes. Every so often, he comes outside and looks out into the woods. I could have shot him twice already. I even aimed my pistol at him, but I can't pull the trigger. Not yet.

I get a glimpse of Blake, and seeing my son is like breathing fresh air. By the looks of it, he's doing well despite his current living situation. He tries to run outside to get some fresh air, but Jayson makes him go back inside. *It's time for me to make my move.*

Jayson follows behind him back into the trailer. As the storm door slams behind him, I get closer to the porch, squatting behind a generator. Next time Jayson decides to peek his head outside, I'm gonna grab him.

My phone vibrates again. Brock has been blowing me up ever since I left. I pull my phone out of my pocket and put it on silent. I ain't got shit to say to Brock or Lera. I know what I did to her was fucked up, but this ain't how you get revenge. I would've rather she put a bullet in my chest than fuck my brother. One is just as painful as the other to me. I always looked up to Brock. He's always been like a second father to us all. So, him doing something like that was nothing I would have ever imagined. The shit is fucked up, and I feel numb. I can't even allow myself to deal with the emotions of it because I don't want to believe it yet. Once I settle things with Jayson, I'm gonna give Lera her divorce and nothing more. I don't plan to see her again ever, and I mean what I say.

Not even ten minutes later, the storm door scrapes the ground as it opens. Out walks Jayson, coming to retrieve the beer he left on the porch. When he reaches for it, I lean out, grabbing his ass and tackling him to the ground. Jayson tries to reach for his gun, but it's too late. I already got him. My pistol is touching his temple.

"Make the wrong move, nigga. I dare you," I say, pressing my gun deeper into his head.

"Chill out," he whispers, holding up his hands to surrender. "Blake is inside."

"You mean my son?"

"Yes," Jayson answers quickly.

"Say it." I push the gun against him harder, ready to pull the trigger. He can feel it, too. He's so close to death he can taste the shit. "Say who he is."

"Your son, man. He's your son," Jayson says, desperate. "I ain't never denied that, man. I was only trying to protect them. They all I got. They the only family I got."

"They all you got?" I repeat.

Pissed by his words, I spin Jayson around and sucker him in the face. He spits blood but stays on his back, holding his hands in the air. The nigga is squirming around on his back like a fucking snake. I'm ready to eliminate him.

"Nobody fucks with my family. Nobody fucks with me." I aim the gun at him, my finger now on the trigger.

"Blake is right inside, man. Please..."

"I mean what I—"

I'm so close to pulling the trigger that I believe I already killed him, but I'm interrupted by a voice I never thought I would hear again.

"Put that thing away," Tara says.

She swings open the door and stumbles outside. As soon as I see her, my heart stops. My arms fall to my sides, and I stare back at her like I see a ghost. She looks frail, but she's alive. Tara has always been tiny, but she's lost at least twenty pounds and looks like a skeleton. The oversized t-shirt she's wearing as a dress hangs off her boney shoulders. She grabs the door to keep her balance. Two seconds later, Blake busts through the door, almost knocking her over.

"Dad!" he screams.

He opens his arms to embrace me, but Tara grabs him by the shirt, stopping him.

"Get back in the house. Now!" She yells so hard that she loses her balance.

"But, Mom, it's Dad..."

"Now!" Tara yells again and then catches her breath.

Confused, Blake looks at me with a sad expression before following his mother's orders.

"Get up, Jayson," Tara orders.

Jayson looks at me and then back at Tara before rolling onto his side and standing to his feet.

"Go inside," she demands, and Jayson does as told.

It's Tara, and she is calling the shots. She's the one keeping me away from them, not Jayson.

Once they both are inside, Tara looks up at me, and a tear escapes her eye.

"Why couldn't you just leave us be," she says through an exhausted sigh, then licks her cracked lips and breathes in heavily. I can see her ribs when she inhales.

"You're my family," is all I can manage. "When you were at the Ranch, I didn't leave your side. Everybody wanted to give up on you, but I knew you were strong. I knew you would live."

I try to explain myself, but she isn't trying to hear shit that I have to say.

Tara waves her hand in the air, silencing me. My words mean nothing to her.

"And the one who did this to me?" Tara's voice is weak. Every word she speaks feels forced.

"He's still on the run, but we're going to find him."

Tara shakes her head at me. "No," she says and squeezes the railing. "Lera."

There is so much hate in her tone when she speaks of Lera. I can feel it vibrating off her tongue.

"No," I say, defending Lera.

She has it all wrong. Maybe she doesn't remember. Perhaps she's confused.

"Lera didn't do this to you. It was Ace Lucky, remember?" I speak soft and slow, hoping my words jog her memory, but Tara's memory isn't the problem. "He hurt her, too. He hurt her bad, T," I add, trying to get her to sympathize with Lera, but it doesn't work.

"Whatever he did to her, she deserved it." Tara points a weak finger at me. "You brought that destructive woman into our home, putting us all in danger, and now you're defending her."

I realize this has nothing to do with Ace and everything to do with my relationship with Lera.

"She's my wife, T."

"She's a whore. A murdering whore, and as long as you are with her, calling her your wife, you won't see our son," Tara replies harshly, giving me a cold stare.

"You can't keep him from me," I respond, trying not to yell.

"I can and I will," Tara says slowly. She's out of breath. "I'll protect him if you can't. We don't need you or your murderous family. I want out. We want out," she adds.

"Please don't do this, Tara. You two are all I have."

"Kill her," Tara says. "Kill her for what she's done to me, and you'll have your family back."

Tara squints her eyes at me. I've never seen her so brutal. She's giving me the same ultimatum that Lera gave, except Tara wants blood. The Tara I know is logical and has integrity. Tara forgets how I betrayed my wife in her bed. She is forgetting how we brought this shit on ourselves, but I don't remind her, and I don't accept her ultimatum. Killing Lera will never be an option. Her keeping Blake from me isn't an option either. Blake and love aren't the only two things that brought me back to Tara. It was also guilt. I feel she needs me. I feel I owe her something, but I can never give her what she expects. Not now. Not ever.

At this very moment, I realize why Tara and I never worked out. The control. The power struggle. The manipulation. The unreasonable demands. I can't get with that.

"Lera is my family." My words hit Tara like a gush of wind. She falls back, the railing catching her small frame. "I'll never let anything happen to her. Not by my hand and not by yours." I give my words time to sink in. "You won't keep my son from me. Nobody will," I warn. "And you know I mean what I say."

I walk past Tara, open the door to the trailer, and walk inside. The interior looks just as bad as the exterior. Moldy carpet and busted walls. Blake is lying on a mattress that looks like it was pulled out of a dumpster. When he sees me, he jumps up and leaps into my arms. I hold my son so tight that he pushes away from me, pulling up for air. I plant my lips on his head.

"I missed you. I want to go home," he says with tears in his eyes.

"You're going home today. I swear," I tell him and look at Jayson. "Gather your things. Pack your momma's stuff, too."

Excited, Blake runs to the back, grabs a trash bag, and starts dumping items inside.

"Bobby—" Jayson tries to speak, but I dismiss him with a flick of my wrist.

"I want them back home today, or you're dead."

Jayson swallows hard and shakes his head, agreeing with me.

"And take me off block."

Jayson pulls his phone out of his pocket and immediately follows my order.

"I'm gonna let you live for now because you're Blake's uncle, but you and I are done."

Jayson gives me a remorseful look, then lowers his eyes and nods. I walk past him, resisting the urge to sucker him in the jaw for allowing Tara to treat him like a little bitch. When I open the door, Tara is still standing outside, holding on to the railing. I stop in front of her, and she tries to turn her head away from me. She doesn't want me to see that she's crying. She thinks she's too tough for tears, but she's human like the rest of us. I lean over and kiss her on the forehead, and more tears escape from her eyes.

"I love you, Tara. I always will. We're gonna get through this. I promise."

While walking down the stairs, I pull my phone out of my pocket. I look at the screen and see ten more missed calls from Brock and one text message: *Call me. Lera's in trouble.*

After reading the text, I don't waste any time calling him back.

32

Lera Badd

I FEEL LIKE I'VE misplaced my mind somewhere. I can almost remember where I left it. I can see it plain as day. Strong. Focused. Balanced. Wise. It's sitting somewhere, waiting to be found. I still can't find it, though. Maybe once I put a bullet in this nigga's brain, my sound mind will reappear, but this trigger is stuck. Every time I try to kill this motherfucker, something goes wrong. There were too many distractions at the Ranch. Whenever I reached for the gun I was hiding in my pants' waistband, a doctor or nurse would come in to check on him. I can't believe they were taking care of Ace, nursing his wounds after all he did to us. After what he did to me. I don't know what the fuck I was thinking by trusting Brock.

I had convinced myself that I had feelings for Brock, but everything I thought I felt for him was residual feelings for Bobby. I buried my feelings for Bobby deep, but they popped back up like a buoy in the ocean. I decided if I couldn't control my emotions, I was going to repurpose them. So, I attached myself to Brock. I still love Bobby, and that angers me. It makes me feel pathetic. He doesn't deserve my love, but I can't control it. My feelings for him are like a knee jerk reaction. It just happens. But that doesn't stop me from trying to deflect every emotion I have for him on to something else. Like anger. Hate. Rebellion.

At first, it felt good to tell Bobby that I fucked his brother, even though it wasn't true. Now he knows what betrayal feels like. Seeing the pain burning behind his eyes still wasn't enough, though. He needs to hurt more. He needs to feel what I feel. The victory I found in his pain was so short-lived that I wonder if it was even worth it. Now I'm back at square one. Deflecting. Thinking about how much I hate Ace is a nice distraction, but it's only temporary. Once I kill him, what's next?

Ace is looking at me, taunting me with a smirk.

"You know why the trigger won't work, right?" Ace says without flinching.

He's pretending not to be afraid, but he knows the end is near. I don't know how I made it this far with him. I took a few of Brock's supplies from the prison to aid me in my escape. I handcuffed Ace's hands together and shackled his ankles. He could barely move when I cuffed him. Now, he's dragging his feet, moving like a snail. It took us forever to get to the second Ranch. I don't know how I let him convince me to bring him here, but really, I had nowhere else to go. He convinced me to leave the Ranch, too. He warned me that security would catch me and that I would never be able to kill him there. I believed him enough to leave. He told me what to do. Guided me to where we are now, where he's about to die. I guess he thought he would be able to overpower me and escape, but that hasn't happened yet. And it won't.

We are standing outside the gate of the second Ranch. I'm not wasting my time going inside; I don't need to. Ace is dying right here and right now, as soon as I get this gun to work. I strain my finger trying to pull the trigger back, but it's still stuck. I hit the bottom of the gun handle. I don't know why, but I don't know what else to do. Ace looks at me and shakes his head. Then he bends over, twisting his face in pain and moaning a little.

"Trust me, I don't mind you putting me out of my misery, but this is getting way more complicated than necessary. There are plenty of guns in the house." Ace nods towards the gate.

I turn around and look at the house, then back at him. Maybe he's right. Maybe there's money inside, too, and enough supplies to get me to my next destination. Wherever that it. I give Ace a considerate look, and he shrugs his shoulders.

"I'm in pain," he says while twitching his eyes and biting down on his bottom lip. "Please, let's just get this over with," he adds through an exhausted breath.

Ace stumbles towards the gate, tripping over his shackles. He grabs the gate to break his fall. He looks pathetic and weak, and for a split second, I feel sorry for him. But then, I have a flashback of him on top of me. I close my eyes tight and reopen them, reality greeting me. *Yeah, it's time to get this shit over with.* I swing the gate open and push Ace through it. He falls to the ground.

"Get up!" I kick him.

Ace slowly pulls himself up from the ground and tries to balance himself. He takes small steps, following behind me as I walk up the driveway.

"Why did you tell them I raped you?"

His question catches me off guard. Spinning around, I lunge at him, pushing him to the ground. Once again, I pull out my gun and squeeze the trigger, but it still doesn't move.

"How dare you," I hiss.

"I can't ask a question in my final hour?" Ace says snidely. "You came on to me. Then you cried rape."

"Fuck you!" I scream. "I told you to stop."

"Yeah, ten minutes into you bouncing on my dick and digging your nails in my back," Ace replies.

I raise my hand to strike him, but just like the trigger, my arm gets stuck. I'm caught in a thought. That night was so tragic; I only remember fragments of it. I do recall trying to take control of the situation. I have a flashback of myself unbuttoning my shirt and walking towards Ace. Then a flash of Tara being stabbed pops in my mind. Then Bobby assuring her that he will make me pay. Then it all becomes one big blur. I remember Ace on top of me. Then I remember wanting him off, but he didn't get off.

"Fuck you!" I say and lower my arm, confused by my own accusation.

Was it rape? I hate that he's making me question that.

"You know what you did," I say like I'm trying to justify my claims. "I told you to stop. It doesn't matter when I said it. I said it! Over and over again!"

"Yeah, it was all a part of your game." Ace leans up. "You thought you were going to be able to manipulate me with pussy, but I ain't that fucking weak. Your plan didn't work, so you cried rape," Ace says, defending himself.

My knees start to tremble. I aim the gun at Ace and squeeze the trigger as hard as I can. I close my burning eyes to keep the tears from falling. I just want this nightmare to be over. Weakness floods my body, and I feel myself about to snap just like I did that night. I try to focus, but it's too hard. It's too much all at once. I look down at Ace through blurred vision, and he's smiling at me. *This is what he wants. He raped my body. Now he's raping my mind.*

"They all know what you did. They saw the tapes." Ace chuckles. "If it's one thing I don't need to take, it's pussy. Unwanted pussy at that. Desperate pussy. Damaged pussy."

My body goes numb. I feel the gun fall out of my hands and hit the ground. I drop to my knees and stare off into blank space, remembering everything from that night like it was yesterday. Ace's words pierce my body like a blade, and I bleed emotions everywhere.

"You know what I felt inside of you?" Ace continues. "Rejection. Muddy waters."

What he is describing is how I feel now.

"I felt sorry enough for you to fuck you. What a mistake. Two seconds into it, I understood why that nigga replaced your ass," he scoffed. "You got the type of pussy that drips with weakness. It felt contagious. I should have been the one screaming for you to stop. Dumb bitch. You were infecting me with your fucking weakness. I still feel that shit in my veins."

Ace turns his head to the side and spits as if he's trying to get the taste of me out of his system like I'm an infectious disease turning his stomach. Ironically, it's exactly how I feel—like a piece of smelly trash that turns up people's noses. At that moment, everything goes blank. I feel trapped in time. The sound of Ace's voice grows faint until it finally drifts away, snatched up by the wind. The sun shines brightly in my eyes as they fill with tears before everything turns blurry. I don't know how much time has passed, but it feels like the world has stopped spinning for a moment. Then I hear another voice.

"Lera…"

The voice lingers in the air and echoes before bouncing off the wind.

"Lera…"

I feel him touch me. Gentle arms sweep across my shoulders, carefully lifting me. *Is he touching me? Is he actually fucking touching me?* I snap halfway back to reality, wiping the fog from my eyes. When my sight becomes clear again, Ace is gone. I look down and see the gun at my side. Leaning down, I grab it, arming myself. All I have left to protect myself is a broken gun.

"Baby, put the gun down."

I squint, shaking away the confusion but not lowering my weapon. When I look closer, I see Bobby stepping towards me. His every move holds caution. His eyes are fixed on me. They're full of compassion, empathy, regret.

Why is he here? How is he here? Where the fuck is Ace? How long was I in a daze?

Bobby extends his arms to me, and in an automatic reaction, I drop the gun and fall into his embrace. He pulls me into his body, and my head rests against his chest. I sob so hard that my body becomes depleted of emotions. Bobby squeezes me tighter, and I let everything out. Anger. Spit. Sorrow and snot. It all soaks through him, but he doesn't pull away. Instead, he soothes me with his touch, rubbing my back. He doesn't try to speak. He doesn't say he's sorry. He doesn't tell me that he loves me. He simply shows me that he's here, and by the way he's holding me, I know he doesn't plan to let me go. After I empty myself of toxic emotions, the healthy ones come out. Some kind of way, I feel at peace in Bobby's arm. His warmth wraps itself around me, and his love seeps into my pores.

I wipe the tears from my eyes and look up at him. I see a softness in his eyes that I didn't know he had. I also see the brokenness that looks just like mine. In that instant, Bobby and I become one. Our emotions and turmoil mesh, forming a knot in our bond that can't be undone. I take a step back; Bobby takes a step towards me. I exhale, and every negative emotion I feel is pulled from my body. I feel so light on my feet that I feel like I'm floating. I stare back at Bobby and then smile. He nods at me before pulling me into a kiss. I've officially been reborn.

BOBBY HANDS ME the gun. "It's loaded," he says and steps back.

Suddenly, the gun feels heavy in my hands. Lifting it is hard.

"You don't have to do this, Lera."

I stare at him and then back at Ace, contemplating my next move. What seemed so effortless less than twenty minutes ago now feels complicated. I'm not so sure that killing Ace will help me anymore.

"I'm here for you no matter what," Bobby says, placing a supportive hand on my back.

His touch fuels me with strength, and I raise my elbow but lower it once I see the fear in Ace's eyes.

"I'll do it for you if you need me to, but if anybody deserves this, it's you," Bobby states with a reassuring nod.

That was all the confirmation I needed. I plant my feet firmly on the ground and position myself like Brock taught me.

I fix my eyes on Ace. Bobby has him tied to a tree, and his mouth is taped shut. He doesn't squirm; he doesn't blink. He knows this is it for him. Even in his final hour, his arrogance shines. The evil slits in his eyes don't soften. They don't plea. His pride is at an all-time high. Ace seems ready to die, but I know it's all an act. He's staring back at me like he wants me to hurry and get it over with. I'm sure his thoughts are haunting him. All the horrible things he's done in the past are taunting him.

I take a deep breath and slowly exhale. I feel Bobby standing behind me; his presence comforts me. I don't know how I thought I would pull this off on my own.

Ace almost got away. He was so close to escaping that he arrogantly stopped to catch his breath. He figured he had time, but what he didn't expect was Bobby pulling up. Bobby also found Ace's mother and sister in the house. He has someone picking them up and taking them to the Ranch for questioning. When Ace's mother saw him, she laughed and called him a fool. His sister almost pleaded for his life but didn't waste her breath. She shook her head sorrowfully at him and told him goodbye with her eyes. He's already dead to her.

"You ready?" Bobby says, encouraging me.

I nod my head, slightly close my eyes, and pull the trigger. When I open my eyes, Ace is dead, his arrogant eyes staring back at me empty and void of life.

33

Brip Badd

"**I**'M COMING WITH you," Taffy says again.

I look back at her and shake my head no. She walks up to me, wraps her arm around mine, and lays her head on my shoulder. Brock just called an emergency family meeting. This will be the perfect time for me to let them know they have to find another goon because this one has retired. I'm trading in my Glock for a briefcase and tie like I promised my wife.

"I just want to make sure you're okay," she says in that tender voice I've been missing.

I look at her and smile. We survived this shit together. That's the kind of shit I cherish. All that matters to me now is my family—her and my little girl, whether she's my blood or not. Fuck everything else. This Ranch included.

I kiss her on top of the head. Her hair smells like coconut oil. I look down at my wife in admiration that quickly turns to lust. Even at six months pregnant, she's looking like a snack in those tight-ass leggings. Her breasts are fuller than I've ever seen them. They're popping out the top of her V-neck shirt, begging to be sucked.

"Sexy ass," I say, and a bashful smile stretches across her face.

Taffy pulls away from me and checks herself out in the mirror. She's so vain, but I love it. She flicks her hair and runs her hands down her pants.

"My ass is getting too big." She frowns at herself in the mirror.

I laugh. "There ain't no such thing as too much ass," I say and playfully smack her on the butt.

She lets out a playful shriek before spinning around in my direction to wrap her arms around my neck. She stands on her toes, stretching her body up to kiss me on the lips. I close my eyes and savor every moment of her. Her natural sweet scent seeps from her pores; it's aromatic. The silky softness of her skin. Her small, delicate frame. I take it all in. For a while, I thought I lost her. I thought we were done. Now I know we're never gonna be done, not even in death. Me and Taffy are forever. I mean that infinity and beyond type of forever.

Taffy steps back and stares at me. She now has a serious look on her face. Placing sassy hands on her hips, she raises her brow. I wait for whatever demand is about to come out of her mouth. She's been giving me many demands lately, and I've been smart enough to listen. Our dynamics have changed a bit. I'm still the man. I always will be, but I ain't afraid to let my woman take the lead if that's the way it needs to be. Taffy has earned that right.

"What's up?" I ask.

"I need to go with you," she replies. "Everything has changed, and they need to see that you and I are stronger than ever, especially if you're going to start working on the operations side of things. They need to know I'm in this with you just like Mona." Taffy tilts her head to the side and pauses, waiting for my reaction.

Her feistiness is so sexy. The way she has my back gives me a feeling of pride that I can't explain. She's right. Brock doesn't make a move without Mona. That's why he's been on top all of these years, but it's time for some new blood. I got more to offer, and so does Taffy. I'm gonna make them see that today.

I look at Taffy and inhale deeply, letting her know I'm considering what she's asking. My eyes drift down to her belly. I walk up to her and place both hands on her stomach. The feeling I get from touching her swollen belly brings me to my knees. Kneeling, I kiss her stomach and then look up at her humbly.

"I don't want you stressing. You've already been through enough. Now is the time to chill. As a matter of fact, I booked a vacation for us to go to Paris. We leave in two weeks."

Taffy's jaw drops with shock.

"I wanted it to be a surprise, but I guess we've had enough surprises. I already got clearance from the doctor for you to travel. The private jet is waiting for us."

Taffy's eyes beam with excitement. She pulls me up from the floor and leaps into my arms, squeezing my neck so tight she suffocates me.

"Are you for real?"

"I wouldn't lie to you," I say and stroke the side of her face. "You need this." I place my hands back on her belly. "Both of you," I add.

Taffy nods her head, agreeing with me.

"Okay, but I'm still coming," Taffy dictates through a smile. "The baby will be fine. She's a fighter."

"What about BJ?" I remind her that she's been playing momma to BJ for the day.

"I already called Billy. He has his nanny coming in. He'll be here to get him soon."

"You think she left her son? After all that?"

Taffy looks at me and shrugs. "You never know with Dalla," she responds and cradles her belly.

"My brothers are going through it," I say to her, grateful that we made it out on top.

Taffy cups my face in her hands and kisses me on the forehead. She knows how much I love my brothers. I hate to see any of them hurt.

"Everything's going to be okay. You'll see."

She seals her last statement with a gentle kiss on the lips.

I'VE NEVER SEEN Mona so quiet. She can barely make eye contact with me. I guess she thinks I'm still mad at her, and I am. But I forgive her. When I kissed her on the cheek, she almost jumped out of her skin. I squeezed her hand to let her know we ain't got no beef. I'll always love Mona no matter what.

To my surprise, nobody objected when I walked in with Taffy. Taffy took a seat next to me like it was assigned to her. She came ready and wasn't taking no for an answer. I was even more shocked to see Bobby and Lera at the table. The last I heard, she had run off with Ace, and Bobby had run off to find Tara. I guess things are falling back into place.

Billy is alone, though. He looks so burdened. My poor brother. He always has some kind of emotional stronghold that he's battling. I hate to say it, but Dalla leaving ain't the worst thing that could happen to him. The woman is bad news. Trouble follows her everywhere, and I don't trust her with my brother. I make eye contact with Billy and give him a reassuring nod to let him know I got his back. He smiles at me with his eyes and then looks away, staring off into the emotional trance he's trapped in.

Now and again, I catch Mona staring at the 'B' necklace around Taffy's neck. Taffy is the only wife rocking the B. That means a lot to me. I'm surprised Mona hasn't put hers back on yet. I wonder if everything is good with her and Brock. I can't concern myself with my brothers and their wives too much, though. I got my own shit to keep together.

We all are sitting at the table waiting on Brock. He's late by five minutes. It's not much, but it's strange because he's never late. Then again, stranger things have happened.

Billy clears his throat and forces himself to be present. Everyone looks at him, waiting for him to speak, but he keeps his eyes fixed on Lera.

"Is he dead?" Billy finally asks, referring to Ace.

Billy seems to want Ace alive more than anyone, including Ace himself. Lera's eyes shift away from Billy. Bobby immediately places his hand on top of hers to comfort her. Lera looks scared, but she seems a lot better than she did before she left the Ranch with Ace. I don't know where she went or what she did, but she's starting to look like the woman Bobby brought home over a year ago. She seems more at peace and less deranged.

Billy waits for Lera to respond, but she doesn't. Instead, Bobby responds for her.

"He's done, man," Bobby tells Billy and then stares at him, waiting for a reaction that never comes.

Billy sighs an exasperated breath and shakes his head in disbelief. He takes a deep breath and opens his mouth to speak, but I guess he doesn't have words because he doesn't say anything.

"It had to be done," Bobby continues. "What he did to my wife—"

"It's all good, man," Billy says, cutting him off.

Billy looks away from Bobby and Lera like he can't take the sight of them. Billy's anger does not faze Bobby. He's more concerned for his wife.

"I would have done the same thing if I had the chance," I say to Bobby, and he nods.

I pull Taffy in closer to me. Billy cuts an annoyed eye at me. He's pissed, but he'll get over. If Mamma's alive, he can find her without Ace. He's relentless that way.

"Where's he at, Mona?" I say, aggravated.

Mona jumps like she's been awakened from a trance. We all stare back at Mona, confused by her behavior. Mona opens her mouth to speak but then just shakes her head like she's confused herself.

"Any word on Dalla?" I ask Billy to clear the air.

Billy swallows hard. His eyes trail away from us before he answers no.

"She'll be back, man," I say, trying to sound hopeful, but really, I hope she stays wherever she is.

"I got mine, man," Billy snaps. "And I got Mamma," he adds.

Bobby pushes back in his seat a bit. I look over at my wife to make sure she's okay. This is the reason I didn't want to bring Taffy. Too much drama. The baby doesn't need this stress. Taffy gives me a reassuring nod.

"We all love Mamma," Bobby says, aggravated. "If she's alive, we're gonna find her, but the man who raped my wife doesn't get to help us do that shit. I'm sorry if you're pissed."

Before things can get more heated, Brock marches in the room, silencing everyone with his presence. Everything about Brock screams leader. Bobby sits up straight in his seat, and Billy straightens his shoulder. Neither of them wants Brock to know they've been bickering because he would find it juvenile. Brock has no time for the bullshit, and neither do I.

"You're late," I say.

Brock gives me a look I've never seen before. It creeps me out so much that I can't say anything else. I just stare at him. We all do.

"I'm here now," Brock firmly responds. "I—" Brock tries to speak, but the words are stuck in his throat.

Mona grabs his hand, and the tension in his shoulders eases a little but not much. Brock places a folder in front of him and stares down at it like he's in a trance.

"I don't know what to say," he says to Mona. "I—"

"What the fuck is going on?" I feel myself starting to get excited.

Taffy grabs my hand, reminding me to keep my cool. My heart starts to race, and my stomach ties into a knot. Something ain't right. I can feel it. Suddenly, I just want to grab my wife and run. But I don't.

Everybody is staring at Brock, waiting for him to speak. We all are sitting on the edge of our seats. When a tear escapes from Mona's eyes, we know that whatever Brock is about to say is going to fuck us all up. After all this shit we've been through, he's about to add to our plates. I can't eat no more bullshit. I'm too stuffed.

Brock takes a deep breath and looks us all in the eye individually before speaking.

"There ain't no easy way to say this."

He forces the words from his tongue, then straightens his posture. Every move he makes is full of effort. The pounding of my chest makes me feel like I'm hyperventilating. My mouth gets dry.

"The results are back," Brock adds and drops his head.

Mona closes her eyes tight and then reopens them. I feel so fucking unsettled that my trigger finger starts twitching. I want to shoot something. Somebody. Anybody. I can't take this anxious shit. I look back at Taffy, and she's looking just as spooked as I am.

Brock forces himself to lift his chin and face us like a man. His hands tremble as he opens the folder. Brock swallows hard like the air is full of nails and takes another controlled breath.

"Say what you got to fucking say, man," I blurt out.

Brock looks at me and nods. He keeps his eyes fixed on me. Only me. The look he's giving me feels like a knife to the chest. Taffy squeezes my hand tighter, but I'm too numb to feel her support. Something ain't right.

"We ain't Badd men." Brock lets the words escape from his mouth, and the entire room stirs.

"What the fuck you mean?" I ask.

"I'm not a Badd," Brock says. "Billy ain't a Badd," he continues while flipping through the papers. "Bobby ain't a Badd." He pulls out the last paper and stops, but he doesn't say anything else.

I start to feel like someone has set my soul on fire. Brock won't take his eyes off of me. Billy is saying something, and Bobby jumps up to grab the papers from Brock. But Brock keeps his eyes fixed on me. Just me.

"All of us are Lucky. All of us except..." Brock stops and lowers his head. "Except you, man. You're the only true Badd."

I hear Taffy gasp. She grabs my hand and is shaking me, but I ain't moving. Mona is crying, and Brock is still staring at me. My brothers crowd around me. I can feel the heat from their bodies but nothing else. Supportive hands are placed on my shoulders while tears drop on my lap. My tears. Taffy's grabbing my face. She's trying to get me to talk, but I can't. I can't speak. Brock's words linger, echoing everywhere.

What the fuck did he just say to me? What does he mean?

I push away from the table, moving everyone out of my way. Anger swells in my chest and fills my lungs with hot air. I'm ready to blow on all these niggas.

Why the fuck did Brock bring this bullshit to me? Is he trying to say I'm not family?

I stand to my feet; my knees are shaking. Taffy is by my side. She wraps her fingers around mine. She's breathing heavily. This is too much for her. It's too much for me.

"You shouldn't have brought this bullshit to me," I say to Brock, then look around at all of them. They would have been better off letting this secret die like Mamma wanted. But, nah, they like to dig. So, dig, niggas. Dig your fucking graves.

"Brip," one of them niggas says, but I don't know which one. "We're still brothers."

"Nah, we ain't shit, and y'all ain't Badd." The words slide off my tongue with ease. This shit changes everything. "Y'all got until tonight to get the fuck off my Ranch, or all y'all Lucky motherfuckers are dead."

I grab my wife's hand and storm out of the room in pursuit of my gun. They really fucked up.

34

Brock Badd

"**N**OW WHAT WE gonna do?" Mona says from behind me.

I'm staring out the window from the living room, looking over the Ranch. We've taken our father's vision and expanded far beyond what he could ever see. This place is a big part of my identity. It doesn't matter whose blood is in my veins. That man's spirit and drive are in my heart.

Mona's worried about Brip's threat to kick us off the Ranch. I'm not worried about my brother. He's just hurting right now. The results hurt me, too.

"We should have never said anything. With all due respect, Mr. Badd, this was the wrong move. No one ever had to know this."

I turn to face my wife. I can see the red strain lines crisscrossing against the white of her eyes. She's tense; she's afraid. Mona was right beside me laying bricks to build this place up to what it is now. She can't imagine losing the Ranch. She can't imagine not being a Badd either, but the truth is the truth. We all have to deal with it.

"We did the right thing," I say and rub my chest.

Mona's eyes land on my hands.

"Your chest still hurting?" She reaches for the phone to call the doctor, but I take it from her hands. "Brock, you've been through a lot. With all this shit going on, I can't bear to lose you. You got to get that checked out," she fusses at me, and I smile.

This woman loves me without fault.

"This ain't a pain the doctor can fix," I tell Mona and pull her into a hug.

She pulls away from me. She ain't in the mood to be loved on right now. I grab her hand and look her directly in the eyes.

"We did the right thing. We told the truth. This was too heavy to take to the grave, Mona. We're gonna work through it."

"Brip means what he said, Brock. You know how he gets when he's upset. If we ain't out of here, he's gonna shoot us all," Mona says and throws her hands in the air before covering her trembling lips, pushing back tears.

"You let me handle my little brother," I tell her. "Everything is going to be okay. We're all gonna evolve from this."

Mona looks at me and gives me a hesitant nod. I stare back at my wife. Every day I see something new about her that I didn't notice before, like the small freckle hidden at the corner of her eye. I smile, and Mona gives me a confused look. My behavior has been throwing her off. She's never seen me so peaceful and easy. That breaks my heart, but change is on the way. I can feel it in my soul.

"Are you okay, Mr. Badd?" Mona places the back of her hand on my forehead to check my temperature, but I pull away from her.

"I'm happier than I've been in a long time because I'm feeling grateful."

"Grateful?" Mona mocks me, throwing her hands on her hips. "We're about to lose it all! Everything we worked for to Taffy and Brip."

I notice how she says Taffy's name before Brip's. Mona is taking this personal. The old me would have waged war against my brother. Maybe even had him killed for this Ranch, but the new me doesn't give a fuck. If I had to choose, I'd chose Brip over all of this in a heartbeat. Maybe Brip's right. Maybe it's time Mona and I step down and just enjoy each other. Reconnect with our children and grow old together. I'm tired of trying to conquer the world. I've missed out on so many things while operating this Ranch.

"Come here," I gently command.

She hesitates at first but slowly walks into my arms. I kiss the freckle and lay her head on my chest.

"It's going to be okay. The biggest loss we can take is losing each other, not this place."

Mona takes a step back and looks up at me like an alien invaded my body. It's going to take her some time to get to know the new me. It will take me some time, too, but transitioning into the man I'm becoming feels so natural. It's effortless.

"I ain't leaving," Mona says through tears. She defensively crosses her arms over her chest. "We don't deserve this. Give them a month, and this place will be up in flames. Papa Badd would never..." She stops herself and gives me a considerate look, searching my face for emotions that aren't there.

At one time, I worshipped my father, but now, I feel like I was serving a false god. All these years, I never understood why I couldn't be exactly like him. Now I know. It's because I ain't him. I forced myself to be ruthless. Coldhearted. Cutthroat. Just plain savage. I fought back the tender side of me that I feel taking over now. I treated emotions like a disease that weakened me. The remedy for emotions was brutality. Blood and fire. I'm done with that now. I'm releasing it. It feels so good to be just me. The part of me that wanted to be like my father was cruel. So cruel that I thought I killed the woman who loved me first—my mother. I had a long time to process what not being a Badd feels like. I had a three-year head start on my brothers, but now I'm accepting it. I'm a Lucky. Brock Lucky, and I want to get to know that part of me. I want to know everything about Carlo Lucky, and if he's still alive, I want to meet him.

Brip never fit in with us brothers. That's why he's always been a misfit. He never felt good enough. He always felt awkward in the group, and he struggled with that until Taffy came along to settle him down. Thank God that he still has her, but I am worried about him. I thought about taking Mona's advice and letting this secret die with us. Not for the sake of the Ranch, but to protect my baby brother's feelings. I couldn't do that to him, though. He has to go through his process like the rest of us. Brip lives for us. Family is everything to him. But, now, he feels alone and isolated, and there ain't nothing I can do to pacify him. If Brip was a Lucky, too, he'd feel accepted. It would soften the blow, but him being the only true Badd hurts him. This Badd life was about all of us. It's what we all had in common. It set us apart from the rest, but now it separates us—a divide. A line in the sand has been created.

"I'm going to give Brip his space. I'll try to talk to him when the moment is right, but that ain't now. And if we have to leave here tonight, then that's what we're gonna do," I tell Mona, and her entire body shudders. "We're gonna be okay, baby. I promise."

I'm at the chapel waiting on Dalla. To my surprise, she called me and said she wanted to talk right before Taffy called crying about Brip, who is not taking the news well. He's at the casino trying to drink away the pain. I thought it was best I didn't bother him there. It would only make matters worse. Let him drink and shoot a few rounds in the air to dispel his anger, and then he can come talk to me.

I told Taffy to stay with Mona for the night. I'm going to have Taffy call Brip and lure him here to meet me. I know he'll come if she asks. I don't got nothing to say to my brother except *I love you* and *I'm sorry*, and that shit ain't gonna make him feel better. But we got to talk our way through this. I want him to know I'm here for him just the same as I was yesterday.

I don't know what the fuck Dalla wants to talk about. The old me wouldn't trust her, but the new me is ready to forgive her. She was supposed to be here fifteen minutes ago. I pray she gets here before Brip. Him seeing us together will only make things worse. He'll think we're plotting. Waiting for her makes me anxious. That weird feeling that's been looming around returns, and I grab my chest and take a few deep breaths until the feeling passes. I wonder if Billy knows that Dalla is still on the Ranch. She has my brother worried about her. I don't like that, and I'm going to let her know she needs to leave because there is nothing else here for her if she doesn't love my brother. I'll even pay her to go.

I walk over to the altar and look up at the beautiful diamond-crusted cross that Mamma had custom made. Many nights, I would find her on her knees praying. I now wonder what she was praying about. Maybe she was praying we'd never learn the truth about who our real father is, or maybe she was praying that we would. Hopefully, Billy will find her, and I'll be able to ask her. I have so much I want to ask her, so much I want to learn about her. My father made me look at her like she was weak. I lost interest in my own mother once I turned fourteen and missed out on so much. I only got small bursts of the best parts of her, like her infectious laugh and the warmth that filled the room when she walked in. All the things I thought made her weak.

I fall to my knees and close my eyes to pray, but I don't know what to say to God. With all the shit I've done, I'm not even sure He's ready to listen to me. So, I just say the first thing that comes to my mind. *"Forgive me."* Then I stand up. When I turn around, Dalla is behind me.

"You're late," I say to her, but she doesn't respond. She looks stressed.

I look down at her clothes and notice they're covered with dirt. *Where has she been?*

Dalla pushes her trembling lips in her mouth and sniffs hard. Her eyes are strained and puffy like she's been crying all night.

"Does my brother know you're here?"

Dalla shakes her head no. She still doesn't speak.

"He's been worried sick about you, but I'm glad you came."

A tear falls from her eye.

"BJ?" she says, her voice shaky.

"He's fine," I respond, softening my tone.

Something's wrong with her. I'm used to Dalla hiding behind a mask, but these are raw emotions I've never seen her show before.

"Let's sit down," I tell her, but she hesitates.

She looks over her shoulder a few times, then turns and gives me a wide-eye stare.

"It's okay. I'm not going to hurt you."

I place my hand on her shoulder to lead her to one of the pews, and she jumps out of her skin.

"Brock," she softly yells.

"What is it?" I ask, confused.

"Billy's at the back door," she says and lowers her head.

"What? Why?"

I look over my shoulder towards the hallway in the back. That dark feeling that's been haunting me returns along with the pain in my chest. I give Dalla a hesitant look.

"What did you do to my brother?" I grab her. "You hurt him?"

I shake her and then push her away from me before running down the hall.

I have to protect my family. I have to. They're all I have.

"Brock, wait!" Dalla yells while running behind me. "Don't open…"

Before she can finish, I open the door to be greeted by Kong and his Glock. I stop, take a deep breath, and focus. I look back at Dalla, who is now by my side mouthing the words *I'm sorry* through her tears. I look at her and nod.

"It's okay," I gently say.

Kong points the gun at me, and I freeze. All I have to protect myself is one mind and two fists.

"We finally meet," Kong says, smiling.

"I'm here," I say back, holding my stance. "Why don't you let her go," I suggest.

I'm trying to get Dalla out of this situation.

"I told her that she could leave once she leads me to you, but I've changed my mind," he says and aims the gun at Dalla.

I charge at him with everything I got, but not before he pulls the trigger three times. Then four. Then five. I jab him in the jaw twice and knee him. Then six shots. After the seventh shot, I hear a body fall and see blood. It's Dalla. He shot her.

I try to grab his gun again, but I can't move. *Why the fuck can't I move?* Kong is standing over me. *Wait. I'm on the ground.* The pain in my chest returns but is more intense. I grab my chest and feel blood pouring out of my body. *I'm bleeding? He shot me.* I try to get up, but these bullets got me on my back. I can smell the gunpowder in my nose and taste the blood in my mouth. I cough a little, and more blood pours out of me like a fountain. *Where is Dalla?* I turn to look beside me and see her laying on her stomach. A large circle of her blood is growing wider underneath her. I couldn't protect her. All I think about is Billy and BJ. This is going to destroy them. I failed them all.

Kong kicks me, and I cough up more blood.

"I've been waiting for this moment for a very long time. This is it," Kong says, chuckling and gloating.

Kong aims the gun at my head. He has his target set. I try to speak, but I feel like I'm drowning. The blood in my mouth won't allow me to form words. Kong smiles at me. He's finally getting what he wants.

"It's over, Mr. Badd," he says through a laugh.

But Kong doesn't see what I see. I smile at him, and he gets angry. Kong isn't focused. He has no discipline. Just anger. When he sees my blood-covered teeth, he goes to squeeze the trigger, but it's too late, Brip blows his fucking brains out. I get the privilege of seeing his skull split and brain matter shoot out of his head like a cannon. After his body falls face first at my feet, Brip empties a round in his back before diving to my side and grabbing my hand. My vision is failing me. All I see is his silhouette. I try to speak to my brother, but my tongue feels like it weighs a hundred pounds. My head falls back, and I just stop fighting.

"Brock. Come on, Brock. Breathe, man. Breathe," I hear Brip pleading. "Breathe, man. Come on. Come on. I need you. We all need you."

This is something I can't fight. I feel myself leaving this place. Brip is leaning over me, but he might as well be a million miles away. His voice is growing fainter by the second.

"I love you, brother," I say to him. "I'm sorry." I force the words out with my tongue, triggering more blood to come out of my mouth in clumps. I can feel the clots sliding down my jaw.

"I love you, too, man. You're gonna be okay. You're stronger than this, Brock. You're stronger than this," he repeats.

Brip always treated me like I was Superman, but I'm not. I'm tired, and I can't fight this shit. It doesn't make sense to try and win a wrestling match with death.

"Mona…" Saying her name feels effortless. "Take care of Mona," I urge. "Tell her…" My pacing heart halts my speech. "I-I…" I try to continue, but the more I speak, the more pain fills my chest. There ain't no more air left in my lungs. I'm all out.

Brip squeezes my hand.

"I love her." I force the words out with all the life I have left in me.

Then everything disappears, and I'm left with nothing but the love I feel for my family. A surge of that love hits me so hard I almost feel resurrected, but then everything stops.

35

Mona Badd

Six Months Later

I WAKE UP EVERY morning expecting Brock to be beside me in the bed, but he's not here. I still reach for him, but I feel nothing. I wrap my arms around air to hug him. I try to embrace his spirit, but I can't feel him. Brock's gone. Mr. Badd did the unimaginable. He did what none of us saw coming. He got himself killed.

Life's been tough without him. I spent three months in this bed. Not moving. Not speaking. Not eating. Only feeling the pain. When Brock left this world, he didn't just take a piece of me with him but a whole chunk. I feel so lost without him. Like I can't breathe right. I open my mouth to speak sometimes, but nothing comes out. My words are lost. I get up to walk, but I have nowhere to go. So, I sit back down. All of this still feels like one big nightmare that I can't escape. I thought my eyes were playing tricks on me when I saw my unbreakable husband lying in the casket stiff and lifeless. He didn't even look real. After the funeral, I had him cremated. All the fullness that made Brock was reduced to ashes and stuffed in a tiny vase that now sits on top of my fireplace mantle.

Brock's funeral was bigger than Papa Badd's. Everybody who was anybody in this city came out to pay their respects to my husband. When the news spread of the legend's death, everyone was in awe. In the world we live in, Brock was considered to be immortal. He still is. Some people don't believe he's dead. The rumors have already started circulating. Pretty soon, the rumors will become myths, and goons and gangsters alike are going to put their children to sleep by telling great bedtime stories about Brock "The Rock" Badd, an urban legend.

Vinchi is taking Brock's death hard, but he won't show it. He's too busy worrying about this Ranch and me. He's already trying to fill his father's shoes. He blames himself, too. Not just for Brock's death but Nicchi's, as well. After we buried Brock. I buried my sister. I lost my sister, and her children lost their mother. While Nicchi's children may have lost their mother, they got me, and I have them all here with me at the second Ranch. All of Brock's sons, too. I'm gonna finish what we started. I'm continuing Brock's legacy.

Before Brock died, he started journaling. He wrote down all of his thoughts, expressing how he felt using words I never heard him speak. Just when I thought I would never get out of bed, Vinchi found his journal and a letter addressed to me. I could hear Brock's voice as I read the letter. It was as if he was narrating it, and for the first time since his death, I felt his presence. That alone gave me the strength to get up and keep living like I know he would want me to do.

In the letter, he talked about how he admired me because of my strength. How my strength can move mountains. How my strength kept him going at his weakest moments. He asked me to keep that strength going no matter what, and that's just what I plan to do.

Brip gave me the second Ranch to run on my own. I'll still operate under the Badd name because that's who we are, but this place is mine free and clear. Getting it up and running is keeping me busy. I already have people clearing land and starting the construction of buildings. It's not going to be anything like the main Ranch. Nothing ever will. But it will be my own. Out of respect for Brip and to keep peace within the family, I'm bringing in my own clients. I don't know where to start yet, but I got a feeling I'm going to be okay. After all, my name is attached to a legend. If I build it, they will come. Once this place starts bringing in money, I'll pay taxes to Brip and the main Ranch just like everybody else.

Brip made an example of Kong as a warning to everybody. He cut off his head, pinned it to a stick, and then planted it in the ground at the East Meadows projects. The act was gruesome and medieval. But it was Brip, and he got his point across. He's really been honoring Brock in his death. I respect that.

Before Brock died, I thought Brip was going to be done with all of us, but to my surprise, he came through for us just like Brock said he would. Every now and again, Taffy brings the baby by and gives me an update about what's going on at the Ranch. I give her a few tips on keeping it all together, but she gets a little overwhelmed. She has a lot to learn, but I know she can handle it. They both invite me back from time to time, but I can never go back there again. When I think about the Ranch, all I see is blood and painful secrets. Without Brock, the Ranch ain't nothing but brick and mortar—buildings sitting on top of dirt void everything I once loved and respected. Too much blood has been lost there. Brock lost blood. Nicchi lost blood. And Dalla. I ain't never been a fan of Dalla, but I hate what happened to her.

It's all good, though. One thing I can say for sure is that I experienced a love of a lifetime, and together, Brock and I made the impossible possible every day of our lives. We built a legacy so powerful that our names will live on for an eternity. This Badd name made us immortal. Unstoppable and undefeated. Even in death, we'll live on. He lives on. My husband may be dead, but his spirit will always be alive.

After Brock, there will be no other. Who can fill his shoes? No one, so I ain't gonna waste my time trying. Brock's love was so strong it still fills me up daily. When I said I was in this shit for life, I meant it. In the end, I will die my husband's wife—a Badd wife.

36

Lera Badd

"I CAN'T BELIEVE WE'RE here," I say to Bobby.

The wind catches my words from the balcony we're standing on and carries them off into the distance. The navy sky is extra beautiful, and the peace that fills the air heals me.

"Right back where we started," he says, hugging me from behind. "Miami," he whispers in my ear and then kisses me on the neck.

"I can't believe we made it," I say more to myself.

After Brock's funeral, Bobby and I traveled the country like nomads, staying in lavish hotels and clearing our heads. Bobby and Brock weren't on good terms when he died because of me and my lie. I confessed the truth before Brock died, but Bobby didn't get a chance to really accept his brother's apology. There were no final words, and I know that eats at him. I pray he doesn't wake up one day and resent me for it. I'm hopeful, though. Bobby and I had to forgive each other for a lot of unforgivable things to make it to this point. Our love is stronger than ever now. Brock and I didn't end on good terms either. I regret that, but when I read the letter he wrote to me, it filled my soul with peace. He wrote several letters to Bobby, too. Bobby reads them every night. The letters are healing him. It's a slow process, but he's getting there.

Everything feels stable now that we've settled in Miami. The other states we visited didn't feel right. They were either too slow or too fast, but Miami feels like us. It's far enough away from the Ranch and everything Badd, but close enough to keep us connected. We're staying in the same beach house Bobby rented the first night we spent together. Being here brings back so many sweet memories—the innocence I felt loving him and the independence I felt as a woman. That part of my spirit still lingers here, and it's nice to reconnect with that old part of me—the woman I was before I became a Badd wife.

"So this is home." I push my back into Bobby's chest, and he embraces me tighter.

"This is it." Bobby kisses the nape of my neck. "This house good enough for our fresh start?"

"I love it," I say, turning around to face him. "I remember the first meal I made you here."

"The steak and the salad with the tomatoes." Bobby chuckles. "I'm glad you like the house, because I bought it for you last week."

I leaned up on my toes and kissed Bobby to show my gratitude.

"Remember that day on the beach? We made love on the sand," I say, flirting with him.

"We're gonna have plenty of nights like that," Bobby says, then parts my lips with his tongue.

I close my eyes and savor every moment. After pulling away, he strokes the side of my face.

"We're both about to get busy," he reminds me.

We've separated ourselves from the Ranch, so we need something to keep us busy. That's when I remember my dreams of owning a nightclub. Miami is the perfect place for that. With Bobby's name and my style, we're gonna have the hottest nightclub in the city. It's all going to be for fun. Bobby doesn't need the money. Brip paid him off. So, we have enough money to last us three lifetimes. And when we get bored here, we'll move on to the next destination. There is no real plan, and I like that. Bobby promised more trips. Vacations. Long weekends. And so far, he's been doing just as he said.

Now that we're settled, he's worked it out with Tara for Blake to come and stay with us in the summer. I'm nervous about being a stepmother, but it will be good practice. Bobby is ready to start a family right away. So am I. I'm so excited about our future, about all the possibilities and the unbreakable bond we've built. Whenever Bobby brings Blake to visit, he stays with us at a hotel. I like the way it feels when the three of us are together. It makes me ready to nest, but before we officially start working on making a baby, Bobby and I are going to counseling.

He found the best therapist in Miami to help keep me grounded, but I was shocked when he volunteered to do couples counseling. Bobby's not much of a talker, but now that we're in counseling, I see him in a whole new light. I didn't think it was possible, but I love Bobby even more now.

"I really love you, Lera," he whispers in my ear.

"Oh yeah?" I play coy just to hear him say what he's about to say next.

"You know I mean what I say."

37
Taffy Badd

"GIVE ME MY grandbaby," Momma demands and reaches out her arms towards me, gesturing a grabbing motion. "Taffy, you too stingy with that baby. You gonna spoil her rotten if I don't do it first," she says, then softens as I place Beverly Brock Badd in her hands.

Momma's right. I am stingy with Beverly. I hold her all day, even when she's sleeping. I still can't believe she's here. I can't believe we're here. We survived it all.

When Brip told me that he wanted to name our daughter after his mother and Brock, I wasn't opposed to it. Brock's death hit him hard, but he's being strong for our family. Brip surprised them all. My man is running this place like he's been doing it his entire life. It feels weird living in the big house. We've renovated it to fit my style, but it still feels strange being on this Ranch without Brock or Mona. There was no separating them and the Ranch.

My heart goes out to Mona. Losing Brock was like losing her religion. Mona loved every part of that man. She believed in him more than she believed in God himself. Part of Mona died with Brock. When I go to see her, she's still no-nonsense and tough as nails, but the fire inside her has burned out. She seems empty and sad, but still strong. Always strong. I still can't believe he's dead.

We all knew Brock was human, but he carried himself like a super-human, and superhumans don't die. Brip had a French artist flown in to start working on a statue of Brock. He's almost finished with it. It's going be the first thing guests see when they enter through the Ranch's gates. The statue is the spitting image of Brock. It's big, bold, and rock hard. It stands eight feet tall and sculpted with beautiful copper-colored stone. It's a sight to see and a beautiful way for Brip to honor his brother's memory.

I hate to admit it, but Brock dying made things easier. When Brip found out he was the only true Badd, he took it hard. He wasn't lying when he gave his brothers the ultimatum to leave the Ranch volun-tarily or be put out forcefully. I knew Mona and Brock weren't going to leave this place easily. It would have been more unnecessary fighting. Bobby and Billy still come around but not much, especially Billy. He has a lot on his plate right now. They both had one foot out the door anyway. Brip gave them enough money to walk away without a fight. He set Mona up real nice, too, but he's still struggling with his identity. He doesn't feel connected to anyone anymore, and with Brock dead, that doesn't help. It's going to take some time, but he'll get better. He's changed so much already.

After Beverly Brock was born, I decided to hold off on the blood test because it would have been too much for Brip to handle. Emotionally, he has a lot on his plate right now, and adding the possibility that Beverly isn't his could break him. When she was first born, she didn't resemble any of us. Now that her facial features are starting to form, I don't need a test because that face is Brip all the way. So much so, it looks like he gave birth to her. When Brip first held Beverly, I saw him transform into this mature, stable man right before my eyes. She brings him so much joy, and it helps soften the blows that reality has thrown at us. Brip is already talking about baby number two. Getting pregnant was a miracle, but the fact that she survived all this proves God can grant as many miracles as He wants. I'm looking forward to giving her a little brother or sister, but we have to settle into our new lives first.

The Ranch has changed a lot in six months. Brip brought in new clients and gave me a job handling all the entertainment on the Ranch.

Not only do we have the casino, but we are clearing land and preparing for a nightclub and an upscale shopping boutique for the elite criminals' wives to frequent. I'm designing it myself. I want this Ranch to be a haven for them. Between managing that process and being a new mom to my angel, I'm pretty busy. Not to mention how busy Momma and Tony keep me. They live on the Ranch fulltime now. Momma lives in our old mansion and Tony in a suite at the casino. Brip continued the help that Brock extended towards him, and Tony is getting better every day. He's retaining more of his thoughts, and his speech has improved a lot. He's almost like the Tony remember. Momma is impressed and happy to be on the Ranch finally. When the gates opened and she finally got inside, it was like she was walking through the gates of heaven. Her eyes beamed with excitement and lust. The staff here treats Momma like a queen, and she eats that shit up.

I feel so blessed to have my family close. I can finally say that Keno would be proud of me.

"Lord, I never thought I'd see the day," Momma says while rocking Beverly, then looks up at me and smiles. "I'm so proud of you, Scrappy. You hung in there for all of us."

Brip walks into the room wearing a button-up shirt and some navy slacks. The knot in his tie is loose. That lets me know he's done working for the day. I smile when I see him. Long gone are the polo shirts and Timberland boots. My husband is a businessman now.

"Where's my girl?" he says and pulls Beverly out of Momma's lap. "My little mini-me," gushes and kisses Beverly on the cheek.

My heart swoons every time I see a big goon like Brip being so tender with our daughter.

"I'm right here," I say playfully, flirting with him with my eyes.

There is nothing sexier than Brip holding our daughter.

Brip smiles at me before leaning down and kissing me on top of the head. He cradles Beverly in his arms, still smiling. Then he looks up and winks at me like he's saying thank you. I blush from the inside out.

I finally have everything I want.

38

Billy Badd

B J PICKS UP a hand full of sand and throws it in the air for the
wind to catch. He laughs, then looks off into the ocean and
points.

"Big waders," he says, trying to form words.

"That's right, big man. Big waters." I lean down and kiss my son
on top of the head and stare at the water's massiveness that seems to be
infinite, like the possibilities of my future.

He points to the sky and says his newest word—Mama. It's his
favorite thing to say lately. He always wants his mother. I can understand that because I always want mine, even now. I pull BJ into my
chest and squeeze him tight. I know I can't fulfill his need with just my
embrace, but I still try.

This is what Dalla wanted—to be near the ocean and far away
from everything. The air in Spain feels calm. Safe. Pleasant. With the
money Brip gave me, I purchased a beautiful ten-acre estate with its
own private access to the ocean. I also bought a big-ass yacht. The
estate needs a little work, but that's the reason I bought it. Working on
it keeps me busy, but it's going to be beautiful when I'm finished. It's
going to be home.

The wind pushes a wave in our direction, and BJ claps his hands, waiting for the water to crash at our feet. When it does, he sinks his little toes deep in the sand and smiles. He's happy. It's like he knows we barely made it out alive, and now he's grateful.

The world doesn't feel the same anymore. There's been too much tragedy, and I feel shell-shocked. But I'm grateful I have something to look forward to. I'm happy I was able to make peace with Brock before he died. It's still hard to fathom living the rest of my life without him. But, in the end, Brock did right by us all. He showed us how much he loved us, and I understand him now more in death than when he was alive. I guess that's just how shit works. You take what's staring you in the face for granted every day until you lose it. That's why I'm learning to cherish every little moment, even this one. Sitting in the sand with my son and staring at the ocean means something to me.

I'm so glad Brock and I were on the same page before he died. I don't have Ace, but he gave me every lead he had on Mamma. Bobby was right for killing Ace. He would have caused more trouble and confusion than helped. I don't need him. I'm glad the motherfucker is rotting. I did interrogate his mother and sister before I left the Ranch. I got a few things out of them that will help me along the way. More pieces to add to the puzzle. It won't be long before this puzzle becomes a picture.

I convinced Brip not to kill Ace's mother and sister. Too much blood has been spilled. Besides, they ain't no threat. They just got caught up in all of Ace's madness. Because I rallied for their lives, Angelo promised to help me with whatever I need during the journey to find my mother. She seemed genuine, so I just might take her up on her offer.

I regret the words I exchanged with Dalla the night she got shot. I made her feel like we were done, like I didn't trust her. Dalla was just afraid. She'd been fighting longer than all of us. It bothers me to think that while she was lying on the ground bleeding and struggling to breathe, my hurtful words could have been replaying in her head. The thought of her thinking I didn't love her while dying pains me. I try not to dwell on the negative, though. Dwelling on the negative shit will only dim the bright light that's shining on my future.

Speaking of the future, I'm already setting up shop and putting things in place to find Mamma. I got a plan, and I'm hopeful. I know Mamma's out there. I can feel her. I just got to figure out what I'm gonna say when I see her. How I'm gonna convince her to come home. Brock told me that Carlo Lucky might still be alive, too. I ain't looking for him, but I understand that finding Mamma may mean finding him.

I don't know how I feel about not being a Badd. I hated my father. I always have, but I identify with the Badd name more than I do anything else. What type of man is Carlo Lucky anyway? He left his children with a madman. He left the woman he loved with a madman. I knew Dalla was mine the moment I laid eyes on her, and it was then that I decided I wasn't leaving her with Ace. I didn't give a fuck about their marriage. Dalla was coming with me. If Carlo Lucky loved Mamma, why did he leave her? He don't sound like a man to me. He don't sound like a father either. He sounds like a bitch. But if he's alive, I'll let him explain. I'll be open to listening just for Mamma's sake.

"Mamma," BJ says and points again.

I lift my son from the sand to wipe him down, but as soon as his busy feet hit the ground, he takes off running. I turn to grab him but catch air instead. He's too quick. The air hits me in the face, blowing her perfume in my direction. I look up and see Dalla stretching her arms out towards BJ. She bends down on one knee, and he leaps into her arms. Her long sundress is floating in the wind, covering the swollen belly that contains BJ's sister. Our daughter. The wind blows through her hair, blinding her sight. She looks angelic. She picks up BJ and pushes her hair out of her face, then smiles at me. My heart skips a few beats. This woman is my everything. I don't know what I would have done had I lost her that day. Brock will always be my hero for catching most of the bullets that were meant to kill her. He gave his life to protect her.

I pick up the pace in my steps until I'm nose to nose with my wife.

I kiss her on the lips and run my hands over her stomach. Dalla beams at me with loving eyes.

I finally gave her what I promised her, what she had been fighting for all these years, and what she deserves. Her family. Her happily ever after. *Our* happily ever after.

The End

The story of Mamma Badd and Carlo Lucky will be continued in Badd Beginnings: A Badd Series Prequal.

✶✶✶SPOILER ALERT✶✶✶

To My Badd Readers,

From books one to four, you held your breath while I took you on a wild ride through the lives of the Badds and all the craziness that takes place on the Badd Ranch. You wore the 'B' necklace with the wives, and you stuck with me through all the many twists and turns, shocking secrets, and heart-wrenching betrayals. Hopefully, you can now exhale knowing that the Badd family has finally found their peace. This truly feels like the end of an era for me. I'll miss these characters as much as you. Especially Brock Badd. He was devious, but he had a loving heart. I hope you were able to see him in a whole new light, but sometimes to understand the end, you have to start from the beginning.

Badd Beginnings, a Badd standalone, is coming soon. Where all the characters' lives may have come full circle, and there's nothing else to share, there is one last story that must be told. Mamma Badd, the originator of secrets, has her own story to tell. And what she reveals will shock you and maybe help you understand Brock a little better. Let's start from the beginning and see exactly how they became Badd. Stay tuned for the final Badd book, *Badd Beginnings*.

Most of all, thanks for your support. If you enjoyed the Badd Series, leave a review on your favorite Badd book (or all of them). Your honest reviews mean the world to me. And hey, while you're waiting on *Badd Beginnings* to drop, check out my other work. I have more characters for you to fall in love with. They may break your heart, but you'll forgive them. (Wink)

Until next time…

-Author Zee. W

PLEASE LEAVE A REVIEW

If you enjoyed this book, please leave a review and/or share this story.

LET'S KEEP IN TOUCH

FOLLOW ME:
FACEBOOK @THISWRITERSLIFE
INSTAGRAM @AUTHORZEE.W

www.ingramcontent.com/pod-product-compliance
Lightning Source LLC
Chambersburg PA
CBHW060400260626
47160CB00006B/2377